PENGUIN BOOKS

No Name Lane

'Howard Linskey is one of the best new writers around and
this is the start of a must-read series' Mark Billingham

'Gripping and convincing' Kimberley Chambers

'Serial killer thrillers don't come much better than
No Name Lane. Old secrets and terrible new crimes
woven into an immensely satisfying, utterly compelling
narrative which keeps you constantly guessing.
Fans of Linskey's critically acclaimed David Blake series
will already know what an outstanding author he is,
everyone else . . . prepare to add another name to your
must-read list' Eva Dolan

'Linskey weaves together a compelling and twisty
tale that gripped me from page one. If you like
Val McDermid's thrillers, you'll love this' Mark Edwards

'A new master of the gripping, gritty thriller. Intrigue
and urban darkness. Howard Linskey takes you right to
the heart of it' Paul Finch

'Howard Linskey's first three novels made him a name
to be watched. *No Name Lane* propels him into the
Premier League. We'll watch him become a major

'*No Name Lane* is an assured novel, brilliantly told by one of the best new authors to emerge on the British crime scene in decades' Tony Black

ABOUT THE AUTHOR

Howard Linskey has worked as a barman, journalist, salesman and catering manager for a celebrity chef. Originally from Ferryhill in County Durham, Howard now lives in Hertfordshire with his wife and daughter.

HowardLinskey.com

@HowardLinksey

Facebook.com/howard.linskey

Also by Howard Linskey

THE DAVID BLAKE SERIES
The Drop
The Damage
The Dead

NO NAME LANE

HOWARD LINSKEY

PENGUIN BOOKS

PENGUIN BOOKS

UK | USA | Canada | Ireland | Australia
India | New Zealand | South Africa

Penguin Books is part of the Penguin Random House group of companies
whose addresses can be found at global.penguinrandomhouse.com.

First published 2015
001

Copyright © Howard Linskey, 2015

The moral right of the author has been asserted

Set in 12.5/14.75 pt Garamond MT Std
Typeset by Jouve (UK), Milton Keynes
Printed in Great Britain by Clays Ltd, St Ives plc

A CIP catalogue record for this book is available from the British Library

TRADE PAPERBACK ISBN: 978–0–718–18154–3
PAPERBACK ISBN: 978–0–718–18032–4

For Erin & Alison

Prologue

Girl Number Four

County Durham – 1993

He watched the girl until he was certain she was perfect. Only then did he risk approaching her. It was never difficult to get them to come with him. The hard part was staying calm, even as his heart was thumping so hard in his chest he was convinced she must be able to hear it.

He drove her somewhere quiet then stopped the car, waiting until he was sure they were entirely alone. Sometimes he'd bundle a girl into the boot so he could drive her miles away but this lane was isolated enough, so he'd climbed into the back seat to get to her. He ignored her terrified pleas and reached for her, easily brushing her weak little hands aside, forcing her head back until the flesh of her tiny neck was exposed. He clamped his hands around her throat and began to squeeze, tightening his grip as her desperate struggle began. He closed his eyes. It was better if he could not see the little girl's face, for she did not understand. How could she even begin to comprehend what he was doing for her? He squeezed harder and harder and wouldn't let go until the moment when her struggles finally ceased and her tiny body went limp.

He looked down at the lifeless young girl in his arms and whispered the special words he always used when he had saved one.

'*Suffer the little children to come unto me.*'

Chapter One

It all began with a phone call, as these things tend to.

'Hello.' Tom answered and there was a pause, as if the person on the other end had suddenly realised the magnitude of what they were doing and decided against it. 'Hello?' he prompted.

'I've got a story,' the woman blurted and he strained to listen to her against the sound of dozens of journalists talking over the tap-tap-tap of busy fingers hitting keyboards while the insistent ringing of competing phones could be heard all across the room.

'Okay,' answered Tom, 'what kind of story?'

There was another pause until finally she said, 'a bloody big one,' and there was something about the nervous, agitated way in which she spoke that made Tom Carney take the woman seriously.

Tabloid stories generally start with a tip-off. This one began because a woman chose the biggest red top in the country to tell her side of it. Aggrieved men and women called its London office every day. Some were wronged, others desperate, some just plain demented. It was Tom Carney's job to perform *triage* on them, as his legendary editor Alex 'the Doc' Docherty put it; 'from the French verb *trier*, meaning to sift and select,' he was told. 'Your job is to separate the shit from the sugar.'

The people who called always assumed their story was

3

worth a life-changing amount of money. It was rare however for their particular grievance to actually make it into print. The tabloid Tom Carney worked for had a daily circulation of four million copies. Everyone wanted to be in the paper; politicians from all sides, models, actors, rock bands, the wannabes, gonnabes, has-beens and never-wasses, along with many thousands of what their foul-mouthed editor called 'the great unwashed', by which he meant the general public. Only the really juicy stuff ended up in the paper. Sometimes though, one of these callers would turn out to be peddling neither shit nor sugar but genuine gold.

The anonymous woman who phoned that morning was randomly connected to one of a large number of journalists manning the news desks. Afterwards, Tom Carney would often wonder about the direction his life might have taken had he not been in the office that morning or if the call had gone to one of the many other reporters in the newsroom. The simple act of answering the phone that day changed everything for Tom, though he could never have known it at the time.

'What's it about then?' he prompted when she was not immediately forthcoming, 'this story of yours?'

'A very famous man, someone high up.'

'Right,' he replied non-committedly, 'can I take your name, Miss?'

'No names, not yet, just listen.'

He could have played hard ball, told her to give him her name or he'd hang up but if she really did have a story to tell, he'd only read about it later in a rival newspaper. Besides, there was something about the way she spoke, the urgency in her voice that compelled him to keep her on the line.

'So, what's this famous man been up to then?'

'Something he ain't ought to have been,' and she snorted a laugh then immediately became serious again. 'He's married, see, and he's been seeing us and he ain't supposed to have been doing that, not in his position.'

'Who's us?' he asked, though he was beginning to get the idea.

'Me and some others,' she said, sounding cagey.

'I see. You and some others,' his tone was thoughtful. 'Would I be right in saying that you have been seeing this man in your professional capacity?' He was trying to be delicate.

'You mean, am I on the game?' she snapped.

'Yes,' he said simply.

'Well, say what you mean then,' she told him. 'Yes, *we* are, 'course we are.'

'And who is this family man who has been spending time with you?'

'I can't say until I know how much it's worth.'

'How can I tell you that unless I know who he is?'

There was a long pause on the line while she weighed up this dilemma. 'He's important, like I said, and I'll tell you everything, for the right price.'

'I understand.' If she was legit then this could be just the kind of kiss-and-tell story the paper might be interested in but who really cared if some town councillor, minor actor or daytime game-show host had been dipping his wick where he shouldn't? 'Is he someone I will have heard of?'

'Everybody has heard of him.'

'He's not a politician then?' The public were notoriously awful at recognising politicians unless they were either the Prime Minister or some lunatic with flog-em and hang-em views that turned them into a 'character', and eventually, a national treasure.

She must have grown tired of his questions. 'He's only in the bloody government, all right?' she snapped at him, 'the cabinet. Now how much is that worth to you?'

Tom Carney straightened. He gripped his pen firmly in his hand and let it hover over the page of his notepad. If this woman really was telling the truth and she could prove it then this was dynamite. The Tory government with its back-to-basics, family values had a cabinet member who was shagging hookers? It couldn't be better. 'Quite a bit I should think,' he said in a voice that was a lot calmer than he was, 'if you can prove it. Now, why don't we meet to discuss this further?'

'I asked how much,' her voice was hard, with a trace of fear behind it.

At this point, Tom wasn't about to let her know his true status at The Paper, a probationer on a six-month contract so the editor could see if he 'had the chops' to make it there, and so he blagged it. 'Top end of five figures, six even, maybe, but you have to be able to prove it.' There was a silence on the line that told him she was still interested. 'So why don't you tell me where you want to meet and I'll be there. That's what you want isn't it, to sell your story?'

Maybe it was the use of the word *sell* that finally landed her.

'All right,' she said.

Chapter Two

Girl Number Five

Six Weeks Later

It had taken Michelle Summers fifteen long and singularly uneventful years to realise it but tonight, as she stood shivering in the dark, beneath the rotting timbers of the ancient bus shelter, while the rain beat down in a steady, staccato rhythm on the roof above her, she finally acknowledged the sad and simple fact: she hated her mother. Hated . . . hated . . . *hated* her . . . the stupid, fat cow.

If her mam ever said anything to her these days it would start with the words, 'you used to'. 'You used to be so nice . . . you used to be fun . . . you used to be such a pretty little thing,' implying of course that she was no longer any of these things. Michelle Summers had little enough self-confidence without her own mother repeatedly reminding her that she wasn't nice, pretty or fun any more.

Michelle watched as rivulets of water rolled down the inner walls of the shelter till they met in pools on the rutted, grey concrete floor. The spreading water forced Michelle out of the bus stop's innermost corners and the wind whistled through the wooden shelter. In Michelle's view, she lived in a shabby village in the middle of nowhere, at the arse end of the north east of England, and there was nothing that wasn't at least a bus ride away, even her home. Michelle swore that when she was finally old enough, she would leave Great Middleton forever, because there was absolutely nothing great about it. Everybody knew everyone else, everybody's parents knew everyone else's parents and everybody minded everyone else's business. You couldn't get away with anything in Great Middleton.

Michelle had arrived at the shelter just in time to see the penultimate bus of the night pulling asthmatically up the hill ahead of her, farting black smoke out of its rear end, as it forced itself slowly over the summit like the little-engine-that-could. Now she was glad she had given in when her mam insisted on her wearing a coat, even though it covered the cool top she had worn that night and the body that was developing very nicely, thank you very much. Even her mam was jealous of that. 'Eh, I wish I had a flat stomach like you our Shell,' she'd say, 'and a bum that small. It's like a peach!'

Denny had certainly noticed the change in her this past year, the dirty perv. Michelle hated her stepdad almost as much as her mam and loathed the way they both called her 'Shell', like she was something washed up on a beach. With a bit of luck her stepdad would be out in his lorry by now. He did more and more night jobs these days, 'to beat the traffic', he said, but she wondered if he was just as sick of living in their house as Michelle. Her mam would likely be asleep on the couch, a lukewarm gin and orange cordial congealing on the table next to her. It would be half-drunk, just like her mam, and Michelle could creep quietly upstairs to her room.

It wasn't a very nice thing to admit you hated your

mother. Michelle knew that. She was supposed to love her mam, go out on shopping trips with her, share jokes, talk to her about boyfriends and stuff, buy her chocolates on Mother's Day, that sort of thing. She knew girls who did have that kind of relationship.

'My mam's pretty cool,' they'd say, 'she talks about sex and everything, she's going to put me on the pill when I'm older.' But Michelle wasn't going to talk about sex with her mam, not in this life. Her sole pronouncement on the subject, once her daughter had started seeing Darren 'Daz' Tully on a fairly regular basis, was to mutter 'don't forget, Shell, nothing below the waistline.'

She didn't want to go shopping with her mam either, the fat cow would probably only want to buy chocolates, crisps or gin. The woman had completely given up. She wondered what Denny saw in her at all. Really, did they even still do it any more? They were both over forty after all. Maybe they just didn't bother. Perhaps you didn't when you were that old.

That would explain why Denny was such a perv; always hanging round outside the bathroom with that stupid grin on his face. The first time wasn't long after her fifteenth birthday and she'd come out of there with only a bath towel wrapped round her. There he was, standing on the landing like he'd just that minute climbed the stairs, but she knew differently. 'Whoops,' he'd said, like it was all a big accident, but his eyes had given him away; they'd lit up like a kid's on Christmas morning, and he had definitely given her the once over, just like the boys at the youth club; his glance travelling south from top to bottom; face, tits then bits. Michelle had wanted to retch. She'd rushed past him to her room, ignoring his 'night, night, pet,' before slamming the door hard behind her. Men were dogs, all of them. She'd learned that much already.

Now she didn't dare go anywhere near the bathroom unless she was fully dressed in neck-to-ankle PJs and towelling dressing gown. Not that it mattered these days, as the house was colder than a morgue. Heating being just one more thing they couldn't afford.

She'd told Suze all about Denny.

'He probably thinks about you when he plays with his thingy,' her best mate had offered matter-of-factly.

'Suze!' Michelle shouted, 'you're disgusting!' But she'd laughed when she'd said it.

Suze was still laughing, 'I bet he does you know, loads. I reckon that's all he does.' She had a point. It had been a long while since Michelle had been disturbed in the night by her mam and Denny rattling the head board. The first time they'd done that Michelle was still a little girl and she'd woken abruptly, filled with concern for her mam's safety because the thumping against the wall was accompanied by moaning sounds. Dull with sleep, she'd wandered into their room, only to discover Denny lying on top of her mother, who screamed when she saw Michelle. Denny shouted then swore and Michelle turned on her heels and fled. Her mother walked into her room moments later, in her ratty old dressing gown. She sat down next to Michelle on the corner of her bed and explained that there was nothing to be frightened of, that Uncle Denny was giving Mummy a special hug and they had both screamed because Michelle had startled them. Not long after that Michelle was moved into the smaller, draughtier back bedroom, 'Uncle Denny' began living with them on a permanent basis and a date for the wedding was set. Things had been okay with Denny before then, when he was trying to wheedle his way into her mother's life by taking her and Michelle on trips to the pictures or the zoo, buying her ice creams and dollies. All that soon stopped 'once he'd got his boots under the kitchen table', as her Nan put it. There were no more trips, precious few presents and the ice creams became less and less frequent. Money was 'tight', her mother and step-father repeatedly explained to her, though she suspected it was actually her new stepdad that was tight.

Michelle was snapped from her thoughts quite suddenly by a fresh torrent of rain water that broke free from the wind-rattled guttering and tumbled to the ground in front of her, splashing her in the process. Why could she not have been born somewhere else, like London or even twenty miles away in Newcastle? At least there was stuff to do in a city. There was nowt to do in a village except smoke cigs and get felt by boys round the back of the village hall. That was all Darren Tully wanted to do. They'd been going together for a little over two months now and already Michelle could only vaguely remember how excited she had been when he first asked her out. Even Suze had confirmed that Darren Tully was officially 'lush' and for once in her life she'd felt special and wanted. But the reality of going out with Daz had been quite different from her imaginings. Tonight had been typical. There was always a bit of snogging, he made that much effort at least, but the persistent thrusting of his tongue in and out of her mouth and his tobacco-flavoured kisses behind the village hall were hardly the stuff of a girl's dreams. The continuous groping always ended with her pushing his hands away and him muttering 'You are so tight,' like she was the last virgin in the village, before informing her that he'd have to dump her soon unless he started 'getting summat'.

'I have to get summat. There's no point if I don't get owt,' he'd informed her that evening, as if this was a suggestion so romantic she would never be able to resist it.

Boys were dogs too.

Daz barely glanced at her as he climbed eagerly into a friend's mam's car, the offer of a lift home to the neighbouring town proving too good for him to pass up in this weather. She'd watched him go, wondering to herself whether she should perhaps give in to him, in order to keep him, or if he really wasn't worth the trouble.

Michelle glanced at her watch. The last bus would be here soon, if it was going to come at all. It was often cancelled without explanation but the weather was foul and it would take a fair while to walk home. There'd been a lot of stuff in the papers about young girls going missing lately too. Some of them had been found later. It made her shudder when she thought about how it must have felt to be them during their last moments. Her mother always drummed it into her, 'Never come home on your own Michelle, it's not safe, always get the bus or make sure that boyfriend-of-yours . . .' she never called Darren by his name, '. . . walks you home if he's s'posed to be seeing you.' That was a laugh. There were few things more dangerous than allowing Daz Tully to walk you home.

Michelle began to tug absent-mindedly at the St Christopher medallion around her neck, stretching its silver chain. The rain took on a new level of determination, whipped down onto the shelter's roof by a malicious, swirling wind, which prevented her from hearing the man, the drops tumbling onto the wooden roof of the shelter masking his footsteps. The first sign of his presence was a slight change in the light, an almost imperceptible darkening of the path in front of her as the glow from one of the street lamps caught his back, casting a shadow that changed shape as he drew near. She looked up just as he reached the shelter. Back lit as he was by the street lamps, she could hardly make out his features. Michelle started, sensing danger but unsure of what to do about it. When he finally spoke, the sound of his voice made her jump. It was deep and undeniably masculine and she realised she was holding her breath, fear and anticipation competing inside her.

'Hello,' he said.

Chapter Three

Michelle's mother snored so hard she woke herself up. Fiona's head lolled onto one shoulder and she opened her eyes suddenly, blinking at the room in a panic as she attempted to get her bearings. Shit, fallen asleep on the couch again. She looked at the little brass carriage clock on the mantel, nearly one o'clock. Bugger it. She should have gone to bed hours ago instead of opting for that last little glass of wine. Now she'd have a thick head in the morning and work would be even more of a drudge than usual.

Fiona had thought that switching from gin to wine had been a good idea. It would get her off the hard stuff and make her little evening tipple seem that bit more innocent. She didn't want anyone to get the wrong idea about it; like her dear husband for example, or her delightful daughter, both of whom seemed to think that she had been put on this earth purely to wait on them. The bottles of sweet German wine had the added advantage of being cheaper than gin and Fiona convinced herself they were doing her body less harm in the long run. After all, wine was made from grapes and grapes were fruit, so how bad could it be to drink fruit? If anyone asked, not that they would, she could tell them she had one, maybe two glasses, two or three nights a week, but in reality she knew she was drinking a lot more than that every night. Since she never finished a glass, always topping it up as she went along, instead of draining it and starting again from the beginning, she could never be sure how many glasses she'd had, which was her intention, because she didn't want to know. Fiona didn't exactly feel that she *needed* a drink every night, it was just that life always felt a lot less stressful after she'd had a couple.

Coming round slowly in a fog of alcohol, she moved her foot and immediately connected with the half-empty wine bottle standing there, which tumbled like a skittle, knocking over the glass next to it. Miraculously they both remained intact, though a little of the wine was lost on the carpet before she could rescue the upended bottle. Fiona swore then walked into the kitchen and stowed the remnants back in the fridge. Already her head had begun to throb. Best not to think about the morning and just go to bed.

Fiona climbed the stairs and, as she neared the top, spotted the tell-tale crack of light coming through the gap under Michelle's door. What on earth was her daughter doing lying awake till all hours with school in the morning? Fiona wasn't having that. She put her hand up, ready to rap her knuckles on the door, then she stopped. Fiona knew she should give her daughter a rollicking but realised she was hardly setting a good example herself, a point her daughter would doubtless use to her advantage, undermining her mother's already fragile authority even further. And there was always the possibility that, being this tired, Fiona might struggle to pronounce the words as clearly as she would have liked. What sarcastic response would she get from Michelle about passing out on the sofa again? Her daughter would have seen her when she came in, sprawled there, hardly at her best. Fiona didn't have the energy for another row with Michelle, a girl who was getting lippier and more ungrateful with every passing day. And to think she used to be such a sweet, nice-natured child. Fiona stood on the landing and leaned in close so that her ear was almost pressed against her daughter's bedroom door. No sound from within. Michelle had probably fallen asleep with the light on, while reading one of those stupid fan magazines she was obsessed with. Her walls were covered with pictures of Take That – another one of Michelle's teen bands that would be here today and gone tomorrow, like the Osmonds or the Bay City Rollers in Fiona's day. She was boy-daft, that one.

It was one of Fiona's recurring nightmares that her daughter would fall pregnant before she was out of her teens. The very last thing she needed right now was to become a grandmother at her age. The thought made her shudder. She was already knackered all of the time as it was and financially they were barely surviving, without a new baby to feed, clothe and buy bloody toys for. She hoped her dippy daughter still had enough sense in her head not to let her spotty boyfriend do what he doubtless wanted to do, but she was far from sure of this.

Fiona turned away from the door and headed for her own room. At least Denny was already off in the lorry, so she wouldn't have to put up with his disapproval or his half-hearted pawing at her for sex. And Michelle would be fine. She'd sleep all night with the light on then emerge in one of her usual, grumpy moods, hating everything and everybody, just like she did every morning.

*

Fiona would always blame herself for not knocking that night. The guilt would stay with her. If she had gone into her daughter's room, she would have realised that Michelle was gone, had never returned in fact. If only she'd known about it then and reported Michelle missing long before morning, gaining the police precious hours in the process, perhaps something could have been done sooner. Then things might have worked out so very differently for everyone.

Chapter Four

Day One

As the Jubilee line train juddered round a corner, Tom Carney gazed at the newspaper's front page with its accompanying banner headline, 'Grady And The Tramp'. A dark-haired, middle-aged man in a blue pinstripe suit angrily attempted to repel a photographer's lens with an outstretched palm. The man in the photograph oozed wealth, status and entitlement.

Tom had been up much earlier than usual, eager to see his first front page lead for a national tabloid – and not just any article. Hell, this was the story of the year. It was a defining moment for Tom, a vindication after long, hard years of puzzled frowns and dismissive comments from friends when he'd told them he was going to be a journalist. No other paper had the story. Tom and his colleagues at The Paper had scooped them all. He imagined it being read on every bus and train in the country. It had already been the breaking news on the radio and breakfast TV channels. In Downing Street, they'd be reading Tom's words in The Paper that morning and fretting over them. It was an exhilarating thought.

Their newspaper was always referred to as 'The Paper' by the journalists who worked on it. That was a golden rule, for to utter its real name was to concede that it was not the only newspaper and there might, just might, be other, admittedly less worthy, contenders for the accolade of paper of the working man. Tom had been on the receiving end of a particularly violent outburst from his editor after just one hour in the job during his first editorial meeting. Unfortunately for Tom, Alex 'the Doc' Docherty had been walking by and overheard the new boy refer to the paper by its actual name, because he had no idea that it was forbidden to do so.

'Who the hell are you?' Tom was shocked to see the legendary Alex Docherty staring down at him with a look of venomous hatred plastered on his face. 'I take it you're the new boy,' he answered his own question, 'which is why you have just committed blasphemy in my office.'

Docherty stared malevolently down at the new boy, 'are you a prole?'

'Pardon?' was all Tom could offer in reply.

'Part of the great unwashed, the ones out there?' and the Doc pointed through the enormous windows that faced the Wapping skyline. 'The folk who don't know who to vote for, what to think, who to love, hate or ignore, the type of person who doesn't even know which hand to use to wipe their own arse, unless we tell them. If you are one of them, then you can call my paper by its name. If, on the other hand you wish to survive here for another five minutes then you can do me the simple courtesy of calling it The Paper, like everyone else.'

The Doc went down on his haunches so his face was level with Tom's, as if he was about to confide something. 'Because my paper is *The* Paper. There is no other,' Tom opened his mouth to say something but Docherty prevented him with a raised hand, 'Oh, I know you might think there are other newspapers out there, you may even be labouring under the misapprehension that they are serious competition but they are not. Fact: we are read on every building site and football training ground, in every office and station platform, council canteen and school staff room in the country, which means we matter. I can ruin careers, put people in prison and keep them there, I can sack ministers, topple prime ministers, swing the vote in marginals by ten, even twenty per cent with a few well-chosen words in my editorials, all of which makes us players.' He looked around at the smiling journos he was now holding in the palm of his hand. He turned back to his sub. 'What is the circulation of our nearest rival, Terry?'

'Nit shit chief,' Terry parroted back instantly.

'Nit shit,' the Doc nodded and he turned back to Tom. 'If you want to go and work on a broadsheet no one reads, except for a few retired colonels from Tewksbury, then join the *Torygraph*; if it's a paper with a history but no future then *The Times* is definitely for you; if you like to goose-step your way into work every morning then the *Daily Mail* will welcome you with open arms; the *Guardian* will have you in a flash, if you can knit your own sandals. But if you want to work for a real paper there is only one, and it's mine. Only I get to call it *My* Paper, you get to call it *The* Paper and if I hear you use any other word in future, you will be out of this door so fast your arsehole will fly past your nose on the way out, got that?'

'Yes, boss,' Tom nodded emphatically, eager to get off

stage and retreat back into his shell again as soon as possible.

'I'll leave you to it then.' And he walked away muttering, 'I've got a country to run.'

'How long have you been here?' asked one of the older journalists, 'an hour?' and he shook his head in wonderment. 'We've had probationers here who never merited a word from the great man in their entire six months,' he drawled in an Edinburgh accent that was barely a whisper. 'Well done son.'

Having barely survived his first day, Tom knuckled down to learn the ropes from his fellow journalists. He quickly learned that they wrote in euphemisms. 'Single-parent' meant scum, 'benefit-claiming, single-parent' meant vermin, 'teenaged-benefit-claiming-single-parent' meant 'council-house-snatching-good-for-nothing-idle-vermin-scum'.

Women who had affairs were 'love-cheats', who took their lovers to 'love-nests' for 'sordid, extra-marital affairs' that were exposed in kiss-and-tell stories, in the interests of public morality, by journalists who were the worst bunch of coke-snorting, binge-drinking shag-arounds Tom had ever known. The paper was the scourge of the unmarried mum, the benefit claimant, the football fan, the Europhile and the paedophile; the latter being two crimes so heinous in the Doc's eyes that they almost shared top billing on the paper's front pages.

Tom Carney kept out of the Doc's way from then on. The next time he stood before the great man, he had a story to tell. Tom had met the hooker, a woman called Trudy Nighton who went by the working nickname of

'Mistress Sparkle', and was convinced she was telling the truth. The Doc took some persuading but eventually he believed it too and personally assigned the team to cover it, on the understanding that evidence, real corroborating evidence, of the 'photos-of-Grady-with-his-todger-out' variety, was what was needed here.

The surveillance operation recorded the comings-and-goings and cumings-and-goings of the uber-respectable and very-married Defence Secretary, Timothy Grady, who until that point had been widely tipped as a future Conservative Prime Minister. His much-vaunted support for 'family values' did not however prevent Grady from meeting 'Mistress Sparkle' and her friends in his London apartment, with her services billed at an eye-watering three hundred quid an hour, though he of course had negotiated a discount. Not for nothing was Timothy Grady known in politics as 'the Lion,' a nickname he had acquired while renegotiating Britain's budget rebate from the EEC. So intransigent had been his stance on this issue that French and German politicians had started referring to him, in a derogatory manner, as the 'Lion from London' and when the right-wing press picked up on it, renaming him 'The Lion of Brussels', Grady did nothing to stifle this heroic image.

Even though he knew every salacious word virtually by heart, Tom Carney sat on the train and read and re-read the story he had co-written all the way along the Jubilee line. For the first time, Tom walked into the newspaper's headquarters like he truly belonged there. As he passed rows of desks manned by veteran reporters he adopted what he hoped was a laid-back demeanour, as if destroying the career of a future Prime Minister *and* landing the front page in the process was all in a day's work for this young reporter. A couple of journos actually bothered to mumble a greeting. A pretty young girl he had once unsuccessfully flirted with by the water cooler even smiled at him.

'The chief wants to see you,' said Terry-the-sub when Tom reached his desk, looking like he begrudged the congratulations Tom was about to receive.

'Careful,' said Jennifer, the Doc's secretary, as he arrived at the huge, glass-walled office that dominated the enormous newsroom, 'he's not a happy bunny.' She made it sound like she'd just invented the nauseating phrase everybody seemed to be using at the moment.

'Well,' Tom said, 'it's nothing I've done,'

His reverie was short-lived however, cut cruelly short by a familiar, booming voice that had more than its usual level of malice behind it. 'Carney, get in here now!'

Tom walked into the office in disbelief.

'Chief?' he asked uncertainly.

'You prat!' shouted the Doc and he immediately threw a folded copy of that morning's edition at Tom, who ducked as it sailed harmlessly over his head and out though the opened door behind him. 'You complete and utter fucking prat!'

Chapter Five

DC Ian Bradshaw was staring at the ceiling again. He'd spent a lot of time looking at ceilings lately, during the long nights of sleeplessness that followed his recuperation. Then there were the hours of listless staring when his depression left him with so little energy he couldn't even stretch out a hand to change the TV channel with the remote control. Instead he would leave the inane daytime chat, stupefying game-shows and saccharin-coated kiddies' programmes running. Every lunchtime in Bradshaw's flat, 'Mr Benn' would go about his business of escaping from the real world, via the magic tailor's shop, before returning to number 52 Festive Road, always with a new souvenir in his pocket, while Bradshaw lay on the couch watching him, wondering how he could similarly escape from reality and just how he had managed to ruin his entire existence so spectacularly by the age of thirty.

It had been a long, slow road to recovery, taken in baby steps and punctuated by small victories; the ability to make a proper breakfast in the morning, two slices of toast with a couple of fried eggs on top, was considered an important milestone. When Bradshaw finally returned to work, months after the 'incident', as his counsellor had taken to calling it, he noticed a change in the way his colleagues regarded him. It wasn't so much what they said, for they rarely said anything to him at all these days. It was more subtle than that; the look in their eyes or the way they pretty much shunned him when he was in the room, as if his ill luck or incompetence might rub off on them if they came too close. He was a wash-up. That's how they saw him and, he had to admit, as he pondered his lot during the many more hours of ceiling-staring which followed while he tried and failed to conquer his insomnia, that they were, on the whole, correct and fair to view him that way. He *had* fucked up, therefore he *was* a fuck-up. There was no denying the cold, hard logic of it. He had messed up and somebody else had paid very dearly for his mistake. As he played the events over and over again in his mind, wondering how he could have been so stupid, it seemed to somehow compound his misery to know that he'd had the best education of any of them. At school, Bradshaw had always found success so effortless. Tall, good-looking and clever, he was never short of a girlfriend, captained the football team and was the hero of the swimming galas. Bradshaw attained good grades and a university degree, literally becoming a poster-boy for Durham Constabulary when during his early days he appeared in an advertising campaign for graduate recruits, under the strapline 'Join the Fast Track'.

And look at him now, still languishing as a Detective Constable. Ian Bradshaw's early run of achievement had left him singularly unprepared to deal with the spectacular failure of his police career. None of the academic or sporting stuff mattered if it turned out that you were basically clueless. Everyone had always told him when he was growing up that he could be anything he chose to be but when it came down to it, he couldn't even become the one thing he really wanted to be; a police officer; or at least a competent one.

Now he was staring at the ceiling once more as he lay on the soft leather couch, while his counsellor, Doctor Mellor – recommended and paid for by Durham Constabulary in an effort to prove they had not entirely washed their hands of him – tried once again to forge some form of empathetic bond between them.

'This is our fifth session,' Doctor Mellor's soft and faintly hypnotic voice drifted over to Bradshaw from his seat in the middle of the airless room, 'and I think we have established enough trust between us to begin to explore the matter of your self-esteem, right?' The doctor had a habit of ending his pronouncements with the word *right*, an annoying little verbal tick that made his voice rise in pitch at the end of every sentence. The good doctor clearly didn't know he was doing it but Bradshaw had taken to answering his questions literally, because he suspected it might irritate the older man.

'Not right.'

'Excuse me?'

'Sixth,' answered Bradshaw. He couldn't see the doctor, he was still looking at the wooden blades of the ceiling fan, but he knew the man would be frowning while he attempted to understand his patient's meaning. 'This is our *sixth* session.'

'Is it?' the voice was disbelieving.

'Yes it is.' Bradshaw wanted to add, 'Believe me, I know!'

'I'm sure you're right,' the doctor's face would be a picture of geniality now but if Mellor couldn't get a simple fact like this right then what chance was there that he could actually help Bradshaw to conquer his 'demons', as they were both encouraged to call them?

'I am,' confirmed Bradshaw.

The doctor cleared his throat and asked, 'would you like some tea?'

Always the same offer, always the same reply. 'No.'

'I *will* have some, if you don't mind,' the doctor said.

'Why would I mind?'

He heard the doctor pad across the carpet then the snick of the kettle as he switched it on. 'So, as a young man, how did you feel about yourself, Ian? Would you mind telling me that? Take as long as you need.'

'If you like.' Ian Bradshaw didn't really care. He just wanted the seconds to tick by until they made minutes, and then for the minutes to accumulate as quickly as possible until there were sixty of them and the hour was up, whereupon the doctor would solemnly announce, as he always did, that 'alas and alack our time is through,' before moving on to his next victim – the money-grubbing old goat.

Bradshaw thought for a long while before answering, so long that he heard the kettle hiss then bubble as its watery contents slowly began to drift to the boil, then the words came out, seemingly of their own accord. 'When I was a boy I used to think the world was a movie about my life and I was its star.'

'Interesting,' said the doctor and he began to pour.

'Is it?'

'Yes, it is,' Bradshaw could hear the clink, clink, clink of the metal spoon against the bone-china cup as the doctor

27

stirred. 'And now, Ian,' he probed gently, 'how do you feel about yourself now?'

Again, there was a long silence before the younger man spoke.

'Like a bit-part player,' answered Bradshaw, 'non-speaking.'

Mellor contemplated DC Bradshaw's response for a time.

'Shall I tell you what I think?' asked the good doctor eventually.

'Isn't that the whole point of the exercise?' replied Bradshaw.

'Therapy is a two-way street, Ian,' Doctor Mellor reminded him, 'you talk to me, we establish a bond of trust, over time. I feel it's only fair for me to repay that trust.'

'So, you're going to tell me about your childhood?' asked Bradshaw.

'No, no, Ian,' a slight grimace of irritation from the usually unruffled doctor, 'that's not what I am going to do and I suspect you know that. No, I am going to tell you what I think. What we have here is a classic case of a life failing to live up to really quite unrealistic expectations. I believe you to be a romantic at heart, Ian, with a romantic's overblown view of the world and I don't just mean where the fairer sex is concerned, though you are currently single,' the doctor needlessly reminded him. 'We have spoken before about your long-held desire to join the police force, which I feel was the nearest thing to your childhood comics filled with heroes who would somehow save the day. You expected that the job of a police officer would be something you could fall into quite naturally and were subsequently quite unprepared for the frustrations of the job.

'Don't you see, though, that there is nothing fundamentally wrong with you,' the doctor suddenly announced cheerfully, 'apart from a quite temporary sense of shock and despair caused by the trauma of the . . . er . . . *incident* of which we have previously spoken at length. Aside from that, the realities of day-to-day life simply fail to live up to your expectations.' The doctor spoke those last words as if he had just discovered a cure for cancer or at least the particular tumour that afflicted Bradshaw. This time the silence went on for so long the doctor felt compelled to prompt the detective constable with a 'right?'

'I know that,' said Bradshaw and he sat bolt upright on the couch. 'I bloody know that. Jesus Christ, six sodding hours for you to finally come out with the bleeding obvious! Life hasn't lived up to my earlier hopes and aspirations; well then, that's just me and about nine-tenths of the rest of the planet isn't it? I don't suppose you wanted to do *this* when you were a kid, did you?'

'Calm down, Ian,' cautioned the doctor.

'Calm down? Bollocks to that!' Bradshaw sat up suddenly, 'I've had enough of this,' and he climbed down from the couch and struggled into his jacket.

'But Ian,' protested the dumbstruck doctor, 'we've barely had forty minutes, you've still got twenty left.'

'Keep the change!' called Bradshaw as he went through the door.

He hadn't gone more than a few yards when the receptionist reached him. They were both moving at speed and almost barged into one another.

'Detective Constable,' she said, 'I have a call for you. They say it's urgent.'

They walked quickly back to the front desk together and Bradshaw picked up the phone. It was Peacock.

'Get your arse back here sharpish, Bradshaw,' the Detective Inspector ordered, 'the boss wants everyone assembled in half an hour.'

'What's happened?' Ian asked, and when Peacock answered, Bradshaw felt a stone where his stomach had been.

'Another girl's been taken.'

Chapter Six

Jesus, thought Tom Carney, what the hell did he have to do to please this man? 'What's the matter?' he protested weakly. The alpha male within him had run for cover at the first sound of the Doc's booming voice and he already sounded like a small child caught licking the icing off a cake by his mother.

'He's suing us!' yelled Docherty, 'and, according to our lawyers, he's going to bloody win!'

Tom rallied then. 'Of course he's going to sue us. What choice does he have? He's not going to admit it, is he? If he does that he's finished. Timothy Grady's a politician, so he's got to sue or at least *say* he's going to sue – but he isn't going to win. He can't win!'

'Oh, can't he? Which law school did you go to? Or are you George Carman in disguise?' Tom kept silent. 'No? Well perhaps you can get me his number because I think we are going to need the best libel lawyer in the country thanks to you, that stupid bitch Anna-Louise and that nugget Jonathan. The only person I blame for this disaster more than you lot is my deputy. He, at the very least, should have known better!'

In that instant it all became clear. Alex Docherty was already distancing himself from the story, the front page lead on his own paper, on the hard-to-disprove point that he was technically on leave on the day it was cleared to run, at a Buckingham Palace garden party of all things, and poor, unfortunate Martyn Tracy had taken on the job of Editor in the great man's absence for a day; a single day that would probably destroy him and everyone who worked on the story, if Grady won his libel case. It mattered little that Docherty was in touch with every aspect of it right up until virtually the hour that it ran. He would only have to claim that he would never have agreed to run the story in its entirety and it would be the deputy editor who'd carry the can. Editors lost their jobs over this kind of thing. Newspapers weren't made of money and their owners did not like to lose libel cases. Juries had a nasty habit of awarding massive pay-outs to the wronged, even when they were as guilty as sin and everybody knew it. It was one thing to know someone was dodgy, another thing entirely to prove it beyond doubt in a court of law. Alex Docherty had consulted the paper's lawyers and he was already running for cover. So much for it being 'his paper'.

'But we've got photos of Grady coming out of his apartment and pictures of her going in,' Tom protested.

'Not the apartment,' the Doc corrected him, 'the apartment *block*. She could have been shagging anybody in those flats, or so his lawyers will claim,' countered his editor. 'I told you we needed a recording of them screwing or at least negotiating the terms of the shag in advance.'

'And I told you there was no chance of that,' said Tom, 'it was his flat and he wasn't daft. He used to just point at the bedroom when a girl arrived and she'd go in and strip off. There was nowhere to conceal a mic on her. He just did the bizzo and handed her the cash. You told us to write it anyway.'

The Doc shot him a warning look and Tom realised he would be expected to erase that little exchange from his memory, which had occurred when Alex Docherty was in one of his egotistical, print-and-be-damned moods.

'Our lawyers are saying it's flimsy,' said the Doc, 'it looks like a tabloid set up and he can just say he has never even seen her or her mates before, much less given them one.'

'He has given her several!' Tom argued, 'and her mates – and they are all willing to swear it was him.'

'They are hookers!' the Doc shouted and he waved his arms in frustration. 'Which means their word counts for a bit less than a cabinet minister's!' He seemed to force himself to calm down then. 'And there's something else.'

'What?'

The Doc seemed pained, 'his lawyers are asking for the exact times and dates we are claiming he was shagging Miss Sparkle and her mates.'

'So?'

'Our lawyers reckon it's so they can go back to Grady and ask him if he has alibis for those times and dates.'

'Well he hasn't,' said Tom, 'has he?'

'Well let's see, shall we?' The Doc made a great show of pretending that he was thinking. He placed a hand to his chin and wrinkled his forehead in a mock frown. 'He's a wealthy, powerful individual who might one day become Prime Minister, which means he can generously repay a lot of favours. There have been rumours of dodgy dealings surrounding him for years, so we already know he's bent. What do you think, Tom? Reckon he'll have any trouble coming up with those alibis?'

'But this is . . .'

'Unfair?' offered the Doc, 'to hell with fair. This tosser is fighting for his political life right now and most probably his marriage as well. He ain't gonna fight fair, is he?'

Tom was feeling bewildered now. Faced with his editor's certainty, he suddenly ran out of arguments. 'What are you going to do?'

'About this? I don't know. I'll probably develop an ulcer and have a heart attack as well but you worry about yourself, not me.'

'How do you mean?'

'We can't have you in the office writing more stories while we are being sued because of your last one. The lawyers would have a fit. I need you out of the building. Take a holiday,' Docherty told Tom. 'Don't look at me like that. You'll still get your money. I'd kill for some paid holiday right now.'

'What about my contract? You know I've only got six months and it expires soon.'

'We'll have to wait and see, won't we?' he told Tom.

'Are you throwing me out? Is that what you're doing here? Just tell me if you are.'

'No, I am not throwing you out, so don't give me any more grief!'

'So why can't you tell me what's going to happen at the end of my contract?'

'Because I don't actually know if I'll be there then, let alone you! I might not even survive the day. Nobody likes to lose a libel case, son; they are way too expensive, even for us.'

Jennifer chose that point to put her head round the door.

'Sorry, Chief, you said you wanted to write that letter to Cryptic Ken.' And when he blinked at her in something like recognition she added, 'I could come back later.'

'No, Jennifer, come in,' he told her, taking a deep breath, 'I'm done here,' He left Tom under no illusion that their conversation was over.

Cryptic Ken was the paper's resident astrologer, a man whose days were constantly rumoured to be numbered because his horoscopes were too mundane for the Doc's tastes. Their last row had been loud enough for half the office to hear every excruciating detail. Alex Docherty wanted to see dreams, wealth and steamy love affairs in each horoscope, every day.

'But that's not how it works,' protested Cryptic Ken, 'life isn't like that.'

'Who cares how it works?' demanded the Doc. 'It's all a load of wank anyway! Horoscopes are bullshit. How can one-twelfth of the population experience exactly the same level of good or bad fortune on the same bloody day, just because they were born during a random positioning of the stars? I'm selling dreams on every twatting page here. I want each and every reader to think it could happen to them; whether it's playing for England or ending up in a threesome with Sharon Stone and the bird behind the bar at their local pub and you, pal, are letting the fucking side down!'

Now Jennifer sat on the edge of the couch and crossed her legs primly, holding a pen close to her notepad, ready to transcribe the editor's latest death warrant.

But first the Doc turned to Tom. 'Do me a favour, son, leave my office now will you, like a good little boy – and don't ever have the temerity to go mentioning your contract to me again or I'll terminate it on the spot.' And he turned back to Jennifer.

'I want you take this down word for word, exactly as I speak it,' he told her. 'Dear Cryptic Ken . . . as you no doubt will have foreseen . . . you're fucking fired . . . fondest regards, the Doc,' then he glanced to one side and realised Tom was sitting there in mute shock. 'Why are you still here?' he demanded.

Chapter Seven

The team was so large they had to go the training room so their senior officers could address them all. The twenty-five detectives assigned to the investigation into the murdered girls filed into the room. DI Peacock was already there and DCI Kane, so too was Chief Superintendent Trelawe. A fourth man Bradshaw had never seen before was standing to one side of the top brass.

'I'm sure you've all heard by now,' Kane began, 'we have another missing girl.' He looked around the room to let that one sink in. 'Now, I'm going to give you the bare facts as we know them,' he continued, 'then I'm going to hand you over to Chief Superintendent Trelawe.'

DCI Kane waited to ensure he had their full attention then continued, 'the latest girl is Michelle Summers, aged fifteen, from Great Middleton. She disappeared last night, her last known whereabouts being the bus shelter at the foot of the hill at the eastern end of the village. She was seen there by a number of witnesses, presumably waiting for the last bus that would take her through the village to her home at the opposite end of Great Middleton, right by the main arterial road. Michelle lives there with her mother and stepfather, no siblings. None of our witnesses saw her walk away from that bus shelter or get into a car with anyone. The driver has already been questioned and swears that nobody boarded his bus from that stop last night. We are looking for passengers who can confirm this.'

'There's a boyfriend, Darren Tully, same age as Michelle, but he got a lift home from a friend's mother. The mother confirmed she saw Michelle alive and well, so we can rule him out. We've spoken to Michelle's mother. She fell asleep on the couch downstairs and didn't hear her daughter come home but there was a light on in the girl's room when she went to bed, so she assumed all was well. It now looks as if it may have been left on when the girl got ready to go to the youth club earlier that evening.' Then he added, 'We're not sure how reliable a witness the mother is.'

'Meaning she's a pisshead,' whispered the officer next to Bradshaw.

Either Kane didn't hear this comment or he chose to ignore it. 'Now it is of course entirely possible that young Michelle is a runaway but she only had the clothes on her back and a few coins in her purse. From the M. O. alone and the assurances of the family that the girl had no reason to run off, we have to accept that this is likely to be the work of the man the tabloids have taken to calling The Reaper. We think it is very possible therefore that Michelle Summers is Girl Number Five.' The room was immediately filled with the low humming sound of twenty-five detectives all offering each other an opinion at once. Kane held up a hand to silence them. 'Like the other victims, she's been snatched from the street. Two were walking home from school, one was waiting by the side of the road for her ride home and another, like Michelle, was taken from a bus stop.

'As you know when a youngster goes missing, the first couple of days are vital. If she *is* a runaway, we'll find her soon enough or she'll be picked up in London and they'll pack her back up here but we can't wait for that; not while there is a killer out there targeting young girls, so we need you to be all over this one – and I do mean all over it. Now the Chief Superintendent has an important announcement.'

'Thank you, David.' Chief Superintendent Trelawe was young for his rank and always struck Bradshaw as a man in a hurry. 'Five children,' he told them sharply, 'five young girls taken from their families in eleven weeks, lifted off the streets they once considered safe.' He paused for effect, 'and not a single lead worth a damn from any of you.' He looked around the room. 'Not one worthwhile scrap of information that has led us anywhere but back here to this briefing room, as we once again contemplate how these atrocities could be committed in our own back-yard. You may feel I am being harsh and if you do, you can tell that to the parents of the last victim.

'Now I expect you all to redouble your efforts. I want you to get out there, find this man and bring him to justice but I have come to realise you are unlikely to achieve that on your own,' added Trelawe and Bradshaw knew that statement wouldn't go down well, 'which is why I have asked Professor Richard Burstow to join us here today.' All eyes turned to the civilian standing next to the senior officers. 'The professor is an expert in the relatively new field of forensic profiling, having worked with, amongst others, the Metropolitan Police and the FBI. He has kindly offered us his assistance and we have asked him to draw up a psychological profile of the man we should be looking for. Professor . . .'

The Chief Superintendent turned to the professor and stepped to one side, allowing the older man to come to the front. He looked every inch the academic, sporting items of clothing – a tweed jacket, blue striped shirt, grey trousers and red tie – that failed to match.

'If there is one thing I want you to keep today,' he told them all confidently, 'it's an open mind.' And his eyes roamed the room. 'Some of you may be familiar with the science . . . for it is a science . . . of psychological profiling . . . and some of you will have doubts about the validity of the notion that by observing the scene of a murder and analysing the evidence contained therein, one can detect consistent patterns of behaviour and, thereby, deduce characteristics the murderer is likely to possess.'

'Bullshit.' The word wasn't shouted but nor was it whispered. Instead, DC Skelton uttered it just loud enough for Bradshaw and his immediate colleagues to hear. Whether the professor heard or not, he chose to continue.

'I have worked with America's Federal Bureau of Investigations in Langley, Virginia on a number of high-profile cases. The FBI is at the forefront when it comes to applying modern technological and scientific methods to crime detection. You might doubt the effectiveness of psychological profiling as an investigative tool but they do not and if it's good enough for the FBI . . .' He left the sentence unfinished but the inference was there, thought Bradshaw. The professor thought the members of this small north eastern police force were all dinosaurs by comparison. 'Remember also that there were those who once doubted the use of fingerprinting or forensic analysis in solving crime. No one queries that now.'

He waited to see if anybody was going to challenge him, asking 'Any questions?' and when none were forthcoming, continuing his lecture. 'Good,' he said, 'the man you are looking for is white . . .'

'In the North East?' hissed DC Bob Davies incredulously, 'never.' And there were a couple of low chuckles. Even Bradshaw had to concede he had a point. It wasn't that migrants were more or less welcome in the North East than any other part of England but they tended to follow the jobs, and there was always a shortage of those around here.

'. . . He's never had a meaningful relationship,' the professor went on, 'he's inexperienced sexually, possibly a virgin or, if he has had sexual relations with a woman, it was a traumatic episode that left him scarred in some way.'

Behind Bradshaw, Trevor Wilson muttered, 'He must have been shagging your missus,' causing the guy on the receiving end of this bit of banter to stifle a laugh by turning it into a fake cough.

'So he's single, lives alone or possibly with an elderly mother. Look for the absence of a father figure, probably from a young age.'

'What makes you so sure about all this?' asked a voice from the back. Bradshaw didn't bother to turn to identify the man. He was more interested in the professor's answer.

'Look at the condition of the four previous victims and the way they were found. There was nothing hidden away, there were no shallow graves. All of them were left on open ground in rural areas. It's as if he wanted us to find them. This man was proud of his work,' he let that sink in, 'but not one of them was assaulted sexually. Their clothes were undisturbed, without even a partial undressing of any of them. Why not? Why is he not curious about them sexually?' he asked rhetorically. 'Because he is not interested in his victims as sexual beings. This man is a misfit. He cannot relate to an adult woman, all that complexity, the hair, bodily fluid, menstruation; all of this disgusts and repels him so he chooses young girls instead. What he wants is an ideal, a dream, an entirely innocent female, something he can cope with, control and contain . . . someone he can manipulate and play with . . . a small child . . . a doll.'

It was a chilling idea and, as the professor continued, Bradshaw sensed the atmosphere in the room begin to change. The detectives were still sceptical but they were listening to him.

'He's physically strong, can strangle a young girl as easily as wringing the neck of a chicken, so there's power there. You are looking for a manual worker, a builder perhaps, this guy does not work in an office. He's blue collar and likely to be frustrated by his work. Perhaps he feels he should be special and cannot understand why the world does not agree with him.' Inwardly Bradshaw winced as he recalled his conversation with Doctor Mellor.

Some of the younger, eager beavers were making notes. It looked like the professor had convinced most of them he knew what he was talking about.

Before he could stop himself, Bradshaw asked, 'How does he get them to come with him?' Everyone turned to look at him and he cleared his throat.

The professor peered back at him and offered an apologetic smile. 'I wish I knew.' And he addressed the whole room. 'I can tell you a great deal about our man but not that, I'm afraid. Any more questions?' He spotted a young female DC who had raised her hand. 'Yes?'

'Will he do it again?'

The question was blunt and so was the answer, 'Oh yes,' and he looked her in the eye. 'Why?' he asked her in turn, 'because he enjoys it too much to stop. He loves the control he has over these young girls. It makes him feel . . .' He paused as he considered a suitable phrase.

'Like God,' someone had uttered the words out loud and, when everyone in the room turned to look at DC Bradshaw, he realised it must have been him.

'Precisely,' answered the professor.

Chapter Eight

Helen Norton looked up from her desk just as Martin, the deputy editor of the *Durham Messenger*, marched purposefully into his boss's office. She was too far away to hear what was being said but it was enough to energise their editor, which took some doing. She could see the two men exchanging words, grim-faced. Malcolm Hardy then picked up his phone and made a call. When Helen glanced up again she could see that Malcolm was laughing and joking with whoever was on the other end of the line. Then he hung up the phone and both men peered out at her. Helen quickly carried on writing up her piece on a charity fun-run. A moment later, her editor was standing over her.

'Helen,' he asked her with a leering smile that instinctively made her want to button her blouse up to the neck, 'remind me how long you've been with us?'

'Ten weeks.'

'Then I reckon it's time for your first death knock?'

'Okay,' she said quickly, getting to her feet and picking up her bag. Helen hadn't even blinked while he surveyed her for a response, not wanting to give him the satisfaction of knowing how she was really feeling. It wasn't just Malcolm; she wanted the other journalists to take her seriously too, even if she did only work on a 'weekly', as Peter had been foolish enough to remind her during their latest argument about her chosen career.

The *Durham Messenger* was a good start as far as she was concerned; a well-respected 'regional' that covered the whole county, with a decent reputation for solid, if unspectacular, journalism that stretched back decades. It certainly beat working for a 'free-sheet' that would be dropped into every letterbox for nothing, whether the recipient wanted a copy or not, its front pages dominated not by news but tacky adverts for cheap carpets or bedroom furniture.

Malcolm held out his hand to offer a slip of paper he'd scribbled a name and address on. She tried to take it from him but he deliberately held on to it. 'You sure you're ready?' he asked with insincere concern.

'Yep.'

'Okay,' he said it as if he wasn't entirely convinced of this but he did at least release the piece of paper into her care and began to brief her, 'Lee Wallace is no more,' he explained, even though he knew she wouldn't have a clue who he was referring to, as she'd not been living in the area long enough to know any of the local characters.

'He's a bit of a hard-knock,' he told her, 'a one-man teenage crime wave – or at least he was.' He actually smirked. 'He's only managed to crash a stolen car into the concrete strut of a bridge at something like eighty miles an hour.' Shaking his head at Lee Wallace's folly, he continued, 'Now he has gone to the great big borstal in the sky we need you to get down to his house and speak to his family, see if you can get some sense out of one of them. Off you go then.' He jerked his head towards the door and she left the news room without protest.

Helen Norton had reserved judgement about her

editor till that point but she was beginning to realise the truth. The man was an idiot. It was not that Malcolm wasn't competent enough to oversee the creation of a new edition each and every week without messing it up entirely but the *Durham Messenger*'s quality was largely down to its journalists and its continued success was despite Malcolm, not because of him.

Malcolm seemed to spend an inordinate amount of his time walking up and down between reporter's desks making what he thought were wisecracks. He was the kind of man who laughed at his own jokes and no one else's and his were never that good.

And he was lazy.

To Malcolm, a strong news story on the last day before going to print was an irritation not an opportunity, something that got in the way of the smooth running of his domestic life. He didn't encourage his journalists or make them strive for greater things. Instead he merely expected them to churn out enough copy so that he could fill the pages of the paper as early as possible in the week then go home. It seemed everyone at the *Messenger* put up with this state of affairs but no one took the guy very seriously.

As she climbed into her car, Helen felt a little sick but she told herself to get a grip. She was twenty-three years old, a mature, educated and intelligent young woman, with a degree in English and a post-grad in journalism that was endorsed by the National Union of Journalists and approved by the NCTJ, the National Council for the Training of Journalists. She even had a press card, a little blue plastic one with her picture on it. Helen was so proud of this that in her first week, she had to resist the tempta-

46

tion to keep pulling it out surreptitiously to take another look at it. It was in her bag right now, next to Peter's apologetic card.

Helen had wanted to be a journalist for as long as she could remember and was now part of a team of reporters on a well-respected newspaper. So why was she filled with dread each morning and not excitement? Maybe because she felt as if she didn't really have a clue what she was doing? Yep, that was it. Sometimes she couldn't shake the feeling that she was an imposter; a little girl, playing a game of dress-up in her mother's old clothes, but now she'd been thrown in the deep end.

The death knock. Every student journalist knows about them and dreads the day they will be called upon to make one. Helen Norton had been expecting this of course but the suddenness caught her by surprise and she was trying hard to compose herself as she drove to the unfortunate family's house.

People killed by terrorists or murdered in lawless parts of the globe, stabbings and shootings, car crashes and pedestrians mowed down by fleeing criminals or, sometimes, the police who pursued them; all of them end up in the newspaper, their photographs looking out at you while their deaths are explained and somehow rationalised in quotes from partners, parents or loved ones. Helen wondered if anyone ever stopped to question how those quotes were obtained and where the intimate photographs came from; those pictures of beautiful brides who drown in the sea on their honeymoons, of promising students killed by hit-and-run drivers, of little boys and girls whose lives are cruelly cut short by accident, illness or murder. There is no database of photographs of the country's population stored on some enormous computer, waiting for the day when an image can be plucked from it to accompany a newspaper's tragic story. Those pictures have to be acquired, taken from the albums of the poor victim's family, prised from the clutches of the bereaved and grieving when they are at their most anguished.

It's not an easy matter to call on someone when they have lost everything, when their world has been destroyed by the death of a son or daughter, a wife or husband and ask them how they feel about it. You must convince someone who is beside themselves with grief to trust you with a picture that was precious before but now more priceless than ever. There will be no new photos of that loved one after all. You have to get them to part with a memory and all the while, at the back of your mind, you're praying whoever takes it from you at the newspaper returns it in the same condition, for these things matter greatly.

Helen parked her car in a long, terraced street on the outskirts of Darlington then went the remaining distance to number thirty-nine on foot. She walked slowly, practising her opening words silently in her head, hoping they were as appropriate as they could be under the circumstances. She reached the front door, took a deep breath, then knocked.

She stood for a moment, half hoping there would be nobody there, then she heard advancing footsteps and, all too soon, the door was pulled open. A woman, who had to be the mother, was standing on the doorstep – but if

Helen was expecting tears, there were none. This woman was big and hard looking and she said nothing, merely surveyed Helen dispassionately.

'I am so sorry to disturb you,' Helen began, 'I really am.' The woman folded her arms and continued to watch Helen, showing no sign that she was a mother who'd been robbed of her teenaged son that very morning. Helen ploughed on somehow, adding, 'I'm from the local paper and I wondered if you might be prepared to talk to us about Lee.'

Helen watched the woman as she unfolded her arms, rolled her eyes and in a voice that held no trace of anguish asked, 'Bloody hell, what has he done now?'

As Tom walked dumbly past the rows of reporters, nobody paid him any attention. The Doc's voice had a way of travelling and he kept his door open for a reason; so that everybody knew who was on the receiving end of his temper and would pray they weren't going to be next. All of a sudden everyone was very busy. If you were on the wrong side of the chief nobody would give you the time of day, they didn't want to be you or even be associated with you. You were a 'Winston', after Winston Smith, the hero of Orwell's *1984*, because sometimes the people on the wrong end of those bollockings would literally disappear and never be seen again.

Tom had witnessed this before and now it was his turn. He felt sick. How could a day have turned from triumph to outright disaster so quickly? He glanced at his watch. Jesus, he thought, not even ten o'clock and I'm already on gardening leave. The girl from the water cooler quickly picked up the phone as he reached her desk. There was no smile this time. She didn't even look at him.

By now Tom couldn't wait to climb into the lift and get out of there. He had almost reached the last line of reporters' desks when a voice came from the end of a row. 'Hey Tom!' It was Angus Boyle, self-styled ace crime reporter. 'You're from the grim old North,' he was reminded. 'Do you know Great Middleton?'

How weird was this? On the verge of his greatest humiliation and he receives a timely reminder of his past. 'Yeah,' mumbled Tom, 'I used to live there, years ago. Moved away when I was still a kid but I covered the area for the local paper before I moved down here.'

'It's your home town?'

'It was. It's actually a village.'

'What's it like?'

Why the hell was Boyle asking him this? Nothing ever happened there and it was hardly a holiday destination. 'Small,' was all he could think to say by way of an answer, 'semi-rural, with a farm at either end,' he could see Boyle was still interested, so he thought he'd better make an effort, 'one junior school, four pubs, a village hall, about twelve hundred people living there. Why do you ask?'

Boyle snorted, 'Don't you read your own bloody paper?' Tom had read it that morning but limited his interest to the first five pages, which dealt exclusively with the supposed downfall of Timothy Grady. 'A young girl's gone missing,' Boyle said it matter-of-factly as journalists tend to, 'so they're saying he's done it again, the Kiddy-Catcher.'

The official tabloid nickname given to the child killer was 'The Reaper' but off the record, journalists and police officers alike had taken to calling him 'the Kiddy-Catcher', using a macho, gallows humour, so they didn't have to ponder the realities of the case.

'That's what?' asked Boyle, 'Girl Number Five?'

Tom nodded. 'Yeah,' he agreed, 'Girl Number Five.'

'How did it go?' Malcolm asked her in front of everyone.

Helen tried hard to contain her fury but her voice was trembling with rage and everyone in the news room turned to look at her when they heard it. 'The next time you send one of us out on a death knock because you've had a tip-off from your mate in the police, make sure they've told the bloody parents first!'

'Oh God,' Malcolm flushed, 'I thought they had,' and he realised that all of his reporters were staring at him now.

'No,' she informed him, 'they hadn't!'

Helen had found out to her cost just how quick the police had been to tell the local newspaper editor about young Lee Wallace's unfortunate demise and how slow they had been to inform the lad's own mother, who had no idea why a *Messenger* reporter was knocking on her door that morning asking for quotes. Helen had made a swift and apologetic exit, mumbling about it all being a mistake.

'Oh bollocks,' Malcolm added, looking as uncomfortable as she had ever seen him.

'And when they do finally inform her,' she added, 'don't send me back there!'

'No,' he assured her quickly, 'I won't.'

Malcolm retreated into his office then and stayed there for the rest of the day.

Chapter Nine

Bradshaw watched as Vincent shuffled into the room nervously carrying a large tray of steaming mugs, his face a picture of concentration. When the big man finally set the tray down in front of his colleagues, not one of them thanked him or even acknowledged his efforts. That seemed to be Vincent Addison's role these days: the office tea boy, tolerated but not respected. He could carry on drawing his salary as a detective constable just so long as he wasn't trusted with any actual police work. It was a sad state of affairs but these days Bradshaw even envied him that status.

'You trying to poison me?' Skelton's face twisted into a grimace.

'What?' answered Vincent.

'There's about three sugars in this,' the detective constable pulled a face, 'and I don't even take sugar.'

'Oh sorry,' Vincent seemed genuinely concerned, rather than angered by Skelton's tone, 'I must have mixed up yours and David's.'

'You really are a waste of oxygen, Vince,' a couple of his fellow officers chuckled at that, enjoying the spectacle of the bigger but weaker man being tormented by Skelton, 'you can't even get the bloody tea right.' Skelton was playing to the gallery now, 'What is the point of you, eh?' and when the older man was stuck for an answer, he repeated, 'Eh?'

'Oi,' said Bradshaw.

Skelton rounded on Bradshaw, 'Oi? What do you mean oi?'

Bradshaw had spoken without really thinking and didn't know what to say next. In the end he settled on, 'Why can't you just leave him alone?'

'You again?' said Skelton. 'Fuck me, every time I turn around there you are, ruining my day.' Bradshaw could see the other men smirking at that. 'What's it to you anyway? He's a big boy. Let him fight his own battles.' Vincent meanwhile had shuffled off with the empty tray.

'Just leave him alone. You have a go at him every bloody day.'

'Oh right, well, since you put it like that, maybe I'll start having a go at you every day instead.'

Bradshaw realised none of his fellow officers was going to come to his aide. 'Water off a duck's back,' he mumbled half-heartedly.

'What?' Skelton was on his feet now, using the mumbled reply as an excuse to stand over Bradshaw to intimidate him. 'What did you just say?'

'I said, it's water off a duck's back.'

'Really? We'll see, eh? Just mind your own business next time Sherlock.' They'd given Bradshaw that nickname years ago, when they heard he had qualifications. Now it had stuck and he hated it. It was another reminder of his failure. 'Else I'll have to knock some sense into you.' Skelton was staring straight at him now, defying him to get out of his chair and take a swing but Bradshaw knew that would end badly. Win or lose, he knew he'd be blamed for starting it.

Instead Bradshaw just stared straight ahead. Skelton

regarded him with distaste then said, 'Yeah, thought not,' before sitting back down with a smirk on his face.

But Bradshaw couldn't let it go. 'You're a disgrace,' he said.

'I'm a disgrace?' replied Skelton. 'At least I never put anybody in a wheelchair.'

The room went very quiet then. Everyone else decided to mind their own business. Bradshaw suddenly realised that Peacock had been watching it all from the doorway, but the DI acted like he'd just arrived. 'Come on,' he said, 'you haven't got time for tea, get yourselves back out there.'

Bradshaw was the last to file out of the door. Peacock stopped him and waited till the others were out of earshot. 'Choose your battles more carefully, son. You ain't got many friends left round here and Vincent hasn't got any. They've been trying to get rid of him for ages. He's a liability and you won't win anyone over by sticking up for him.'

'Thanks for the advice, boss,' Bradshaw said in a neutral monotone.

Peacock looked exasperated but he let it go.

The underground was eerily empty at this hour. Tom Carney chose not to re-read the 'Grady and the Tramp' story. He didn't want to be reminded that if the Doc's prediction was correct, Timothy Grady's highly paid lawyers were about to bring his career as a reporter to a swift, inglorious end.

Tom had never seriously considered any other line of work. Journalism was the only thing he had ever wanted to do or been any good at. It had taken six long years on the *Durham Messenger* before he'd finally landed his big break at The Paper. Six years of non-stories about summer fêtes and beauty queens, planning rows and non-league football matches, mind-numbing council meetings and a daily diet of self-important press releases from local businesses or their egocentric MP. After six months writing real news for a national tabloid, he could never go back to his local paper – and they wouldn't take him either, not the way he left. Christ, what would he do if he ended up taking a share of the blame for this catastrophe? It didn't bear thinking about.

Though it annoyed Tom to admit it, the Doc was right. 'It doesn't really matter whether Grady is guilty of spending his spare hours throwing money at hookers, three at a time,' his editor assured him, 'it doesn't even matter whether the average man in the street considers him to be guilty. The only thing that does matter is how far down the garden path a bunch of highly remunerated advocates can lead a jury of simpletons. The Paper might just survive a seven-figure pay-out but we certainly won't!' All those years Tom had waited for a shot at the title then, when he finally got one, he'd screwed up and it looked likely to destroy him. It couldn't be more humiliating.

In an effort to take his anxious mind away from his troubles, Tom picked up the paper and flicked through it until he reached the pages that dealt with the missing girl from the north east. Five young girls, aged between ten and fifteen, had vanished from small towns and villages across the county and four bodies had already been found. Now everybody was expecting a fifth. It was hard to hold out much hope for victim number five.

The latest location surprised Tom. Great Middleton was so small, had seemed so even when he was a child, living there with his mother, father and sister, several lifetimes ago, before everything went to rat-shit. His father moved them to a town ten miles down the road afterwards. Nobody could face staying there any more, because Great Middleton was full of ghosts.

There was an out-of-date picture of Michelle in the paper, aged about twelve; a school photograph of a girl with long dark hair tied in two tight, neat plaits, either side of a pale, freckled face. Michelle wore a forced smile for the photographer with an obvious self-consciousness about the metal teeth braces that filled her mouth. She was dressed in a white shirt and a black and yellow tie with her secondary school crest on it.

Tom noted how careful his fellow journalist had been about reporting Michelle's fate but you could easily read between the lines. The police had dropped enough hints about fears for her safety for all of the journos to link the vanished girl with the other missing children. Most likely the poor lass would be found in a ditch a few miles from her home. The nation would be collectively appalled at the story and for a moment, everyone would feel for the girl and her family. How could you ever get over something like that, they would ask themselves, tutting over their cornflakes, before turning their attention to the more mundane matter of getting ready for work that morning. It would be the family who would have to live with her disappearance for the rest of their lives, long after everyone else had forgotten the girl's name. Of course, there was always the hope of a miracle; but Tom had been in journalism long enough to know that they were in very short supply.

Tom returned home and watched Timothy Grady on the TV news as the politician emerged from his London home to fight his way through the media scrum outside. There was no mistaking his absolute fury as he stomped down the steps of his Kensington townhouse. The man from the BBC thrust a microphone through the crowd of paparazzi, jabbing it at Grady. 'These allegations are absurd and deeply defamatory,' Grady barked at the nation, 'but I shall have my day in court. The mighty cannons of the British justice system shall blast apart the flimsy foundations of these baseless, slanderous lies, consigning them where they belong,' there was a dramatic pause from the Defence Secretary, 'in the gutter!'

Grady tried to force his way to his waiting car but a newspaper reporter demanded an answer. The reporter's voice could not be heard but Grady's tetchy reply was audible to all, 'I might very well have met Miss Sparkle. She is apparently a constituent!' he blustered, before adding, 'No, I will not be resigning, no, no, no! There's no question!'

The former golden boy of the Conservative party finally succeeded in forcing his way through the throng and into a waiting state car, a black Jaguar Sovereign, his face like thunder, cheeks redder than one of his ministerial boxes.

'Twat,' said Tom as he watched the politician speed away.

He walked into the kitchen and flicked on the kettle, then thought better of it and turned it off again. He walked back into the living room and leaned against the door frame just as the BBC news began to cover the other story of interest to him.

Tom watched as the same photograph of a smiling Michelle Summers in school uniform appeared, the news-reader regurgitating the well-worn, pat phrases that were always employed when the police feared the worst. '*Concern was growing last night following the disappearance of a fifteen-year-old girl from County Durham. Michelle Summers has not been seen since leaving her local youth club in the village of Great Middleton, at around ten p.m. on Thursday evening.*' There then followed a brief physical description of the girl. '*Police have appealed for anyone who may have seen Michelle to come forward.*'

Tom made an instinctive decision then that spurred him into action. He went up to the tiny spare room he rented from Terry-the-sub. Tom dreaded the thought of staying in this cramped room, waiting for the paper's lawsuit and his future to be resolved, while not being allowed any-where near the office. He knew the legal case could drag on for months and he had to face facts. He was more than likely finished at The Paper and perhaps even as a journalist altogether. Maybe he could freelance for a while but he wouldn't be allowed to do that under his own name. Any-thing he wrote could have no by-line and The Paper could never find out but the tabloid world was a small one and if he was seen popping into the office of a rival newspaper, the Doc would go loopy and he would be out for good.

He reached under the bed and grabbed his sports bag, dusty from months of lying there undisturbed. He dropped it on the bed then removed the entire contents from each of his drawers and threw them into the holdall;

socks, T shirts, underwear and pairs of jeans. Next he went to the bathroom and scooped up his razor, deodorant, brush and toothbrush and dropped them into a washbag that followed the clothes into the holdall.

Tom grabbed his notebook and pen, quickly scribbled a note on it and tore off the page then he wrote a cheque for the rent. He threw on his leather jacket and filled the pockets with his notepad, pens, camera, wallet and keys then finally picked up the bulky cell phone they'd given him when he joined The Paper and stuffed that in a side pocket. He looked around the room and noted that he'd managed to remove every trace of his existence in less than five minutes, a realisation that was both gloomy and liberating at the same time. Tom went downstairs, placed the rent cheque and note on the mantelpiece then headed for the door.

There were bits that appeared to be falling off the body of the black Mark Two Ford Escort and other sections that seemed to be held to it only by a stubborn coating of rust but Tom still had a deep affection for the decrepit old heap. He prayed it would start. Journalists on The Paper prided themselves on taking taxis everywhere, claiming back fistfuls of receipts every month, even when it was easier to go by tube, and his car had barely been used lately.

It took four goes and each rasping, scraping turn of the key sounded like the Escort's final death rattle, but the ignition finally fired and the car suddenly spluttered into life, like an elderly colonel woken abruptly from his afternoon nap. He told himself it was a sunny morning in London and he was being paid to take a holiday. That was the glass-half-full approach he forced himself to adopt.

Tom Carney was heading home.

Chapter Ten

The TV reporter surveyed the massed throng of newspaper photographers in the village hall. 'Bloody paps,' he muttered under his breath but it was loud enough for Helen to hear.

'Hurry up,' he instructed a harassed-looking cameraman who was hurriedly assembling a tripod. Another photographer brushed past the two men in a hurry, barging the TV reporter in the process, 'vultures, the lot of them,' he mumbled. Helen watched him issuing instructions to the cameraman ending with a 'quickly ... quickly ... quicker ...' as a senior police officer emerged in uniform, followed by a plain clothes detective then finally, Michelle Summers' mother and stepfather. 'You'd better be ready ...' the TV reporter warned the cameraman as he continued to line up his shot.

The senior officer sat down in front of a microphone and, before he spoke, the TV reporter had just enough time to give a final instruction to his cameraman. 'And remember, if the mother starts to cry, zoom in on her face, nice and slow.'

The TV reporter turned then and noticed Helen surveying him with a look of distaste. 'What?' he asked. Helen opened her mouth to say something in reply but before she could speak she was drowned out by the first words from the uniformed policeman.

'I am Detective Superintendent Trelawe,' he told them importantly, 'and this is Detective Chief Inspector Kane. With me are Michelle Summers' mother Fiona and her stepfather Darren. We will begin this press conference with an appeal from Fiona.'

Michelle's mother stared nervously out at the ranks of photographers and journalists then down at the table, which contained a half dozen microphones set up by radio stations to capture her words. She had a piece of paper in her hands and she stared at it but did not start to read. Michelle's stepfather, a bulky man with an impassive face, put a hand on her shoulder for support or perhaps to prompt her, and she managed to begin, her voice quivering with emotion.

'Michelle, if you are listening to this,' she read, 'whatever's happened, it doesn't matter, we can sort it out, love. Just come home; please, darling, get in touch with us or just call the police to tell them where you are and they'll come and get you.' And she started to cry then. Later, Helen Norton would watch the TV coverage of that same press conference and notice that, as directed, the cameraman would choose that moment to begin a slow zoom into a close-up of the poor woman's face. Unable to continue, Fiona was helped to her feet by her husband, who led her from the room.

When the distraught mother had gone, Detective Superintendent Trelawe gave the journalists the simple facts, including Michelle's last known movements before she disappeared and a physical description of the girl, right down to the St Christopher medallion she wore round her neck on a silver chain. Then they took the first question. There was a flurry of hands and the detective superintendent pointed to a male reporter in the first row.

'Do you believe that Michelle Summers is Girl Number Five?'

'We can't be sure of that at this stage of our investigation,' answered Trelawe, 'but there are certain similarities between the previous cases and this one.'

'So you do believe it?' the reporter persisted.

'It is one of several lines of enquiry we are currently pursuing.' Trelawe quickly pointed to another journalist, hoping for a different line of questioning.

'Is Michelle the latest victim of The Reaper?' asked a reporter with a London accent.

'I think I just answered that question. That is a line of enquiry but we cannot categorically state . . .'

'Michelle Summers is an underage girl who has been snatched from a public place without anybody seeing or hearing a thing and she has not been seen since,' added the reporter, 'that sounds identical.'

'The detective superintendent was quite clear,' interrupted DCI Kane, 'we are rightly keeping an open mind and pursuing a number of different lines of enquiry, as you would expect us to. We would urge any member of the public with relevant information to contact us on one of the incident room hotlines.'

This just made Kane the focus of reporter's questions. 'Detective Chief Inspector, how are you going to catch this man and how can you prevent him from striking again?' another voice called from the back of the room.

'We are doing absolutely everything in our power . . .' Kane began but he was interrupted.

Reporters began shouting over each other as they competed to be heard. Trelawe knew he'd lost control. 'That is all for now ladies and gentlemen, thank you!' He quickly gathered his papers and got to his feet. 'You will be kept informed,' he assured the reporters who did not let up, continuing to call out to him as the police officers left the room.

Tom Carney followed the landlord up the narrow, creaking staircase to a gloomy first-floor landing with four small rooms. It had taken him five and a half hours to get from London to Great Middleton, which included a short rest for a soggy bacon sandwich and a cup of overpriced instant coffee that still tasted faintly of washing-up liquid. He was tired but at least his car hadn't broken down on the way.

'You're at the end on the right,' Colin explained, handing him the key, 'bathroom's opposite.'

'Thanks Col,' said Tom, 'you sure you don't want any more for the room? I feel bad.'

'How many times have you put my pub in the local paper?' the landlord demanded. 'Karaoke nights, charity do's, pool contests, darts matches, leek shows and football games; you've had them all on your district page over the years. I owe you.'

'A pint would have done.'

'I don't usually let the room out,' Colin explained, 'there's no real demand for it. It's yours for as long as you need it,' he shrugged, 'what you're paying is covering my costs. I don't need any more.'

'Cheers mate.'

Tom let himself into the room. It was tiny but it would do: containing a bed, an old wardrobe and a wash basin set against a wall. A portable television was perched on a chest of drawers next to a small kettle with two mugs, a few sachets of coffee and some tea bags. Tom put his bag on the bed and walked to the window, drawing a net curtain aside for a view of the street below and the rusting pub sign with a lean grey dog on it and the word 'Greyhound'.

'This'll do.' He quite liked the idea of staying above a pub.

Tom went down to the bar, where a pint of the Greyhound's famous IPA was poured for him by Colin. Tom accepted it gratefully. Someone had left a copy of that week's *Messenger* on a table and he picked it up and read it for the first time since he'd left the newspaper for London. It was strange to read a copy that did not contain a page lead with his name on it and he realised that, like countless other journalists at thousands of other newspapers, his contribution had only ever been a fleeting one and would soon be forgotten. As far as he could see, the *Messenger* seemed to be surviving perfectly well without him.

He took a long sip of beer, finished his pint and paid for another.

Two more pints slipped down fairly quickly and Tom was starting to feel much better about himself and the world. There was nothing like beer to give a man a temporary uplift, even though he was not in the habit of

64

having so many this early in the day. The bar started to fill up with the lunchtime trade, swelled by journalists who'd attended that morning's press conference and stayed on looking for an angle.

'Tom,' called a voice from somewhere over his shoulder and he half turned to find Mike Newton smiling at him, 'I didn't know you were back.'

'Oh yeah,' Tom stammered, 'I'm covering this story,' he would have been far less bothered about bumping into somebody from the *Messenger* if his position at The Paper had been halfway secure.

'Your old stomping ground,' Mike nodded, 'makes sense,' and it was clear he believed Tom had been sent back there by The Paper, 'so how's it going?'

'Great, mate, great, absolutely loving it.'

'Yeah?'

Mike seemed keen to hear all about the legendary Alex 'The Doc' Docherty and seemed mightily impressed that Tom dealt with the great man on a daily basis. 'Hey, it's good to see you,' he said. 'Malcolm took an age to replace you,'

'That's because I'm irreplaceable.'

'Could be,' Mike smiled, 'or he was just dragging his heels so he could cut the wage bill while he got the rest of us to do your work?'

'Sounds like Malcolm. So what's the new girl like? I heard she's a bit of a princess, parachuted in from down south?' Mike's face froze and he looked deeply uncomfortable then. Tom was just about to ask him what was wrong when a second voice interrupted him.

'I drove here actually,' and Tom turned to see a young, attractive, well-spoken woman regarding him with something like disdain. She was holding a pint of beer, which she handed to Mike.

'Thanks,' he said. 'Tom, this is Helen Norton.'

Tom Carney normally prided himself on his ability to think quickly and dig himself out of any situation but not this time. He'd had no idea Helen was standing behind him. She must have gone to the bar to get the drinks then quietly joined them without introduction. In her other hand Helen held a glass of wine and she took a sip while Tom tried to think of something to say to rescue the situation.

The best he could come up with was, 'Pleased to meet you, Helen.'

'I'll bet,' she said, without enthusiasm.

Chapter Eleven

When their sandwiches arrived, Helen and Mike took them to a corner table but Tom made no attempt to join them. Instead, he went round the room, chatting to the locals and renewing old acquaintances. He quickly noted that, although some were happy to see him again, others treated him with suspicion now he had graduated to working for a tabloid, as if he had somehow crossed over to the dark side and could no longer be trusted. None of them could tell him anything about Michelle Summers that he did not already know, so he left the pub and let the fresh air sober him up. He needed to speak with someone who actually knew what was going on in this village.

Tom tried the old vicarage but Mary Collier's housekeeper informed him she had a hospital appointment. Next he went to Roddy Moncur's house and banged on the door but there was no answer. Tom's two best contacts weren't around and he felt he was getting nowhere.

Tom had hoped to spend the afternoon sniffing out new leads on the disappearance of Michelle Summers but he'd drawn a complete blank. He had assumed that contacts and local knowledge would give him a head start over the cloud of reporters who'd descended on Great Middleton but nobody he'd spoken to had anything to say about Michelle, except how awful her disappearance was.

Tom trudged through the village, trying not to think about Timothy Grady as he took in the surroundings, experiencing the mixed feelings of an exile returning home. He didn't know if he was gaining comfort from the familiar or feeling the dread of being trapped in a small, provincial place he had spent years trying to escape. The several pints he'd consumed meant that at least he didn't feel the difference in temperature. It had to be at least three or four degrees colder here than in London. Nothing like a beer blanket, he thought to himself as he headed for the only sensible port of call after the dispiriting day he'd had; the Red Lion.

The Greyhound was a good choice for a quiet lunchtime pint and a handy base while he was back here but if you wanted a decent atmosphere in the evening it had to be the Lion, with its younger, slightly rougher crowd. Everything in the pub was hazy, obscured by the thick veil of cigarette smoke which always hung over the place. The Lion was half full already and Tom knew virtually everyone in there. Soon the older guys would drift home and the young ones would come out to take their place. He squeezed into a gap at the bar and ordered a pint of bitter from Harry the landlord. He was immediately pulled up on his accent.

'No way,' he protested.

'It's changed man,' Harry assured him, 'you've gone posh on us.'

'Bollocks,' he said but there were smiles from regulars who were going along with the wind-up. Tom endured a few minutes of good-natured banter on the subject of him turning into a soft southerner after just a few months in London.

'If it's any consolation, I get even more grief,' the comment came from the bar stool next to him, from a man Tom had never spoken to before. The guy was way too young to be an alkie but he was a definite barfly: one of those fellas whose leisure time pretty much consisted of hours spent in one pub. Tom had noticed him before, sitting quietly in the corner, nursing a pint while reading a book or gazing off into space, lost in his private thoughts. He looked out of place among the other, far older regulars; mostly retired guys who'd been shooed out of their homes by wives who wanted a bit of peace or some cleaning time without their men getting under their feet.

'Not from round here then?' asked Tom.

The man, who was about Tom's age, replied, 'I'm from that mythical place known as "down south", which covers anything the wrong side of Scotch Corner. Everyone's been great since I arrived but if I stayed another twenty years I reckon they'd still all think I was just passing through.'

'You could be right,' admitted Tom, 'but I am actually from here.'

'And now you're back?'

'I'm a journalist. I go where the news is,' Tom said quickly. 'It just happens to be here right now.'

'I never read newspapers,' he said it matter-of-factly, 'news depresses me,' and when he noticed Tom's disbelief, he added, 'I'm serious, it's only ever bad. If newspapers or the TV news ever covered anything happy, I'd pay more attention but they don't, so I won't.'

Tom was taken aback by the innocence of that statement. It was so unusual it was almost refreshing. 'Blimey, doesn't it feel a bit strange not knowing what's going on in the world?'

'I do know what's going on in the world. I just don't get it from newspapers. I read specialist stuff, magazines.'

'Specialist stuff?'

'Rugby, fishing, history,' he shrugged, 'all kinds of things. I just can't be bothered with politics or other people's tragedies.'

Tom contemplated a world without newspapers or the TV bulletins and wondered how long he'd be able to survive without them. 'I'm one of those people who has to walk miles to get a copy of yesterday's English newspaper when I'm on holiday.'

'Can't remember when I last opened one.'

'I'm glad you are in the minority or I'd be out of a job. So how did you end up in Great Middleton?'

'I'm a teacher.'

'A teacher who doesn't read newspapers?' Tom was even more surprised.

'I teach the little ones. They're not big on world affairs. I'm at the junior school.'

'I used to go there,' said Tom. 'I'm Tom Carney. I didn't get your name.'

'Andrew Foster,' answered his new friend. 'I spend my days with nine-year-olds and most of my evenings in this pub. I'm sure those two facts are not entirely unrelated.'

'I'll bet. Do you know this missing girl then: Michelle Summers?'

'Before my time, mate, never taught her. She was at the local comp.'

It was almost a relief. Freed from the necessity of speaking professionally to the school teacher, Tom began to relax. The two men drank together and exchanged stories on the perils of teaching gobby infants or interviewing gormless models who'd been shagging footballers. Despite having absolutely nothing in common with this solitary, young man, except perhaps their age, Tom found Andrew Foster to be excellent company. He had a dry sense of humour and what could only be described as a healthy cynicism that dovetailed neatly with Tom's own world-view.

Someone tapped him on the shoulder then and Tom turned to see Boring Bryan, as he was known locally, 'I need a word,' the old man said importantly.

'Okay,' but Bryan indicated Tom should follow him to a quiet corner. Reluctantly he left the bar stool and followed the pub regular to a table. They sat either end of a large ashtray piled high with stale cigarette butts.

'You want to find out what happened to poor little Michelle?' he asked conspiratorially once they were seated.

'Well, yeah.'

'Did you see the press conference?'

Tom shook his head, 'I was driving up here.'

'Take a look at it on the late news,' Bryan urged him, 'take a good, long look.'

'Why?'

'Because *he* did it,' announced the old man firmly.

'Who did?'

71

'The stepdad,' he told Tom, as if it was obvious.

'Right,' said Tom, hesitantly, 'and what makes you think that, Bryan?'

'I saw it on the telly at lunchtime. He showed no emotion. His stepdaughter's gone missing, his wife is in pieces and he just sits there staring out with those dead eyes of his like all's well with the world.'

'Yeah but that's not evidence, Bryan, just because he wasn't crying in a press conference. Those things affect people in different ways.'

'He did it,' Bryan jabbed a finger into Tom's chest, 'you mark my words.' Then he got to his feet and ambled off to the gents.

Tom was left to ponder the fact that Boring Bryan's conviction, that Michelle's stepdad looked shifty so he must be a murderer, was the strongest lead he was going to get that day. 'Christ almighty,' he muttered as he wandered back to the bar. The school teacher held up his empty glass and mouthed the word 'pint?' at him. Tom nodded. Maybe just a few, he thought, for where was the harm in that?

Chapter Twelve

Day Two

'Get away from there, you small boys!' the headmaster's voice was loud and so full of implied threat that the half dozen seven-year-olds immediately turned and fled, dashing away from the enormous vehicle that captivated them. They ran all the way back up the hill and across the playground, without looking up to meet the disapproving gaze of Mister Nelson. He watched them go, the last stragglers from the morning break, before continuing to walk down the hill towards the freshly dug earth. He turned his head to address Theo Hutton, who was frowning at him. The headmaster belatedly realised the borough councillor wasn't used to seeing his more aggressive side, the one he saved for unruly children, and that it might not exactly be the image he wanted to convey to one of the north east's more renowned political power brokers.

He forced a smile to crease his face. 'Boys will be boys.'

The two men watched the yellow JCB with its enormous, sharp-toothed iron bucket on the end of a long metal arm, as it came crashing down once more to chew the ground in front of it. A huge scar stretched behind the digger, marking its progress across the land, its body juddering each time the mechanical arm dipped and scraped the bucket into the ground, turning green sod into rich, dark soil. Some way behind the digger, another vehicle followed at a more measured pace, its front end ploughing the earth into a flat surface.

'Making quick work of that,' said the councillor.

Councillor Hutton glanced behind him at the primary school; a single-storey building with a flat roof, and walls made almost entirely out of glass and metal frames.

'This all used to be part of Mackenzie's farm,' he told the headmaster.

'I know.'

'And that,' said the councillor, pointing out at the land being dug up by the JCB and carrying on regardless, 'used to be nowt but a bloody marsh. You could walk on it half the year, but a lot of the time it was covered in tadpole-infested water.'

'So I hear,' answered the headmaster. He lacked the patience for one of Councillor Hutton's 'it-were-all-fields-round-here-when-I-was-a-lad' speeches today. 'And the decision to drain it has been the most cost-effective part of the new building project, transforming useless marsh into prime building land.'

'We're not facing the planning committee now,' Nelson was a self-satisfied prick, thought the councillor, determined to bask in the success of his pet project, a new building incorporating two additional classrooms, as well as a swimming pool and dining room that could accommodate children from the neighbouring village, dooming their own school to closure.

As they drew nearer to the digger, both men's thoughts were interrupted by a harsh squealing noise as the driver hastily applied the brakes and it lurched alarmingly. The driver leaped from the vehicle, losing his yellow hard hat in the process, which bounced along the ground. He ignored it and ran round to the front of the digger. The head teacher experienced an illogical fear that a child had somehow become trapped under the digger but surely they would have seen him. They drew nearer as the driver peered down at the freshly dug hole. They couldn't see what had alarmed him but they could hear his panicked murmurings.

They advanced cautiously until the driver sensed their presence and turned. 'Get the police,' he called and when they simply stared back at him, he swore and started to run towards the school building. Councillor Hutton and the headmaster looked at each other then walked towards the hole, the rich, wet soil clinging to their shoes.

They drew right up the edge and peered in.

'Oh my good God,' said the headmaster.

'Jesus-Christ-almighty,' added the councillor for good measure.

Chapter Thirteen

Ian Bradshaw took the call. The first voice he heard was a woman's, the police sergeant on the front desk, asking to speak to Kane.

'Detective Chief Inspector Kane is at Michelle Summers' mother's home,' he said precisely.

'DI Peacock then?' she asked hopefully, as if she couldn't possibly entrust her news to the station half-wit.

'He's with the DCI. Perhaps I can help?' he added reasonably, knowing their absence had painted her into a corner.

There was a pause while she weighed this up. Was he considered that much of a liability these days? It seemed he was. Finally she spoke and there was a trace of resignation in her voice. 'They've found a body,' she told him, 'at Great Middleton School.'

Bradshaw was determined to be discreet. He would take the DCI to one side and quietly inform him the girl's body had been found. He would spare the family any unnecessary anguish until the time came when they could be spared it no longer. He knew if they realised Michelle had been found their first instinct would be to go to her, but how could forensics pick up anything if the grieving relatives contaminated the crime scene? Bradshaw climbed out of the car, straightened his jacket, marched purposefully up to the front door and rang the bell.

'Who found her?' asked DI Peacock moments later as Bradshaw's car sped down the hill towards the school.

'A JCB driver,'

'Where is he now?' DCI Kane was in the back seat, with DI Peacock riding shotgun in the front.

'In the headmaster's office with a cup of tea and a biscuit, so he can't blurt anything to the press or passers-by.' He could tell by their silence they were happy with that. 'The kids are all in the main hall in the centre of the school, for a "special assembly" until they work out the best way to get them out of there with the minimum of fuss,'

'Anyone else know about this?'

'Another workman, he's also in the building,' Bradshaw repeated virtually every word the desk sergeant had told him, 'and there is a local politician – a borough councillor who was walking the grounds with the headmaster when the body was found,'

'That's all we need,' muttered the DI

They got out of the car then walked round the building towards the playing fields at the rear. Bradshaw told himself that the outcome had been entirely predictable. Nobody expected poor Michelle Summers to turn up alive and now they would concentrate on finding her killer. In a strange way, as he walked side by side with the DCI and his DI it almost felt like he was back in the fold.

There was a uniformed officer standing by the JCB and

newly ploughed earth piled up by its digger. Bradshaw could see the rim of a distinct but uneven hole and he began to prepare himself for the sight of the young girl's body.

They walked briskly across the first playing field until they reached the spot the JCBs had been levelling. The ground was muddy and their progress slow. The uniformed officer looked as if he wanted to snap to attention when the three detectives reached him. 'It's over here, Sir,' the PC told Kane unnecessarily as he gestured towards the hole.

Kane reached the spot and peered over the edge to survey the scene. Then he froze. 'What's this?' the DCI rounded on Bradshaw sharply. 'What the hell is going on?'

Bradshaw was behind him and had no way of knowing what he was referring to. He could only watch as DI Peacock stepped forward and looked down into the hole.

'You have got to be kidding me?'

Detective Constable Ian Bradshaw stepped forward then, almost lost his footing on the soft pile of earth. He peered down into the hole made by the digger but couldn't begin to comprehend the sight that greeted him.

Mary Collier didn't believe in a sixth sense but some form of instinct must have drawn her to the rear window that afternoon, just as the police cars started to arrive.

The old vicarage overlooked the school fields from an outcrop at the very top of Church Lane next to St Michael's church. The house had been used by generations of clerics until the Church of England had decided it could make more money from selling the place and putting the vicar in a humbler property at the foot of the hill. Mary had lived here first with her father, when he had been vicar of Great Middleton, then later with her husband when he became headmaster of the old junior school. Henry had somehow managed to scrape together the money to purchase the property. Mary's husband had been dead for almost twenty years now, her father for more than forty, but, to the people of Great Middleton, who seemed to still regard her with a combination of mild deference and suspicion, Mary was always the vicar's daughter or the headmaster's wife, never a person in her own right.

Mary often watched as the children swarmed across the playing fields during their break or spilled noisily out of the building at home time. The ambitious, modernist, self-publicising headmaster was almost always in her local paper these days; full of grand ideas but not a patch on her Henry. He'd been a real teacher and a proper headmaster. This one was all crust and no meat, as her father would have said.

The gnarled, arthritic knuckles of one hand gripped the heavy velvet curtains for support in case her ageing legs betrayed her. She watched as men walked purposefully to and from a vivid, dark brown scar that had been carved into the field that morning. Call it instinct, call it a premonition or a ghost from the past but whatever it was, Mary Collier watched the events unfolding below her with a sad and heavy heart and a growing sense of trepidation.

Chapter Fourteen

Fiona Summers was alerted by a loud banging on her front door, the volume alone indicating its urgency. She was closer than the female police liaison officer and had a head start. 'I'll get it,' she told her.

Fiona opened the door to find her sister standing on the doorstep, wild-eyed with a tear-streaked face, 'Susan,' was all Fiona could manage, 'have they found her?'

Susan had dashed to her sister's house as soon as word reached her that the police had discovered something at Great Middleton junior school and that something was a body. Now that she'd arrived on her sister's doorstep, panting, breathless and tearful, she realised she didn't know what to say. How could she find the words to tell Fiona that her precious daughter was gone? Instead all she managed was a nod.

'Oh my God,' gasped Fiona, 'where?'

It was becoming an overcrowded crime scene and DI Peacock took control, telling the uniformed officers to move back and fan out to keep everybody away from it. Kane, Peacock and Bradshaw moved away to let the forensics guys do their thing.

Bradshaw felt sick. How could he have been so stupid?

When Ian Bradshaw had taken the call he hadn't bothered to check if the body was a young girl. Instead he worked on the understandable assumption that two bodies in one week, in a place the size of Great Middleton, was a statistical impossibility and that it must have been Michelle Summers who had been found dead in the school grounds.

Bradshaw had concentrated on the current whereabouts of the JCB driver, the headmaster and councillor, then shot down to the house to pick up his DI and DCI. When they had all stepped forward to peer into the hole however, it did not contain the remains of young Michelle Summers. Instead they were confronted by the spectacle of an ancient skeleton, one that, even to Bradshaw's untrained eye, had clearly been underground for decades, judging by the state of its yellowing bones, dirt-encrusted eye sockets and the greying rags wrapped round its body. The gaping mouth, as if caught by surprise at the moment of death, mirrored Bradshaw's own shock.

'Bradshaw,' asked DI Peacock, once he'd realised this was not the girl, 'are you a complete moron?' and Bradshaw was unable to answer him. Instead he stood back as the field began to fill up with cars. Just when Ian Bradshaw was thinking his life could not conceivably get any worse, there was a blur of movement and he watched helplessly as Fiona Summers came barrelling down the hill towards them, sweeping past a slow-moving uniformed constable in the process. 'Shit,' he muttered and Peacock turned towards her.

'Jesus,' he hissed, 'that's all we need,'

'Michelle!' the poor hysterical woman was screaming her daughter's name as she powered towards them, dress flapping in the breeze, 'Michelle!'

Bradshaw moved instinctively to block her path to the body. He'd played football and rugby at school but tackling Fiona Summers wasn't easy, even for a man of his size; she was a short but bulky woman who crashed into him at speed and she wasn't going to allow anyone to prevent her from reaching her daughter. Bradshaw managed to grab her but she twisted and wriggled in his grasp, flailing her arms at him, all the while shouting her daughter's name.

'Let her through, Bradshaw,' his DI told him calmly and when Bradshaw looked at his boss he was told, 'What difference does it make?'

He meant that a crime scene as ancient as this one couldn't be contaminated any further if Fiona Summers ran over the ground they'd already trampled underfoot. It would be easier to let her see the corpse than try to convince her it was not Michelle. She was hardly likely to jump in the ditch and embrace it. As soon as he released her, Fiona went straight to the hole in a stumbling run, peered down into it then froze, before turning back to them.

'What?' gasped Fiona and it was left to the DI to state the obvious.

'It's not her,' he told the panicked mother, 'it's not Michelle.'

When they returned to the station, DI Peacock took Bradshaw to one side and gave him some clear direction, 'I want you to go and sit in the canteen,' he told the detective constable, 'I want you to take that big file with you, the one with the details of all the known kiddy-fiddlers and rapists on our territory and I want you to lay it on the table in front of you. I want you to take a pen and a pad so that anyone who looks in on you will think there is s a man who is working incredibly hard on DI Peacock's case. He's checking out suspects, trying to find a lead, looking for a breakthrough.'

'Yes, Sir.'

'But do you know what I really want you to do in there?'

'Er . . .'

'Nothing,' he told Bradshaw, 'not one thing. I want you to sit there all afternoon, drinking tea and keeping well out of my way. I don't want to see your face again until tomorrow. Even then it will be too soon. I don't want you under the feet of real police officers who know what they are doing. Do you know why?'

'Yes, Sir.'

'Why?'

'Because I messed up, Sir.'

'No,' Peacock assured him, 'incorrect, Bradshaw. That's not the reason. Anyone can mess up from time to time, even me. No, I don't want you around because you are an idiot Bradshaw. Despite all of your A levels, you don't know what fucking day it is. I don't have qualifications like yours but I do have the sense I was born with. I have worked extremely hard to get as far as I have and I'm not going to allow you to fuck it all up for me, do you hear?'

'Yes, sir.'

'So what are you going to do now?'

'Go to the canteen?'

Peacock nodded, 'and . . . ?'

'Stay there?'

'Congratulations Bradshaw, you finally got something right.'

Chapter Fifteen

Helen dropped her bag on her desk and was about to sit down when Mel, the reporter who occupied the desk next to her, said, 'They found a body at Great Middleton while you were gone; in the field behind the school.'

'Shit,' said Helen, cursing the fact that she'd wasted half a morning interviewing a teenage cross-country runner who been picked for the county and immediately throwing her bag back onto her shoulder.

'I wouldn't bother,' Mel told her, 'he's just asked Martin to cover it for you.'

'It's my patch,' Helen told her firmly.

Helen stepped out in front of Martin's car and waved him down. He made a point of braking theatrically and lurching forwards. Then he slowly wound down his window.

'Bloody hell, Helen, it's a good job I was watching where I was going.'

'They told me Malcolm asked you to cover for me at Great Middleton,' she said breathlessly.

'Yeah,' he said.

'Well I'm back now, so there's no need.'

She could tell from the look on his face that he wasn't happy with that but if he wanted an argument he'd picked the wrong woman in the wrong week.

'I'm on my way now,' he said stubbornly, as if this was a massive inconvenience.

'You haven't even left the car park,' she told him.

'Look, love,' he began, 'you're still the new girl and I've been doing this since God was a boy. Why not leave this one to me, eh? If you mess up a murder, Malcolm will not be impressed. We don't get many of them.'

'Thanks for the offer, Martin,' she managed, 'but I won't mess it up.'

'I don't know, love,' he said it thoughtfully, like he was Helen's dad contemplating the wisdom of allowing her to go to her first teenage party.

Helen decided she'd had enough of this conversation, 'Look, Martin, this story is on my patch. If you want to race me down there to cover it, that's up to you, but I am going. We can arrive together if you want, then we'll both look like idiots.' And before he could answer, she headed for her car.

He leaned out of his window and called after her, 'There's no need to talk to people like that!'

She whirled round then, 'Isn't there?' she said. 'Oh sorry, love, can't you take a joke?' she was mimicking the loud hectoring tone the older men on the *Messenger* used towards young women in the office.

'Bit sensitive, aren't you? What's the matter? Time of the month?' And Martin's head ducked quickly back into his car.

He was busily parking it once more when she sped past him.

Tom Carney had only been back in the North East for one night but he woke that morning with a hangover that would have felled a lesser man. How had he managed that?

He had virtually decided to give himself a day off when Colin the landlord informed him that the police had found a body and it was all everyone in the village was talking about. He managed to force himself to leave the Greyhound and arrived at the scene moments later, flashing his press card at a young, uniformed bobby who was manning the school gates. 'Is it her?' he asked with no preamble.

The constable shook his head and this surprised Tom. 'What exactly *have* they found then?'

'You'll have to ask them,' and the constable jerked his head towards the school building, 'they're in the field out back.'

'Can't you just tell me?' asked Tom, knowing that cooperation from stressed detectives at such an early stage in proceedings was unlikely.

'You'll get me shot if I do,' said the bobby. 'Get your arse down the hill and ask them. Maybe they'll tell you something.'

Whatever they'd found it must have been important, judging by the number of police officers moving backwards and forwards between the field and the school building, many of them dressed in protective clothing to ensure they did not pollute the crime scene. A large white canopy had been erected to keep out prying eyes, while a JCB stood idle by the spot.

Tom approached a detective. 'I can't tell you anything at this stage,' he was told firmly. 'This is a crime scene, give us room to do our job,' and when Tom tried to ask a question he was told, 'and I do mean now.' The response was so emphatic there seemed little point in arguing, so Tom did as he was told, walking back up the hill away from the scene. He still couldn't say with any certainty whether there were human remains under that white tent or if something else had aroused police suspicion. He could hardly come up with a news story based on a rumour overheard by Colin.

Tom hung around the periphery, taking pictures of the activity on his old Olympus camera. It was ten years out of date but still worked and suited him because it was small enough to slip into a jacket pocket, along with its compact telephoto lens. He spotted her then, as she walked down one side of the school building, questioning a detective who was batting her enquiries away. Even from this distance and without hearing a word, he knew she'd be getting the usual, non-committal bullshit replies with nothing ruled in or out, by a police force that was becoming highly sensitive to journalistic criticism right now.

Tom raised his camera and took a picture of Helen. Maybe she sensed it, for she turned to look straight at him before asking the detective another question. Tom went back to the school gates and the uniformed police constable.

'Thanks,' he told the bobby, 'I got everything I need,' before adding, 'How long will you be stuck here then?' as if he was just passing the time of day. 'These things must take an age.'

'They do,' confided the constable, 'I'll probably be here all day.'

'Really? Will you not even get a lunch break? Do you want me to grab you a sandwich from the shop round the corner?'

'One of the lads will sort me out,' he replied, 'but thanks anyway.'

'No bother,' said Tom. 'Oh shit.'

'What's up?' asked the copper.

'I forgot to ask who found it,' said Tom, 'and I don't really want to go back down there again and annoy your lot when they're busy. You don't need them in a bad mood, today of all days.'

'Too right,' said the constable, 'it was the JCB driver. He was flattening the land for the new school building. His digger went into the soil and up it came.'

Tom wondered how far he could push this without giving himself away. 'Must have been a shock?' he offered.

'You're telling me. It's not every day you accidentally dig up an old corpse.'

Tom felt a surge of excitement. He now had confirmation that a body had been found on the school grounds and, if it was old, it couldn't have been Michelle Summers. He almost had a story but he would need more than that.

'It's one to tell his mates down the pub I suppose,' and the copper smiled at this. 'Must have been there a while?' Tom ventured.

The constable sniffed, 'Didn't they tell you that?' There was suspicion in his words.

'They didn't have to,' said Tom casually, 'if he dug it out of Cappers Field. It's not much more than marsh half the year, always has been.'

The constable seemed satisfied with that explanation. 'They won't know exactly how long he's been down there until the forensic guys have had a prod but they're guessing fifty, maybe sixty years or more. Who knows whether we'll ever be able to identify the guy?'

'It's difficult when he's been down there that long if there isn't anything distinctive about him.'

'Apart from the knife in his back, you mean,' and Tom experienced another thrill as he was given this key information.

'Shame he didn't have a wallet or something. Still, a village this size, someone's got to know who he is. Here one minute and gone the next. I mean, it can get a bit rough round here when the pubs are turning out but people don't usually get stabbed in the back.'

'I don't know about witnesses,' the young constable was dismissive. 'They'll all be coffin dodgers: senile or dead already. Most of them don't know what they did yesterday, let alone half a century ago.'

'Oh well, good luck with it.' Tom thought it best to make a quick exit before anyone witnessed him tapping the constable for information.

Chapter Sixteen

He didn't like swearing. There was no need for it but he had to force himself not to utter a curse word as they narrowly failed to beat the lights. He'd been going a little too quickly and had to brake harder than usual to avoid passing through on a red and his daughter made a big deal out of it, as she did with pretty much everything now she was almost a teenager.

'Woah!' said Lindsay, as if the car was an out-of-control horse. He would have chastised her for being overly dramatic but he didn't have the energy, having already quarrelled with her bitch of a mother when he'd come to pick her up that afternoon. This wasn't even an official visit. Instead he had to take Lindsay shopping for school shoes because her mother insisted this was somehow his responsibility, even though he was already giving his ex-wife virtually all of his money.

Now they would have to wait ages because these lights were on a crossroads and they always took an eternity to marshal cars from all directions.

'Dad?' Lindsay asked him in that sing-song voice she always used when she wanted something, turning one syllable into two, 'Da-ad.'

'What?'

'When I come and see you for my next visit,' she began and he felt irritated because this one had barely begun and she was already talking about the next, 'would it be okay if I had money instead of a present?'

'Money? Why do you need money?' he couldn't conceive of a reason.

'So I can get something I really want,' she told him, 'clothes and stuff.'

'We'll have to see.' He hoped his tone would be enough to convey his disappointment with her and she'd drop it.

'Oh go on,' she'd gone all smiley then, almost flirty in tone, which made him want to cuff her across the face with the back of his hand, 'it *is* my birthday,' she reminded him and for a moment he was struck by how close she was to turning into one of them. A dirty slag, using her smiles and her eyes and her cajoling ways to get what she wanted. He took a deep breath and tried to blot out the thought but he was sure it would all start soon enough. First there'd be boys, then grown men. There'd be tears and manipulation until she got what she wanted and then his daughter would be just like all of the others. It was an unbearable notion.

'I said, we'll see,' he snapped and this time she had the good sense to shut up about it.

How did it begin, he wondered . . . with the first plea for a new dolly? As early as that? And it would go on forever; a new house, then a new kitchen to put in the house, new clothes and jewellery; never satisfied. Right up until the day she grew tired of her husband and lay down and did disgusting things with the next man, just like her slag of a mother had done. For a fleeting moment he was revisited by the image of Samantha lying on their living room floor with their neighbour's hand wedged down the front of her jeans, all the way down into her knickers, touching her most private place, sticking his fingers in her as if it meant absolutely nothing, like they were simply shaking hands. Disgusting, dirty, filthy . . . and what had *he* done when he had discovered her lying there?

Nothing.

And, as she had struggled to remove their neighbour's coarse hand while she sat upright and tried to compose herself, still he had said nothing, even as he watched his whole life slide away from him in a moment.

Paul, their neighbour, had walked right past him and out of the front door without a word.

Even then; nothing.

He had realised it almost immediately. He wasn't a man. Not any more. Thanks to her. He had been one before but she derailed him, knocked him off-kilter, emasculated him to such a degree that he couldn't even raise a hand against the man who had debased his home and debauched his wife. The one consolation he clung to was that they would both go to hell and burn in agony forever for what they had done to him. For it is set down in the commandments, written by the finger of God himself on stone tablets, that he will judge all adulterers.

And when it was over she didn't even look at him, couldn't probably, wouldn't say a word either, just pulled up the zipper on her jeans then walked into the kitchen and got on with doing the dishes, eyes fixed forwards. He had watched her for a moment, his mind racing, a sick feeling in his stomach, for he couldn't think of anything to say. In that moment when he found his wife and his neighbour together he realised everything he had ever believed until that point was a lie.

He had perhaps been guilty of placing his wife on a pedestal, he knew that now, but wasn't that what a husband was supposed to do: love her, adore her, worship her? She had proven herself so completely unworthy of that love. His eyes had gone to the knife block and, for a moment, he had seriously contemplated taking the largest one and plunging the sharp point of it deep into the soft flesh at the back of her neck. He was sure he would have done it too if it hadn't been for little Lindsay. He couldn't have left her with a dead mother and a father behind bars for life.

In the end he had been unable to put words together to form a sentence. His voice had broken and he had asked her, 'why?' in a high-pitched, whiny voice he hated, for he was on the verge of tears.

'Jesus Christ!' she slammed down a plate on the work top. How could she be angry? 'You have to ask "why?" You have no idea, have you? You're not a man, you're a bloody robot.' And she'd burst into tears then, 'I am so trapped!' she concluded before storming out of the kitchen and marching upstairs to their room, slamming the door behind her like an ungrateful teenager.

He slept on the couch that night, though of course he didn't sleep at all, just lay awake torturing himself, replaying images of his neighbour's grubby hand down his wife's knickers, his fat fingers wedged deep inside her. He churned it over and over in his mind, wondering how many times they had done this while he'd been working late. How many times had he returned from a shift to find her calmly preparing dinner with another man's seed dripping out of her? Was their neighbour the only one or was there a queue of men turning him into a laughing stock? How many more had there been? The realisation that he would never know hit him with the suddenness of grief and he knew there was no going back for him.

He never returned to the marital bed.

The terms of the divorce had been the real scandal. He'd agreed to her suggestion that they stay 'civilised' for the sake of their daughter, even though he felt anything but towards her. Instead of 'my whore of a wife's adultery' the grounds became 'irreconcilable differences', a helpful suggestion by her solicitor to prevent their daughter from discovering that her mother's a dirty slag. So he had gone along with the idea, but he had been an idiot. They had used his wholly natural concern for his daughter against him and taken the little girl from him. It was decided she would stay with her mother and he was ordered to move out of the family home; his home, the one he had spent the best part of his free time fixing up. He had not been the one who had spread his legs for a stranger in that house, so why did his wife get to keep it?

But he was the one who had to pay for his wife and daughter to have a life as good as the one they'd always known, while he lived off beans on toast and fried eggs in a shitty one-bedroom flat because he had never been much of a cook and hadn't the money for anything decent. *They* were doing okay, because almost all of his money went on them. They could afford the mortgage and the heating and to put good food on their plates and, before long, just when he thought his resentment couldn't reach a higher level, the bitch-whore-slag started 'seeing some-one'. And how had he found this out? His own daughter had told him. 'Mam's got a boyfriend,' she'd said matter-of-factly, as if her mother had just bought a new pair of shoes. He didn't know why he was so shocked. He already knew she was a whore but perhaps he hoped she might not be so blatant about it while she was living off his money.

He was handing over nearly all of his wages so she could raise his daughter without him, paying for a house that another man was screwing his wife in. Where was the justice in that? It made him sick to his stomach whenever he thought of them doing it in his home, with his daugh-ter asleep in the next room, his ex-wife rutting like a pig with a new man. It made him want to kill them both.

'Dad? Dad!' Lindsay was calling and she was agitated. He hadn't heard her at first. Sometimes he got so lost in his dark thoughts about his ex-wife that he let his coffee go cold or forgot there was food in the oven, until an acrid smell of burnt plastic reminded him that his super-market ready meal was ruined. He became dimly aware of a sound then; a continuous jarring noise that was compet-ing for his attention along with his daughter's urgent voice.

'What?' he asked her groggily and he felt as if he had just been woken from a very deep sleep.

'The lights,' she informed him, 'they're green.'

And when he finally looked he realised she was right, they were, and the noise in his head was the sound of a car horn blaring continuously, as if the owner of the car behind them had finally lost all patience. He thought it best not to acknowledge his foolishness to his daughter, so instead he drove silently away.

Tom drove to the highest point in the village and parked up by the church. He even had to climb out of his car to get a signal. 'Please work, please work,' he told the phone, and it did. It rang three times then, to his great relief, Terry answered. He sounded like he was at the opposite end of a wind tunnel and Tom was forced to shout to be heard. He told Terry about the body in the field, silently praying he would be interested in the story.

'We're on it already,' said Terry and Tom realised he'd been wasting his time, 'our Northern correspondent's got it. He has a contact at police HQ, someone high up. He wouldn't be much of a correspondent if he didn't. You haven't given me anything I don't already know.'

'I figured as much,' said Tom with forced cheerfulness, 'thought I'd better call it in anyway, just in case,' he was trying hard to hide the crushing disappointment he was feeling, 'how are things there?'

'Awful,' he was informed, 'we're not just dealing with a cabinet minister here. It's his wife too.'

'His wife?'

'She's a barrister and a psycho from hell. Her nickname in legal circles is "The Bitch", which is quite something, coming from other lawyers. They reckon even the PM is shit-scared of her. Everybody is.'

'Including the Doc?'

'Especially the Doc,' conceded Terry, 'she phoned him this morning, had his balls in a vice for over an hour. We might as well have put a white flag on the roof of the building.'

'So what will he do?'

'You did not hear this from me,' Terry told him, 'but we might have to settle.'

'You're kidding?' This couldn't be happening. Surely the legendary Doc wasn't really going to roll over at the first mention of a libel case.

'It's a strong possibility,' admitted Terry, 'substantial damages, a retraction, an apology.'

'Doesn't this woman care that her husband was shagging hookers?' Tom was incredulous.

'Doesn't believe it,' said Terry, 'or chooses not to. She's tied her entire life, her future and the future of her children to that man. If he rises they rise, if he falls, they come crashing down to earth with him. So, if he's been dipping his wick elsewhere, that's not her priority.'

'Jesus, I can't believe the Doc's going to settle. The man's as guilty as sin.'

'It's under consideration,' Terry lowered his voice to a whisper, 'the atmosphere is terrible here right now. There are people crying in the toilets and I'm not just talking about the women.'

'I must be pretty popular.'

'Don't expect an invitation to the Christmas party.'

'How did it go?' asked Peacock, who'd been waiting in his DCI's office for Kane to return.

'Four men,' Kane told him.

'What?' Peacock didn't bother to hide his frustration.

'But we can choose them.'

'Right,' his tone became more measured, but DI Peacock still wasn't happy, 'so the Super actually wants us to remove four men from an ongoing investigation into a missing girl to put them onto this?'

'Look, John,' Kane lowered his voice as a uniformed WPC walked by the opened door, 'he's basically given me the go-ahead to take our most feeble blokes off the Michelle Summers case and plonk them onto the-body-in-the-field. Draw me up a dead-wood list, containing the four men least likely to provide us with any kind of breakthrough. I'll reassign them to this . . .' he was searching for the right word, '. . . skeleton.'

'I can think of four I wouldn't shed any tears over and that's just off the top of my head.'

'Who?'

'Vincent obviously.'

'Obviously,' Kane nodded, 'he's as much use as a condom machine in a nunnery.'

'Davies, because he's always on the sick; Wilson, because he's always on the sauce, and Bradshaw because he's always bloody wrong.'

'I wouldn't argue with any of those.'

Betty Turner was sitting upright in her bed, her back ramrod-straight, waiting. It was late and raining outside but that didn't matter. Nothing mattered, except letting the other woman know that she knew.

She knew all right.

The old lady had waited till the house was silent and her three grown sons all asleep, before she padded softly down the stairs and slipped the raincoat on over her nightie. She opened the door, the rain was coming down hard. She stepped out into it and closed the door softly behind her. Betty walked over the wet pavement in her slippers, ignoring the cold, thinking only of her destination.

The streets were empty at this hour and nobody witnessed the old lady's slow and unsteady progress across the village. Her slippers were sodden and her feet soaking but she did not turn back. Betty was soaked through by the time she reached the front door of the old vicarage.

'It was you,' Betty told the locked, heavy wooden door as she slapped her palm hard against it, knowing that somewhere within those walls, someone was listening. She banged again, harder this time, 'It was you!' The rain stuck Betty's hair to her scalp and she wiped it away with an impatient hand, 'It was you!'

Betty had been right. Mary Collier wasn't sleeping. She was lying in bed with the covers pulled up to her chin, eyes tightly closed and she could hear the slap of Betty's hand on her front door, as regular and insistent as a drum beat, 'It was you . . .'

Mary knew who was out there, taunting her. The voice was muffled by the door and the rain but the words were still audible, '. . . it was you . . .' and each one of them pierced Mary Collier like a blade.

Chapter Seventeen

Day Three

DC Bradshaw didn't have to be told he was on the subs bench. One glance around the room that morning at his fellow misfits was all it took for him to realise he was no longer part of the first team. There was the pot-bellied, permanently booze-flushed figure of Trevor Wilson, who made no secret of the fact that all he really wanted was a quiet life. Bob Davies was probably contemplating how soon and with what ailment he could feasibly go back on the sick again. In the past couple of years, Davies had taken long spells off work with a number of complaints, including backache, neck-pain, anxiety, stress, depression and, impressively, Crohn's disease. The one common factor all of these ailments shared, aside from the fact that Davies claimed to be afflicted by them, was the difficulty in diagnosing or, more importantly, disproving them, which meant Davies' suspiciously lengthy absences from work continued to go unpunished.

'I've got stress,' he protested once, when challenged by a colleague in the canteen, as to whether he was ever coming back for more than a week at a time; then he'd searched the room for a potential ally until his eyes rested on Bradshaw and he announced loudly that 'he knows what it's like,' instantly giving Bradshaw an association with a lazy, skiving bastard he could ill afford at that point. When Bradshaw failed to give a response, Davies had hissed, 'Thanks for your support,' at him, ensuring that nobody in the room retained any respect for Bradshaw, not even the malingering Davies.

The rest of the group was made up of Vincent Addison and Ian himself. We are the misfits, thought Bradshaw, too old or too young, too lazy, too sick or too damaged. He knew what this was. It was a dead-wood squad.

DI Peacock briefed them. 'You are to conduct a thorough and methodical door-to-door in Great Middleton, in an attempt to identify the corpse in the school field and uncover a possible motive for this murder. Your presence on the streets sends an important message to the population of the village and crucially, the media, as to how seriously this case is being taken. However, we do not want you to rush this enquiry, in case you miss something vital and all leads will be reported back to me before any follow-up action is taken. Is that clear?'

In other words, acting on their own initiative was actively discouraged. None of the other men seemed bothered by this limitation, but Bradshaw still itched for the opportunity to prove he was not a complete idiot, even though he had begun to doubt that himself.

DI Peacock concluded his briefing by conceding their task was far from easy, 'Forensics reckon the body has been there for nigh-on fifty or sixty years, so this killing could have happened during the war or even before it, which obviously means the usual plea for witnesses is going to be redundant. However, you have got a sizeable retired population in Great Middleton, so find the old fogies and question them, see if we can't find something out about this man. Who was he, who did he fall out with and why, when did he die, why was he killed and how come nobody reported him missing all those years ago? Didn't he have any friends or was the whole village delighted to see the back of the poor bastard so they all kept quiet in some big criminal conspiracy? I doubt it, don't you?' Nobody replied, Peacock continued, 'Was he living there or passing through? Did he con someone, fall out with somebody or knock someone's daughter up? Remember, it was a very different world back then. Stuff we'd consider trivial now was a big deal half a century back, so change your outlook and think differently. A lot of those old dears can't remember their own names but I've got an aunt like that and all of a sudden she'll start telling you about the coronation or World War Bloody Two as if it happened yesterday, so use that.' He noted the men's lack of enthusiasm. 'If nothing else, you'll get a few cups of tea and the odd slice of Battenberg cake.' And he looked at the apathetic faces before him, 'maybe that'll motivate some of you,' before he gave up and left them to it.

The four men stood silently looking at one another for a moment, then Vincent spoke.

'I'll put the kettle on, should I?' Christ he couldn't even make that decision without checking with everybody first, 'I mean, he said there was no hurry and it's a bit early for a door-to-door.'

Nobody bothered to give Vincent the courtesy of an answer, nor did they contradict him. He shuffled away to make a brew. Wilson and Davies sat back down. Davies even picked up a newspaper and started to read the sports pages.

'I think I'll get going,' said Bradshaw to universal disinterest, 'make a start,' and he left before any of them could summon up the energy to tell him he was wasting his time.

Helen called into the police station for her meeting with Inspector Reid. Each day one of the *Messenger*'s journalists went through the same routine; Reid would detail every crime reported in the previous twenty-four hours and they would write down the numerous acts of vandalism, burglary and TWOC, hoping for a story.

Inspector Reid was close enough to retirement to not mind spending fifteen minutes every day in the company of a young, female reporter but even he seemed to lack enthusiasm that morning. Perhaps he felt excluded while his plain-clothed counterparts searched for missing girls or dug up ancient corpses while he manned a desk at HQ. His voice was a monotone, 'Burglary in Newton Hall, not much taken; set of golf clubs and a bike.'

'Did they break into the house?' asked Helen hopefully, thinking that sleeping residents terrified in the night by burglars might make half a story.

'Garden shed,' he answered, shattering that idea, then he glanced down at his list again, 'Got a car taken without consent from Coronation Avenue? Joyriders probably,' he looked up at her, 'no?'

'Not exactly the great train robbery.'

The Inspector smiled at her, 'I'd have thought there'd been enough excitement on your patch lately.'

'There has,' she conceded, 'but we've still got our district pages to fill. Is there nothing else,' she was almost pleading now, 'that doesn't involve stolen cars, golf clubs or broken pub windows?'

'Nothing out of the ordinary,' he said, 'well … one incident … but it was nothing really.' Her face told him she was interested. 'Our lads escorted an old lady home,' then he stopped himself, 'I'm not sure I should be telling you this. No crime was committed.'

Helen smiled. 'Between us then.'

'I doubt you'll be able to do anything with it. An old dear in Great Middleton walked half the length of the village in the pouring rain in her slippers and dressing gown. Our lads got her back home before she caught pneumonia. It's not really news, but you did ask me if there was anything out of the ordinary and that doesn't happen every night.'

'I did,' she admitted, 'and you're right, I probably couldn't use it; wouldn't be fair on the old lady, if she's senile.'

'I wouldn't say Betty Turner was senile exactly.'

'You know her?'

'I know the family,' he said, 'she's a nice old dear but she's got three sons and no control over them. We've been to the house countless times, nothing serious but you know,' and he shrugged to indicate that Betty Turner's off-spring were basically low-lifes.

'And she's not senile?' asked Helen. 'So what was she doing out in the pouring rain in her nightie?'

'That was the weird part,' said the Inspector, 'she wouldn't tell us but when our lads caught up with her she was standing outside the old vicarage, banging on the door and shouting.'

'Really?' asked Helen, 'what was she shouting?'

'"It was you",' he said.

Chapter Eighteen

Bradshaw drove down to 'the cottages', a series of council-owned old-folk's bungalows filled with ex miners. The ones who survived thirty-odd years of cave-ins and coal dust could spend a humble retirement here, in a simple one-bedroomed property with a small, rectangular, allotment-style garden at the rear. Bradshaw was not from Great Middleton but knew from his years as a County Durham police officer that he was more likely to engage with the pensioners who lived here if he went round the back of their properties, avoiding the formality of a knock on their front door. Sure enough, at the first house in the street, an old man was sitting out the back on a tiny porch overlooking neat rows of vegetables, while he read the racing pages of his newspaper. He could have been in his early seventies. Old enough, thought Bradshaw.

He hoped for a head start over the rest of the dead-wood squad. If he was extraordinarily lucky, perhaps someone would even tell him who the dead man was. Bradshaw had not known optimism for a while but he experienced the merest flicker of it as the man with the paper looked up while he bent to open the tiny gate and enter the garden, calling a cheerful 'hello,' as he did so.

'What do you want?' asked the old man suspiciously.

'Sorry to bother you, Sir. I'm a police officer. You

probably heard we found a body in a field next to the school and it's very old. We're trying to find out who it might be.'

The man put down his newspaper and rose to his feet. Maybe Bradshaw would get that cup of tea after all. 'You're a police officer?' he asked calmly.

'That's right,' confirmed Bradshaw.

'Well you can fuck right off then.' And without another word he turned his back on a stunned DC Bradshaw, closed the door of his home firmly behind him then turned the key in the lock. Bradshaw had not known exactly what to expect from his door-to-door, but he wasn't expecting that.

A little wooden sign had been added to the gate of Roddy Moncur's home since Tom last paid the man a visit. It had the word 'Dunroamin' painted on it. Tom watched from his parked car with interest as Helen Norton emerged from Roddy's house. He'd been about to climb out when Helen walked through that gate, stuffing her notebook into a leather bag that was slung over her shoulder. Roddy didn't seem to be in too much of a hurry to close the door behind her. Instead he followed the girl with his eyes, only finally closing his door when she was in her car. Tom waited until she had driven away.

Judging by the smile that was fixed on Roddy's face, he must have assumed Helen had forgotten something. It vanished when he saw Tom on his doorstep.

'Police been round yet?' asked Tom, with no preamble.

Roddy Moncur blinked at Tom. 'Oh,' he said, 'you're back,' then he added, 'no but I don't think they are aware of . . .' he thought for a moment before settling on the right words, '. . . my little hobby.'

Roddy Moncur was in his mid-fifties, with greying hair and a beard. He was wearing the type of chunky sweater favoured by fishermen and real ale aficionados. He quizzed Tom about his reappearance and received the same story as Mike Newton from the *Messenger*.

'Can I come in then?' Tom asked, 'or do you only admit blondes in tight jeans these days?'

'You saw her,' Roddy looked a little sheepish, 'well, she's got your old patch.'

'What did she want?'

'Same as you, I should imagine,' Roddy held the door wider, 'howay in then.'

Tom walked into one of Great Middleton's larger houses. When the old junior school finally closed its doors in the seventies, replaced by a new building built on former farmland, the shell of the old Victorian school remained. For a while nobody knew what to do with the place; a dark and imposing, dirty brick building with small windows that blotted out the light, as if it was specifically designed that way so that generations of schoolchildren, trapped in dingy classrooms with creaking floorboards, could not be distracted by the outside world. Finally a developer stepped in, turning the old school into not one but three houses. Floorboards were sanded and varnished, windows ripped out and replaced by large double-glazed ones, the ancient boiler was carted off on a lorry for scrap, with modern central heating installed in its place.

One of the buyers was Roddy Moncur, a man whose work sometimes took him to foreign climes for months at a time, his engineering skills being constantly in demand in exotic, far-off locations like Oman and Dubai, where his salary was said to be large and his tax bill negligible, due to some little-understood bending of the rules on ex-pat allowances. Soon after Roddy turned fifty however, his globe-trotting ended when he returned to Great Middleton, ostensibly to bury his mother. A week after the funeral, he made an offer on the remaining house.

'There's not many round here get to retire at fifty,' Tom had told him then.

'I've enough to see me out,' Roddy said, 'you don't need a lot round here and you can't take it with you. I'm not one of those blokes who's willing to break his back till he's sixty-five then drops down dead a year after he retires. Not my idea of a life, that. Anyway, I keep myself busy.'

Roddy's way of keeping himself busy was the reason he was an important name in Tom Carney's contact book. If Tom wanted to know what was going on in Great Middleton, he could ask any number of people; including councillors, policemen, pub landlords and their regulars. If he wanted to know what happened in the village at just about any point in the past century however, he'd go and see Roddy Moncur.

Evidence of Roddy's little hobby was all around them. The man's house contained piles of old newspapers and magazines and there were programmes from long-forgotten amateur dramatic theatre productions. Every surface of every wall housed framed black-and-white photographs of the village and the county it lay in, while some were stacked in piles awaiting a more permanent home. There were old books everywhere, even piled on the stairs because he had nowhere else to put them. Roddy was a collector and amateur historian. He also viewed himself as a custodian of village life, keeping alive memories of the place he was born and raised in. Tom thought of Roddy as a hoarder, a man with a bizarre obsession about the past that left his house a disorganised mess, but he was an invaluable source of local trivia.

Tom followed Roddy down the hallway towards his kitchen, which was as cluttered as the rest of the house. The sink contained the previous evening's dirty dishes; further evidence that Roddy Moncur lived alone and didn't give a monkey's what anybody thought of his way of life. They sat at the kitchen table.

'I'm surprised you've not volunteered your services.' Tom said.

'To the police? I would have,' he assured Tom, 'if I thought I'd be any use, but I don't see how I can be.'

'Come on Roddy, you must know something,' and Roddy gave him a blank look, 'or know someone who knows something?'

'I'm as much in the dark on this as anybody.'

'I thought if anyone farted in this village in the past hundred years you knew about it.'

'I thought that too,' and Tom could see it pained Roddy to admit his ignorance where the body-in-the-field was concerned.

'All those school fêtes, beauty pageants and am-dram productions, W. I. meetings and parish council minutes, you've got them all at your fingertips, but look at you now,' and Tom shook his head.

'Don't knock it. I've been filling your local history pages

for years,' it was true that when Tom had been given the poisoned chalice of the local history column, a double-page spread in the *Messenger* that needed nostalgia pieces each and every week, it was widely seen as a punishment for one of his misdemeanours but Roddy had continually bailed him out. Week after week, he provided Tom with photographs and background information on all kinds of long-forgotten events that could grace the pages of the Messenger's 'Days Gone By' column. With Roddy's help, Tom managed to boost the popularity of the almost forgotten column to the point where the *Messenger* actually started to get letters from readers about it. This was a double-edged sword, as Malcolm made sure he kept the column thereafter. Tom also became something of a pin-up for ladies of a certain age, receiving Christmas cards and even chocolates from the 'blue rinse brigade,' as the elderly readers were known. He took a bit of stick for that from the girls: 'One of your lady friends left you a chocolate orange in reception. You're such a stud, Tom.' The lads were even more direct, accusing Tom of being a 'Granny-shagger'.

'You know I'm grateful but there's an old murder on your own doorstep and that just doesn't happen round here. Are you seriously saying you've never heard anything about it?'

'No I haven't. You grew up here too, Tom,' Roddy reminded him tetchily, 'you never heard about it, the police didn't and nor did the *Durham* bloody *Messenger.*'

'Have to hold our hand up to missing that one; must have been a busy news week. Perhaps Germany invaded Poland.'

'Well you wouldn't have run that story, would you?' replied Roddy drily. 'Hitler wasn't a local lad.'

'True,' and he grinned at Roddy, enjoying the banter. 'What's your gut feel then?'

'About what?'

'Those bones in that field were walking around once. He was a living, breathing person. So who was he?'

'That's the weird thing,' admitted Roddy, 'the village hasn't got that many people in it. Aside from two world wars and a couple of pit disasters, most people round here die of natural causes, some of them long before their time but not usually in suspicious circumstances. A murder would have stood out a mile and if somebody went missing without an explanation the police would have been all over it, the newspapers too.'

'So it was a murder nobody knew about. You're the expert; why would someone's sudden departure from the village not throw up any questions?'

'A man could enlist in the forces, join the merchant navy or go and work in ship-building on the Tyne. Swan Hunters took a lot of men and blokes followed the work when it was scarce, which was most of the time, unless you wanted to go down the mine and not everybody fancied that.'

'Isn't that a bit close to home? Wouldn't it look odd if someone never came back, not even for a visit?'

'People didn't travel much, pre-war. They tended to stay put, as long as there was work, but you're right, you'd expect them to come back and see family.'

'What about someone just passing through?' offered Tom.

'Perhaps,' admitted Roddy, 'but who?'

Tom realised he had no idea who, 'it would be unusual to make enemies that quickly,' he admitted, 'look, do us a favour and ask around, will you? It would be a massive help to me if I could get a lead on this one. Somebody in this village must know something.'

'Will do, mate.'

Tom scrawled the number of his mobile phone onto a piece of paper from his notebook then gave it to Roddy, who put it into his pocket and followed Tom to his front door. Halfway down the path, Tom turned back to him.

'By the way,' he asked, '*did* she want the same thing as me?'

Roddy just smiled inscrutably at Tom, then slowly shut the door.

Chapter Nineteen

Helen hadn't received much of a briefing when she started at the *Messenger* but she did learn that Tom Carney used two main sources for local information in Great Middleton. One of them was Roddy, the local amateur historian. The other was just letting herself back into her home when Helen approached her.

'Miss Norton,' said Mary Collier, retaining that air of formality she'd picked up from years in the staffroom, 'looking for material for the local history page?' Helen had already visited Mary's home on a number of occasions to piece together articles for her district page or the 'Days-Gone-By' column she'd inherited from Tom Carney. 'Well, don't let the draught in,' added the old lady as she ushered Helen through her front door.

She stood in Mary's living room, perusing her bookcase while she waited for her host to organise some tea. There were rows of classic novels in matching leather-bound editions, as well as a complete set of Encyclopaedia Britannica and Gibbons' *The History of the Decline and Fall of the Roman Empire*. One volume in particular caught Helen's eye and she retrieved it from the bookcase for a closer look.

When old Mary Collier walked back into the room she seemed a little affronted to find Helen holding one of her books.

'*Wuthering Heights*,' Helen smiled, 'I read it at school.'

'What did you think?' Mary's tone was neutral, giving no clue as to her own view on the book's literary worth.

'I really liked it.'

Mary snorted, 'I thought it was absurd.'

'Really? It was quite romantic as I remember.'

'All of that fire and ice, that passion,' Mary said sharply, 'sentimental rubbish.' Helen was a little taken aback by the strength of Mary Collier's feelings on the subject of *Wuthering Heights* in particular and romance in general. 'You have to work on love – and it *takes* work. That's what the young ones never realise,' Helen couldn't help wondering if the 'young ones' Mary mentioned might include her and she braced herself for a lecture. 'You ask anybody how they stayed with their husband or wife for years and they'll all tell you the same thing: "give and take". It can't just be take,' and she snorted, 'Cathy and Heathcliff; all that anger, all that passion and how long did they last? Five ruddy minutes. He was a monster and she was a spoilt brat. If everybody studies those two for their O levels, or whatever they're called these days, they'll come out of school at the end of it looking for something that's just not there.'

'Do you really believe that?' asked Helen, 'that romance is stupid and love is just some practical thing to be worked at?'

'The young know nothing of love,' affirmed the old lady, 'they all think they do, of course, but it's just a fantasy conjured by Hollywood for silly little girls. Real love is waking up next to the same man every morning for thirty-five years and still caring whether he goes off to work with a good breakfast inside him and a clean shirt on his back. It has nothing to do with S. E.X,' Helen noted that Mary felt compelled to spell the word rather than say it, 'or *fancying* somebody. All of that is so fleeting, yet the young obsess about it, poets and writers waste their lives on it and not one of them has the faintest clue. Why do you think all of those romance novels and films end with marriage? Because they can't think of a way to make the time afterwards seem exciting. Well it isn't exciting and it's not meant to be, but it is love and love doesn't have to be exciting. Rollercoasters are exciting but I wouldn't want to spend thirty-five ruddy years on one.'

Helen didn't know what to say after that and Mary looked quite weary after her tirade. Instead of speaking they both surveyed the framed black-and-white photograph on the bookcase.

'Is that your husband?'

'Taken just after he was made headmaster,' and there was pride in her voice. The couple were standing in the garden together, the man in a grey suit and Mary in a dark blue dress. Helen guessed she'd have been about thirty but she was still a beautiful woman, with long dark hair and striking features.

'The children loved my husband,' Mary said.

'You have children?' asked Helen, 'I didn't know.'

Mary shook her head, 'at the school. The pupils always loved him,' she said, 'but not me. I think most of them were a little scared of me. There were some that respected me, learned from me and were grateful for that learning because it helped them get away from this ruddy place but they never loved me. Not like they loved Henry. He was one of that very rare breed; a teacher who is both loved and respected. There are a number who are one or the other but to be both? It's hard, you see, to be loved and respected at the same time in any walk of life, let alone ours. I think it's because he started out among them,' she added before saying almost absentmindedly, 'he did well for himself, did Henry.'

Helen had spent some time in Mary's company before now but this was the first time the older woman had opened up to her in this way. Perhaps the surprise showed on the young reporter's face, for Mary suddenly said, 'Shall we sit down?'

Ian Bradshaw crunched Polo mints as he drove. He was, as usual, contemplating the hole he had dug himself into. You're damned if you do and you're damned if you don't. It's always the same, thought Bradshaw. If he hadn't taken the call about the body in the field, if he'd left it to someone else, waited for the message to reach the DI, he'd have still been in the dog house right enough, because he resided there pretty much permanently these days, but the ill-will directed towards him wouldn't have been quite so intense. But Bradshaw had taken the call and acted on it, in a final, misguided effort to redeem himself, and his reward? To be stuck in the dead-wood squad. He really was in the dog house now, with the windows boarded up and the door nailed firmly shut.

You're damned if you do and damned if you don't – and it was the same with the visits. Oh God, how he dreaded the visits; every one of them excruciating, every one of them, without fail. He knew, however, they were a small price to pay. After all, he only had to endure the effects of his stupidity for an hour a week. Alan Carter had to live with them for the rest of his life and so would his family.

Carol met him at the door. Carter's wife used to be a pretty little thing. Bradshaw had secretly fancied her. He'd envied his colleague and quite enjoyed the thought of ending up with a wife like Carol. She was in her mid-twenties, looked better in denim jeans and a simple T shirt than most women did made up to the nines and always had a smile on her face back then.

Carol didn't smile any more though. These days she didn't even bother to brush her hair. It was always tied back, unwashed and a little greasy. Her face was pale and bare of make-up and she had deep, black grooves under her eyes that told of ruined sleep.

'Go on through,' was all she said and Bradshaw trudged across the living-room carpet like a man walking to the gallows.

There was a conservatory on the back of the house, somewhere nice for Carter to sit and look out at a garden he could no longer tend.

'How are you doing, mate?' said Bradshaw. They weren't really mates though. They'd been colleagues who never really had that much in common. If it hadn't been for the incident they would have worked together for a while then eventually parted when one of them was assigned to new duties. There'd have been a small leaving do down the pub, a few jokes and some banter, the obligatory collection for a leaving gift and they would have gone their separate ways, destined to exchange Christmas cards for a year or two until they both lost interest. Instead, because of what had happened, they were now trapped together forever in a circle of guilt and despair. The guilt was all Bradshaw's, the despair they shared and most likely would do until the grave.

'I'm great,' Carter replied in his familiar, dead voice, as he spun the wheelchair round to face Bradshaw, 'up early, walked the dog, playing five-a-side later.'

As usual, Bradshaw didn't know what to say in return. Instead he looked around helplessly to see if Carol was nearby. Perhaps he could offer to go and make the tea but she was nowhere to be found. Carol had initially encouraged the visits, so Bradshaw was never sure what her husband had told her about the events of that night. Perhaps Carter didn't blame him entirely. No, that wasn't true, Bradshaw was sure that he did. It was one of the unspoken aspects of the godawful visits. They both knew they were part of Ian Bradshaw's penance. There was a tacit understanding between them that one of the few pleasures Alan Carter had left in life was to sit in that wheelchair, watching his former colleague squirm while he judged him. Look at me, he was saying, every time he put his hands on the wheels of that damned chair and manoeuvred his way clumsily around the room, I'm useless, shot, fucked for life and it's all down to you. This is what you have done to me. This should be you.

When Tom pulled up outside Mary Collier's house the first thing he noticed was Helen's car parked outside it. He decided to wait it out until she left. To kill time he read articles from that day's Paper, noting there was nothing new on Michelle Summers' disappearance and precious little about the body-in-the-field. The Paper's Northern correspondent may have contacts in the police, thought Tom, but the reporter didn't seem to have any more information than he did.

Tom had read the paper from front to back when Helen finally emerged and drove away.

Mary Collier answered her own door this time. 'Oh,' she said, with little warmth, 'I wasn't expecting you.'

'I'm back in the area,' he explained, 'for a little while.'

'I've just been talking to your successor,' she told Tom as he followed her into the old vicarage, 'have you met her?'

'Briefly.'

'What did you make of her?' Mary stopped in the hallway and turned back to face him while she asked the question.

'Seems nice enough.'

'She's pretty *and* intelligent,' Mary's eyes narrowed. 'A lot of men would be frightened by that combination,' she eyed him for a moment, 'but not you.'

Mary ushered him into her lounge. The tea things had yet to be cleared away. 'It's been like Piccadilly Circus here this morning,' she observed.

'Who else has been round?'

'As well as you and Helen Norton? The police.'

'The police?'

'Betty Turner has lost her marbles,' Mary said, 'she came looking for them here,' then she added, 'in the middle of the night.'

'Oh,' he said, 'what brought her to your house?'

'Who knows? You might just as well ask what possessed her to go out in the pouring rain in only her carpet slippers and dressing gown.' She gave him a look that indicated she had no idea what motivated Betty Turner, beyond madness of some kind. 'The police found her thumping on my front door. I can only assume she wanted to come in out of the rain. Thankfully, I slept through the whole thing. They came round this morning to see if I could shed some light on her peculiar behaviour. Obviously I could not.'

'Are you close friends, you and Betty Turner?'

'Hardly.'

'Then why choose your house?'

'I have no idea. We were friends when we were children, if you can possibly imagine that far back, but not for a very, very long time now.'

'Why not,' he asked and she gave him a look as if that was none of his business, 'if you don't mind me asking?'

'People change, Tom,' she said with finality.

'Is she all right?'

'They took her home. I assume she has dried out by now. Anyway, what did you wish to see me about? It's hardly going to be the local history page now that you've left for pastures new.'

'It's about the body,' he said, 'in Cappers Field. I was wondering if you had any idea who it might be.'

'None,' she replied quickly. 'That's exactly what Miss Norton just asked me. It could be anybody. I might know a great deal about this village Tom but I'm not Miss Marple.'

'It was just a thought,' he said, when he really wanted to

challenge her assertion that it could be anybody. Not in a village this size. He wondered why she hadn't offered him tea or cake like she usually did when he called. She didn't ask him anything about his new life in London either, which he would have expected her to do out of politeness if nothing else. Tom came to the obvious conclusion that she didn't want him there. For a moment, he was tempted to ask her why Betty Turner had chosen that very night to walk across the village in a downpour then bang on Mary's door, less than twelve hours after police found the body-in-the field? But he sensed she would clam up, leaving him with nothing, 'I'll not keep you then,' he said.

'Could you lift something out of the garage for me before you go, Ian?'

'Of course,' he was relieved to be asked, desperate to get out of that room. 'See you next time eh, mate?' he said to Carter.

'I'm not going anywhere.'

As Bradshaw followed Carol down the driveway he had a premonition that something important was about to happen, he could sense it. Her tone had been too self-consciously matter-of-fact and the task assigned him too vague. 'Ian, could you give me a hand getting *something* out of the garage please?' Not, 'can you help me get the lawnmower out', or 'the wheelie bin shifted'.

Had her husband finally told her the whole truth? Was she about to inform Bradshaw that he was vermin who had ruined their lives forever? If she was, he would stand there and take it until she was done then he would tell her how sorry he was, for he knew she was well within her rights.

He watched her hips swivel as she padded towards the garage in her tight jeans. Carol still had the 'nice, tidy arse' Carter used to joke about before he became a paraplegic. Bradshaw found himself wondering how long it had been since she last had sex, had they tried anything since the accident, could Carter even get it up now or, if he could, would he still want to? Everyone wondered that but no one dared to ask. Perhaps one day Carter would ask him to take care of Carol. 'I'd rather she was safe and not out with a stranger, you'll be doing me a favour, mate.' Bradshaw couldn't deny the thought excited him.

Oh God, what was he thinking? What was wrong with him? Here he was, following the wife of a man he has crippled into their garage and all he can think about is picking her up, lying her down on that work bench and slipping her one. Christ, was there no dark pit too deep for him to sink to in his own mind? But it wasn't as if he had been getting any either. He hadn't been near a girl since the incident and that was more than a year ago. It didn't seem right somehow – and who the hell would want him anyway?

More guilt.

Was there no end to it?

Carol bent down to place the key in the lock of the garage, turned it then pulled the metal door upwards. But when Carol turned round she didn't pull off her T shirt or unzip her jeans. She didn't beg him to take her here before Carter suspected a thing. Nor did she begin to berate him for crippling her husband.

Instead, she just put her hands on her hips and said, 'I don't think the visits are helping.'

'Oh,' he said simply, and all at once he felt a surge of joy, at the tiniest prospect of being released from this obligation and at her request. He would be free *and* blameless. Bradshaw now concentrated hard on trying to put the right disappointed look on his face then he immediately felt guilty again. What kind of human being was he to find joy in being released from a commitment to a man he had crippled?

'I thought they were a good idea,' Carol continued, 'a bit of human contact to take his mind off things, to stop him from just sitting there, hour after hour.' Was there a trace of resentment in the words 'hour after hour'? She must have been trying so hard to make Carter feel better, while single-handedly keeping the house going, then wondering why she was bothering if all he wanted was to feel sorry for himself day after day, week after week, month after month. Bradshaw assumed she would look back on her irritation later and feel bad about it.

More guilt.

Her guilt, his guilt, guilt piled onto guilt.

'But I think they are doing more harm than good. He gets really sullen after you've gone, like he's reliving what happened,' she added.

Who wouldn't? Bradshaw had, countless times, and he wasn't the one stuck in a metal chair for the rest of his days.

'I could leave it a while,' he hoped he hadn't sounded too eager, 'if you think that's best,'

'Would you?'

'I only want to do what's right by you and Alan.' Perhaps he need never knock on their door again, God he felt elated for the first time in months. 'You could always call the station if he wants me to pop by.' It was a nice open-ended offer that hopefully she would never take him up on.

'I will,' she said. 'Could you wheel the lawnmower out onto the back lawn and plug in the extension cable, so he doesn't think we've just been talking about him?'

"Course.'

She didn't thank him. Why should she?

He wondered when the lies had started. He didn't think Carol was the kind of girl who would have gone behind her husband's back before his 'accident'. Now he was in a wheelchair she must find herself telling him lie after lie, talking about him behind his back to the doctors, her family, her friends, his friends. There'd be many more lies from Carol before Alan Carter found any peace in this world.

'I don't think the visits are helping,' she'd said.

You're telling me, love.

Damned if you do and da. ned if you don't.

Chapter Twenty

Back in his car Tom couldn't shake the feeling that Mary Collier seemed rattled and that she knew a lot more than she was letting on. Perhaps he could get Betty Turner's side of the story.

Betty was an old stalwart of the Women's Institute and he'd been to her home, a two-up two-down council house she shared with three middle-aged sons who refused to grow up, on a number of occasions in his early years with the paper to publicise W. I. events. Betty had always been nice enough but her late husband had been 'a bit of a one', as Tom's own grandmother had euphemistically put it, meaning he was a drinker, a lay-about, a petty thief and a fighter to boot. Betty's lads seemed to have taken after their father and their names had all featured in the *Messenger*'s court reports at one time or another.

That morning Betty's house seemed quiet but Tom couldn't be sure if she was on her own until he knocked. Betty was a well-known figure in Great Middleton and not just as the ageing matriarch of the infamous Turner clan, for she had run the village shop for more than twenty years, which had made her a celebrity to every kid in the village when Tom was a boy. If you wanted pear drops, cola bottles, wine gums, love hearts or Refreshers you went to Betty's shop and got a ten-penny mix-up in a white, paper bag. She'd been retired ten years or more by now but the woman who answered the door didn't look senile.

'Hello, Betty,' he said, 'remember me? Tom from the *Messenger*,' he didn't tell her who he worked for these days, 'I used to publicise the W. I. meetings for you.'

She stared at him warily then said, 'What do you want?'

'I was wondering if I could come in,' he said but she didn't move, 'I wanted to have a word with you,' then he took a risk, 'about last night, when you went to the old vicarage.'

'Oh,' he was expecting resistance but instead she said, 'come in then.'

She went to the kitchen automatically and started to fill the kettle, as if it wouldn't cross her mind to invite anybody into her home without offering them a drink. While it began to boil he asked her, 'So, what was it all about then? Were you trying to talk to Mary Collier?'

Betty thought for a moment. Tom was sure there was more to her nighttime trek to Mary Collier's house than early senility but would she give a journalist her reasons? While Tom waited for her to answer, he heard a sound from upstairs. One of her sons must have been moving around up there. They were all the same; large, thick-set men who liked to throw their weight around, bullies who'd barely worked a day in their lives between them. He knew they weren't likely to take kindly to this intrusion. Tom needed answers from Betty and he needed them quick.

'Not talk to, no.' she finally answered. She seemed uncertain now he had challenged her about it.

'Why did you go there then?'

Upstairs, a door slammed and male voices were having a muffled conversation. There was more than one of them in the house but they were unaware of his presence.

'To tell her I knew,' said Betty simply.

'That you knew what, exactly?'

'That it was her.'

There was the sound of another door opening, then footsteps across the landing above him. Please don't come down, thought Tom. Not now.

'What was?'

'That it was all down to her,' Betty said it as if he must surely know what she was referring to. Tom began to wonder if maybe she *was* losing it after all. 'I wanted her to know that I knew,' she said firmly.

There was a creak from upstairs that sounded as if someone had trodden on a loose floorboard, then heavy feet were on the stairs. Someone was coming down.

Tom only had seconds, 'Was this something to do with the man?' he asked quickly, 'the body-in-the-field?'

'Of course,' she said, as if he was an idiot, 'that's what I'm telling you.'

The footsteps grew louder and a voice called, 'Mam? Who are you talking to?'

Tom ignored this and ploughed on. 'Who is it, Betty? Do you know? Who was buried in that field?' Betty looked visibly upset, her bottom lip came out like a child's and she looked as if she was about to cry. 'If you know then tell me,' urged Tom, just as the thump-thump of heavy boots ended. Someone had reached the hallway and would be with them in an instant. 'Please,' he said.

'Sean,' was all she managed to say before the tears began to fall.

'Sean?' repeated Tom, hoping he might get more than this but just then the kitchen door flew open.

'What the hell are you doing?' a well-built and very angry middle-aged man, who Tom recognised as Frankie, Betty's middle son, was standing in the kitchen doorway. Then the man noticed the tears on his mother's cheeks. 'Have you been upsetting her?' demanded Frankie and he set his face in a snarl and took a step towards Tom.

Tom held up a hand to placate him. 'No, it's okay,' he said, 'I'm a journalist.'

With hindsight, Tom would realise this was not the best response he could have given. 'I know who you are and it's not okay,' hissed Frankie Turner and he grabbed Tom's jacket by the lapels. 'You've made my mam cry.'

'Simmer down, man,' Tom urged him, 'I was only asking her some questions . . .' but he wasn't allowed to explain further. Instead he was flung forcibly from the room and propelled through the hallway. 'She was happy to talk to me,' Tom protested but another shove sent him closer to the door, then Frankie seized him by the hair and banged his head against the front door, causing him to cry out in pain.

'Don't come back here, you bastard, or I'll break your back,' and with that Frankie Turner released him, opened the front door and pushed Tom out through it, hard. He left the house so quickly that he tripped on the stairs and fell, landing heavily on his side. 'Now fuck off!' The door was slammed in his face.

Tom lay there for a moment to see how badly he was

hurt but there seemed to be no lasting damage, apart from a sharp pain where his head had connected with the front door before he went through it and a bang on his arm where he had landed roughly. He picked himself up gingerly.

There was a row going on inside the Turner home now, with a shout of 'Why did you let him in?' from one male voice, then another joined in. It crossed Tom's mind that a second member of the Turner clan might think he had been dealt with too leniently, so he didn't hang about.

Welcome home, Tom thought, as he dragged his bruised body back to the car.

Chapter Twenty-One

Day Four

Though the dead-wood squad were now working another case, their presence in the morning briefings was still obligatory, in case they came up with something that might help in the search for Michelle Summers. Detective Superintendent Trelawe was giving them all what he considered a much-needed kick up the arse.

'We have had twenty-five detectives working on this case and still not a single lead worth a jot,' he told them. 'It's not good enough and it won't do. So far, we've all been asleep at the wheel,' by *we*, he of course meant *they* had all been asleep at the wheel, 'so from now on, I shall be conducting the morning briefing myself, every day, until the case is cleared up.' He knew they wouldn't appreciate that. 'Thoughts, gentlemen?' he demanded.

There was a long pause, during which Trelawe wondered if everyone was actually going to ignore him.

Finally, it was DC Skelton who broke the silence. 'Well,' he said, 'has anyone given some thought to the fact that it might not actually be the Kiddy-Catcher?'

'Please don't use that offensive nickname in this room,' Trelawe told him.

Skelton continued unabated, 'I mean there's a stepdad isn't there?'

'Yes,' confirmed DCI Kane, 'there is.'

'Well, there you go,' Skelton said with some finality, 'that's got to be worth it,'

'Worth what exactly?' asked Trelawe.

'A look, Sir,' Skelton frowned, 'well I mean, if there's a stepdad and the girl was what? Fourteen?'

'Fifteen,' DCI Kane corrected him.

'Even better,' Skelton nodded emphatically, 'fifteen, all those hormones, and what with her not really know-ing what it's for and him having it paraded up and down in front of him all the time like that, and her not a blood relative,' Skelton shrugged. 'His missus is no looker either,' he looked around him, as if drumming up support for his view. 'Well I mean, that's got to be worth a look, hasn't it?'

Some of the men chuckled. The detective superintend-ent showed no emotion.

'He's a lorry driver isn't he?' it was DS O'Brien's turn to pipe up.

'Yes he is,' confirmed Kane.

'There you go,' said Skelton.

'What do you mean by that, Detective Constable?' asked Trelawe.

'Most of them are dirty pervs, for starters,' Skelton told him. There were more chuckles from the squad, who were clearly loving this. 'It's all that time they spend on their own,' Skelton added.

'You're saying that all long-distance lorry drivers are potential murderers?' asked Trelawe.

'Well, not all of them,' Skelton qualified his statement, 'not murderers, no,' then he looked to his DS for support, 'but, I mean, how many of them have we banged up over the years, for all kinds of things?'

'A fair few,' answered O'Brien, a shorter, squatter man who was slumped so low in his chair he was almost horizontal. The two men were affectionately known as Durham's Regan and Carter, by colleagues in awe of their cavalier attitude to the law they were sworn to uphold. Bradshaw despised them both.

Skelton started counting the crimes off on his fingers, 'assault, lewd conduct, gross indecency, sexual assault, rape, whore-battering . . .' he said the last one like there was an official criminal offence of 'whore-battering', '. . . domestic abuse . . . incest . . . and, yes, murder, at least one I can think of,'

'At least,' mumbled DS O'Brien.'

'Wasn't the Ripper a lorry driver?' asked someone and Trelawe looked at them as if he couldn't be sure whether they were joking or not. Here they were, trained detectives, and all ruminating on the weirdness of lorry drivers per se versus the rest of the population. Thousands of men out there all day, every day, driving lorries, delivering the goods that kept British industry afloat and the nation's larders stocked and they'd all just been dismissed as sickos and perverts.

'Come on, Sir. Let us sweat him a little?' urged Skelton.

Trelawe shook his head, 'No, nothing official. No formal questioning.'

'At least let us take a look around the house,' urged Skelton. 'Who knows what we might find?'

The detective superintendent thought for a moment.

All eyes were on him. Finally he said, 'no,' and the sighs from the men were audible. They didn't even bother to hide their disgust. Trelawe looked rattled but he held up his hand to silence them. 'There will be no warrant to search the household, not without any evidence linking either of them to Michelle's disappearance. If we do that the press will find out about it in a heartbeat . . .'

'Is that all we care about, Sir?' sneered DS O'Brien, 'what the press think?'

The detective super appeared on the verge of rebuking O'Brien for the tone of his question but he obviously thought better of it, 'if the press report that we casually searched their home, and they have a nasty habit of find-ing that sort of thing out, the family will be tried and convicted by a million armchair jurors whether they are snowy white or not. You know that. Now let's get back out there, people,' he urged them as he abruptly termi-nated the briefing.

Bradshaw was last to shuffle out of the room. As he followed the departing detectives he was surprised to see Vincent Addison hanging back, as if waiting for the younger man. By the time Bradshaw reached him they were alone.

'What?' he asked, not expecting much in return, 'what is it, Vince?'

To Bradshaw's surprise, Vincent looked eager to con-fide in him. He first checked that no one was in earshot then lowered his voice.

'We don't need a warrant to look round their house.'

Chapter Twenty-Two

Helen was sitting alone in a quiet corner of the Greyhound, with her head down, feverishly scribbling on a notepad, and he knew what she was writing. She didn't notice Tom until he placed a fresh glass of wine on the table in front of her. Without even looking up at him, she slid the glass away from her with an outstretched hand. Tom reasoned she was either massively preoccupied, incredibly rude or both.

'I bought that for you,' he informed her.

She stopped writing then and glanced up at Tom, 'Oh, I thought you were one of the locals,' she said, but her face did not soften.

'I am,' he said.

'Unlike me,' she bridled, 'I was parachuted in, remember?' Then she regarded the drink he'd bought her. 'What's this?' he opened his mouth to reply, 'and don't say it's a glass of wine.'

He closed his mouth again, for that was exactly what he was about to say. Instead he shrugged, 'A peace offering,' and when she said nothing in reply, he explained, 'Look, I'm sorry. I was a prat. I'd had more than a couple of beers and I was showing off but I didn't mean a word of it. I don't even know you.' She was watching him with what seemed like interest. 'There, I've admitted it. I'm an idiot. Can we start again?'

'Apology accepted,' she said stiffly. She used the same hand to slide the wine glass back towards her, then carried on writing, leaving him standing there. He realised the regulars would be watching this encounter from the bar by now and he felt a little foolish.

'Busy?' He was determined not to be thrown by her indifference.

'Very.'

'If I guess what you're doing, can I join you for five minutes? There's something I want to ask you.'

Helen sighed, covering her notes with an arm as she did so. She was pretty sure her spidery scrawl, all squiggles in boxes, with arrows pointing to random, supporting notes, was indecipherable to anybody but herself. 'Go on then,' she challenged him.

'You're writing up your district page,' he told her confidently.

'How could you possibly have known that?' she asked. 'I could have been writing up any story.'

He took the seat opposite her. 'You're sitting in the Greyhound on your lonesome, which is unusual for a woman. Don't give me that look. Women don't normally sit in pubs on their own, especially boozers like this one,' he told her, 'you've got my old patch and it's Monday, which is the usual day for panic about the district page because you've only got forty-eight hours till the next edition. All week long we worked on the big stuff, well biggish stuff, it's all relative after all.'

'All right mister hot-shot tabloid man. I know you think the *Durham Messenger* is crap.'

'No, I don't,' he assured her, 'I worked on the *Messenger*

for six years, remember. I was a lot older than you before I managed to take the next step up.'

'Well, you took it so good for you.'

'I recognise district page panic when I see it. We always left it till the last minute because it's so damn dull and difficult to fill.'

She looked down at her scrawl of notes and let out a long sigh. 'You're right,' she admitted, 'I am panicking. This happens every week and it never gets any better. How did you do this for six years?'

'The district page is a Catch 22,' he explained, 'once you understand that, you're halfway there.'

'Yes,' she agreed eagerly, 'that's exactly what it is.' The district page was the bane of every reporter's life on the *Messenger*. As well as reporting on general news, each journalist was assigned a territory, comprising a few villages and expected to fill a page devoted to news solely from that patch, 'if your story isn't good enough, it won't get on the district page but if it is good enough . . .'

'The editor nicks it for his news pages?'

'Exactly!' he was amused by her frustration at the newspaper's defiance of logic, 'every week I spend hours on it. It's driving me mad.'

'Like I said, it's a paradox. You've just got to find stories that occupy that middle ground.'

She shook her head, 'you make it sound easy,' she said. 'Maybe it was, for you,' and she took a sip of the wine. 'Anyway, what was it you wanted to talk to me about?'

'We keep meeting.'

'And you're worried people will talk?' she answered drily.

'No, I'm worried we'll get in each other's way.'

'I believe I was here first,' she waived a hand airily.

'Today, yes, but technically I beat you to it by years.'

'Want me to leave?'

'This isn't about the pub.'

'I gathered that.'

'I'm talking about the way that whenever I go to see someone you've just been there.'

'We are both journalists,' Helen said, 'I assume we are covering the same stories?'

'Perhaps but people are less likely to open up if we are both door-stopping them.'

'It used to be your patch, now it's mine. Maybe you resent that?'

'He won't let you run with them,' he said. 'Malcolm will either spike your articles or tone them down so much people will fall asleep on the bus reading them.'

'You speak from experience?'

'Oh yes.'

'Maybe so but I have to at least try, otherwise I might as well pack up and go home and I'm not about to do that.'

'I wasn't going to ask you to stop. You are reading me all wrong, Helen.'

'What did you want then?'

'I figured, since we keep on bumping into each other that we might as well use this to our advantage.'

'How?'

'By working together.'

'Together?' she surveyed him for signs he might be mocking her. 'You're serious?'

'Totally.'

She took a long sip of wine while she was thinking. 'What would you get out of it? You're the whizz-kid journalist who works for the famous tabloid, I'm just the girly cub-reporter.'

'That's not how I view you. You've got a brain on you, you've only been here five minutes and you're already speaking to the right people, contacts it took me six years to accumulate, and I've read your stuff. It's good, you can write, not everybody at the *Messenger* can. Plus you've still got the local-paper credentials.' When she appeared unconvinced, he added, 'I do work for the biggest tabloid in the country but that's a double-edged-sword; sometimes it opens doors, sometimes I get them slammed in my face.' The memory of being thrown out of Betty Turner's house mid-interview was still a fresh one.

'Okay, so what do I get out of it?'

'I know the area and I know people, particularly around here. I've been doing this a while. I figure we have different strengths and I'm suggesting we share what we find. There are two big stories here and a lot of doors to knock on.'

'The police are already doing that.'

'They won't get very far round here.' She wondered why he was so certain about that. 'It wouldn't be such an ordeal would it? We could make a pretty good team.'

'I'd be taking a risk,' she said.

'Why?'

'If my editor found out I was teaming up with the infamous Tom Carney he'd hit the roof.'

Tom smiled, 'How I have missed Malcolm. Well I won't tell him if you don't. Tell you what; if I write your district page for you in two minutes will you spend some time looking at these stories with me?'

'Two minutes? How could you . . .'

'Trust me,' and when she gave him a look that clearly indicated she did not trust him, he added, 'or you are no further forward. I could solve your problem like that,' and he clicked his fingers.

'I don't see how you can,' she informed him.

'Okay, well, there are a series of staple local non-news stories you can run again and again with subtle variations.'

'Like?'

'Grass verges.'

'What?'

'The county council used to cut the verges once a week. About four years ago they changed it to once a fortnight to save money and the parish councils have been up in arms ever since.

'Then there's dog fouling,' he told her.

'Are you serious?'

'Perfectly and be sure to mention toxocariasis.'

'What's that?'

'A disease caused by worms that live in a dog's intestines. When they crap, on playing fields and the aforementioned grass verges, they can leave eggs that contaminate the soil. If a kid is playing nearby and he touches the dog shit then accidentally puts his hands in his mouth, eggs can hatch in the child's intestines and the larvae then head for the brain, liver and eyes, which can cause blindness.'

'Oh my God, that's disgusting,' she said. 'Has it ever happened?'

'Not to a kid on the *Messenger*'s patch thankfully, no, but it's a theoretical possibility that dog fouling can cause blindness in children in Great Middleton.'

'But it is *unlikely* to,' she said.

'But it *could*,' he laughed and pointed to her notes. 'Phone the bus company and ask them if they are planning to increase fares or alter services. If they answer no, truthfully, you can run with "Bus Company denies plan to increase fares".'

'But is all this ethical?' she sounded exasperated again.

'Most newspaper editors think ethics is a county near Hertfordshire.'

'I don't know.'

He folded his arms and looked at her. 'Well, that district page isn't gonna write itself.'

She thought for a moment. 'You're right,' she admitted, 'it won't and I don't have anything else.'

'Precisely,' he said, 'write that all up and you're almost there.'

Helen realised her first impression of Tom Carney had been wrong. He may have exhibited a certain cockiness but he knew his stuff. 'Thanks, I didn't know any of this before you told me,' she admitted, 'nobody ever tells me anything at the *Messenger*.'

'Well, they won't,' he said matter-of-factly.

'Why not?'

'Because knowledge is power and if they tell you everything they know you might turn out to be much better at the job than they are – and where would that leave them?'

'But that's stupid.'

'It's the way some of them are,' he said. 'Listen, Helen,

don't waste your time like I did, just get the experience you need and move to a bigger paper as soon as you are ready.' He took a deep breath and smiled at her. 'Here endeth the lesson.'

'Thanks,' she said, 'I think.'

'Now come and have lunch.'

'What? I can't.'

'Sure you can,' he said. 'We had a deal, remember? I just wrote your district page and now I get to talk to you for a while. I don't know about you but I'm starving, so I figured we could talk and eat.'

'Can't we eat here?'

He lowered his voice, 'I know a much better place and it's cheaper. What's the matter?' he asked her. 'It's not a date.'

'I know it's not,' she said firmly.

Chapter Twenty-Three

Fiona and Denny answered the door together. They'd found that Michelle's mother was asked slightly less offensive questions by journalists if Denny's giant frame was filling the door behind her.

'Fiona?' he said, when she showed no sign of recognizing him from their earlier encounter on the playing field, 'Detective Constable Ian Bradshaw and this is Detective Constable Vincent Addison' and he showed her his ID. 'Do you mind if we come in?'

'Have you got some news?' she asked, eyes like a frightened animal.

'I'm afraid not,' and her body slumped — but was it relief or sadness? 'We were hoping to have a little look around your home if that's okay with you?'

She looked at him uncertainly. 'Why?'

'Purely routine,' said Vincent dismissively, 'you'd be surprised what you can find when you look closely. We thought we might start with Michelle's room, if that's okay.'

'Well I suppose . . . but what are you looking for?'

'Won't know till we find it, love,' Vincent told her, 'but there's usually something; diaries, letters to boyfriends, magazines with destinations highlighted in red that, lo and behold, the missing person has run off to.'

'Your colleagues have looked already, but if you think it will help?'

'As long as you and Michelle's father don't mind?' added Bradshaw.

'Oh, he's not . . .' she began, '. . . this is Denny. He's my husband but not Michelle's dad.'

'That's right,' agreed Bradshaw, 'my mistake,' and he looked Denny right in the eye then. 'You're not related to Michelle at all, are you Denny?'

Was there the faintest flicker of guilt or perhaps fear in Denny's eye then? 'No,' Denny admitted then he mumbled, 'like she said.'

Fiona led the way upstairs to Michelle's bedroom with Bradshaw next, then Denny. Vincent made as if to follow but hung back at the foot of the stairs.

'Is it always like this?' Bradshaw said as he reached the girl's room.

'How do you mean?'

'Bit tidy isn't it?' he asked, 'I thought most teenaged girl's rooms looked like someone threw a grenade into them.'

'I tidied,' Fiona said.

'It's usually a right mess,' said Denny and his wife shot him a look that told him he was being disloyal.

'That's kids though, isn't it?' Bradshaw indicated the posters on the walls: 'Likes her music then.'

'Yeah,' her mother's mood lightened for a moment, 'if you can call it that.'

'Take That,' he read the name on one of her posters, 'I was into The Jam myself at her age. What about you?'

'Eh?' asked Denny.

'What music you into?' he said, as if this was a normal question in a missing girl's bedroom.

'I like country.'

'Oh yeah,' answered Bradshaw, 'I s'pose you would.'

'How'd you mean?'

'Being a lorry driver, all that open road; bet you like Glen Campbell or a bit of Charlie Rich?'

'Yeah, I do,' he said brightening, 'she prefers The Carpenters.'

Bradshaw could see the irritation on Fiona Summers' face. There was tension here between them but was it the understandable stress caused by a missing daughter, or something deeper? Bradshaw spent the next fifteen minutes quizzing Fiona and Denny about their home life, Michelle's friends and boyfriend, whether she liked school and any hobbies she may have had, aside from an interest in pop groups. None of this mattered to Bradshaw. He just wanted to give Vincent enough time.

'Should I put the kettle on,' said Fiona after he had run out of questions.

'Tea, thanks,' said Bradshaw, 'milk and no sugar.'

When she had gone Bradshaw walked round Michelle's room. Denny watched as the detective constable picked up some of the girl's personal items, looked at them then put them carefully back down again; a book, a snow dome, a music box.

'Can I do anything?'

'Mmm?' replied Bradshaw absent-mindedly.

'To help?' asked Denny, 'can I do anything to help?'

'Why don't you give your missus a hand with the tea?'

Denny didn't look as if he felt comfortable leaving Bradshaw alone in Michelle's room but he went anyway. As he was going down the stairs he remembered the other police officer. Sure enough when he reached the hallway,

Vincent was coming back through the house towards him. Where had he been while they were in Michelle's room?

Vincent didn't say anything as he passed Denny.

Bradshaw was holding a school exercise book covered with a page from a copy of *Smash Hits*, so that the boyish faces of Take That were staring out at him. 'Didn't think they were your type?' Vincent said self-consciously, as if it had been a while since he'd engaged in laddish banter with a colleague.

Bradshaw dropped the exercise book back on the chest of drawers and said, 'There's nothing here,' then he realised his colleague was looking very pleased with himself.

'Guess what I found?'

They went in his car and there was certainly nothing flash about that. The Rosewood café was a single-story building on the outskirts of Durham city, with whitewashed walls and blue and white checked curtains hanging either side of steamed-up windows. The place was half full.

Tom ordered an all-day breakfast, while Helen chose a BLT before asking the waitress, 'Do you do cappuccino?'

'We do tea and we do coffee,' she was told, as if she had just asked for Lobster Thermidor.

'Tea will be fine.'

They took a small table by the wall. 'I like this place,' he said, 'it's good for people watching.'

'Why would you watch other people?'

'Don't you do that? I like to try and work out who they are what they are up to. It's good practice for a journalist to try and read people.'

'You can't know people just by looking at them.'

''Course you can,' he told her, 'give it a go.'

'Are you serious?' she asked.

He realised she was taking the bait. 'Pick one.'

She glanced around the room. Two guys who looked like builders were demolishing all-day breakfasts. Next to them was a harassed young mum, with a sleeping baby in a buggy and a toddler. Two elderly ladies were gossiping about someone and an old couple sat opposite each other silently having a cup of tea and a toasted teacake. They looked like they'd run out of things to say to each other years ago but Helen chose a younger man.

'That guy by the window,' she said, 'he works in a bank or an office, probably the latter because he doesn't have a name badge pinned to his shirt. He's a bit of a Billy-no-mates, happier reading the paper than hanging out with colleagues. Probably looking at the jobs section so he can leave.'

'Wrong.'

'Wrong?'

'Wrong,' he assured her.

'How do you know I'm wrong? How can you be so sure?'

'He's not here on his own. He's meeting someone for lunch. It's a woman. He's afraid she isn't going to show up. It matters.'

Helen's forehead creased into a frown. 'How could you possibly know that, just from looking at him?'

'He keeps looking at his watch,' he told her, 'he glanced at it twice while you were watching him.'

'If he's on his lunch hour he would look at his watch.'

'Every few minutes but not every few seconds? Anyway, that isn't the only thing.'

'Dazzle me with your powers of observation.'

'He hasn't turned the page of his newspaper since we walked in. It's a prop. He's pretending to read it. He's waiting for someone and he doesn't know if she's going to show up.'

'I'm not sure if you are really good or just winding me up. If his lunch date doesn't turn up we'll never know anyway.'

'True,' he admitted.

'What about me then?' and she folded her arms.

'You mean apart from the defensive arm-folding?'

She immediately unfolded her arms. 'This could get annoying.'

'That's why I don't normally do it to my friends.'

'Are we friends?'

'We could be.'

'Why do I suspect you don't have very many female friends?'

'I have lots of female friends. I like women.'

'No you don't,' she told him, 'sleeping with a woman does not make her your friend.'

'Harsh.'

'But fair, according to the girls in the office.'

'Who obviously all know the inner me,' Tom said drily. 'I thought we were doing you though.'

'Okay,' she allowed, 'so do me then.'

'Right,' he said it unsurely, 'and you won't get pissed off with me?'

'That depends on what you say, obviously.'

'I'll bear that in mind,' they were looking right at each other now, 'I'd say you weren't the oldest in your family but not the middle child either.'

'I have an older sister. How did you know that and why am I not the middle child?'

'She's a bit of a high-flyer, works for some blue chip company?'

Helen nodded. 'She works in marketing.'

'So you had something to live up to,' he said, 'but you wanted to do something different, not just follow in her footsteps?'

'That's factually correct but it's not the reason I wanted to be a journalist. And the middle child?'

'You don't look like you suffer from middle-child-syndrome. You're not the afterthought. You know, when the oldest child is the first to go off to university so it's a big deal and the youngest can do no wrong, because they are the baby of the family. The middle one can feel a bit irrelevant. I don't see that in you.'

'What do you see?'

'A serious person.'

'Oh yes, I'm immensely serious.'

'Bet you never bunked off school.'

'What's that got to do with it?'

'You're not the type. I bet you even liked it, school I mean.'

She sniffed, 'It was okay.'

'You've not had lots of boyfriends.'

'Haven't I?'

'Two or maybe three, the first when you were eighteen.'

'Seventeen,'

'Seventeen, and you went out with him for at least a year, made him wait before you slept with him, you had to be sure it mattered. You broke up when you went to university, tried the long-distance thing but it didn't work out, you drifted apart, became two different people.'

'You could be describing thousands of people my age.'

'You broke it off though, not him. He was gutted.'

'How do you . . .' she stopped herself but not in time.

'He just would be,' he chuckled. 'You broke it off because you began to fancy someone else, probably an older guy, a mature man of say . . . twenty,' she gave him a lopsided look as if she was about to ask him how he knew all this, 'and it wouldn't be right to cheat on your boyfriend so you broke up with him before you started seeing the new guy and you were head over heels with this one.'

'Was I?'

'Yeah, you were but I'm guessing he was a dick.'

'What was wrong with him?' She folded then immediately unfolded her arms.

'He wasn't as keen on you as you were on him, which was great at first because it was exciting but, after a while, you realise it's going nowhere and he's never going to be the *one*, so you break up with him,' she let out something between a snort and a mirthless laugh, 'and then you stay off men for a while, concentrate on your studies, spend time with your friends. Then, probably in your final year, you meet someone who doesn't take you for granted but won't idolise you either. You can rely on him, he's ambitious like you, wants to make a name for himself and you can see yourselves together way off into the future; the house, the kids. Am I right?'

'Some of that was right and some of it wasn't.'

'Which bits were right?'

'Not telling.'

'Spoilsport. You do have a boyfriend then?'

'Yes, but I met him in my second year, not the third.'

'Damn it,' he said, 'I'm no good at this at all, am I?'

'You are disconcertingly good at it,' she admitted.

'He must be very proud,' Tom said, 'of you I mean; being a journalist,' and when she hesitated before replying, he added, 'or not.'

'He's fine with it,' she replied.

'Fine with it,' he nodded, 'that's good then.'

'You can stop now. We are supposed to be talking about Michelle Summers and the mysterious body-in-the-field.'

'Okay,' he said. 'You went to see Mary Collier and you asked her if she knew about the body.'

'Yes.'

'And you did that because . . . ?'

'She seems to know everything that goes on in the village.'

'Like Roddy Moncur?'

She nodded, 'I found their numbers in your local history file.'

'Malcolm gave that page to you?' She nodded again. 'You poor sod. So that's why you went to see Mary?'

'Yes.'

'It had nothing to do with Betty Turner washing up on her doorstep in the middle of the night?'

'You know about that?'

'Yes,' he said, 'but I would have preferred to have heard it from you. We *are* supposed to be sharing.'

'Point taken.'

'How did you know Betty Turner went down there?'

Helen told him about her meeting with DI Reid.

'And she was just banging on Mary's door?'

'And shouting.'

'What was she shouting?'

'"It was you."'

'And Mary Collier dismissed the incident as the ramblings of a senile old dodderer?'

'Yes,' she said.

'I got the impression she was being economical with the truth.'

'That's interesting,' she said, 'so did I.'

Tom thought for a moment. 'So, we have an ancient, unidentified corpse accidentally dug up in a field and that very night, old Betty Turner treks all the way across the village in her jim-jams in the pissing-down rain, so she can bang on Mary Collier's door and tell her "it was you"?'

'Yep.'

He smiled at her then, 'Well, I'm intrigued. Don't you think this has the makings of a heck of a story?'

'Possibly.'

'Did you follow this up with Betty Turner?'

'I didn't get the chance. I was called back to the office, to interview the new Miss Darlington.'

'I bet that was riveting.'

'It was,' she said drily, 'she's "over the moon", her mum and dad are over the moon and as for her boyfriend . . .'

'Over the moon?'

'How did you guess?'

'A teenage beauty queen's take on the world is always worth recording.'

'How about you? Did you follow up with Betty Turner?'

'I did.'

The food arrived then. 'I'm starving,' he said as he covered every square inch of his plate with ketchup.

'You can take the boy out of the North . . .' she said.

He shrugged then proceeded to eat like a man in a hurry while she took a bite from her sandwich.

'So what have you got for me?' she asked, 'since we're sharing?'

'Not much,' he told her through a mouthful of his breakfast, 'just a name.'

'A name?' she asked uncertainly, 'you have a name for our body-in-the-field?'

'According to Betty, his name was Sean.'

'Oh my God. Have you told the police?'

'Not yet.'

'But shouldn't we? I mean, the man was killed. This is an actual murder investigation.'

'I don't think there's much danger of the culprit fleeing the country on his Zimmer frame. He's probably six feet under.'

'Did she tell you anything else?'

'A first name was all I got,' he said, 'before her son threw me out, literally, which was a shame because I reckon she had a lot more to tell, so I was thinking . . .' He gave her a look.

'What?'

'I can hardly go back there. I'd probably leave through the window.'

'Rough family?' she asked and he nodded, 'but you want *me* to go down there?'

'Well, they've never beaten up a woman,' he assured her, 'at least, not to my knowledge.'

'There's always a first time.'

'I've got your back,' he promised her.

'Why does that not reassure me?' she asked.

Just then the door to the café was flung open and a young woman appeared, looking flustered. She was in her mid-twenties and could easily be described as beautiful, with long, blonde hair and a figure that caught the eye of the two builders. Her face took on a pained expression and she mouthed the word 'sorry' at the young man in the shirt and tie.

Helen said quietly, 'Don't you want to say I told you so?'

'I don't have to, you saw how he leaped out of his chair to greet her, how he didn't mind her being late. The man's besotted with her, poor sap.'

'Okay, you were right. But there's no need to be horrible. If he loves her, it doesn't make him an idiot.'

'You didn't spot her wedding ring,' he told her, 'and he wasn't wearing one.'

'Oh.'

'Those two aren't married,' he assured her, 'at least, not to each other.'

Chapter Twenty-Four

When Bradshaw caught up with Vincent Addison, his colleague was staring out of the window by his desk. There didn't seem to be all that much to see; just skies darkened by a fine rain the consistency of mist that coated the surrounding buildings, greying them in the process.

'You all right, Vincent?'

'I, er . . .' Vincent began unsurely, still gazing out of the window, 'it's just, I've not done this for a while.'

'It'll be okay,' Bradshaw assured him, 'how do you want to play it? Good cop, bad cop?'

'How about bad cop, bad cop?'

The pavement was slick and shiny from a rain storm they'd missed while they were in the café.

'Did the police not think Betty going to Mary's house and banging on her door was significant?' Tom asked, 'you'd think they'd have followed it up.'

Helen thought for a moment. 'Betty was taken home by uniformed officers. They logged it but maybe they didn't tell the detectives investigating the body-in-the-field . . .'

'Sean,' he corrected her.

'. . . investigating Sean, sorry. Perhaps nobody has actually linked Betty's little walk in the night to the body.'

'Left hand, right hand,' he told her, 'it's the same in

every large organisation, including the police, which means we are one step ahead.'

'If Betty really knows something,' she reminded him.

'She knows something all right and I'd have found out what if her knuckle-dragging sons hadn't been home.'

'So now you need me to go into the lion's den?'

Vincent broke the rules. He lit a cigarette in the interview room, took a drag then flicked the end into an ashtray on the table between them. The lorry driver's eyes followed his movements. 'Do you know why we asked you to come down here?'

'You said it was to help find Michelle,' said Denny.

'We just wanted a word, Denny,' said Bradshaw, 'it is *Denny*, isn't it?'

'Yeah.'

'What's that short for then?' asked Vincent, 'not Denzel?'

'No,' answered Denny sullenly and they both regarded him with suspicion. Denny felt a pang of fear. Perhaps it would be better if he tried harder to cooperate. 'It's my name . . .'

Bradshaw interrupted him, 'your name is Denny?' he peered at the papers in front of him. 'No, it isn't.'

'No, it isn't,' Denny almost stammered.

'That's what I said,' answered Bradshaw.

'My real name is Darren,' he said it quickly before they could interrupt him again, 'but when I was small my little brother couldn't pronounce Darren,' they both frowned at him, 'he used to run round after me 'cos I was a bit older and he was always shouting "Denny! Denny!"' they continued to regard him as if he might be making this up, 'and when the adults heard, they all thought it was funny, so they started calling me Denny too . . . and it just sort of stuck. Now everyone calls me Denny, always have done.' He shrugged apologetically.

There was a long silence. Finally Bradshaw spoke, 'Denny, you are one hell of a storyteller. That was riveting.'

'Well, you asked me . . .'

Bradshaw interrupted, 'There was no need to write a book about it.' Denny looked into the policeman's fierce eyes and tried to make some sense of what lay there. Why were they treating him like this? It wasn't fair. He wanted to go home. When Bradshaw received no reply from the nervous man in front of him he shouted, 'was there?'

'No!' Denny shouted back in reply. God they could have asked him to stand to attention right then and he'd have done it, he was that nervous.

'All right, Denny,' and Vincent laughed, giving him a twinkly, all-lads-together smile, 'no need to shout about it, eh? We're only over here.'

'Sorry, sorry, it's just I'm a bit . . .'

Vincent smiled again, 'Nervous?'

'Yeah,' Denny nodded, grateful for the empathy.

'Why are you nervous, Denny? What have you got to be nervous about?' Vincent's face was as hard as stone now and just as unforgiving.

'Nothing.'

'You sure?' asked Vincent. 'It'd be better if you told us everything, better for you, better for Michelle, wherever she is.'

'No,' Denny was shocked. 'I haven't done anything. I just mean you make me nervous, that's all. I'm not used to this.'

'Used to what?'

'Police.'

'You got something against the police, have you, Denny?'

'No! God no, course not.'

'We're the good guys,' Bradshaw reminded him, 'aren't we?'

'I know, I never meant . . .'

'You don't have to be nervous about us, mate,' said Vincent, 'not unless you're hiding something,' Vincent cocked his head to one side, which made him look like an inquisitive dog. 'Are you hiding something, Denny?'

'No.'

'You sure?'

"Course I am.'

'Well we think you are,' said Bradshaw, 'we know you are in fact,'

'I'm not hiding anything. I don't know what happened to Michelle. I don't.'

'Michelle?' asked Vincent innocently, 'who said we were talking about Michelle?' and he feigned surprise.

'Well . . .' stammered Denny, 'what else could . . .'

'We are talking about what you've been hiding in the shed,' said Bradshaw.

Denny tried to look innocent and uncomprehending but he made a pretty bad job of it. His eyes widened, he even licked his bottom lip in a nervous gesture. 'I've got no idea what you're talking . . .'

'Sod off, Denny,' said Bradshaw.

'We found your stash,' Vincent told him calmly, 'the one you'd gone to so much trouble to hide.'

Denny tried to look as if he hadn't a clue what they were on about, but he was fooling no one and he knew it.

Bradshaw reached under the table and picked up a familiar-looking carrier bag. He upended it and its contents fell onto the table in front of Denny, a dozen magazines, each one with a young girl on the cover, a very young girl.

'I don't ...' Denny seemed to be searching for an explanation but he couldn't come up with one.

'This is only a few of them,' Vincent informed him, 'I left the others in the shed in case we need to make it official.'

'Official?'

'It's all right though, isn't it Denny? I mean, we are all lads together. No one minds a bit of grot, not these days. It's 1993 not the 1950s,' Bradshaw assured him, 'who hasn't got a bit of the old porno?'

'I used to want my very own Playboy model when I was a lad,' admitted Vincent, 'like that bird off *Baywatch*. That's just my personal preference.'

'I'm more partial to the amateur ladies,' Bradshaw followed Vincent's lead, 'the mucky bird next door with her filthy fantasises about the window cleaner. I'm more of a realist. I'm not likely to wake up next to Pamela Anderson but I've got half a chance of finding some dirty housewife in Darlington whose old man's away on business and, when I do, I'll be ready for her, believe me.'

Denny couldn't hide his relief. At least they understood.

'Can't beat *Readers' Wives*,' said Bradshaw matter-of-factly, 'know what I mean?'

'Yeah,' said Denny shyly, 'I s'pose.'

'Only you don't though, do you, Denny,' said Vincent, 'know what he means,' and the mood seemed to change again in an instant.

Bradshaw was regarding him with those piercing, emotionless eyes, 'You see, what we are talking about is some honest-to-goodness pornography for the red-blooded, adult male. The kind of thing any fellah would be proud to have in his stash, just so long as his old lady doesn't find out about it. And even if she does, well, "I'm very sorry, darling but . . ." and you can laugh it off, front it out. She might not speak to you for a day or two but that's . . . well, that's just an added bonus in most modern marriages. But what *you've* got hidden in your shed is a bit different. That's very far from all right.'

'It's just the same,' said Denny but his voice came out too high, 'just a bit harder, that's all.'

'Where in God's name did you get it all from?' asked Vincent.

'Amsterdam,' squeaked Denny, 'I do long-haul jobs, some of them in Europe. They've got loads of that stuff out there. Everybody looks at it.'

'No they don't, Denny,' Vincent told him.

'Girls in white cotton panties,' tutted Bradshaw, 'in school uniforms?'

'Lollipops in their mouths,' muttered Vincent in disgust.

'They're all over-age,' Denny assured them, his voice cracking again.

'You sure?' asked Vincent.

'Yeah, course.'

'How could you be, unless you took the pictures?' Bradshaw lifted one of the mags and leafed through it, 'Most of them look like they could be fourteen, fifteen at the outside,' and he shook his head at the depravity of the world. 'Michelle is fifteen, isn't she, Denny?' Denny's face was red, the shame burning him, like a physical sensation. What would Fiona think if she knew about his sordid little secret? She'd never understand and these two would probably tell her for the fun of it. Finally he said, 'I want a lawyer.'

'Why would you need a lawyer?' asked Bradshaw. 'You've not been arrested, let alone charged with anything,' and he paused. 'Why do you need a lawyer, Denny? What have you done?'

'Nothing.'

'Only guilty men ask for lawyers, Denny,' said Vincent.

'Was it her fault?' asked Bradshaw, his tone suddenly reasonable again. 'I bet it was,' and he nodded as if he had accidentally stumbled upon the truth. 'Did she wander round in her skimpies? Perhaps she didn't realise what she was doing,' Bradshaw offered, 'or maybe she did. Was that it, Denny? Did she enjoy rubbing your nose in it?'

Denny shook his head. 'Did you want to teach her a lesson, show her what it was for, eh, while her mam was out at the shops?' asked Bradshaw. 'Did she act like she wanted it at first then suddenly change her mind? Is that why you had to force yourself on her? Is it why you killed her afterwards? If she was going to tell her mum, we'd understand.'

'I didn't . . .' stammered Denny in protest, '. . . I never touched Michelle.'

'Come on, Denny, not even once?' chided Bradshaw, 'all that time under the same roof? You must have thought about it.'

'Where is she, Denny? What have you done with her?' asked Vincent. 'You know you want to tell us and we'll find out anyway, so spare us all a lot of time and bother.'

'You'll feel much better when you do,' added Bradshaw, 'believe me. It'll be like a great weight lifted from your shoulders.'

'I want . . .' There were tears in Denny's eyes now and he sniffed them back before continuing.

'What do you want?' asked Bradshaw. 'Tell us, Denny,' he urged.

'I want a lawyer,' said Denny emphatically then the big man wiped his eyes.

Bradshaw slowly rose to his feet and he hung over Denny like a black cloud. 'I wasn't sure until just now,' he told the terrified lorry driver, 'I was willing to give you the benefit of the doubt until I watched your reaction to your . . .' he seemed to be searching for the right words, 'dirty little secret,' and he leaned even closer, 'and then I knew, I just knew. You're a wrong 'un. You're hiding something and we know what it is. What have you done with her? What have you done with Michelle?'

'I . . .' Denny's voice was a squeak and he cleared his throat. 'I want a lawyer.'

Vincent and Bradshaw exchanged looks.

'No need for that Denny,' said Vincent amiably, 'we're done, for now.'

'We've been sitting here for over an hour,' she told him.

'That's journalism.'

'No, it isn't,' Helen said, 'journalism is writing things. Staking out people's houses, waiting for them to leave is police work or private eye stuff.'

'You could try knocking on their door but I suspect that might not work. I speak from experience,' Tom reminded her.

They sat for a while in silence, watching Betty Turner's house through the windscreen of Tom's car.

'How does he do it?' asked Tom suddenly, as if Helen was privy to his innermost thoughts.

'Do what?'

'Get them to come with him,' he shrugged and she realised he was talking about the Kiddy-Catcher. 'They're not little girls. They are ten or eleven years old. They know not to talk to strangers. All girls do at that age. Don't they? Didn't you?'

'I suppose,' she thought for a moment, 'yes I did know at that age, of course I did.'

'You would,' he said. 'The most naïve girl in the world would know not to get into a strange man's car,' and he looked at her, 'wouldn't she?'

Helen nodded. She tried to remember how much she really know about men and rape and murder when she was twelve years old. Not much but enough, even then. It was drummed into you. You did not speak to strange men or get in their cars and go for a drive. If you did, something awful could happen.

'I don't know. Unless he is snatching them from the streets, bundling them into his car . . .'

'No,' he said with the kind of finality that brooked no objection, 'no struggles, no witnesses, nobody has ever reported seeing the Kiddy-Catcher dragging a lass into a car. Not once. Despite what people say, if a young girl screams loud enough, people come running. Of course they do.'

'So how is he doing it?'

'Dunno,' he admitted, 'and why have the police not found Michelle's body yet? All of the others were found quickly. He doesn't burn or bury them, just leaves them out in countryside and waits for the first person to find them.'

'Perhaps the spot is more isolated and nobody has stumbled across her yet.'

'Or he still has her – or she isn't a victim of the Kiddy-Catcher at all. Perhaps someone else took her or she just disappeared.'

'People don't just disappear,' she said, 'not like that.'

'Yeah they do. People disappear all the time, loads of them. You just don't notice it. No one does. You know how many people were reported missing last year in this country?'

'No.'

'Guess,' he urged her.

'I haven't the faintest idea.'

'Try, you're an educated lady. How many people do you

163

think just upped and disappeared into thin air, leaving their friends and families with absolutely no clue to their whereabouts or even if they are alive or dead.'

'A lot I should imagine,' she answered, 'it must be more than we would think, so I'm going for three thousand.'

'Not even close.'

Her eyes widened at that, 'and she thought for a moment, recalibrating her expectations, 'forty thousand then.'

He shook his head. 'More than two hundred thousand.'

She seemed genuinely shocked. 'I'd no idea it was so many.'

'We tend to think of it as teenagers running off to London and getting mixed up with drugs or prostitution but they come from all ages and walks of life. Some come back within a few days or weeks but others disappear for years. You get middle-aged guys who crack under the pressure of a job or a mortgage and they just vanish.'

'Leaving their poor wives to pick up the pieces.'

'Women disappear too.'

'Bet it's mostly men.'

'Not always,' and his mood seemed to darken at that.

'You have an example?' she asked him. 'I'll bet it's the exception that proves the rule.' She wasn't going to let him get away with thinking that women were as likely to run off and abandon their families as men.

'Yes, I do,' Tom said. 'My mother.'

Chapter Twenty-Five

Helen felt like a complete fool. In her keenness to challenge Tom Carney's prejudices, she had gone charging in with both feet and now she was mortified. 'I didn't realise . . .' She began, but he interrupted her.

'How could you?' he asked reasonably.

She tried to continue but he put a finger to his lips then pointed out of the window. Betty's front door had opened and three stocky men, aged between forty and fifty, emerged, including the son who had ejected Tom.

'Barry, Mark and Frankie,' Tom said, 'which means the only person left in that house should be Betty Turner.'

'But you're not sure.'

'I'm as sure as I can be,' he said.

'That's not very comforting.'

'They're probably off to sign on,' Tom said, as the three men climbed into an ancient red Datsun Sunny and drove away.

'What if they've just gone round the corner for a newspaper or some cigarettes?'

'The Turner clan can't read and they'd never run out of fags,' he told her with conviction. 'Go on, off you go.' Then he added, 'Better be quick, mind, just in case.' Helen sighed and got out of the car. 'Don't worry,' he said, 'I told you, I've got your back.'

It was as if Tom's visit had never happened. As soon as

Helen explained who she was, Betty Turner admitted her. They sat opposite one another in the old lady's front room. When Helen asked about her early-hours visit to the old vicarage, Betty did not disappoint.

'Mary bloody Collier? She's no better than she ought to be.' Betty was using the understated code of the elderly Northern gossip, leaving her listener to fill in the gaps but giving enough of a hint for Helen to draw the right conclusion.

'What do you mean by that?' asked Helen.

'The headmaster's wife . . . with her airs and graces . . . thinks she's Lady Docker.' Betty fell silent again as if she had said her piece.

Helen prompted her. 'What about Mary?'

'Vicar's daughter,' she mumbled, 'had them elocution lessons and called herself a teacher but we knew what she was,' she said it like Mary Collier was a secret the village owned.

'And what was she?' asked Helen.

Betty carried on as if she was talking to herself and Helen wasn't in the room, 'Gadding about like that when she was supposed to be nearly wed, making a show of herself.'

'Gadding about? Who was she gadding about with?'

'Sean, of course,' snapped Betty, as if she had just mentioned this and Helen had forgotten already.

'Why don't you tell me all about that?' asked Helen.

Tom had been waiting in the car for a good ten minutes. He'd tried to phone The Paper three times on his mobile but the signal was too weak at this end of the village, rendering it useless. He gave up then glanced in his side mirror as another car came into view. This time it was a red Datsun Sunny. 'Oh shit,' he said.

The Turner brothers hadn't been gone long and now Tom didn't know what to do. His first instinct was to intervene to make sure Helen was all right. Catching a journalist from the local paper in their house wouldn't please them but maybe they'd go lighter on a woman. However, knowing she was working with a man who had already been thrown violently out through their front door might provoke them into a more extreme reaction, so maybe he should let her try and talk her way out of this one. 'Damn it,' he said, banging the steering wheel with his fist in frustration but electing to stay in his car for now.

Tom watched as the three brothers went into their home and closed the door.

Then he waited.

And waited.

Moments passed, which became minutes. Tom had his window down listening intently, but he could hear no raised voices, no cries of alarm from Helen or shouts of rage from the Turner brothers. He would give her five minutes, no more. Then he would bang on their door and somehow force them to release her, whatever the consequences. He couldn't even phone the police, thanks to the non-existent mobile signal.

Every few seconds he glanced at his watch, so he would know when five minutes had passed. He lasted four before he was out of his car. He walked quickly, eyes fixed firmly on their front door. Tom crossed the road and was almost at their front gate when the door suddenly opened and he stepped to one side, shielding himself behind the bushes that ran between the Turner's garden and a neighbour's house. It took two words to banish the worry from his mind.

'Thank you,' Helen said brightly, as she stepped onto the path and the door was closed quietly behind her. Tom waited for Helen to spot him as she came through the front gate.

'I thought you had my back?' She frowned at him.

'I did,' he said. 'I do. I was just giving you a few minutes to see if you could wriggle out of it.' Helen looked sceptical. 'What happened?'

'They weren't happy to start with,' she said, 'when they realised I was a journalist.'

'What did you say to them?'

'I told them I was doing a piece for the *Messenger* on the effects of long-term unemployment on hard-working families.'

'"Hard-working families"?' he said. 'There's a lot of those round here but I wouldn't include the Turner clan amongst them.'

'They seemed flattered to be asked,' she confirmed. 'I got quotes,' and she held up her notebook to prove it.

They crossed the road and climbed back into Tom's car. 'Did you get anything out of Betty?'

'I only had a few minutes with her but she did confirm our man was not a local. If she is telling the truth and isn't entirely barking then Sean was an Irishman who visited Great Middleton one summer a few years before the war.'

'Why would he do that?'

'I never got that far but, according to Betty, Sean was her beau; her first love in fact.'

'Really?'

'She was smitten,' confirmed Helen, 'and guess who stole him away from her?'

Tom smiled, 'Mary Collier.'

'Got it in one.'

'I knew this would make a great story,' he said, beaming. 'So what happened? Why does Betty blame Mary for Sean's death?'

'That's when it all got a bit vague. Betty is old and more than a little confused. She told me "Mary Collier killed him" then a moment later, she said "as good as killed him", I pressed her, but she wasn't making much sense at that point, then her sons came back. I don't think she really knows what happened to Sean.'

'Damn it.'

'I did get one thing though,' she said as he started the engine.

'What?'

'His full name. The body-in-the-field is Sean Donnellan.'

Chapter Twenty-Six

Roddy Moncur took in the sight of Helen and Tom standing on his doorstep together. 'If you can't beat 'em, join 'em, eh?' he said, then he invited them in.

'Sean Donnellan?' he repeated when they gave him the Irishman's name a few moments later. They were sitting at Roddy's kitchen table surrounded by the detritus of his disordered life, quietly hoping. Helen and Tom watched him expectantly, waiting for Roddy to blow the case wide open and singlehandedly solve the mystery of the body-in-the-field.

'He came to the village before the war,' Helen prompted, 'we don't know why.'

Roddy shook his head slowly. 'I'm sorry,' he said, before finally admitting, 'it doesn't ring any bells.' Then he pointed towards the front of the house. 'Come on,' he told them.

They followed Roddy down the hallway. 'Where are we going?' Helen asked.

'To consult the oracle,' replied Roddy. He climbed the stairs with a 'mind how you go' over his shoulder. They stepped gingerly around piles of old books stacked helpfully on the stairs in Roddy's own unique brand of filing system before he found them a more permanent home.

They climbed a second set of stairs and emerged into a large, low-ceilinged loft which was Roddy's share of the old school attic and was now partitioned so that each house had its own loft space. Roddy flicked a switch and a bare bulb hanging from the centre of the room illuminated a chaotic scene that made his kitchen seem neat by comparison. The dusty room was filled with ancient machines that looked as if they had been stolen from a museum: a mangle, a solid metal frame housing an old sewing machine, a pile of vinyl 78s stacked next to a gramophone in a walnut cabinet that cohabited with an ancient rocking chair, a 1930s wash stand in a wooden surround, a battered dressing table, an upright lamp of singular ugliness and two bedside cabinets. Here and there vases and old pots, toby jugs and pewter tankards were dotted amongst other pieces of memorabilia from a bygone age. Everything had been arranged in a haphazard manner against the low, sloping walls of the attic and there was a musty smell in keeping with the age of the building and its ancient contents. This appeared to be Roddy's private collection, his pride and joy in fact.

'Ta-da!' said Roddy.

'What?' asked Tom.

'The archive,' Roddy told him, surprised that Tom hadn't understood the significance of the place, 'it's all in here.'

Tom looked again and noticed a large pile of cardboard boxes stacked at the far end of the attic. Then his eyes adjusted to the relative gloom and he spotted two metal filing cabinets nearby. Roddy strode towards them, the floorboards creaking alarmingly beneath his feet, and Tom half expected Roddy to plunge through the floor, but he reached the cabinets and pulled out a drawer to illustrate his point. 'If it happened in this village,' he told them proudly, 'it's in here.'

Helen wanted to say something encouraging but she felt dwarfed by the sheer amount of paper Roddy had amassed. If every box was full, it would take hours, even days to go through it all and there was no guarantee they would find anything, 'I thought you'd be pleased,' he said.

'That's great, Roddy, thanks,' she managed.

He gave her a proud smile. 'Newspapers, parish magazines, minutes of council meetings, school records, amateur dramatics productions, births, death and marriages. It's all there; the hatched, matched and despatched,' he smiled again. 'If this fella made any impact during his time here, he'll get a mention some place. I've got to go out for a bit but I trust you to treat my archive with the respect it deserves, so you're welcome to stay and get cracking. I'll be back in a few hours.'

Roddy climbed back down the stairs. When he was gone, Helen stared at the piles of records then she looked at Tom, who shrugged. 'Okay then,' he said, 'I'll start with the boxes, you take the filing cabinets.'

Tom dragged the first two boxes towards him and sat down on the floor. He began to pull out the papers and sift them though them one by one, sorting them into neat piles that could go straight back in the box once he had finished with them. 'Once you've read something, for God's sake put it in a pile at the other end of the room, I don't want to look at any of this twice.'

'Okay,' Helen said as she started to tug documents from Roddy's filing cabinet, 'but this could take hours.'

Tom smiled then, 'and you can think of a place you'd rather be than here?' he asked waving his hand expansively at the musty room.

'Nowhere that springs to mind.' She gave him a rueful grin then flopped into the old rocking chair, pilling the first heap of dusty papers onto her knee as she did so.

The birthday visit had not gone well. This was not what he had wanted. He had planned it all in advance, even taken a day off work, and it was meant to include all of the ingredients she usually loved on her special day, her surrogate birthday; for she would be spending her actual twelfth birthday with her bitch of a mother.

Lindsay had always enjoyed the park when she was little, even when it was raining and her mother would always blame him when their daughter came home in muddied clothes when all he had tried to do was please his little girl. Predictably, this time it also rained, but he didn't think she would mind. They could still feed the ducks and he'd promised her ice cream afterwards but this only made her roll her eyes. He was not sure why. Now he thought about it, his daughter often rolled her eyes when he said things. It made him feel foolish, even though he was an adult and she was still a child who knew absolutely nothing of the world.

They hadn't spent long in the park but she had complained incessantly. 'Dad, it's freezing,' a childish exaggeration, when the air was merely crisp, or 'Dad, it's raining or haven't you noticed?'

'Don't be cheeky, Lindsay,' he'd told her but this just led to more eye-rolling and the simultaneous positioning of hands on hips.

Lunch had to be brought forward due to her lack of interest in the outdoors. And no, she did not want to go to the café they had always visited on special occasions. 'But you loved the place when you were little,' he protested.

'Yeah, and that's the point, Dad.' He felt hurt, put out. He had been looking forward to going there. It was a treat after months of living off cheap crap and would have brought back memories of a happier time when the three of them were still a family, before all of the unpleasantness, the nastiness and vileness he tried not to think about.

'Well, where do you want to go then, Lindsay? We have to have lunch somewhere,'

'Can I go anywhere?' she'd asked pleadingly.

'Within reason,' he'd answered, then chastised himself for thinking she might be asking to eat somewhere expensive. His little girl wasn't like the women he had tried dating since his marriage imploded. The ones who thought you had to ply them with presents and meals before they would let you do things to them. Lindsay wasn't like them.

'Can we go to McDonald's?' His daughter was excited at the prospect but he couldn't stomach the idea of more stodgy, greasy food.

'Oh no, Lindsay, not McDonald's. Can't we go somewhere a bit nicer than that?'

'Oh, please!' and her face took on a pained expression, as if he was being the most unreasonable father that ever lived. Sometimes he felt he didn't really know his daughter any more, not really. That's what came from no longer living under the same roof. She was like a stranger to him now. He wanted to grab her and shake her and tell her to stop changing like this, to stay the way she'd been when she was Daddy's little girl. Instead he just looked back at her and said, 'All right then, just this one time,' and she beamed again but for him the day was already ruined. He was getting one of his headaches, a searing pain behind the eyes he'd been told was stress-related.

'Yay!' she shouted once he'd given in, her moods as fickle as the weather and just as hard to predict.

He wasn't sure how it all went quite so badly wrong from there but it started when they saw the older boys she knew. Lindsay immediately went to them then stood flirting while he queued alone for their lunch, which seemed to take an age even though it was supposed to be fast-food. When they finally served him, he carried the wobbling plastic tray to a table by the window as far away from the boys as possible. Lindsay didn't even notice, having seemingly forgotten her own father existed. He watched as she waved her arms excitedly while she told them some silly tale; as she giggled and flicked her hair and basically acted like her mother. He wondered if it was too late for her already. How long until he would have to save her? The boys just smirked, trying to play it cool, but he knew what they wanted.

'Suffer the little children to come unto me,' he spoke the words while he watched his daughter making a fool of herself. He hadn't even realised he'd said it aloud until he caught the eye of a woman close by and she quickly looked away. No one else heard him, thankfully, but he felt foolish now and angry.

'Lindsay,' he called but she either didn't hear him or chose not to, 'Lindsay!' then finally 'Lindsay! Your food's getting cold!' at a volume that made other diners turn to look at him and he realised his face must have been contorted with anger. A young couple on the next table did that lowering of the eyes and exchanging glances thing, as if he was some kind of nutter to be silently tolerated and that enraged him even more. Then he saw the look Lindsay was giving him and it made their disapproval seem trivial. Her face was a picture of embarrassment and shame. She marched over to the table, sat down theatrically and asked, 'Can't you ever just be normal?'

'The food you wanted, the food you ordered,' he was almost grinding his teeth now, 'in the place you asked me to bring you to . . . is getting cold.'

'Yeah?' she replied. 'Well, I'm not hungry any more.'

Chapter Twenty-Seven

By now each of them had large piles of discarded papers stacked neatly to one side or placed back in their boxes and dragged out of the way to avoid confusion. Between them they had surveyed records of all kinds but found no mention of any missing Irish man.

'If I see another flyer for the 1953 Coronation and its accompanying street party, I'm going to tear it into small pieces,' Tom said.

'I'll gladly trade you,' she told him. 'You can take thirty years of Women's Institute meeting minutes. I'll swap your tea and buns for my jam and Jerusalem.'

They continued to work in silence for another half hour until Tom finally revealed his thoughts. 'There's no pattern, as far as I can make out,' Tom said, 'with the Kiddy-Catcher, I mean. I've read all the articles and the crimes seem random, unplanned.'

Between them they'd been through every article they could find on the victims of the Kiddy-Catcher, looking for a link.

'I had a look on a map,' she said. 'I don't know the area as well as you so I thought it might help if I marked everything: the victims' homes, where they were taken and where they were found, and it does look random,' she agreed, 'apart from the fact that they are all within the county boundary. Sarah Hutchison was taken from a bus stop right at the edge but it was still in County Durham.'

They continued to speed-read their piles of papers while they talked, dropping the pieces of paper onto the floor when they were done with them.

'So there's no pattern,' he said, 'unless that's the pattern.'

'How do you mean?'

'People understand more about police work these days. It's all on the telly. They know they'll have a map on their wall with the locations of the abductions on it and the sites where the bodies were discovered. They'll be trying to spot a trend or seeing if they can mark the centre of the killer's zone. He wouldn't want to murder on his own doorstep so he'd head out. Maybe the next time he'd choose a different direction. If he continues like that you end up with a pattern that's like spokes on a wheel, with a victim at the end of each spoke and the killer's home right in the centre.'

'But that's not happening here, so he doesn't think like that or perhaps he has offended before,' Helen said, 'been to prison, for something less serious and learned from the experience.'

'And he doesn't want to go back.'

'If he's assaulted women or girls previously and they tracked him down, maybe he'd know how they did it and that would explain why he avoids a pattern.'

'Possibly,' he agreed, 'I've heard that serial killers don't normally start with murder. There's usually some minor offending that gradually gets more serious until . . .'

'They go the whole hog and kill someone.'

He nodded. 'And if he has been to prison before and doesn't want to go back that would be another reason to kill the girls after he has taken them.'

Helen felt no comfort from that realisation. 'No witnesses,' she said.

'Of course what we really need are Malcolm's files,' he said.

'What files?'

'Your editor might be an anally retentive idiot but he is a very organised one. He keeps clippings of files so he can check things if the top brass panic about something that could get them sued. Every front and page lead has a little file that contains the first unedited draft, contact details of the people in it, the photographs and any notes deemed to be significant, such as the information that didn't end up in the final story.'

'You mean stuff that was too contentious?'

'Yes.'

'You think there could be something useful in there?'

'Who knows, but it's not as if I can ask him for it. I'm persona non grata at the *Messenger*.'

'And I'm not, but I soon will be if I hang around with you.'

'I just thought you could borrow the files for each victim,' he announced.

'"Borrow" them?'

'Only for one night,' he assured her, 'just stay until everyone has left, slip them in your bag and walk out of there. You can go in early the next day and return the files after we've looked at them.'

'I'm not sure I like the sound of this.'

'They won't be missed for one night, I'm telling you.'

'You can't be sure of that.' She was recalling her experience with the Turner brothers.

'I am and it's the only way we are going to get the inside track. You know he edits out loads of stuff. We need to see the unedited version of the reports.'

'I'll think about it.'

'Great,' he said, 'thanks.'

'I didn't say I would do it,' she reminded him. 'Jesus Christ,' she said.

'Okay, if you feel that strongly about it.'

She shook her head irritably, 'no, no,' and he watched her uncomprehendingly. Helen was staring at a notice from her W. I. files; a single piece of paper amongst thirty years of detritus.

Tom got to his feet and walked over to her. She handed him the ancient notice. It was quite clearly a rudimentary poster used to advertise an event. On it was written, '25th August. Village Hall. A talk to be given on the subject of sketching local landmarks for publication by Mr S. Donnellan – artist.'

DI Peacock was trying hard to contain his fury. 'What in the name of . . .' He clenched and unclenched his fists, took a deep breath, thought better of what he was about to say, forced himself to calm down then exhaled and settled on, '. . . were you thinking?' He glowered at the two detective constables in his office.

Bradshaw looked at his colleague for support but Vincent was staring blankly ahead, seemingly content to admit their wrong-doing and accept the latest in a long line of bollockings. Bradshaw realised he was on his own. 'The chief super told you not to bring him in for questioning,' Peacock added, in case they'd forgotten who gave the order.

'We didn't bring him in,' protested Bradshaw, 'we invited him to come to the station voluntarily to assist us with our enquiries. He was cooperating.'

'Don't give me that,' hissed Peacock, 'you knew what you were doing and you disobeyed a direct order when you were supposed to be on another case.'

'We were told to work both cases.'

'Only if something fell into your lap!' shouted Peacock, 'you weren't supposed to knock on their door, search their house and drag the stepdad down to the station.'

'But he's hiding something,' insisted Bradshaw, 'I know it.'

'What exactly?' asked the DI, 'apart from a few porno mags?'

'We don't know.' It pained him to admit it, 'but something is not right in that house. I can sense it.'

'Oh well, that's all right, for a minute there I thought we had no evidence of wrong-doing but you can sense it. I say we arrest the bastard. What do you think, Boss?'

Peacock was finding it difficult to retain his composure but DCI Kane had been watching the reprimand calmly. Finally he spoke. 'Has he made a complaint?'

'Not yet,' admitted Peacock.

'Will he?' he was asking Bradshaw.

'No, Sir.'

'You sure about that?'

'Yes, Sir.'

'You bloody better be.'

When it appeared more was required of him, Bradshaw asked, 'Would you complain if someone found a load of magazines in your shed full of naked, adolescent girls?' before adding, 'Sir.'

'Probably not,' conceded Kane, 'so perhaps we're okay,' he told Peacock. 'But if we're not, we'll know who to throw to the wolves, won't we?' He was addressing DI Peacock but staring malevolently at Bradshaw and Vincent, then he sighed. 'Maybe, just maybe, these two half-wits have stumbled on something,' he said then he turned back to the two subordinates, 'not that I'm happy with the way you went about it.'

'I'm telling you, Sir, there's something not right about that Denny,' Bradshaw was almost pleading now.

'Do you think he killed her?' asked the DCI.

Bradshaw instinctively wanted to say 'yes' but thought better of it, offering 'it's possible' instead.

'Then we'll keep a closer eye on him,' Kane told them. 'Now you two, go and get on with the job you were given in the first place. Knock on some bloody doors. Go on, piss off.'

The two detective constables got to their feet and left Kane's office. Vincent hadn't spoken the whole time. Bradshaw overtook him in the corridor. 'Thanks for your help in there, Vincent,' he muttered as he swept past his colleague.

Chapter Twenty-Eight

'What are we looking for now?' she called down the loft stairs when he failed to answer her the first time.

'Something . . .' Tom began but he tailed off absent-mindedly, so she sighed and followed him downstairs. When she reached the second-floor landing, Tom was emerging from one of the rooms with a determined look on his face.

'He must have moved them,' he muttered, to himself as much as to Helen.

'Should we be exploring Roddy's home like this while he is out?' she said, but he ignored her and headed down to the ground floor with no further explanation. Once again Helen followed him.

Tom walked towards a room Helen hadn't seen before. 'He doesn't use the front room much,' he explained, 'because he keeps the parlour for best. That's what folk used to do way back when and, as you know, Roddy lives in the past. You kept the parlour for entertaining, usually on a Sunday afternoon,' and he led her into a dark front room, the light from the window obscured by thick net curtains. Tom swept them back. Immediately the gloom was lifted. 'There you go,' he said, indicating the wall opposite, which was a jumble of old paintings and drawings. 'That's quite a collection.'

It was an odd assortment of work, with pictures of varying sizes all sharing a common theme: local landscapes you would recognise if you were familiar with the rural land around Great Middleton – farmhouses, fields, woods and of course the river. The quality varied, from enthusiastic amateur to talented professional. More than a dozen frames cluttered the wall. Helen and Tom peered at each in turn. 'Take a look at these two,' she said finally.

Tom transferred his attention to the two black-and-white line drawings in the middle of the display. Both were framed illustrations of the river that ran by the village and were of a high standard. They were rich in detail, every stroke of the artist's pencil a perfectly proportioned realisation of the water, river bank or surrounding countryside. 'They're really good,' said Helen. 'There's a date here,' and they leaned closer to peer at the bottom left-hand corner of the first drawing.

'August 1936,' said Tom, 'same on the second one and there's a signature,' he squinted at it then smiled at her, 'looks like it could be S. Donnellan to me.'

'It could,' Helen agreed.

Ian Bradshaw was just about to pull out of the police station car park, following a fruitless afternoon knocking on doors in Great Middleton, when he spotted Professor Richard Burstow exiting the building. No doubt the forensic psychologist had been sharing his opinions with Detective Superintendent Trelawe. Bradshaw moved quickly across the car park towards Burstow but was careful to look about him first, to make sure nobody saw him intercepting the professor.

Bradshaw reached the professor's car just as he was placing his briefcase on the back seat, 'Professor?' he called and the older man looked up. Perhaps he recalled Bradshaw's contribution to that first briefing, which had been more positive than the young detective's more sceptical colleagues', for he gave Bradshaw what could have been a slight smile of recognition.

'Detective,' Burstow said. 'What can I do for you?'

'I'd like a word,' Bradshaw answered, 'if I may.'

'How did you get these, Roddy?' asked Tom. The three of them were looking at the drawings now. They hadn't even let Roddy close his front door on his return before virtually dragging him into the parlour to show him the scenes of the river and the accompanying signature.

'He left them behind,' said Roddy, frowning slightly as he remembered, 'hadn't paid his rent up on his room. His landlady was widowed in the Great War, so she took in lodgers to make ends meet. People used to visit Great Middleton because it's on the walking route, close to where the river swells, which was exactly what he was drawing,' he pointed at one of the pictures. 'Elsie Robinson put him up in her home then one day he did a moonlight flit, or so her son told me. She thought he just took off and left some of his drawings behind. She kept them for years.' Roddy paused for a moment while he gathered his thoughts. 'Elsie died in the mid-sixties, I reckon. Her son had these on a stand at the summer fête when I was just starting to collect. I had these two framed but I'm sure there were more,' he said it absentmindedly, as if talking to himself, 'they must be somewhere,' but he didn't seem entirely certain.

'It would be good to see them,' said Tom, though he

didn't hold out much hope of Roddy locating anything amongst the clutter. 'This would explain why the guy wasn't missed. If he wasn't from here, if he was just passing through and everybody, even his landlady, thought he'd done a runner to avoid paying the rent.'

'It would,' agreed Roddy.

'Now we know Betty wasn't making all this up,' said Helen. 'We have a name and an identity and, thanks to you, Roddy, we've even got some of the man's drawings.'

They took a moment to survey the pictures, appreciating the delicacy of the work while silently wondering about the man who had created them and how he came to be brutally murdered in this village without anybody knowing about it.

'You did good, Roddy,' said Tom, 'but you got one bit of the story wrong. Sean Donnellan didn't leave these pictures behind,' he reminded the older man, 'because he never left.'

'There are two schools of thought on this one,' ruminated the professor, as he took a long sip from the pint of beer Bradshaw had bought him. If he had been puzzled by the request to speak away from police premises he had made no comment about it, instead following Bradshaw to a pub close by but just far enough from HQ to avoid bumping into anybody they knew. 'Some believe pornographic images have absolutely no long-term effect on the viewer, that they are just a harmless form of sexual release. There is an awful lot of easily available pornography out there but, mercifully, only a very small percentage of the male population turns into a rapist or murderer. In fact, there is no statistical evidence linking porn to any increase in sexual violence. Some even believe that porn and prostitution prevents men from offending who would otherwise do so, without the outlet they provide.'

'Right,' said Bradshaw, trying to hide his disappointment that the science didn't back up his theory about Denny's possible guilt. 'You did say there were two schools of thought?'

'There's another argument,' conceded the professor after another large gulp of beer, 'backed up by more recent research, which cites a link between extreme porn and violent behaviour. That kind of pornography can have a desensitising effect on men, leading to less empathetic behaviour towards women and even a tolerance of rape or sexual violence.' He drained his beer and surveyed his empty glass. 'Thanks for the drink by the way.' Bradshaw had barely touched his.

'Let me get you another one, Professor.' Bradshaw quickly drew the barman's attention to the professor's glass.

'Thank you.'

'What about the kind of person who secretly hoards indecent images of young girls or women pretending to be young girls?' he asked, 'what would a craving like that tell us about a man?'

'Well,' the professor thought for a moment, 'it would tell us that man could not possibly be The Reaper.'

'Why?'

'Have you forgotten what I told you? The man taking these little girls has no interest in them sexually. Remember his God complex. He is doing this so he can have the power of life and death over his victims. That is his thrill.

So whoever you have in mind now cannot be The Reaper,' the professor concluded.

'Which just proves my point,' confirmed Bradshaw.

He no longer subscribed to the view that Michelle Summers was a victim of The Reaper. Bradshaw was sure it was someone much closer to home.

Tom knocked on the door and once again it was the housekeeper who opened it and answered with a single word. 'Doctors.'

'Again?'

'She's got arthritis,' the sullen woman reminded him.

He turned to Helen. 'We should wait.'

The housekeeper ignored the hint to admit them and closed the door, so instead they sat in the car.

'It's funny,' Helen said, 'it seems more real now, seeing his drawings. It turns him into a real person, not just . . .'

'A load of old bones?'

'Yes,' she said.

Tom was staring at the old vicarage intently. 'What is it?' she asked him.

'Every time I come here she's either at the doctors or a hospital appointment, according to the housekeeper,'

'She probably has a few things wrong with her,' reasoned Helen, 'she's quite old.'

'I suppose she is,' he said, 'but she hasn't changed a bloody bit, still speaks to me like I'm one of her pupils, even now.'

'She taught you? What was she like?'

'Strict,' he said, 'you couldn't get away with anything. Some of the other teachers had no authority. Kids can detect that. If they smell weakness they'll run you ragged but not her. She was always too quick with the slipper.'

'The slipper?'

'She used to keep this old slipper in her drawer and she'd use it, even if you were just talking when you shouldn't.'

'I don't agree with hitting kids, whatever they've done.'

'Mary Collier's from a different era,' he explained, 'she used it on me often enough. I'll never forget this one time; I was about nine and I was being picked on by this bigger kid. It went on for weeks. He was a nasty little shit. Anyway, cutting a long story short, he hit me one day and I just saw red.'

'Somehow I can imagine that,' she said.

'Yeah well anyway, he hit me hard, so I picked up the tray we kept all of our exercise books in and I lamped him with it.'

'Oh my God, was he all right?'

Tom shrugged, as if the bully's fate was of no importance. 'Eventually,' he looked a little sheepish then, 'bust nose, split lip, there was some blood and quite a few tears. Mrs Collier was the first one on the scene and she went ballistic. I got slippered like nobody had ever been slippered. Then she called my dad in and I had to wait outside the office while she told him how unacceptable my behaviour was.'

'Were you scared of your dad?'

'At that age? Terrified,' he admitted, 'He never said a word when he came out, just jerked his head in the direction of his car. After we'd pulled out through the school gates he asked me, "Was this kid bigger than you?" and I said, "Yes, Dad," and there was a pause then he asked, "And did he hit you first?" and I'm nodding vigorously and saying, "Yeah, he did Dad," then he finally asks me, "And instead of just punching him back, you picked up a big, heavy tray and lamped him in the face with it in front of your entire class and your teacher?" and I had to admit my stupidity and I said, "Yes Dad." He didn't say anything for a while and just when I thought he was going to erupt he just said, "Good."'

'Good?' asked Helen.

'Good,' Tom confirmed, 'and when I asked him why, he said, "Because nobody will ever fuck with you again."'

'Wow,' she said, 'that's pretty intense for a nine-year-old.'

'I know. I don't think I'd ever heard him use the F-word before, much less say it to me. I told him how cross Mrs Collier was but he just said, "Teachers don't live in the real world", like her opinion was of no consequence. I think he was pleased I'd not let the bigger lad kick me around. It's the one time I can actually recall him being proud of me.'

He hadn't said it with any kind of edge but the way Tom said 'the one time' made Helen feel incredibly sad.

He was forced to drop Lindsay back at her mother's early and she was in tears. He stood on the doormat while his wife blocked the front door of their old home, like she was single-handedly manning Checkpoint Charlie. It was all right, he didn't want to come in, had no wish to see the evidence of her new man; a different newspaper folded on his old armchair, someone else's shoes by the fire.

'Don't do this,' she told him, 'for once can't we just be . . .'

'Civilised?' he snorted.

'Yes.'

'I wasn't the one with my jeans round my knees and another man's hand . . .'

'Stop it! Just stop it! Do you want your daughter to hear you?!'

'I don't know, maybe that wouldn't be such a bad idea. Perhaps she wouldn't be so hard on her old dad if she knew that!'

'I think you should go right now,' she hissed, 'and if you start poisoning her against me with that kind of talk, I'll go back to court and they'll bar you from coming anywhere near her.'

He snorted. 'On what grounds, because I told her the truth? Your mam and me split up because she couldn't keep her knickers on till I got home.'

She turned mean then, nasty and spiteful, like she always did when they had a fight and he was actually winning for once. She stepped off the doorstep towards him and fixed her gaze on his. 'What grounds? I don't need any grounds. I'll make something up. I'm her mother and she doesn't hate me but you, you're a basket case. You can't even take a twelve-year-old to McDonalds without causing a row.'

'You weren't there,' he countered, 'you didn't see her chucking herself at those two older boys.'

'She wasn't chucking herself at them. They are both in her class at school. She's just told me. They are all going to a birthday party next week and she's excited for God's sake. That's normal at her age; to be excited about something. Now she's crying in her bedroom.'

'A birthday party? Whose birthday party? Will the parents be there? Are you just going to let her go?'

'Jesus Christ! What's wrong with you? She's a normal girl, with nice friends. Leave her alone,' she demanded, before adding, 'or God help me, I'll keep you away from her for good!'

He couldn't believe she was mentioning God now; the nerve of the woman.

'How are you going to do that? You're not keeping me away from my own daughter.'

'You're losing the plot and you've got a history of outbursts. What did you call that magistrate; a twisted bitch? Do you think they didn't write that down and put it in a file somewhere? You had a breakdown, for God's sake! You say one word to Lindsay about me and I'll tell them you hit me or tried to touch her where a father shouldn't ever touch his daughter.'

'You wouldn't do that,' he spluttered but he knew from the look on her face that she would. 'You're a monster.'

'I'm her mother. I'd say and do anything to protect her from you. Who do you think they'll believe? They'll keep you away from her for so long she won't even recognise you in the street.'

'You wouldn't do that . . . no one could say that about the father of their child . . .'

'Wouldn't I? If you ever want to see Lindsay again, let alone on alternate weekends, then you are going to keep your mouth shut, or I'll drop you so far down in the shit, you'll think you are in hell.'

He looked at her for a long time and, from the hatred he saw there, knew she meant it. He closed his eyes for a moment, the way the doctor had taught him when he needed to combat the rages, but it was no good this time.

Instead he reached out and grabbed her by the hair and pulled hard, forcing her down onto her knees even as she shrieked in protest. He got down there with her and closed his eyes tightly as he began to dash her skull hard against the driveway. He could hear her screams right enough but he didn't stop, couldn't stop. Instead he carried on and with the action came a glorious feeling of release as he smashed her evil, twisted head against the cement over and over again until finally the screams stopped and there was nothing left of her sick brain but mush, smeared all over the concrete, the blood running in pools. Then he felt dizzy and he blinked and opened his eyes.

He was surprised to see her still standing there unharmed, regarding him closely, with a look that was a combination of pity and suspicion.

'What is wrong with you?' she asked him.

When he didn't immediately answer her, the look became one of disgust. For a moment the image had been so vivid, so real, he actually believed he had done it. His heart was racing and he was grinding his teeth together so hard they hurt. He had to take a deep breath, then another, and start the counting, slow and silent in his head . . . one . . . two . . . three . . . just like his therapist had told him 'to manage his anger' . . . four . . . five . . . six . . . preventing it from bursting out of him like a wild animal released from a cage . . . seven . . . eight . . . nine . . . she was looking at him like he was nothing, like shit on her shoe, the bitch, the dirty, little . . . ten . . . eleven . . . twelve . . . the expression on her face changed as she slowly became wary of him. He closed his eyes again for a moment . . . thirteen . . . fourteen . . . fifteen . . . he was tired now . . . he so badly wanted to lie down. He felt like he always did when he had just saved one.

'I think you should go now.' He realised she was scared. Well, she should be. Perhaps he would use a knife when it came down to it. Cut her up a bit. Mess up that face so that no man would ever want her again, show her what she looked like in the mirror before ending her. Or perhaps he would just do it quick, finish the whole damn thing and burn the house down with all of them in it. 'Please,' she said it firmly, 'I want you to go.'

A knife, or maybe a hammer, smash her teeth in with it, knock them all out. If he took her somewhere quiet, secluded, where no one could hear them, he could keep her alive for hours, days even, then she would regret everything she'd done to him, he'd make her sorry, get her to beg him for forgiveness but he would not forgive, he would never forgive.

'I said I want you to go.' Was she about to disappear into the house and phone someone? Perhaps she would cry out for help, tell more lies about him. Who knew what she was capable of. So not now – but one day. One glorious day, he would take back everything she had stolen from him, one blow at a time.

'I'm already in hell,' he said it softly.

'What?' She'd already forgotten her promise. 'You'll think you're in hell.'

He took a step forward and she flinched, he leaned in close so that his face was almost pressed against hers and she looked frightened then. He breathed in the sweet smell of her and relished her fear.

'I'm . . . already . . . in hell.'

Chapter Twenty-Nine

Mary Collier had to be helped from the private hire cab that pulled up outside her home, the driver holding his arm rigid so she could lean on it. She waved away his offer of further assistance and went to her front door unaided. Mary was just turning the key in the lock when she became aware of the presence of someone and she turned to see Helen and Tom standing at the end of her path.

If Mary was surprised to see them both together she hid it well. 'Back so soon?' she said. 'What's Betty Turner been saying about me now?'

'Sorry to bother you again,' said Helen, ignoring the question, 'but we have some more information.' She hoped this would be vague enough to engage the old lady's curiosity.

'You'll have to wait till I get in.' Her tone was scolding, as if they were impatient children but she opened the door and they followed her inside, with Mary keeping up a commentary as she walked slowly and unsteadily across the carpet. 'I used to go for long walks across the fields. Now it takes me half a day to get out of my chair,' she said, 'ruddy arthritis, in my hands and hip. It's why I don't leave the house much. Mrs Harris *does* for me; gets my groceries, pays my bills and what not. I get a taxi to the doctors; my one little indulgence but I'd give a month's pension to run across a field in my bare feet, just one more time,' and she winced as she turned to face them again.

Tom couldn't imagine his old teacher running barefoot across a field. 'Go on through,' she waved her hand impatiently at the next room but made no move to follow them. Neither of them moved and she snapped, 'At least let me put the kettle on before you interrogate me. I'm gasping.'

'We have a witness,' Tom told Mary, once they were finally seated and clutching ancient bone china cups filled with tea, 'several, in fact.' Tom didn't want to reveal that his only source was Betty. 'They say that, when you were young, you were friendly with an Irishman called Sean Donnellan.' Both Helen and Tom watched Mary Collier's face closely to gauge her reaction but she gave none, 'an artist from Ireland who visited Great Middleton back in 1936 so he could draw the river. We think Sean Donnellan is the body-in-the-field.'

Tom paused for a moment to let that sink in. Mary's face was a mask, revealing nothing. She was regarding Tom as if she wanted to know just how much of his homework he had completed before committing herself to an answer.

'Really,' she said, as if he had merely commented on the weather, 'witnesses,' she scoffed, 'you mean mad, old Betty Turner?'

'But you did know the man?' Tom insisted.

'Yes,' she said but that was all.

'So do you think it's Sean Donnellan who was buried in that field?'

'I have no idea. Up until yesterday, like everybody else,

I didn't know there was a body buried anywhere in the village,' she said, 'except in the cemetery.'

'So are you surprised it's him or not?'

'I'd be surprised whoever it turned out to be, since the word is that he was murdered.'

'Betty thinks of Sean Donnellan as her first love,' said Helen, trying a new tactic.

'Ha!' the old lady let out a loud, mocking exclamation, 'does she now? Well I suspect it was a little one-sided.'

'She also said you stole him from her.' Helen added.

'My, my, what fantasy world has she been living in lately?'

'But you knew Sean Donnellan?' said Tom. 'You just admitted that.'

'When you grow up in a village, everybody knows everyone else. He was an outsider. Visitors of any kind were an exotic species. You have to remember there were barely three cars in the whole of Great Middleton back then and one of those belonged to the doctor. We used to get a few folk passing through on the walking routes but they'd stay for a day. Sean Donnellan was here for a whole summer. He was an Irishman and an artist, in a pit village. Of course I remember him. Everybody did.'

'And when he was no longer there?' asked Tom, 'what did everybody think?'

'That he had gone,' she offered obtusely, 'back to Dublin, most probably. Certainly nobody thought he was dead.'

'That he'd been murdered you mean,' Tom reminded her, 'Betty seems to think that was your fault by the way, which is why she was banging on your door in the middle of the night shouting "it was you".'

'Well you know my view on Betty,' she replied, 'and her missing marbles.'

'So you didn't have a relationship with this man, Sean Donnellan?' asked Helen.

Mary Collier narrowed her eyes. 'People didn't flit from one man to the next in those days, not like now, courting was a serious business, which almost always ended in marriage and woe betide the girl if it didn't. I was already engaged to Henry. We were married in 1937. Henry and I grew up together and always had an understanding that one day we would marry. I can't even remember a time before that. Everybody will tell you it was so.'

'Not everybody,' he corrected her and when she turned her angry eyes towards him, he added, 'since it was more than half a century ago, there won't be many left who could tell us.'

'So Betty Turner is lying?' asked Helen.

'Or her mind is puddled?' offered Mary, 'if we're going to take the charitable view.'

'Can you think of any reason why anyone would want to kill Sean Donnellan?'

Was there a slight hesitation from Mary, a tiny wavering in her voice? 'I cannot think of a reason why anybody would want to kill anyone.'

'Did he make any enemies?' asked Helen.

'Not that I can remember but it was such a long time ago.'

'So tell us about this Sean Donnellan,' said Tom, 'when did you meet him and what was he like?'

'Why should I?' Mary snapped suddenly.

'No reason,' admitted Tom, 'I just thought you'd prefer to tell us rather than the police.'

'The police?' She looked rattled then.

'This isn't just a story,' Helen reminded her, 'it's a murder enquiry. We have to pass on any information we hear to the police.'

'And right now we are hearing that you and the dead man were more than just friends. If you're saying that isn't so then we'll hear you out.'

'I don't want the police on my doorstep for a second time,' Mary said. 'Every curtain in the street will be twitching.'

'Can you remember Sean Donnellan coming to the village?' asked Helen, 'I realise it was a very long time ago.'

'Miss Norton,' said Mary Collier, 'everyone old enough to recall that time will remember Sean Donnellan coming to the village, particularly the girls.' It was the first time Helen had seen the faintest trace of a smile crease onto the old face but there was warmth there, buried deeply.

'Handsome chap, was he?' asked Helen.

'You might say that,' conceded the old woman.

'You recall that much,' Helen said it in a teasing tone. They were a couple of teenagers now, discussing the best-looking boy in class and Tom decided to let them talk.

'Since not very much of importance happens to me these days, memory is all I have left.'

'What else can you remember about him?'

She cocked her head to one side and seemed to be staring into a space somewhere above Helen's shoulder. 'Where to begin?' she asked herself. 'With poor old Betty, I suppose.'

Chapter Thirty

1936

There was childish excitement in Betty's voice. 'Wait till you see him,' she told her young friend, 'he's tall, good looking and his voice,' she giggled and shook her head in wonderment, 'it's like he's singing to you. I could listen to him for hours!'

'I'm not sure I want to go down to the river just now,' replied Mary, 'it looks like rain,' and Betty's face fell. 'I thought I might stay in and finish my book.'

'But you said you'd come,' Betty reminded her, 'please say you will,' she implored. 'I can't go down there on my own. What would people say?'

'Hurtful things, I should imagine.'

'Exactly,' said Betty, 'it wouldn't be proper. But if I went with you . . .' and she gave Mary a hopeful smile.

Mary closed her book and stood up. 'All right, I'll risk catching a cold in a downpour, so you can make cow-eyes at Mr Blarney Stone.'

'Thank you, Mary, you're a true friend.' Then she added, 'And don't be like that. He's a lovely man.'

'How can you tell? You've only just met him.'

'Sometimes you just know,' Betty replied dreamily.

'Love at first sight?'

'Perhaps. Don't you believe in it? Wasn't it love at first sight when you met Henry?'

'We were children, so I hardly think so.'

Betty was as excitable as a child, wittering on about Mr Sean Donnellan every step of the way, only finally falling silent about him when they rounded a bend in No Name Lane and saw him up ahead, sitting on the river bank, intent on his work.

'A good day to you,' he said as they reached him. He must have heard them but still he didn't look up, which Mary considered the height of rudeness.

'Good morning, Mr Donnellan,' Betty addressed him with a formality she might have reserved for one of her old school teachers.

His pencil darted one last time over the drawing he was working on then he looked up at them. A handsome face squinted against the sun, which was behind them.

'Becky, is it?' he asked the younger girl.

'Betty,' she reminded him a little desperately.

'Betty! Of course you are,' and he gave her a huge smile to make up for forgetting her. He climbed quickly to his feet and took one of her hands in his. 'Please forgive me. I've been engrossed in my work. I can forget my own name when that happens.' The smile grew broader and there was a gleam in his eye, which set Betty to laughing and blushing at the same time. Mary could see through the charm and knew very well she would not be falling for it – unlike her silly friend who knew nothing whatever of the world or men like Sean Donnellan. Mary turned her attention to his drawing, which she had to admit was a fine representation of the river bank, with not a detail excluded.

'That's very impressive, Mr Donnellan,' she told him.

'Why thank you, miss,' he smiled at her now, 'but you have me at a disadvantage; you know my name but I haven't learned yours.'

'This is Mary,' Betty answered for her.

'Mary,' and he fell silent as if trying her name on for size.

'Don't worry,' Mary told him, 'I'll remind you of it next time we meet.'

He laughed at her cheek and said, 'I have a feeling I'll not be forgetting you in a hurry.' He seemed oblivious to Betty's obvious disappointment, even though it was written all over her face. He was regarding Mary as if Betty was no longer there. She felt satisfied that she had read the man correctly. Whatever he had said earlier to Betty, when he stopped her in the village to ask for directions to the river bank, it had been enough to turn her head. Mr Donnellan however had forgotten her a moment later and was now turning his insincere Irish charm on Mary. Well, it wouldn't have worked on her, even if she wasn't already promised to another.

'I understand you are here for the river,' her tone was deliberately formal.

'That's correct. I have a contract to do some work for an Edward Cummings,' he told her, 'or rather, a commission from his publisher.'

'You're illustrating a book?' Mary asked him.

'Quite so,' and there was something about the lyrical tone of his voice that even Mary was forced to admit was endearing. Betty was right about that. It was hard not to enjoy the way he had of making the commonest words sound poetic, '*More Essays on Nature and Topography*,' he announced, 'that's the title of his book; *more* because there has been one previously and it sold enough for a second to be commissioned, which keeps me gainfully employed at least.'

'It sounds lovely,' said Mary without conviction.

'Do you think? I'm not so sure. I'm not one for reading essays about anything. I like a good book as much as the next man but I'd want a story in there. Mr Cummings has a terrible dry way with words and there's only so much a man can take in about rookeries, hedgerows and village characters. However his writing has enabled me to make an honest living, outdoors in the summer time, so who am I to complain? Your countryside is as close to the area described in Mr Cummings' new book as can be. Apparently he walked here while he was writing it.'

'People do,' explained Mary, 'they walk the river banks because Great Middleton was built on one of its widest parts. The water swells here and it floods from time to time, covering the fields during the wettest part of the year.'

'Are you staying with us long?' asked Betty and Sean Donnellan answered her without taking his eyes from Mary.

'For a time; I've been asked to submit a fair few drawings for their consideration. They'll choose the ones they want and discard the rest. Sure as hell, they'll only pay for the ones that end up in the book.'

They talked a while longer, while Sean Donnellan

explained the iniquities of the publishing industry and the difficulties of earning a living as an illustrator, with work in short supply and demand so variable. Betty didn't say much and Mary assumed she felt out of her depth.

'I read a quote,' Mary told him earnestly, 'that an artist cannot be a true artist unless he is hungry, because nobody ever created anything truly worthwhile on a full stomach.'

Sean Donnellan nodded. 'I know who said that,' he told her.

'Who?' asked Mary.

'An idiot.' Against her better instincts, Mary laughed. 'It might be true that some artists need to be hungry in order to work, but not me. If I'm not fed I lose all powers of concentration, by which I mean that I'd stop drawing trees and start drawing sausages.'

Despite herself, Mary found that she was warming to this trivial man, so she decided it must be time to leave and made excuses for both of them.

'We didn't have to go so soon,' Betty told her.

'If you feel kindly towards a man,' Mary replied, 'then it's best to leave him before he's heard everything you have to say or he'll tire of you.'

Betty thought for a moment. 'You really think so?'

'I know so.'

'But you and Henry talk for hours,' Betty reminded her, 'on your walks.'

'We are on a higher plane,' and Mary immediately regretted sounding so haughty, 'by which I mean, we have known each other for a long time and have reached a point of mutual love, respect and admiration.'

Betty smiled at her then. 'That's what he said.'

'What is?' asked Mary, irritated by her friend's smirking.

'By which I mean,' Betty reminded her.

'Mr Donnellan does not have sole rights to the English language,' Mary scolded.

'Doesn't he have the most beautiful way with words though?' Betty sighed, 'and such a talent for drawing. I think he'll be a great and famous artist one day. Isn't he just amazing?' and she hugged herself in excitement.

'Oh come on, Betty. Mr Donnellan may have a certain roguish charm but he's as common as rain.'

'Well, I like him,' snapped Betty, 'and we don't all have the chance to marry school teachers.'

After that, they walked the rest of the way back along No Name Lane in silence.

Chapter Thirty-One

They listened to the local news as they drove back to Helen's car but there was nothing new about Michelle Summers, so Tom turned off the radio.

'She is definitely hiding something,' he said at last, as he guided his car to the side of the road.

'Betty might not be all there but she is more convincing than Mary Collier,' agreed Helen.

'Thanks for today. It was interesting.'

'Couldn't have done it without you,' he told her, 'literally. I wouldn't have survived another visit to the Turner clan.'

'I want to find out more about this Sean Donnellan. We might need to put his name into play, get it out there. I'm going to have to move quickly on any information we uncover. I can't just sit on something while I wait for the *Messenger* to catch up, no offence.'

'I know,' she admitted, 'I realise you can't wait a week so we can share an exclusive.'

'So how do you want to play this?'

'One day at a time,' she offered. 'You were right. We learned a lot today by working together, so I'll keep going,' then she added, 'for now. Maybe something will land in my lap at the right time. It's not ideal but I'm still learning.'

'You learn fast,' he told her. 'I didn't have a clue what I

was doing in my first six months,' and that admission, more than anything else she had learned that day, cheered Helen.

'I am not gay,'

'Okay,'

'I'm not!' declared Ian Bradshaw.

'Fine,' said the doctor, 'though I never said you were.'

'You did,' insisted Bradshaw, 'in so many words.'

Doctor Mellor shook his head, 'no.'

'You inferred it.'

'I don't think so, Ian.'

They'd only been in Doctor Mellor's room for twenty minutes and already Bradshaw was sitting up in a state of agitation.

'You asked me about my relationships with the opposite sex, you reminded me I hadn't had one for a while, you hypothesised this might be because of my former police partner and the feelings I had towards him,' he sent the doctor's words tumbling back to him, 'you implied I might be a homosexual man in denial.'

The doctor regarded him for a moment, as if he was trying to decide whether this argument was worth continuing. 'Then I apologise.'

As he often did when he wanted to take some tension out of their sessions, the doctor went to the kettle and turned it on. 'Since you were good enough to apologise to me,' the doctor reminded Bradshaw of his earlier humiliating climb-down, forced upon him when his request to end his sessions with the doctor had been turned down flat by his superiors, 'for your outburst and premature departure from our last consultation, I would like to repay the compliment.' He picked up a cup and added a tea bag but did not offer any to Bradshaw this time. 'I'm sorry if my words were clumsy, Ian. I did not wish to imply you were a homosexual in denial,' he fished the milk out of the little fridge in his office, 'though I don't think everyone would have reacted quite as violently as you did just then.'

Bradshaw sighed. 'Meaning I'm a homosexual?'

'No,' the doctor sounded exasperated now, 'though perhaps you are a little prejudiced against them.'

'Rubbish, I'm not prejudiced against anyone. I've got nothing against gay men, or lesbian women, come to that. I think you'll find my generation is a lot more tolerant about that sort of thing than yours.'

'That sort of thing?'

'Gay sex,' Bradshaw clarified. 'I don't give a toss what two consenting adults get up to in their own bedroom, I'm merely telling you I'm straight, that's all. Christ, half of Durham Constabulary is homophobic. Pick on one of them for a change.'

'I'm not picking on anyone, Ian. This is merely part of your therapy.'

'My private life and personal relationships? Are they really that valid?'

'All human relationships are important,' countered the doctor. 'The closer the relationship the more relevant it becomes and currently you do not have a close relationship with anybody.' The doctor held up his hand in a placatory manner. 'I am merely stating a fact. You have no one to share the burdens of this life with you. You face them alone. I'm not sure that's entirely healthy.'

'Look, I wasn't in a very positive frame of mind when I broke up with Angela. I wasn't good for her.'

'That was shortly after the incident,' the doctor reminded him, 'and understandable. But since then?'

'I just haven't met anybody.'

'No one?'

'Nobody I really liked.'

'Mmm, yes; well, I can't help but feel there is a little more to it than that. Have you made any effort to meet anybody?'

'Not really.'

'Why not?'

'Because . . .' he began and realised he had not given the matter any thought himself. '. . . it's not a great time . . . I'm busy, I'm *always* busy and . . .'

'Too busy to go out for a drink with a lady friend? Surely there's time enough for that. Even detectives have personal lives, Ian.'

'I just . . .' and he ran out of words.

'I think it's something deeper. I'm wondering if, since the accident, you have been deliberately shying away from female contact?'

'Well I've been depressed, haven't I?'

'Yes, indeed, but maybe there is another reason?'

'Which is?'

'I think at this point it's very important for you to be open and honest with yourself and with me. I think if we are to make progress here, if we want these sessions to work, we need to let the barriers come down and I would really like you to tell me the reason. Could you do that, do you think? Please.'

Bradshaw took such a long time to answer he was expecting Mellor to lose his temper at any moment, but instead the doctor merely waited. He made his cup of tea, sat down and waited some more.

In the end Bradshaw answered him without being fully conscious that he was doing so. 'I don't want any of that right now.'

'Why not?'

'Because it's not something I need.'

'Need or . . .'

'Want,' Bradshaw said.

'But why not, Ian? Please tell me. You know it will stay with us, inside this room. No one else will ever know.'

'I don't think I . . .'

'Say it, Ian,' urged the doctor, 'say what's on your mind.'

'I don't think I deserve it,' and Bradshaw's face creased slightly in apparent confusion, as if the words had been spoken by someone else, for this was not something he had been consciously aware of.

The doctor nodded, 'I thought so,' he said, 'you don't think you deserve to be happy, do you, Ian.'

'No,' said Bradshaw and he was far more surprised than the doctor to finally discover the truth.

His heart was racing and he was breathing hard. Was he having a heart attack? Was this what it felt like to die? No, he was just spooked. They'd been so close to catching him.

The girl was standing outside the village hall, like a tethered goat, just waiting for him when he drove past her. Had she missed her bus or was the adult tasked with collecting her running late? Could he risk approaching her, to coax the girl into his car before anyone saw? Then he remembered Isaiah: *The prey of the terrible shall be delivered for I will contend with him that contendeth with thee, and I will save thy children*, and this spurred him into action.

He pulled over by the side of the road and watched her in his passenger side mirror. She was the right age but it was still a risk. He looked about him and the streets were silent and empty. She was entirely alone, so he decided to chance it, his heart thumping as he made a U-turn and drove back towards her. She was shielded by stationary cars so he had to park a little way from her and risk getting out. The girl didn't notice as he started to walk towards her. She didn't even look up when he was a few yards away. He opened his mouth to speak to her.

'Andrea!' someone called then and the girl turned towards the voice, 'what are you doing?' asked a man who was approaching her from a path that ran down the side of the village hall, 'I told you I'd pick you up at the back.'

'Sorry, Dad.'

'Come on, let's get you home,' her father said impatiently.

Neither of them paid him any attention as he went by. He made a point of walking round the block so it looked like he was just out for a stroll but his heart was pounding. He made sure no one was watching when he returned to his car. He didn't want anybody reporting a suspicious man or recording his licence plate.

The girl would never know how close she'd come to being saved but he knew how close he'd been to being trapped. He'd almost given himself away and he vowed to be far more careful from now on. He wasn't ready to be caught.

Chapter Thirty-Two

Tom went back to his room in the Greyhound and wrote up his story in longhand. He had to admit it didn't amount to much but he was now convinced Sean Donnellan was the body-in-the-field. On re-reading it however, the piece lacked authority. So far all he had was the word of a half-batty old lady.

This wasn't good enough for The Paper, or anybody else. What if Tom was wrong and it wasn't Sean after all? He'd look like a complete idiot. If he had still been at The Paper, he could have done some digging. Remaining members of the victim's family could be traced to see if he really had disappeared back in 1936. There was no way Tom could manage to do that on his own though, with no contacts and a mobile phone that could barely manage a signal.

Tom just couldn't risk calling the story in as it was. It was too damn flimsy. For all he knew, Sean Donnellan could be sitting in a pub in Dublin right now, nursing a Guinness.

Helen had a cover story but as they left the news room not one of her colleagues asked her why she stayed. She decided to wait half an hour in case a reporter or photographer returned late from a job.

When the time had elapsed she stood up and

tentatively approached the cabinets, which contained Malcolm's famous cuttings' files. Helen opened the drawer of the first cabinet and peered in. She then tackled the alphabetised filing system and withdrew the necessary documents one after another until she had a small stack of files, each one relating to a missing girl. She opened the first and began to read when she heard a sound from the reception area just beyond the newsroom's double doors. Helen froze. She could dimly make out a muffled conversation. Someone was heading her way.

She quickly pushed the heavy drawer closed and ran back across the room, still clutching the files. She was halfway to her desk when the buzzer sounded to indicate that someone had swiped their pass across the electronic lock of the newsroom door. Helen threw herself into her seat, wedging the files between her knees and the underside of her desk so they could not be seen then sat straight in her chair just as the door opened.

Malcolm was standing in the doorway and he did not look at all pleased to see Helen, nor was he alone.

Ian Bradshaw bought a pint of bitter and walked to a quiet corner of the pub. He sat down heavily and pondered the fruitless day he'd just spent investigating an ancient murder nobody seemed to know anything about. His strange session with Doctor Mellor, which had actually forced him to think about his personal life for the first time in a long while, had been sandwiched between several hours of knocking on doors and getting exactly nowhere,

Being a police officer, Bradshaw was used to hostility

from sections of the general public and not just the criminal element. There were a fair number of folk who should have known better; including left-leaning students and even some of their tutors, who routinely labelled him and all of his colleagues as 'fascists', without ever stopping to contemplate what their world would actually be like if they were left unprotected by a police force. Bradshaw could live with that, but Great Middleton was an unusual place to make door-to-door enquiries. Nearly everyone seemed suspicious of him and his routine questions. Some refused to talk. Others didn't even bother to hide their contempt. There were a few who were friendly enough, usually the younger ones with small children, but they were in a clear minority and, importantly, none of them had any information. Everyone, young and old alike, denied knowing anything about the identity of the body-in-the-field, much less the reason for its presence there.

Thank God he was finally off duty. He was halfway through the sports pages of a discarded newspaper when someone spoke to him.

'Ian Bradshaw?' He looked up to see Tom Carney staring down at him. 'It is, isn't it?'

'Yeah.' Bradshaw was sure he did not know the man standing opposite him and that could only mean trouble.

'I thought so,' Tom smiled at him. He had a pint of IPA in one hand and a bowl of chips in the other. 'Tom Carney,' he told the bemused Bradshaw, 'you were at my comprehensive, the year above me, or maybe two. You won't remember me but I saw you play football a couple of times. You were bloody good.'

Not quite good enough, thought Bradshaw. 'Thanks, I was okay I suppose, many moons ago.'

'Mind if I join you?' Bradshaw did mind but he slid a chair out with his foot and Tom sat down. 'Cheers. So what you up to now then?'

'Police.'

'That explains it. Are you investigating the missing girl or the body-in-the-field?'

Bradshaw didn't want to admit the truth. 'Both.'

'Then maybe we could help each other out,' offered Tom. 'How's that?'

Tom explained what he did for a living and Bradshaw visibly tensed at the word 'journalist'.

'I'm not suggesting anything dodgy, Ian. I might come up with some information you'd value and you could repay the compliment,' and he smiled, 'in the time-honoured tradition of these things.'

Bradshaw knew that members of the police force had been tipping off reporters in exchange for a second income for many years now but he wasn't sure he wanted to go down that route. It wouldn't matter that the practice was widespread, it was still against the rules and it would be just like him to be the one who was caught and made an example of. His superiors could then use it as an excuse to get rid of Ian once and for all.

'What makes you think you could uncover something I can't?'

'The locals round here aren't too forthcoming where the police are concerned.'

'Maybe not.' Tom was certainly right about that, though

Bradshaw had no idea why. 'We have had a few leads though.'

'Go on, admit it,' grinned Tom, 'you might have had some help with your missing girl, they'd want her back obviously, but I bet you've had radio silence on that old murder.'

Bradshaw lacked the will to lie to Tom's face and hoped the shared school connection might mean the younger man was less likely to stitch him up in print. 'They're saying bugger all about it.'

'Unsurprisingly.'

'Why unsurprisingly?'

'Because people have long memories and they haven't forgotten what your lot did,' said Tom.

'What do you mean my lot? What are we supposed to have done?'

'The battle of Orgreave,' Tom said, 'during the miner's strike. The police went in hard on the pickets and I do mean hard.'

'That was miles away and it was the South Yorkshire Police, not us.'

'Yeah but striking miners travelled from all over, including a fair few from this village.'

'Some of those striking miners were a bit of a handful from what I've heard.'

'I'm sure they were but the blokes charged with keeping the peace went in like World War Three had just started. One of the lads from this village took a right beating, ended up with a fractured skull and almost died.'

'Bloody hell.'

'The police denied all responsibility then threatened to do him for obstruction and assaulting a police officer. At one point the bloke was going to be charged with rioting. He'd have been sent down for years if that had stuck.'

'They were probably just trying to scare him.'

'They succeeded and it wasn't an idle threat by the way. Nearly a hundred miners were charged with rioting after Orgreave but here's the thing: all of the charges were mysteriously dropped when they went to court, because it turned out that serving police officers had made most of it up.'

'That's a bit strong isn't it?'

'Is it?' asked Tom, 'then why has South Yorkshire Police paid out more than four hundred grand of taxpayers' money in compensation to those men, without ever admitting liability and not a single police officer has ever been disciplined over it?'

'I don't know,' Bradshaw replied truthfully.

'Because it was probably orchestrated from the very top,' said Tom. 'They never identified the officers who did the beatings and concluded there was no evidence of wrong doing. Your lot always do that though, don't they?'

'Will you stop calling them "your lot"? It wasn't Durham, it was South Yorkshire and I wasn't even in the force back then.'

'No but you know what I mean. There are always enquiries and nobody is ever held accountable or, if they are, they're allowed to retire early, though ill health.'

'Some police officers are actually ill you know,' Bradshaw bridled at this, 'stress and depression are real.'

Tom nodded. 'But there are a fair number who aren't. Everybody knows you've pretty much got to kill somebody to get thrown out of the police force and even then.'

'All right, you've made your point,' conceded Bradshaw, 'journalists aren't exactly saints though, are they? A small minority of police officers might be caught telling lies but your lot have turned it into a profession.'

Tom smiled, 'I have to concede there are some tabloid reporters who stretch credibility at times.'

'You're telling me.'

'Thank God there are still honourable men like us,' he grinned, 'to make up for all of those rotten apples,' he clinked his glass against Bradshaw's. 'So is it a deal then?'

'Is what a deal?'

'You and me, helping each other by sharing information?'

'What kind of information?'

Tom leaned forward, 'I need something other journalists don't have: police theories about Michelle Summers' disappearance, leads you are following, anything that's better than the bland old crap about exploring numerous lines of enquiry.'

Bradshaw thought for a moment. He was still annoyed at Tom Carney's casual tarring of every police officer with the same brush. Even if Bradshaw could quite easily imagine Skelton and O'Brien cracking heads on a picket line, he didn't like to hear criticism from outsiders. Then he remembered Tom's words about Orgreave and thought about spending the next week having doors slammed in his face. 'Tell you what,' he said, 'you find out something of significance about either of those cases and I'll give you something nobody else has. How does that sound?'

'Something of significance?' asked Tom cautiously while he regarded Bradshaw for a moment to see if he was serious. 'How about his name then?'

'Whose name?'

'The body-in-the-field.'

This had to be a wind-up but Tom Carney didn't look like he was kidding. 'Are you serious?'

'I am if you are.'

'How the hell did you manage to get a name?' challenged Bradshaw.

'I'm not the police, which gives me a distinct advantage in a pissed-off mining village. I have my contacts and little ways of teasing out information.'

'Go on then,' urged Bradshaw.

'Hang on a minute,' Tom told him, 'this is a deal, right? I expect something from you in return.'

'You can't just hang onto a name in a murder enquiry,' Bradshaw told him. 'I could have you arrested for obstructing the police.'

'I don't think a couple of hours is a serious delay in a case that's sixty years old, do you?' challenged Tom. 'And my story might have a bit more credibility if I can add the words "Police are working on the assumption that . . ." to my claim about the identity of this man. So it's in my best interests to leak it in advance to a trusted police source but, I'll be honest with you here, I'd rather choose someone I trust, so I can further their career,' and he took a sip of his pint before adding, 'not some tosser who threatens to have me arrested.'

Bradshaw sighed, 'I'm sorry,' and his head dropped. 'I didn't mean that. It's just . . . I've been having a very bad week.'

'Well, your week is about to become a whole lot better. Now pin back your lug holes because I have a story to tell.'

Bradshaw did listen then, as Tom explained Sean Donnellan's visit to Great Middleton and his sudden disappearance.

'Sean Donnellan,' repeated Bradshaw, 'and they reckon he did a moonlight flit?'

'That's what people thought, at the time. Obviously he didn't. He was murdered.'

'If it's him.'

Tom shrugged. 'Who else could it be?'

'How did you get this?' asked Bradshaw.

'A journalist never reveals his sources,' and when he saw the impatient look on the DC's face he added, 'that works both ways. How can you trust me with information if I give you up as soon as somebody asks me?'

'I suppose,' he conceded reluctantly.

'What do you think?'

'It sounds feasible,' admitted Bradshaw.

'I'd say it's more than feasible,' Tom told him, 'it's all you've got and in the absence of anything else I'd call this a strong line of enquiry, wouldn't you?'

'I wouldn't say it's strong.'

Tom said, 'none of the other villagers could go missing without anybody noticing.'

'True, but do we have a motive? Why would anybody kill this guy? He was Irish but it couldn't have been political back then?'

'He was an artist from Dublin not a rebel from Belfast and this was thirty years before Bloody Sunday but . . .'

'But what?' probed Bradshaw.

'He had a way with the ladies by all accounts.'

'That's not a bad way to make enemies in a small village.'

'Exactly and I'm going to write this story regardless,' bluffed Tom. 'I'm going to say that it's him but can I also say that the police think it could be him?'

Tom held his breath and watched as Bradshaw considered the implications of this. Finally the detective constable concluded he had nothing much to lose. 'I'll tell my DI about it in the morning. There's enough there for us to run some checks into this man.'

'Which would make it a line of enquiry?'

'Yes,' agreed Bradshaw, 'it would.'

'Then I have a story and you'll get a pat on the back for excellent police work.'

'Something like that,' said Bradshaw without enthusiasm.

'Look,' said Tom, 'I'll sit on it for a day. Just call me when your lot confirm they are looking into it, will you? I'm staying here,' and he indicated the pub.

Bradshaw nodded and they both sipped their beers reflectively then Tom said, 'So, go on then.'

'Go on then what?'

Tom gave Bradshaw a disbelieving look. 'Give me something good, something nobody else has.'

'Oh,' Bradshaw sounded sheepish.

'A deal is a deal.'

'I know,' admitted Bradshaw with the dread of a man waiting to be called from a dentist's waiting room. 'Well, okay,' he said, 'there is something that nobody knows about.'

Chapter Thirty-Three

1936

Mary watched the young couple from the road. They were standing in the doorway of St Michael's church, framed by its gothic archway, smiling out at the well-wishers who had gathered to share their big day. As well as family and close friends who had spilled out of the church following the service, there were passers-by, like Mary, who took a moment to gaze on 'love's young dream', while children stood around, hoping the best man would throw pennies into the street.

The groom was a local boy; tall and good looking but with few prospects. The bride was not much older than eighteen. Mary noted her shyness and the way she clung onto her new husband's arm uncertainly, as if the act did not yet feel altogether natural. The term 'blushing bride' could have been invented for her and Mary thought she knew why. Surely Mary was not the only one wondering about a time after the wedding party was over when the guests had all departed. The bride was almost certainly a virgin, unless of course she had foolishly allowed herself to be swept away in a moment of weakness, and if that was the case it would be a surprise if the man still wanted to marry her. However the bride's assumed virtue meant the whole village knew what they would be up to that night if the marriage was to be consummated. This seemed to Mary like a dreadful intrusion into their privacy, but she had to concede she was as guilty of that intrusion as anyone.

Mary couldn't help trying to picture the scene in her own inexperienced mind. Would she undress for him or would he do it for her with his big rough hands? What would it feel like when he finally lay her down on the bed and took her? Would he be gentle or behave like an animal, as she had heard men sometimes did when passion overcame them?

'A penny for them?' asked Henry for he had crept to her side without Mary noticing.

'I wasn't thinking about anything in particular,' she said.

The best man threw a handful of pennies into the air then and they landed on the road. Several young boys scrambled to pick them up as they rolled in all directions.

Mary's father came out of the church, still dressed in his vestments. He left his congregation to speak to Henry, which caused Mary's soon-to-be-fiancé to stand a little straighter, as if he was on parade.

'Will we see your brother in church this Sunday, Henry?' asked the vicar.

'I will ask him,' Henry assured the vicar, 'again.'

'No man needs the solace and comfort of religion more than one who has been to war,' the Reverend Riley assured Henry, then he made a point of looking heavenward while he strained to recall a quotation. '*Put on the whole armour of God, that you may be able to stand against the schemes of the devil.*' he recited at Henry. 'I think it would reflect well on your family should Jack choose to join us at prayer,' he told the young man then he smiled, 'but you are not your brother's keeper.'

'No,' answered Henry, 'but I will try.'

'You can do no more than that,' the reverend informed him.

'We were about to go for a walk, father,' Mary told him, to spare Henry any more discomfort.

'Don't be late,' he told her. Everyone in the village knew that immoral acts always happened after dark. Young, courting couples were particularly susceptible to their urges then and could easily 'fall wrong', so Mary and Henry were only allowed to conduct their wooing during respectable hours.

'We won't be long,' Mary assured her father, though she couldn't help but think that they would be gone long enough should they wish to get up to something.

He had the knife in his hand and he was staring intently, gazing down the long blade with its razor-sharp point, 'it won't be long.'

'This is silly,' she told him.

'No one will see,' he told her, 'nobody will know.'

'Then what's the purpose of it?'

'We'll know, won't we?' Henry reminded her. 'I didn't think you'd want everybody to see it.'

'I don't,' and it worried her how emphatically she'd said that.

'We're well off the beaten track. The only people who'll come out here will be doing what we're doing.'

'Carving their initials on a tree,' Mary observed drily, 'with a heart around them.'

Henry looked hurt then. 'I thought you'd like it.'

'I do,' she said quickly when she saw the disappointment in his face, 'really I do,' and in an effort to encourage him she added, 'you've not finished our heart.'

He gave the tree one last scrape with the lock knife, leaving their initials framed by a rough, uneven heart. 'There,' he said, pleased with his handiwork.

Henry folded the lock knife and put it back into his coat pocket before gently drawing her closer to him. The kisses that followed felt clumsy and one-sided. Henry expected to take these liberties by now, for they had been walking out together long enough and she would grant them but sparingly, towards the end of their walks and not for long. They both knew they must wait until their wedding night, a mythical time that would involve the instant shedding of all of their joint innocence in one go.

Henry would sometimes be left flushed and flustered by her insistence that they stop but Mary never found herself getting too carried away and she wondered if there was something wrong with her for not feeling his embraces more intensely. It was not that they weren't pleasant enough but that was all they were. That day, however, Henry did get carried away.

'Henry!' Mary warned him wide-eyed as she felt the stirring then the hardness pressing against her. Henry was mortified and immediately took a step back from her.

'Oh Mary, I'm sorry,' he seemed distraught, 'please forgive me.'

Mary wanted to laugh but contained herself for his sake, for she knew enough about men already to know that they did not care to be laughed at; Henry more so than most. 'Of course I forgive you,' she said, 'I understand and we didn't go too far. It's all right.'

'It's not all right,' he seemed on the brink of tears. 'I don't think of you like that, Mary. A beast in the field would have more restraint.'

Mary took hold of his hand. 'Let's say no more about it. Walk with me,' and she steered him away from the shelter of the trees.

Mary returned home alone just as Mrs Harris was leaving the vicarage. 'I'm off to my sisters,' she reminded Mary as she bustled down the path. 'Your father is at the Dean's. Mind you stay out of mischief,' she said that last part as if it was a joke, but she wasn't really joking. Mrs Harris's biggest fear was that Mary would end up disgraced in some way before she was safely secured in wedlock.

Mary watched Mrs Harris leave, then went into the vicarage, fully intending to read for a while until her father returned from the Dean's, but then she noticed his study door was ajar. Reverend Riley never left his study door open. It was his private space where he composed his sermons and attended to the business of the parish, a serious room whose threshold Mary had never been allowed to cross. Perhaps it was the forbidden nature that prompted Mary to push open the door and step inside.

Mary entered her father's study quietly so she could listen for any sound of a premature return, from him or Mrs Harris but once inside, she revelled in the intrusion. The room smelt of pipe smoke and old leather from bookcases filled with heavy, bound tomes on religious reading and ancient history but no novels, for they were frivolous and could not lead to self-improvement. There was a gramophone so that music could be played while her father wrote his sermons and an old, ornately carved desk with a wooden chair, which had a dark red, cushioned seat that matched the inlay of the desk. Mary touched the chair but did not sit in it. She noticed her father's drawer was not flush with the desk and it protruded slightly. She knew her father always kept his desk drawer locked. When she came to summon him to dinner it was the last thing he did after placing his papers in order and he kept the key on his person. She took hold of the small, wooden handle and gently pulled. The drawer slid open.

The contents were a disappointment at first; some official-looking papers that appeared to relate to their occupancy of the vicarage, a pocket watch and two old fountain pens but precious little else of note apart from a metal strong box. Mary made a mental picture of the contents of the drawer and the manner in which they were arranged, so she could restore them to their exact position. She carefully lifted the box onto the desk then opened it.

Inside were a substantial number of gold coins of a type Mary had never seen before but each had a portrait of the king on one side. She realised they must be sovereigns and that each one was valuable. No wonder her father was normally so careful to lock the drawer. The Reverend Riley did not trust banks and Mary deduced that this was her father's life savings from his church salary and parents' legacies plus her late mother's estate.

She was about to close the lid and return the box to the

drawer when she noticed a small brown envelope that was half hidden by the coins towards the back of the box. She removed it carefully and opened the envelope with a premonition of excitement, instinctively knowing that something forbidden was housed here. At first she thought they were simple postcards but Mary soon realised they could never have been purchased in any normal shop.

In the first postcard, a young Japanese woman was lying on her side being tightly embraced by a man. Both figures were still wearing kimonos but they had been allowed to slip loosely open and the woman's had been pulled up to show her bare legs and a full view of the area between them, including a thick, downy triangle of pubic hair. The man was forcing a hand beneath her kimono to grasp at her breast while pushing a huge penis inside her. Mary was both shocked and intrigued by the sight, particularly when she realised that what she first took to be a rape scene was contradicted by the look of contentment on the woman's face. But was she concubine or whore, wife or slave girl – and what was she doing in her father's locked, desk drawer?

Mary slid the card to one side, to reveal a different one, which showed another man about to take a second girl, her clothes hoisted conveniently around her upper body, leaving the lower part bare. He was thrusting forward towards her and she seemed quite content to accommodate him.

Mary looked at each of the cards in turn, a dozen oriental scenes of copulation with nothing hidden from view, and somehow knew her father had not merely confiscated these banned images from a parishioner. They were his secret, guilty pleasure, something he had to keep hidden and locked away, her discovery of them revealing something new to Mary about him and men in general.

She carefully slid the cards back into the envelope and put it in the box, covering it with the right number of gold sovereigns, then she put the box back in the drawer and slid it into its original position, before quietly leaving the room.

Mary liked to think that she and Henry had no secrets and later she would tell him about the gold sovereigns she had discovered in her father's strong box, but she neglected to mention the postcards.

Chapter Thirty-Four

Tom did not linger in the bar once Bradshaw had departed. Instead he went up to his room, removed his shoes, socks and shirt and lay down heavily on the bed, hoping to sleep for an hour. He was dozing fitfully when he was awoken by a loud knock on the bedroom door. The sound made him sit up sharply and groggily take in his surroundings. Disoriented, he realised he was still in Great Middleton. Then there was a second knock. What the hell did Colin want?

Tom answered the door, but it was not Colin. Instead Helen was standing there on the landing. Because he was shirtless, they both apologised at the same time. 'Wait a sec,' he said and he retreated to pull on a T shirt then returned to let her in.

Helen walked into the room and stood awkwardly for a moment. 'I didn't realise you were sleeping,' she said.

'Just dozing, sit down,' he told her but there was no chair so she perched on the edge of the bed.

'Are you okay?' he asked.

She nodded unconvincingly. 'I got the files,' and he realised she was carrying a large shopping bag.

'Great,' he said, 'so why do you look like somebody just died?'

'Something weird happened,' she told him, 'at the office. Everyone was gone. I was the only one left in the building . . .' she began, '. . . I was just about to lift the files out when I heard voices and then the door went. I made it back to my desk but only just.'

'Who was it?'

'That's the weird part.'

'Go on.'

'Malcolm,' she said.

'Right.'

'But he wasn't on his own,' she told him, 'there was this woman.'

Tom grinned, 'Malcolm? Coming back to his office after hours with a woman? Oh that's priceless.'

'Not for me,' she assured him. 'When he saw me he did not look happy.'

'Well, he wouldn't be. What did he say?'

'He didn't say anything.'

'What did you say?'

'"Hi Malcolm, just finishing off, got a good piece on council cutbacks for you,"' she parroted cheerfully, 'as if I was a simpleton who hadn't noticed the woman he was with.'

Tom laughed. 'What did he say to that?'

'He just nodded but he looked like someone had slapped him across the face,' she said, 'and that's not all. The really weird bit was that *they* weren't alone. I mean I can sort of understand it if Malcolm has somehow managed to persuade a poor woman to be his bit-on-the-side but . . .'

'Who was with them?' And there was something in his tone that made Helen wonder if Tom already understood the situation.

'Jim.'

'Jim the photographer?' she nodded. 'Where did they go Helen?'

'Into the dark room.'

Tom looked distinctly amused now. 'Was this woman in her late-thirties with dyed red hair and, shall we say, a fuller figure, by any chance?'

'Yes, how did you know?'

'That's Rita-the-man-eater,' he told her then he chuckled in disbelief. 'I can't believe they are still doing it.'

'Doing what?'

'Back when Malcolm was a reporter he met Rita. She is a . . . model . . . of sorts, an amateur who does glamour photography.'

'Oh,' said Helen, cottoning on.

'Malcolm and Jim used to make a few bob on the side taking photos of Rita of an artistic nature then selling them to low-end men's magazines. Somehow word got out that they were doing this and we all knew about it but I thought he'd stopped years ago. However, on the evidence of tonight, I'd say you just caught your editor in the middle of one of his porn shoots.'

'Oh dear God,' she groaned.

He laughed then, 'You know, it took a few years before Malcolm absolutely hated me,' he said. 'Looks like you've achieved the same status in less than three months,' he nodded towards her bag. 'Come on. Let's see what you got and whether it was worth it.'

She took out the files and Tom sat next to her, leaving a gap so she could place the first file on the bed.

'Susan Freeman,' she said. She removed a photograph

of a smiling young girl from the file and placed it face up on the bed. She was dressed in what was possibly her first school uniform and it was hard not to be touched by such a natural, unforced smile, knowing that it would never be seen by anyone again.

Helen continued to remove the photographs from each file, placing the images of each young girl on top of the relevant folder so they could view all four of them together. 'Katie Sykes.' Another girl in school uniform, this one was dark haired and her smile more of a reluctant grimace, an unsuccessful attempt to hide the metal braces on her teeth.

'Sarah Hutchison.' The third victim was dressed in casual clothes in the photograph, which could have been taken by the kind of professional photographer you'd find on the high street of any small town. Sarah was dressed in a green T shirt and blue jeans; she might have been trying to look a little older than her years but she was still demonstrably a young girl.

'Jenny Barber.' The last girl had pale skin, ginger hair and freckles and her face held a startled expression, as if she was not expecting the picture even though she'd been posing for it.

Seeing actual photographs of the victims made the murders more real somehow. A picture in a newspaper keeps a distance, as if the tragedy of their death only occurred in newspaper-land, a fictional place far away, only glimpsed briefly during the snatched cup of coffee before the day's commute, or the few rushed moments between stops on the morning train.

Tom stared at the photographs for a long time without saying anything.

'What is it?' she asked.

'I dunno,' he shook his head, but there was clearly something troubling him.

'Why did you want to see their photos?'

He exhaled slowly. 'It was just something . . .' He stopped speaking and there was such a long pause she wondered if he was going to start again. Eventually he asked, 'How old was Susan Freeman? Eleven?'

'Yes.'

'And Katie Sykes?'

'Twelve.'

'Sarah Hutchison? She looks about eleven.'

'She was thirteen actually. I read the files.' What was he getting at?

'And the last one?'

'Jenny Barber was thirteen too.'

'Okay look at them all here,' and he opened his palms towards the pictures beneath him, 'what strikes you about them?'

Nothing struck her about them, apart from the obvious, 'aside from the fact they are all girls?'

'Yeah.'

Helen thought for a time and finally admitted, 'Nothing.'

'Okay, bear with me,' he tapped the photo of Susan Freeman, 'Susan here is eleven, we know that from the clippings but, if we didn't know it, how old would you make her: old for her age or young for her age?'

'About right,' she said instinctively.

'You sure?' he asked. 'She looks confident, a pretty girl, I'd maybe make her a year older, say twelve?'

'She could be.'

'What about the next one?' he asked, 'Katie Sykes? Older or younger?'

'Well she was twelve and I would say she looks twelve.'

'You sure?' he asked.

'Yes,' she said confidently.

'Good,' he replied, 'so would I.'

Helen was puzzled. What morbid game was he playing here?

He tapped the picture of the girl in jeans and T shirt, 'Sarah was what? Thirteen? Older or younger.'

'Mmm, I'd say she is a bit younger looking than her actual age, maybe a year or so.'

'Again, I agree and I think Jenny also looks a bit younger than thirteen. So they were all different ages but one was older looking, one was about right for her age and two looked younger. If we add a year to Susan, keep Katie where she is and take a year off Sarah and Jenny that would make them all twelve years old.'

Helen let this sink in. 'I suppose.'

'And we knew their ages.'

'Yeah,' she said uncertainly.

'And he didn't. The killer, I mean. He just saw them standing there in the bus shelter or outside the chippy, from his car, across the street.'

'What are you getting at?'

'I'm saying he has a type. He wants girls who are about twelve years old. He wants them . . .'

'What?'

'On the cusp,' and he actually looked a little embarrassed, 'you know, of puberty. I mean they are demonstrably girls but they aren't *very* young and they aren't teenagers either. He gets them just before they reach that stage.'

Helen was silent for a while and then she admitted, 'You could have something there,' and she thought for a moment, 'but I'm not sure how that helps necessarily. I mean what does it tell us about him, really?'

'I don't know,' he admitted, 'but it tells us one thing.'

'What?'

'Michelle Summers was different. From what we have read or heard about her and the pictures we've seen, she's not the same.'

Helen let her mind go back to the snapshots the police had issued to the media, hoping to jog the memory of potential witnesses who may have seen a runaway or an abduction; a girl well past the first onset of puberty, a girl nearer a woman than a child, a fifteen-year-old with a defined, womanly figure just waiting for the puppy fat to disappear before she would start to receive the unwelcome attention of every construction worker she had the misfortune to walk by.

'She was older,' said Helen, 'two or three years older but,' and she paused while she took in the true significance of what he was saying, 'she looked much older, even in that photo the police blew up for the press conference.'

He nodded. 'That's what I can't get my head round. If it's the same guy, the same motive, the same warped and twisted logic then why has he suddenly gone from skinny, little pre-pubescent girls to curvy teenagers who could pass for seventeen with a bit of lippy on? It doesn't ring true.'

Tom transferred his attention to the clippings files and they both began to silently read their contents.

'There's a fair bit of information here but does any of it actually help?' Helen asked but he didn't answer. He was too busy reading and she sat near him in silence for a time while he looked at the notes in the clippings files.

'Well, let's see,' he finally answered, 'are these cases all the same?' he pondered. 'From what we can see here, the victims are all young girls,' and he held up a finger to denote this first similarity, 'they were all taken out in the open, from bus shelters, roadsides and the like,' his second finger went up, 'and nobody saw or heard a thing,' the third finger, 'the first four girls were all killed in the same way, by strangulation,' the fourth finger went up, 'but there was no rape or sexual assault of any kind, all were found fully clothed.' His thumb marked the fifth similarity then he put his hand down by his side. 'If Michelle Summers fits the pattern then they should find her body soon, she will have been strangled but there won't be anything sexual about it, which makes you wonder why he does it, what he gets out of this?'

'You're assuming he's a frustrated guy who can't get sex or only likes it when his victim struggles or is helpless,' Helen said, 'but this isn't about sex at all. It's about power. He gets his excitement from killing them. He must get off on that.'

'Maybe,' and he thought for a second. 'So far the police and all of the papers have focused on the similarities between the Michelle Summers case and the other four victims of the Kiddy-Catcher – but what about the differences?'

'Well, I'm not sure there are any, except the obvious fact that Michelle was older than the other girls,' she said.

'By at least three years,' he reminded her. 'Why was this girl older? She wasn't his usual type,' and when she looked uncomfortable he added, 'of victim, I mean.'

'The others were all aged between eleven and thirteen,' she noted, 'whereas Michelle was nearly sixteen. That could be important but . . .'

'But . . . ?'

'Maybe she was the only girl he could find. We haven't considered that. He's driving around looking for victims when everyone knows there's a strange man out there abducting and murdering young girls, which makes parents more vigilant than normal. They won't let their daughters go out on their own until he's caught.'

'They'd drive them around instead or make sure the girls travel in groups when they come home from school or to youth clubs and the cinema,' said Tom.

'But Michelle's mother didn't think to do that because she was older.'

'She was fifteen,' he said, 'and she would know better than to step willingly into a car with a stranger. If it is the Kiddy-Catcher that's taken her, it brings us back to the question of *how* he is convincing the girls to go with him.'

'I've been thinking about that,' Helen said. 'Something happened a while back and it came back to me today.'

'What?'

'It's probably nothing.' She felt self-conscious now, as if her instincts couldn't entirely be trusted.

'Tell me,' he urged.

Helen hesitated at first. 'I stopped to grab a sandwich at the supermarket on the edge of town. I was in a hurry so I just ate it in my car. While I was parked there a little girl came running out on her own. She was only about three years old and I remember I was worried she'd get knocked down by a car. Then a woman came chasing after her. Everybody stopped for a moment to see what was wrong but then the woman caught up with the little girl, grabbed her and told her off. As soon as she did that everyone relaxed and carried on as if nothing had happened.'

'Right,' he said uncertainly, 'well they would, wouldn't they, once they knew she was safe.'

'How could they know she was safe?' Helen asked. 'How did I know she was safe, come to that?'

'I don't get it,' he said, 'you saw her mum.'

'Did I? Was it her mum or a child molester trying to kidnap a fleeing toddler?'

He gave a little laugh then. 'Well, I mean . . .'

'Because it was a woman,' she told him firmly, 'it never crossed our minds that it could be anything sinister because it was a woman. If it had been a man the whole scene would have looked very different.'

'So, what are you saying?'

'I'm saying that could be how he gets them to go with him so easily.'

'By using a woman?' Tom asked and she nodded, while his mind raced at the thought of smiling women luring young girls into cars, feigning messages from their parents or a manufactured emergency of some kind. It slowly registered with Tom that Helen could be right. 'Jesus, you know what that would mean?'

'Yes,' she said, 'we'd have another Myra Hindley on our hands.'

Chapter Thirty-Five

Day Five

'You,' Trelawe addressed the young detective in front of everyone, 'what do you think you're doing, coming late to my briefing?' Trelawe broke off to focus on Bradshaw's tardiness. 'You'd better have a damn good reason.'

'Sorry, Sir,' answered Bradshaw. The truth was he hadn't been able to drag himself out of bed that morning, unable to shake the feeling that nothing he did seemed to matter any more, but he could hardly confess to that. 'I was in Great Middleton, following up a lead.'

Trelawe looked momentarily confused. Lateness for the morning briefing was a capital offence but he could hardly chastise an officer who had taken the trouble to go out onto the streets already that morning. 'Which case?' asked Trelawe, postponing Bradshaw's public humiliation till he had heard him out.

'The body-in-the-field, Sir,' answered Bradshaw and he felt the pressure that comes when every ear in the room is listening to you.

Trelawe felt a pang of disappointment. He should have known it would be the less more important case. Clearly this detective had been assigned to Kane's dead-wood squad and it was little wonder. He remembered Bradshaw because of the reams of paperwork following the previous year's incident. 'So you have a lead?'

'Possibly, Sir.'

This was the wrong answer. 'Is it a lead or isn't it?' Trelawe demanded.

'It is, Sir,' and Bradshaw found an ounce of defiance from somewhere, 'I have a name for the victim.'

This information was greeted by a surprised murmur from his fellow officers, who'd obviously assumed the likelihood of Bradshaw coming up with anything worthwhile was next to zero. Trelawe raised a hand to silence them. 'Go on,' he urged Bradshaw.

'It will need checking of course.' He knew he was in deep now. All Bradshaw really had was Tom Carney's half-baked theory, 'but I think the dead man is Sean Donnellan, an artist from Dublin who visited Great Middleton back in 1936 to produce illustrations for a book. I don't have a suspect or a motive yet but it could be sexual jealousy. He was quite a hit with the ladies apparently.'

When Bradshaw had finished he was aware that everyone in the room was staring at him silently, including the detective superintendent. 'And how did you come by this information?' asked Trelawe.

Bradshaw was never going to admit that. 'I picked it up from the door-to-door,' he said, hoping that would be vague enough, 'a little bit at a time.'

Trelawe said nothing at first. Instead he glanced at DCI Kane, then looked round the room at his officers. Finally his gaze settled back on Bradshaw and he nodded, 'you see that is what I am talking about: proper police work, information gained from diligent, door-to-door questioning and a strong lead to follow up. What a pity Bradshaw is the only one who has been listening to me.'

At the earliest opportunity, Tom rang his editor. He used the pay phone in the corner of the Greyhound's empty bar before it opened. As expected, the Doc's PA intercepted the call.

'Jennifer, it's Tom.'

Her silence told him everything.

'Can I have a quick word with the Doc?'

'He's busy.'

'Yeah, I know he's busy,' said Tom, 'he's always busy. I was just hoping that I could squeeze a word in with him between everything else.'

'And I just told you no,' she was being the gatekeeper, protecting her boss from unwanted interruptions. 'He doesn't want to speak to you, Tom.'

'Did he tell you that?' Tom demanded. 'Did he use those exact words?'

'I know the Doc,' she said, 'he doesn't want to speak to you.'

'Bitch,' Tom whispered to himself but his mouth was still too close to the phone.

'What did you just say?' her voice was shrill with indignation.

'I said "son-of-a-bitch",' he answered quickly. 'Look, I've got a good story here and I need to speak to the Doc about it. He's going to like it. Can you at least tell him that and get him to give me a call?' he implored her. 'Please, Jennifer.'

She took so long to answer he wondered if she had cut him off because he'd been stupid enough to call her a bitch. Eventually she said, 'I'll pass the message on.'

'Thank you,' and before he let her go he made sure she took down the number of the Greyhound's phone in case the Doc couldn't get through to him on the mobile.

'Are you doing this to me deliberately?' Peacock asked Bradshaw when he hauled the younger man into his office.

'Doing what, Sir?' he asked uncomprehendingly.

'Ignoring the chain of command,' Peacock told him, 'going over my head.'

'But I haven't . . .'

'You just did!' Peacock snapped, 'out there, in the morning briefing.'

'But the super asked me . . .'

Again, Peacock interrupted him, 'I know what he asked you. You should have said you were pursuing a number of leads and were hoping for something concrete soon.'

'I don't get it,' Bradshaw protested, 'I thought you'd be pleased I'd come up with something.'

Peacock sighed, 'I know you don't get it, son, so at least I can put this latest round of stupidity down to ignorance and not malice. When you uncover something you come to an adult; meaning, me. What you don't do is offer it up to cover your own arse in the middle of a collective bol-locking. You made me and the DCI look like clueless tossers and gave everybody else in your squad another reason to hate you. *Now* have you got it?'

And he had.

The familiar, debilitating weariness enveloped Bradshaw, along with the realisation, reinforced on a daily basis by his superiors until he had started to believe it himself, that he was useless. All he wanted was to accept this latest kicking, get out of Peacock's office, go home and pull the covers over his head. He was pretty sure they would neither notice nor care if he did. 'Yes, Sir.'

'We will check out this fellah Sean Donnellan. You get back on the streets and carry on with your door-to-door.' Bradshaw supposed he should have been grateful to have avoided another afternoon sitting in the canteen. 'Now get out.'

A little before midday, Tom walked back into the bar of the Greyhound.

'A lass phoned for you,' Colin told Tom, 'Helen-something; said she couldn't meet you.'

'Thanks,' muttered Tom. His day, which had started promisingly enough, was not panning out the way he had intended. By now, he had hoped to have given the Doc a new story for The Paper, based on Ian Bradshaw's confidential tip-off, which would have reminded his editor that Tom's contract might be worth renewing after all. He had also hoped for confirmation from Bradshaw that his superiors were treating Sean Donnellan's name as a promising new lead in their enquiry into the body-in-the-field. But Bradshaw's silence was deafening, Helen had blown him off, and the Doc still hadn't called him back. He was reluctant to leave the Greyhound in case he missed a return call from his editor and he couldn't trust the mobile phone, which meant he was stuck here in the pub.

'Been stood up, have you?' asked Andrew Foster, who was smiling at him from a stool at the end of the bar.

'Aren't you supposed to be teaching unruly kids?'

'School's closed till they've finished with that body.'

'As if you lot don't get enough holiday,' said Tom. 'Ain't you got better things to do than hang round here with us natives?'

'Only dropped in for a swift one,' Andrew told him, 'joining me then?'

'Why not?'

When Helen returned from interviewing the mother of a 'miracle baby', her intention had been to write up the story as quickly as possible then creep out to meet Tom in the village. Instead she was intercepted by her editor.

'The bloody baby can wait,' Malcolm informed her. 'Get yourself down to Great Middleton Junior School. I want some reaction from the headmaster about that body in the field.'

Being sent back to Great Middleton certainly suited Helen but her positive mood did not last long. On her way out, Jason, one of the more experienced reporters, gleefully informed her that, 'You'll not get him to say owt. Nelson's always happy to talk to us when it suits him; if it's the school sports day, prize-giving or summer fête you won't be able to shut him up but if it's anything negative he won't speak to you. Malcolm's already had a go and so has Martin.'

Helen immediately realised she had been given this thankless task because others had tried and come back empty-handed. She was expected to fail.

As she drove to Great Middleton she thought about Peter. They had argued again, this time over the phone. When she'd called him the previous night she'd been eager to tell him all about the cases she was looking into. She had thought that, if he could hear the details of the work she had been doing he might understand the buzz it gave her, but Peter wasn't interested. At first he made no comment if Helen said something and she thought he was waiting patiently to hear her out but each time she mentioned something about her week, he started telling her something about his day instead.

Perhaps, Helen reasoned, Peter, with all of his ambition, sometimes felt threatened by her own. Maybe all men did. She didn't think this was right or justifiable but Peter had certainly become a different person since she had left to take on her job at the *Messenger*.

Their phone call had continued in a similar vein. It was like a tennis match where, every time she tried to insert a topic into the conversation, he hit back with something irrelevant that he or his mother and father had done recently. She persisted though, in the vain hope that he might at least feign interest but it was clear he was still irked with her for taking a job so far away, even though he had repeatedly told her it was fine.

'Can you stop going on about this bloke please?' he'd asked suddenly in a tone that belied the seemingly polite request. 'I thought you were ringing to talk to me.'

This bloke was of course Tom Carney and perhaps Helen had mentioned him once too often but it was hard not to talk about the man she had been working with so closely. Her assurances that he shouldn't be jealous of her fellow journalist were met with a surly, 'I don't feel threatened, Helen, just a bit bored of hearing about him.'

The argument escalated then and, though they both attempted to end the conversation politely before she hung up, Helen had been particularly hurt by his lack of interest in a career she was so passionate about.

By the time Helen reached Great Middleton School she'd managed to convince herself the argument was her fault. Perhaps she had been insensitive in failing to ask Peter more about his new job, though she knew he did not face half the obstacles she had to contend with when he was working for his father.

Possibly she had been too gushing in her assessment of Tom Carney, a man Peter had never met. He was many miles from her back in Surrey and must be imagining all kinds of things. Peter's jealousy was understandable then, even if he denied feeling threatened, and she would tread more carefully in future. It was one of the many little compromises Helen had been training herself to make recently. You had to work hard at a relationship and put the other person first sometimes. Wasn't that what she had always been told? Her mother often explaining that 'give and take' was the secret to the long marriage she had maintained with Helen's father, though in her daughter's view Mrs Norton had always been more likely to give than take. Perhaps all women did this. Maybe it was the great, unspoken secret they all shared. Women backed down and gave in, at least on the little things, the ones that didn't matter so much, and they hoped that the big things would naturally sort themselves out as a result. Maybe that was just how it was.

She'd been made to wait on the mat like an unwanted tradesman while the caretaker sent for the headmaster. The school was eerily silent today. Normally at this hour she would have been able to hear the whoops and excitable screams of dozens of young children enjoying the last remnants of their morning break but the school had been closed to pupils while the body was examined and photographed, samples taken and the corpse removed for forensic analysis.

Mr Nelson however was still 'manning the barricades' as one wag at the *Messenger* had put it, neatly summing up the siege mentality of a headmaster who liked to control everything in his domain, even when there were no pupils prowling the corridors. Nelson probably preferred the place this way, thought Helen, with no children and just a skeleton crew of caretaker and school secretary to support him while he tackled his admin. The first Helen knew of the headmaster's impending presence was the sound of his shoes on the wooden floor as he strode purposefully towards the front door. Was there anger in that unstinting stride? She was about to find out. Helen had spoken to Nelson before and figured he wasn't the kind of man to despatch a messenger to turn her away. He was the sort who would want to speak to you while he told you he was not going to speak to you, enjoying the power of a refusal. She was struck by the realisation that the headmaster wouldn't talk to her because he didn't need to. He had no reason to say anything, so she would have to give him a reason. But how was she going to do that?

'Headmaster?' she started brightly when he opened the

door. 'I'm writing a story for the *Messenger* about the body that was found in the grounds of the school and it would be a big help to me if I could just get a short quote from you on . . .'

'Good God,' he hissed, 'do you people never learn? I have told your editor and your deputy editor that I have absolutely no comment to make on this matter and now they send *you*,' he made the last word sound deeply insulting, as if the *Messenger* really had resorted to scraping the dregs from the very bottom of their barrel.

'That's fine,' she said, smiling, 'no problem at all,' and he seemed momentarily taken aback by this response, 'I can write the piece without any quotes from the school. It really doesn't matter.'

'Oh,' he said. Was the ego dented by her dismissal of his contribution? 'Good then.'

'It's just,' and she gave a contrived grimace, 'I was a bit worried about how it might look.'

'What do you mean?'

'Well,' she continued, in a confiding tone that made it sound as if the school's best interests were her prime concern, 'obviously if I don't get a quote from you, I will have to put "the headmaster of Great Middleton Junior School refused to comment",' she let that sink in for a moment, 'but I always think that sounds as if you have something to hide, which of course you don't.' She definitely had his full attention now.

'But what could I say about the discovery of a body on land we didn't even own when it was placed there?'

'It might be appropriate to express some form of sorrow for the departed individual,' Helen offered, 'or perhaps a few words of sympathy for family members who may have lost a loved one?'

'Mmm,' he said unsurely and she could tell the cogs were whirring, 'perhaps,'

'I'd be happy to assist you with the preparation of a statement,' she said, 'if you think it would help?'

'Well,' he was weakening and Helen was silently praying, for he had no idea how wonderful it would be if she could return to the *Messenger* with a quote when her editor and his experienced deputy had failed to secure one. 'All right then,' and she had to stop herself from punching the air in triumph, 'perhaps you should come in. Would you like a cup of coffee, Miss Norton?'

'Coffee would be lovely.'

Chapter Thirty-Six

Andrew Foster had long since left the Greyhound, but he promised to be back in a few hours, 'It's quiz night at the Lion!' he reminded Tom, as if this was the undisputed highlight of the week. Tom was still sitting there, nursing a beer, making it last. He didn't want to spend too much money or end up drunk at lunchtime. It was more than four hours since he'd left the message with Jennifer and still the Doc had not called him back. He couldn't wait any longer.

He left the Greyhound to get some air then bought a phone card from the village shop, which he used in a draughty telephone box that had half of its windows missing.

Jennifer was even less amused this time. 'I gave him the message,' she assured him through what must have been clenched teeth.

'You told him I had a story, one he would like?'

'That *was* the message,' she seemed to think he was questioning her professionalism now.

'And what did he say?'

'Nothing.'

'Nothing? He must have said something.'

'He just grunted, like he does when he's preoccupied.'

'But is he going to call me?'

'*Has* he called you?'

'No,' he said and she waited for him to cotton on. 'He's not going to call, is he?' and when she didn't even bother to answer, he added, 'Jennifer, it's been a pleasure speaking to you, as always,' then he hung up before she could respond.

When Tom got off the line, his first instinct was to slam the receiver into the phone repeatedly until it shattered into dozens of tiny, plastic pieces. It took him a minute or two to calm down and come up with a plan B and even longer to wonder if he had the balls to actually implement it. If the Doc ever found out what he was about to do he'd fire Tom on the spot, maybe even take legal action against him. Tom would be blacklisted forever in the tabloid world but it looked as if that might be about to happen to him in any case and, if his contract expired without renewal, in a few weeks he'd be broke. He desperately needed money and he had to get the story he was sitting on out there before someone else did.

Tom fished inside his jacket pocket for his contact book, leafed through it until he found the number he was looking for, then dialled.

'*Daily Mirror*,' said an unfamiliar voice.

'Put me through to the news desk . . .'

There was a begrudging acceptance at the *Messenger* that Helen had done a good job. She had returned with quotes from the headmaster of Great Middleton School and woven them into an insightful news story about the mysterious body-in-the-field, which had shocked a village already reeling from the disappearance of one of its children. It would probably knock everything else off the next morning's front page. She was however left with the impression that she was no better thought of for any of this and that took much of the gloss from what should have been a big moment for her.

The passive hostility of the newspaper's older, male colleagues stopped her from telling them everything she knew about the body-in-the-field. If she wrote that the body was Sean Donnellan, Malcolm would have spiked it before a word had been written. He wasn't the type to idly speculate on the identity of a corpse before the police had come out with an official statement, so for now she decided to keep this information to herself.

When her working day was over, Helen quietly left the office and went straight to the Durham University library. Writing up her first front-page lead had forced her to postpone her time with Tom Carney and she was keen to make amends. She had some digging to do on the Sean Donnellan case.

'The thing about the quiz . . .' Andrew Foster was talking too loudly for a quiet residential street after kicking-out time, '. . . is that it makes you both a winner and a loser,'

'How do you mean?' asked Tom who was enjoying the combination of fresh air and a beer buzz.

'We won 'cos we knew all the history questions and the trivia; the films, the books, the songs and the sport, which makes us basically . . .' and he looked at Tom as if he were prompting one of his slower pupils to come up with the answer.

'Losers?' asked Tom and Andrew nodded emphatically. 'Aw, don't be like that. We just pissed off all the old buggers who've been winning the quiz week-in, week-out for donkey's years. We are the champions!' Tom roared those last words.

'Stop it, man,' Andrew was laughing, 'before people draw back their curtains and realise I teach their horrible kids.'

'What did you say?' shouted Tom.

'I said I teach their horrible kids!' and he cracked up laughing. Andrew sneaked a look around him at the lifeless streets and silent houses then he made a shushing noise and said, 'let's have a nightcap.'

'Where?'

'My house. It's on your way. Come on, you've nowt to get up for have you?'

'That's very true!' said Tom emphatically. 'Go on then. I'll have a small, sweet sherry.'

'You'll have vodka and like it.'

Helen had spent her evening at the library staring at ancient pages of the *Messenger*, dating back to 1936. It was pretty desperate stuff and she knew it, but she was hoping for anything that might relate to the disappearance of a young man in Great Middleton that summer.

Hours later, when her eyes had grown tired from the effort involved in endlessly staring at the blurred pages on the microfiche machine, she was about to give up. Helen had seen no reference to an Irish artist. Nor was there any reported quarrel, grievance, fight or assault in Great Middleton that might have led to a murder and she was beginning to feel foolish for even thinking there might have been, when something caught her eye.

Helen read the piece carefully and straightaway she knew it must have involved Sean in some way, even though he was not mentioned in the story by name. The date was around the time he was meant to have disappeared, so she took out her notebook and copied the small news item word for word.

Helen had left the library eager to share her discovery with Tom and was disappointed when she couldn't reach him at the Greyhound or on his reliably unreliable mobile phone, so instead she returned to her tiny home: a gloomy, one-bedroom, ground-floor flat in a crumbling part of town, whose rent she could only barely afford. She microwaved a rubbery lasagne then washed the taste away with two glasses of cheap white wine before finally heading for her bed.

'I love this movie,' Tom told him as they watched *The Godfather*, which was one of the videos from the school teacher's extensive collection. You could tell Andrew was single the moment he turned the key in his door. There wasn't a sign of a woman's touch anywhere. Instead there were plain wooden shelves filled with videos, some bought, some taped from the television onto blank cassettes with handwritten movie titles scrawled on them. The décor was pure teenage-boy-with-money, even though Andrew was in his mid-twenties. On the wall were two World War Two-era bayonets and Tom did a double take before realising they were the real thing. They took pride of place above Andrew's mantelpiece, just below the paintings of a Spitfire and an England rugby match. Andrew owned a turntable and a large collection of vinyl albums. There were car magazines on the rickety coffee table, along with a dog-eared, paperback copy of Frederick Forsyth's *Day of the Jackal*. An old bus ticket served as a bookmark. Andrew was a great guy but all any woman would see if she visited his home was a big kid locked in an adult male's body.

They were drunk enough to be sitting on the floor, with their backs against the couch and armchair respectively while they watched the film.

'Thanks Andrew,' said Tom, 'for taking my mind off stuff.'

'What stuff?' enquired the teacher.

'Oh, you know, problems.'

'You don't sound like a man who has too many problems, Tom.'

'Don't bet on it.'

'What have you got to worry about?'

'Not much,' and before he really knew what he was doing, Tom found himself telling Andrew all about his banishment from the paper and Timothy Grady's potentially ruinous lawsuit. He also explained that his master plan was to unearth a story big enough to convince his editor to keep him on but now the Doc wasn't even returning his calls.

'So you need a big story?' asked the teacher.

'Yes.'

'Have you got one?'

'No,' before adding, 'well, not yet.'

When he was done, the school teacher thought for a moment then said, 'well, it doesn't sound all that bad,'

'Really?' Tom was incredulous.

'No,' answered Andrew, 'actually it sounds awful. I'd say you're pretty much fucked.'

And for some reason that he couldn't quite explain, Tom started to laugh. The brutal honesty of Andrew's deadpan appraisal and the seriousness of his predicament hit him all at once and he laughed some more, Andrew started laughing too and pretty soon they were both in hysterics.

'Thanks for that, mate,'

'No problem,' spluttered Andrew, wiping his eyes, 'any time.'

'You should work for the Samaritans,' Tom told him and that set them both off again.

Chapter Thirty-Seven

Day Six

Detective Superintendent Trelawe reached his office at his customary early hour. He liked to get a head start on the paperwork before everybody else arrived. Trelawe went to place his briefcase on his desk then stopped as he realised there was something there already. A copy of a newspaper had been placed neatly on the desk so its occupier would see the front page as soon as he sat down. Trelawe paused then glanced suspiciously around his empty office, as if he expected the culprit to still be hiding somewhere. When he was satisfied this was not the case he took his seat then picked up the paper.

There, on the front page of the *Daily Mirror* was an exclusive story about the latest development in the hunt for the missing schoolgirl Michelle Summers, accompanied by the helpful headline, 'Psycho Hunter' and the strapline; 'Desperate Police Hire FBI Super-Shrink to Hunt Reaper.'

Trelawe read the article quickly, hoping for a positive angle, for it had been his personal decision to enlist the help of a proven forensic psychologist to help track this serial child abductor. He was to be disappointed.

The *Mirror* journalist Tom had called was an old acquaintance from the North East who, like him, had moved to the capital. He'd given Tom his number so they could meet for a pint some time. Paul Hill had listened with interest to Tom's story about Durham Constabulary's hiring of the professor and promised to call him back. One of the *Mirror*'s contacts, a detective in the force, corroborated Tom's claim and, twenty minutes later, Hill rang him at the Greyhound to buy the story, on the proviso that Tom's name would not appear on it, since he was still contracted to the rival newspaper that had suspended him. After waiting in vain for hours for the Doc to show an interest, the process had been remarkably straightforward. Hill even stated that it might make the front page, as it had been a slow news day.

Unfortunately for Trelawe, Paul Hill's editor decided the story was nowhere near spicy enough and he rewrote the whole thing till it became a scathing critique of a hapless police force that was so desperate it was shelling out taxpayers' money on an FBI shrink, using pseudo-scientific techniques as yet entirely unproven in the UK. The *Mirror* even paid a retired former Metropolitan Police detective of some standing to dismiss the new-fangled methods as 'completely bonkers'. The final nail in the coffin was the picture of Anthony Hopkins playing Hannibal Lecter that had been helpfully inserted next to the article, which made it look as if Trelawe, who was named in the story, had been influenced more by Hollywood than science in his choice of expert.

'Oh dear God,' muttered Trelawe, for he knew his day was about to go downhill rapidly.

Ian Bradshaw took a break from his latest door-to-door to buy some cigarettes. As he waited for his change, his eyes went to the rack of newspapers and, more specific-ally, the *Mirror's* front page lead. 'Jesus Christ,' he exclaimed when he saw what they had done.

'You all right?' asked the newsagent as he handed over the cigarettes.

Bradshaw snatched a copy of the newspaper and dropped some change onto the counter to pay for it before hastily leaving the shop without another word. A moment later he was sitting in his car, re-reading the art-icle for a second time to see if it got any better.

It didn't.

How the hell had the newspaper taken an innocuous piece of information like the recruitment of an FBI expert and twisted it into such a negative piece? Bradshaw knew that if this was traced back to him, he would be fin-ished. He was going to kill Tom Carney.

'Please tell Helen Norton that Tom called,' he told the receptionist at the *Durham Messenger* with his hand between his mouth and the receiver to disguise his voice, 'Miss Darlington's brother. I'm at the Rosewood café this morn-ing if she wants to stop by. Tell her I'm over the moon.'

The bemused receptionist took the message. Tom hung up his mobile phone and walked into the café with the papers under his arm. He ordered coffee and a double bacon sarnie then sat down, swallowed two ibuprofen for his hangover and turned his attention to that morning's headlines. He surveyed the front page of the *Daily Mirror* with grim satisfaction. He had just written his second front-page, lead story for a national tabloid but was happy that his name was nowhere to be seen on this one. Then he read the piece through and quickly realised it had changed a great deal since Paul Hill jotted it down. His thoughts immediately went to Detective Constable Bradshaw.

Ian Bradshaw was staring straight ahead, trying to make his face into a blank canvas as he listened to an increasingly irate DCI Kane.

'By now most of you will have seen the front page of a certain national newspaper,' Kane told the detectives at the morning briefing, this time without Trelawe, who was busy fielding press enquiries. 'Once again this force has been subject to ridicule. What pains me most is that the story must have come from somebody inside this room,' he paused to let that sink in before adding, 'and we will find the culprit, believe me.' He scrutinised them all carefully and Bradshaw found himself frowning at this act of treachery to try and avoid outward signs of a guilty conscience.

'If it was you,' Kane told them all, 'you'd better come and see me afterwards with a damned good explanation; do that and you might avoid crucifixion. If you don't, you'll be sorely wishing you had when we find you.'

Kane seemed to take their deep and heavy silence as comprehension and when the briefing was over, he took O'Brien and Skelton to one side. 'I reckon this is a job that's suited to your skills,' he told them, 'pull up some stones until you get me a name. The super's in the mood for a human sacrifice so you'd better find me one quick. Otherwise it's the Siberian gulag for me,' and he gave them a meaningful look, 'and you two won't be able to take a piss round here without getting Trelawe's permission in advance.'

'Leave it to us,' O'Brien assured him, 'we'll ask around, see who's been cosying up to journalists. You'll have that name in twenty-four hours.'

'I'm really sorry about yesterday,' Helen told Tom as she joined him at the cafe, 'I just couldn't get away.'

'I read your front-page lead,' he told her then he repeated the headline, 'Headmaster's Shock at Playing Fields Murder, by Helen Norton,' and he smiled at her.

'Thanks,' she said, without enthusiasm, 'that's why I couldn't meet you. I had to write it up.'

'You got Nelson to talk. Well done you.'

'Malcolm sent me down there expecting me to fail,' she admitted.

'But you didn't?' he reminded her and she nodded. 'And of course they were gracious and full of congratulations,' Tom added drily.

She didn't want to admit it: 'Not exactly.'

'Let me guess,' he said, 'Martin sulked, Brendan didn't believe you and good old Malcolm accused you of flashing your tits at him?'

It wasn't far from the truth. 'What Malcolm actually accused me of was using my feminine wiles on the headmaster, but you're close enough,'

'Malcolm must like you or perhaps he still hopes you'll go to bed with him because he is normally much cruder than that.'

Tom was right about that too. Helen had often overheard snippets of the conversation coming from the editor's office when his door was ajar. 'Tits' were a recurring theme, as was 'shagging' and 'cock teasers'. For variety, the senior editorial team liked to tell jokes about 'arse-bandits' as well. When Helen had been in the middle of her post-grad in journalism, this was not how she had envisaged her first newsroom.

'I don't think any of them actually like me,' she said.

'They are the ones with the problem. They don't like it when they're not the biggest heroes in the room, that's all.'

'It doesn't matter,' she said. 'I got my first front-page lead and we have a week till the next edition, which means I have time to work on more important things,' she said significantly, 'like this,' and she took out her notepad and handed it to Tom.

'Thieves plunder vicarage,' he read aloud then he looked up at her.

'From the university library,' she said, 'they've got all the old *Messenger*s on microfiche. This story is from 1936.'

He gave her a look that told her he was impressed then went back to reading. 'Desperate thieves forced their way into the vicarage at Great Middleton in the night, to steal a quantity of gold sovereign coins belonging to the Reverend Albert Riley. The criminal act took place Thursday 10th September while the reverend was absent. The money has not yet been recovered nor anyone detained by police.' Tom stopped reading and looked back up at Helen.

'It's too much of a coincidence, isn't it?' she asked.

'Gold sovereigns being stolen from Mary Collier's dad around the same time Sean Donnellan was murdered? I'd say so.'

'But what does it actually mean?' she seemed to be thinking aloud, 'are we thinking Sean stole them?'

'That's my assumption,' said Tom, 'he didn't have enough money to pay his rent, he was close to Mary.' 'Suppose she told him about the money or he found out somehow, then he helped himself?' He was speaking slowly, piecing it together in his mind. 'Somebody found out and . . .'

'They killed him?' she asked, 'Murdered by the vicar?' she offered flippantly.

'I know,' he said, 'and it's usually the butler.'

'I'm not sure this gets us much closer to the truth,' she said.

'I wouldn't say that,' Tom told her. 'You might just have found us our motive.'

Chapter Thirty-Eight

'The DCI's not happy with you,' announced O'Brien as he brought his lunch tray down hard on the table in front of Bradshaw's. Skelton joined O'Brien and they sat opposite Bradshaw, who looked about him. The canteen was almost empty so they had plenty of other seats to choose from. Vincent was still at the counter and didn't seem to have noticed the intrusion. More likely he was ignoring Bradshaw after his harsh comment in the corridor following their bollocking. Vincent kept his back to them as he waited for a fresh supply of treacle tart to be brought out from the kitchen.

'Really?' answered Bradshaw, 'and I thought he wanted me to marry his daughter.'

'Listen, Sherlock, we all know what you've been up to,' Skelton told him, 'so why don't you just admit it. Come clean and you'll get what you want . . . what we all want, in fact.'

'And what's that?'

'A ticket out of here,' O'Brien told him. 'There won't be a fuss, as long as you 'fess up but if you deny this and we prove it was you then you are for the high jump.'

'Really? Right, okay,' Bradshaw was nodding his head as he spoke. 'I heard someone pinched a Kit Kat from Trevor Wilson's lunch box the other day but I can assure you it wasn't me. I'm more of a Twix man myself, as you can see,' and he indicated the chocolate bar on his lunch tray.

'Someone has been leaking,' O'Brien informed him, 'and we've been asked to find the mole.'

Bradshaw merely blinked back at him, as if awaiting further information. 'What's it got to do with me?'

'That local lad, Tom Carney, the hack who went off to London then came back with his tail between his legs. It's him, isn't it? We've been checking him out and asking around. All it took was a couple of phone calls. We found out a lot about him, in fact.'

'Including who he drinks with,' added Skelton, before adding, 'QED.'

'Now, we are going to give you one last chance to admit what you did, Sherlock, and you can leave quietly,' O'Brien told him. 'After that, you are on your own.'

Bradshaw opened his mouth to say something in denial, then he stopped. It would be so easy. All he had to do was cop for it and he'd be off the stupid body-in-the-field case, out of the dead-wood squad and away from the force for-ever. There'd be no more grief from colleagues who despised him or hassle from senior officers who con-sidered him a liability. Perhaps he could find something more useful to do with his life. He could start again, maybe even go abroad, work in a bar, some place hot. All he had to do was admit it.

They were both watching him intently now. Waiting to see what he would do.

'School,' said Bradshaw simply.

'Eh?' asked Skelton uncomprehendingly.

'I know him from school,' Bradshaw explained reasonably. 'Tom Carney was in the year below me at my comprehensive,' he explained, 'or did your extensive enquiries not yield that bit of information? I hadn't seen him in years but we both happened to be in the Greyhound at the same time, along with a bunch of other journalists and coppers. He came up to say hello. I must have spoken to him for all of five minutes.'

There was a moment's pause while Bradshaw waited for their response. Inwardly he was holding his breath. He knew they were bluffing him with the offer to confess and leave without a fuss, which meant they merely suspected he was the mole but couldn't prove it. He in turn was bluffing them to see if they had anything more than a sighting of him drinking in the pub with Carney, which wouldn't be enough to damn him on its own.

When they didn't reply Bradshaw said, 'That all you've got? Good, now why you don't you piss off and leave me alone. Better yet, I'll piss off instead shall I? I'll eat my Twix in the car.'

He got to his feet and took his tray with him. As he made to go, Skelton said, 'This isn't over by a long way, Sherlock. You're history and you know it.'

Roddy placed a large roll of papers bound with string onto his kitchen table. 'I've got something for you,' he said, 'two things actually,' and he fished a scrap of paper from his pocket and unfolded it. 'I've been asking around about Mary Collier and her late husband Henry. There's not many left who remember him before he became headmaster but this fellah will.' He handed Tom the scrap of paper, which had the name Sam Armstrong written on it, along with a phone number.

'Who is he?' asked Tom.

'Remember Armstrong's farm at the end of the village?'

'Of course,' said Tom.

'He only sold up eight or nine years back. Tough as old boots, he was. I remember playing in his hay bales when we were kids and he chased us out of there, effing and blinding. I've never run so fast.' He was grinning at the memory.

'What's his connection with Henry Collier?' asked Tom before Roddy could be distracted by any more childhood reminiscences.

'Best friends when they were kids, by all accounts.'

'Are you sure about this, Roddy?'

Roddy looked hurt. 'I checked it out, man. I gave the old fellah a call and it's true. He confirmed it.'

'Blimey, what does he know about Henry then?'

'I didn't ask.'

'Eh? Why not?'

'I'm a historian not a reporter, that's your job. I'm just opening the door for you.'

'Will he see us?' asked Helen.

'He says so. Give him a ring. He only moved ten miles away.'

'Nice one, Roddy,' said Tom, 'you said there were two things?'

'Yes,' and Roddy slid the piece of string off the rolled-up papers and let them open so they were facing upwards then he flattened them down with his palms. The first sheet was a line drawing of the woods behind the river bank.

'Another one of Sean Donnellan's landscapes,' said Tom.

'It's good too,' observed Helen.

'Told you I'd find them,' said Roddy, as if it was never in doubt. 'A couple of these are unfinished. I guess he wasn't happy with them,' and he let them look at each of the half-dozen drawings in turn. There were four of the surrounding area but when he reached the last two drawings he placed the landscapes carefully on the floor so he could position the final pictures side by side. Both had the same subject; a very pretty young woman was gazing unsmilingly back at the artist. 'Good, aren't they?' said Roddy, adding, 'unfinished like the others, but a damn good likeness.'

'A likeness?' asked Tom.

Roddy regarded Tom as if he was missing something obvious then he smiled. 'You're a lot younger than me so you can't see it but that,' and he tapped the end of a finger against one of the pictures, 'looks a lot like a young Mary Collier.'

Tom peered at the drawing for a while then said, 'you're right, Roddy, it does.'

Helen, Tom and Roddy stood in silence for a moment, contemplating the drawing of the serious young girl Sean Donnellan had captured in a moment long ago, forever frozen in time.

Chapter Thirty-Nine

1936

'Ow.'

'Keep still then.'

'I am,' Mary assured her, 'ow.'

'You're all knots this morning,' Mrs Harris told her. 'What have you been doing in the night?'

'Nothing,' Mary flushed, 'sleeping.'

'In a thorn bush? I can barely get the brush through these rat's tails.'

'You are full of sweetness and light.'

'I hardly slept a wink last night. I envy you. You sleep the sleep of the innocent.'

'Ow!'

'You have to suffer to be beautiful.'

'Who said so?'

'My mother used to say it and she wasn't often wrong. There's a few in this village who should listen to their elders and betters if you ask me.' Mary knew Mrs Harris must have been building up to this, 'I've seen that Betty,' she said ominously, 'we've all seen her, even if she thinks we haven't, walking out with that Irishman.'

'Is that such a terrible thing?' asked Mary, 'for Betty to go for a walk with Mr Donnellan?'

'As long as that's all she's been doing, but tongues

wag in this village and people could see those walks as something they're not. A girl always has to be careful, particularly a silly little one, like Betty. Some men have a way with words and a woman can be swept away if she's not careful. Her reputation destroyed forever in a single day.'

'Why am I under the impression we are no longer talking about Betty? Is this because *I* go on long walks with Henry? You don't have to worry,' Mary assured her, 'he respects me.'

'I'm sure he does,' Mrs Harris answered stiffly, 'but men can't always control themselves, which is why a lady has to ensure . . .' She struggled to find the words.

'That her honour is never compromised?'

'You always say it better than me,' she admitted, 'which shows the value of your education, but I know what I'm talking about, so just you take heed.' She seemed to soften then. 'I know your Henry is a good man. He thinks the sun shines out of you and I expect you'll run him a merry dance when you're married.'

'I will not,' retorted Mary.

'Now, his elder brother on the other hand,' and Mrs Harris coughed, 'let's just say I wouldn't want to bump into him on my own on a dark night.'

Nor he you, thought Mary, before she immediately scolded herself for being unkind.

When Mary went for her walk that morning down No Name Lane, she found herself hoping to bump into Sean Donnellan again by the river. She found him there sure enough, bent over his work, but when he saw Mary he put it to one side and they talked of mundane things for a while. Then he said, 'I was about to stretch my legs. Will you walk with me for a time?'

'I don't think so.'

'Why? Would that be improper?'

'The whole village knows you are walking out with Betty.'

'Does it? I have walked with young Betty but I'm not walking out with her,' he told her.

'More fool her then,' answered Mary, 'for making it seem so.'

'Can a man not walk down a lane with a woman without getting betrothed at the end of it?'

'Not round here,' she said but it was not a reprimand, more an admission of the parochial outlook in her village.

'I'm not the right sort for a gal like Betty. She will never leave Great Middleton, nor even contemplate it,' Sean said, 'but I will leave, because there's a whole world out there that wants seeing and I intend to see it before I lose the light.'

'The light?' at first she thought this was an artist's term.

'Most people have a light inside them when they are young but it soon goes out.'

It was obvious she didn't understand him. He looked exasperated, because he hadn't explained himself well enough.

'I'm talking about hope, Mary and the way it has of dissolving, usually to be replaced by fear. Young people think anything's possible, God love them, then they go out into the real world for five minutes and they're cowed by what they see, by what they're told they must contend with.'

'What do you mean?'

'The need to make a living, put a roof over their head and food in their bellies, it takes over. The fear of starvation, of being put out on the street, replaces any dreams they might have once had, so they settle for less. It's a sad fact but true. How many people do you see who are living the lives they dreamed of when they were young?' he asked rhetorically, 'but I won't settle for less, Mary and nor should you. There's nothing for you here.'

And though they spoke no more that day and there was no physical contact between them, Mary would look back on the exchange and realise that was the moment when it all began.

Chapter Forty

Tom steered his car off the main road and into the lane, bringing it to a halt. Sam Armstrong's house was situated at the end of a long, rutted track at the top of a hill. It was steep, full of puddles from the rainstorm and slick with mud. Clearly Sam had not left the countryside entirely behind.

'I don't think my car is going to get us any closer,' he said and they looked at each other.

'We'll manage,' she told him, not wanting to turn back now.

They left the car where it was and climbed the hill. Within seconds their trousers were speckled with wet mud. As they walked, they were forced to tread carefully, to avoid the pools of water in the broken road surface. Halfway to the house Helen slipped and Tom instinctively shot out an arm to prevent her from falling.

'Thanks,' she said, 'not my most practical pair.' She took another tentative step but her shoe immediately slid again.

'Here,' he took her hand in his and they began a slow and unsteady trudge towards the house. The road grew steeper and they both nearly slipped several times. As they neared the top of the hill, Helen had to stifle the urge to giggle as she realised how it must have looked, the two of them walking along the road together holding hands like a couple of soppy teenagers.

Tom finally let go of her hand to bang on the door. Immediately a dog began to bark ferociously somewhere inside the house. 'I hope he's bloody in,' he muttered as he looked at their filthy shoes.

The door was opened by an old man with a heavily lined face and rough calloused hands from years of working outdoors. He looked them up and down and said by way of greeting, 'Roddy should have told you to bring your wellies, you're covered in clarts.'

Though not as cluttered as Roddy Moncur's place, Sam Armstrong's home also spoke of a solitary existence. Sam was a widower who didn't seem to have much interest in housework. He left Helen and Tom for a moment to silence his dog then returned and set about moving things so they could sit down. Several newspapers, a pile of clothes set aside for washing and some small, oily mechanical parts from an old machine he'd been tinkering with on a coffee table were all removed. The room was cold but he did not make use of the ancient paraffin heater in the corner.

The old man listened silently while they explained the purpose of their visit. 'Sean Donnellan,' he said slowly, 'until Roddy mentioned it, I hadn't heard that name in a long time. You reckon he's the bloke they dug out of Cappers Field?'

'We're not sure,' said Helen, 'but it looks likely.'

'I wouldn't be surprised,' said the old man placidly.

'What makes you say that?'

'That man had a knack of getting on the wrong side of people,' said Sam. 'He was cocky and had a way with words. The lasses round here hadn't heard anything like it before. They acted like he was a film star or summat and the blokes weren't too fond of that.'

'We heard Betty Turner fell for him,' said Tom.

'She wasn't the only one,' answered the farmer pointedly, as if he was waiting to hear what they knew before revealing more.

'Mary Collier too,' Helen stated.

'Aye, her an' all, and one or two more besides. Some were crafty about it, others hadn't got the sense. The whole village knew he was walking out with a few of them while he was there.'

'So Mary was just one of a number he was stringing along?' asked Tom.

The old man thought for a while as if he was trying to remember or perhaps he was choosing his words carefully. 'No, she was more than that. Whatever they got up to it was enough for her to turn her fiancé over, which caused quite a storm at the time. Not many in the village liked the Irishman for that; leading the vicar's daughter astray in a place as small as our village . . .' and he shook his head as if they wouldn't be able to sufficiently comprehend the seriousness of it back in those days.

'Sounds like you remember it pretty well?' asked Helen.

'I do,' said the farmer, 'Henry Collier was a good friend of mine. We used to go fishing together.'

'From what you're saying there'd be quite a few with a grievance against Sean Donnellan.'

'There was,' he agreed, 'but not many who'd kill him over it.'

'Who do you think did it then?' asked Helen.

'It could only have been one of two people,' said Sam, 'if you're asking me.'

Helen and Tom were both surprised by his certainty. 'We are asking you,' Tom told him, 'who do you reckon killed Sean?'

'Either Henry Collier,' he said his old friend's name quite calmly, 'or his brother Jack.'

Chapter Forty-One

Sam Armstrong had a story to tell but he decided he required a drink first. Tom turned him down because he was driving and Helen because she was no fan of whisky. Sam shuffled over to a rickety old wooden cabinet, which opened to reveal a half-drunk bottle of Bells and a small glass jug of cloudy water with a stopper in it. He poured himself a large measure of the whiskey and added the merest splash of water before retaking his seat and taking a sip.

'Henry Collier gambled everything on Mary,' he explained, 'his whole life really. We were just kids when she moved to Great Middleton with her da and she was a right proper princess even then, haughty and full of herself. I saw right through her but Henry didn't. He thought she was the best thing since sliced bread and so did she,' and he took a big sip of his whisky. 'He set his stall out to land her from day one, started studying like he was off to Oxford or something. Most of the other boys thought it was pointless. They were all going to end up in the mines anyhow, so why bother. All the young men in the village went there once they left school. I would have gone too if we hadn't had the farm. Don't get me wrong, farming's a tough life but it's better than the mine. At least the air is fresh and you're not underground worrying about the roof caving in on you all the time.'

'How did Henry avoid the mine?'

The farmer smiled ruefully. 'Got a scholarship, didn't he? Turns out he had a brain on him after all but it was her that encouraged him and her father who put a word in for him at the school. They were respected back then, you see; the vicar and headmaster, nobody questioned them, so if they thought Henry Collier was bright enough to teach the kids in the village that's just what happened. He started teaching the little ones at first, worked his way up to the bigger kids, till he finally became headmaster back in the fifties.'

'Tell me about this brother of his.'

'He had two brothers in point of fact; Jack and Stephen, Stephen was the middle brother but he was touched.'

'Sorry?' Helen asked uncomprehendingly.

The farmer tapped the side of his head with a finger. 'He was simple, not all there, born like that he was,' he said, as if this was Stephen's own fault somehow.

'What happened to him?' asked Helen.

'Carted off to Springton years ago.'

'Where's that?'

'It's the loony bin, pet,' explained the farmer. 'He was caught peeping and that was the last straw.'

'Peeping?'

'Looking in through windows,' Sam told her, 'watching lasses getting undressed for bed or in the bath. One day he got caught, got a good hiding from the girl's father and admitted he'd been doing it for years then they took him away.'

'When was this?' asked Tom.

'A few years after the war.'

'So he was still living with his family in 1936?' the farmer nodded. 'They closed that old place down a while back,' said Tom, 'I wonder if he's still alive.'

'Doubt it,' said the farmer, 'he'd be . . .' he did the sums in his head, '. . . about eighty. It's possible I suppose but not likely.'

'And Henry Collier let them take him?' asked Helen.

'Of course; he was a teacher who wanted to be head and Stephen was an embarrassment. You can't have the headmaster's brother peering in at lasses when they're in the nuddy, can you?' he spoke as if Stephen being institutionalised was the only sensible outcome.

'Did he ever hurt anybody?' she asked.

'Not seriously,' it was a reluctant admission, 'but he'd throw tantrums like a bairn and couldn't remember anything about them afterwards.'

'What exactly was wrong with him then?' asked Helen, hoping for a more specific diagnosis.

'I told you,' snapped the old man, 'he wasn't right in the head. He was harmless enough I suppose, apart from the peeping. I doubt he killed Sean Donnellan, if that's what you're asking. His older brother Jack was the dangerous one. *There* was a man you didn't mess with,' the farmer folded his arms, 'hardest bloke in the village.'

Tom's eyes narrowed, 'bet he had to prove that a few times.'

The farmer nodded. 'In a place full of miners? Oh yes, Jack Collier cracked a few heads before he proved himself cock of the north. There was nearly always a fight somewhere on a Saturday night and Jack was involved in more than a few. He was a soldier, see, trained and battle-hardened in the Great War, as hard as bloody nails. If you're wondering about someone who's capable of killing a man then look no further than Jack. He'd done it before.'

'He'd killed someone?' asked Helen in surprise.

'In the war,' Sam explained.

'So Jack Collier was hard as nails but every village has someone like that. Why would he have killed Sean Donnellan? He doesn't sound like the kind of bloke who would fight his brother's battles for him. Wouldn't he have told Henry to be a man and fight the Irishman himself?'

The farmer chuckled, 'He probably would have if Henry Collier had been a fighter but, I told you, he was a scholar. He and his older brother were as different as could be. There was more than fifteen years between them, for starters. I don't think anyone was more surprised by Henry than old Ma Collier. She'd already lost two babies then had Stephen, who came out all wrong, so God knows where Henry got his brains from but no,' he said, 'Henry Collier couldn't fight his way out of a wet paper bag.'

'But why would a battle-hardened war veteran give a damn about a young girl like Mary ditching his brother,' asked Tom, 'family pride?'

The farmer gave a sly smile. 'Maybe, but perhaps Henry Collier wasn't the only one who'd pinned all of his hopes on Mary.'

'How do you mean?'

'Jack Collier might have been a hard man but there was one thing that did frighten him.'

'What was that?'

'The mine; they used to say that's why he joined the army. He'd been a soldier in a war but he wasn't keen on being a miner. He was from a mining village though and left with two brothers to support when his mother and father died.'

'What did he do then?'

'Learned the blacksmith's trade. Hard to imagine it now that everybody's got a car, but every village had one once.'

'Could he make a living out of being a blacksmith?'

The old farmer nodded. 'At first, yes, there was all sorts needed doing. Pit ponies needed shoes,' he said by way of example, 'but as the years went by there wasn't as much demand for anything coming out of a forge. Jack wasn't daft. He could see it wasn't going to last but he was too young to give it up and too old to learn anything else.' He looked at Tom then. 'Do you see?'

'Do I see what?'

The old man sighed. 'If his brother does well, *he* does well. If Henry becomes the school teacher and marries the vicar's daughter, Jack gets a toe-hold in the village.'

'I don't understand,' said Helen.

'Work could be found, schools need repairs, maybe even a caretaker. A vicar had influence back then, he could have a word in someone's ear, make sure his son-in-law's brother didn't want for work.' He smiled. 'Have you ever heard of a vicar or a school teacher starving or being evicted?' he asked.

'So if his brother doesn't marry Mary,' said Helen, 'that all gets derailed?'

'It was worse than that,' explained old Sam, 'when Mary told Henry it was over he gave up.'

'Gave up what?' she asked.

'Everything,' he observed, 'it was like nothing mattered any more. I saw him once, out walking over the fields. He looked like someone who'd had a bereavement and I asked him, "Aren't you supposed to be teaching?" He just mumbled something and walked off like he barely knew me. This was my best friend,' he recalled, his face betraying how shocked he had been at the time, 'but I thought he was going to lose his mind with jealousy. Of course everyone reckoned the Irishman was tupping her by then.'

'So you really think Jack Collier killed Sean Donnellan because his brother losing the plot was ruining some master plan he had for their future?' asked Tom.

'You're a bright lad, a reporter; a miner's son so Roddy tells me, who bettered himself so he doesn't have to get his hands dirty like a working man. Good for you, I'm not knocking you for it but you've really got no idea how hard it was back then for a working-class lad like Henry Collier to drag himself up by his boot straps. It was a different world, man,' and his tone changed then as he began to recite, '"The rich man in his castle, the poor man at his gate, God made them high and lowly and ordered their estate."' He glanced at Tom meaningfully. 'Know where that's from?'

'"All things bright and beautiful",' answered Tom.

'That's right. They even told you in your bloody hymns that you were where you were because God intended it. You weren't supposed to change that but Henry Collier was bright enough and polite enough to do it without them even noticing or caring who he was when he started out. Even with two brothers like Jack and Stephen Collier he was accepted, because of that scholarship,' he told them, 'then Mary turned him over for a Mick and everything came crashing down.'

'Yet he ended up married to Mary in the end,' said Helen.

'He did,' acknowledged Sam, 'no bugger else would have her after Donnellan left her in the lurch.' And then he frowned, as if remembering that Sean Donnellan hadn't actually left anyone in the lurch because he was murdered. 'At least that's what everyone thought.'

'People thought Sean had done a moonlight flit and left Mary behind?' asked Tom.

Sam nodded. 'That's exactly what they thought.'

'Did they also think he'd stolen her father's money?'

'You two catch on quick, don't you? How did you hear about that then?' he must have noticed Helen straighten at this. 'That was you, was it pet? I should have known. You know what they say: if you want to get a secret out in the open; telephone, telegraph or tell a woman,' and Sam laughed until he started to cough and had to stifle his choking with another sip of whisky.

'He disappeared one day, along with her da's money. They reckon the vicar didn't trust banks, not so many did back then, if they went under you lost everything, so he had a box of gold coins instead. Police searched high and low for the Irishman but couldn't find him. They reckoned he robbed the vicarage then slipped on board a ship and got clean away. He convinced Mary Collier he was going to take her too but he was just after her father's money. Went to America, or so they said. He used to talk about going there.'

'Except he never left the village,' Helen reminded him.

'No, he didn't,' admitted the old man, 'he was murdered.'

'By Jack or Henry Collier,' said Tom, 'or so you reckon?'

'Who else would have done it?' asked the farmer, 'and since they are both long dead, we are never going to know, are we?'

'Probably not,' agreed Tom. 'When did Jack Collier die?'

'In the second war. He re-enlisted but never came back.' There was silence for a while then the old farmer said, 'I don't think there's much more I can tell you.'

There was a finality in that statement and Tom said, 'We'll leave you to it then.'

Sam went with them to the door and let them out. As they were about to leave, Tom turned back and asked, 'Was Jack Collier known for carrying a knife?'

'A knife?'

'Sean Donnellan was stabbed in the back.'

'He may have done,' said the farmer, 'he was a black-smith, probably carried all sorts on him, I don't know.'

'He was more likely to carry a lock knife than Henry,' Helen reasoned, 'a teacher wouldn't need one.' Tom noticed a change in Sam's face that was almost imperceptible.

'No, he wouldn't,' agreed Tom, 'but a fisherman might carry a lock knife, eh, Sam, and you told us Henry used to go fishing with you?' The farmer said nothing but the old man's eyes seemed to narrow just a little then.

Chapter Forty-Two

'Who do you think did it then?' asked Helen. She clung on to Tom's arm again, to avoid sliding down the hill. 'The soldier or the school teacher?'

'My money is on the soldier,' he said. 'Old Sam said it himself, Henry Collier wasn't a fighter.'

'It wasn't a fight. Sean was stabbed in the back.'

'I was only a bairn when our old headmaster died,' he said, 'but I seem to remember Henry Collier was a gentle sort of bloke.'

'Who was driven half mad with jealousy when he was a young man,' said Helen, 'and giving up on life because nothing mattered any more, according to his best friend. Does that not sound like a man capable of murder to you?'

'I don't know,' Tom admitted, 'but you seem pretty sure.'

'It's just . . .' and she sounded annoyed then, '. . . if Sam's right . . . even if it was his older brother and not him, Sean Donnellan died because of Henry Collier and his stupid jealousy.'

'True. The way Sam tells it, whichever brother stuck the knife in, he died for the same reason,' then he added, 'and they are both dead too now anyway.'

'Which means they got away with it.'

'You're taking this very personally,' he told her as they reached the car.

'Well, I'm angry. Aren't you? It might have been a very long time ago but Sean Donnellan was just a young man at the time and he was brutally murdered. He missed out on the life the Collier brothers enjoyed and all because a woman chose him over another man. That sort of thing happens all the time. It doesn't normally lead to murder.'

'Jack Collier didn't have that long to go and Henry Collier was in his fifties when he croaked.' He was doing up his seat belt and silently praying the car would start.

'Henry got thirty more years than Sean Donnellan,' she said indignantly, 'and Sean's only crime was to be popular with women.'

'It sounds to me as if he still is,' he told her but she didn't rise to it. To his relief the engine fired first time.

'I thought we were a team,' Bradshaw reminded him. Vincent Addison was literally on his knees but he looked up at his fellow detective constable and blinked at him. 'You and me, we were working well together, getting under the skin of that Denny.'

'Yeah,' agreed Vincent, 'we are,' but he immediately turned his attention back to the vending machine. Bradshaw watched as he put his hand under the flap at the foot of the machine then slid his arm through and bent it upwards in an attempt to retrieve the chocolate bar he'd paid for, which had somehow lodged itself between the metal coil that previously restrained it and the glass front of the machine.

'I've not seen you around for a couple of days.'

The chocolate bar they were both surveying seemed to hover now, against all laws of gravity, and Vincent tried to stretch his bulky arm up to reach it but Bradshaw could already tell it was beyond his clutches.

'You're not still sulking because I had a dig at you for not speaking up for us?' asked Bradshaw, 'because if you are . . .' He was about to defend his previous comment but before he could, Vincent shook his head.

'I'm not sulking,' he said quietly, 'I don't sulk.' Vincent stretched further and splayed his fingertips but it was no use.

'Well, what then?'

Vincent sighed deeply and withdrew his arm. He still wasn't looking at Bradshaw. Instead he forlornly regarded his lost chocolate bar, 'I'm just going through a bit of a tough time at the moment, that's all,' and Bradshaw could tell by Vincent's demeanour that he was a fellow sufferer. He should have spotted it sooner. It was partly the way he withdrew from conversations or seemed to retreat into a shell for protection when the top brass were tearing strips off him but it was also the way he carried himself, like he was a man of no consequence. Vincent often walked with his head down and looked at his shoes when he spoke to people, avoiding their eyes. You could tell he felt worthless most of the time.

'Keeping a low profile lately?' Bradshaw asked, 'is that it?'

'Yeah.'

'I like to do that too sometimes,' he assured the older man, 'but I could use your help, you know, when you're feeling better.'

'Sure,' Vincent looked up until he had eye contact, 'will do.'

'So we're okay?'

Vincent nodded, 'I've got to be getting home now though.'

'That's okay,' said Bradshaw, 'I've got get off now too. There's someone I need to have a word with,' and a deep frown of concentration crossed Bradshaw's brow then.

'What is it?' asked Vincent.

Without any warning, Bradshaw took a step closer and kicked out with great force. Vincent flinched as the younger man's boot shot past him then it connected hard with the metal plate where the money was fed into the vending machine. The machine absorbed the blow but it rocked alarmingly backwards until it hit the wall behind then almost immediately righted itself. As soon as it did so, the maverick chocolate bar was dislodged from the grip of the metal coil and slid serenely into the dispensing tray at the foot of the machine.

'You see,' Bradshaw smiled at Vincent, 'teamwork.'

As Tom emerged from the gents in the Red Lion, still zipping up his fly, Ian Bradshaw was waiting for him. He took a step towards Tom, seized the journalist by the throat and slammed him back against the wall.

'What the fuck?' he protested, the words distorted by the policeman's grip. He grabbed Bradshaw's wrist but the bigger man held firm.

'I've been looking for you!' snarled Bradshaw. 'I read that bloody piece in the *Mirror*!'

'It wasn't me,' Tom croaked and at the flicker of doubt in Bradshaw's eyes, he saw his chance to pull the detective's arm away. 'It's not my fault,' he said, rubbing his neck, 'they rewrote the bloody thing, to make it sound bad.'

'You're telling me they did,' Bradshaw was wild-eyed. 'My lot are after someone's guts for this.'

'I'm sorry. I'll make it up to you. I promise.'

'How?' demanded Bradshaw.

'I don't know yet,' said Tom, 'but I will. I owe you one Ian, all right?'

And Bradshaw gave him a look that said it most definitely wasn't all right.

'Everything okay, Tom?' asked Helen. Neither of them had heard her come up behind them, but now both men turned to find her watching them uncertainly.

'Everything's fine. This is DC Ian Bradshaw,' he told her, 'an old friend from school,' and he made a point of straightening his jacket, which had become creased when the police officer grabbed him. 'This is Helen Norton,' he told Bradshaw, 'the *Messenger*'s finest.'

'Pleased to meet you, Helen,' Bradshaw mumbled sheepishly. 'I've got to be off now though.'

When he had gone, Helen said, 'I could hear the shouting from the bar. What was that all about?'

'I upset him,' said Tom, 'inadvertently,' and he shook his head like it was of no importance. 'Come on, let's get a drink.'

DC Skelton and DS O'Brien watched the front door of the Red Lion with interest. They'd just seen Ian Bradshaw leave the place but their real target was still in there.

'He could be hours,' observed Skelton.

'Stop moaning,' O'Brien told him.

'He'll be chatting up that bit of skirt from the *Messen-*

ger,' sighed Skelton. 'All I'm saying is, it would be a lot warmer on the inside.'

'We're not going to carry out surveillance from the bloody bar,' O'Brien told him.

'Why not?' asked Skelton. 'He doesn't know what we look like.'

'He was on the *Messenger* for years. How many times have you testified in court with journalists in the gallery?' Skelton groaned at this, which O'Brien took as an admission that Tom was likely to recognise them from his court reporting days. 'Look, Kane needs a name and we ain't going to get Bradshaw to cop for it, so we have to go at it from another angle.'

'Well I hope he doesn't spend all night trying to get that posh bird into bed.'

'She's not the sort,' said O'Brien.

'How do you know?' asked Skelton.

'I can tell,' O'Brien replied, 'intuition,' and he tapped his finger against the side of his head.

'Fiver says you're wrong and he's knobbing her by the end of the evening.'

'You're on,' said O'Brien.

Chapter Forty-Three

'I've been meaning to apologise,' Helen told Tom when they were seated at a quiet table in the bar.

'What for?' he asked.

'I feel bad about that conversation we were having,' and the look he gave her showed he had no clue what she was referring to. 'You know, on people going missing,' she reminded him, 'and your mother.'

'Oh,' he said , 'I'm fine about it. It's no big deal.'

'What happened?' she asked then immediately her tone changed. 'No, it's none of my business.'

'I'm not defensive about it,' he said calmly. 'I think she probably had what is now known as postnatal depression but Nan just told me she couldn't cope; with kids I mean and life in general to be honest. My dad was working and earning and not drinking much back then. She had a home and two kids. Everybody figured she should be grateful for that but she just kept breaking down in tears all the time. I don't remember that much about it, or her. Then one day she dropped us with Nan and didn't come to collect us. She just upped and left.'

'That's awful.'

'My dad was an idiot basically and a sucker for lost causes. He married late, to a much younger woman. He was about thirty-five I think and she was twenty-three or something. It's a sizeable gap now; it must have been like the Persian Gulf back then. Obviously I wasn't around to see this but I heard what happened later. I sort of pieced it together from things he said, stuff my nan mentioned when she let her guard down or was feeling particularly bitter about my mother and things other folk said about her because they thought I was too young to understand.'

'Always the journalist, piecing together the story?' she noted.

'No one had ever seen her before. He just brought her home one day, said he'd met her at a dance and announced they were engaged. God knows how long he'd known her but, judging by how things panned out, I'd say it wasn't long.'

'A whirlwind romance was not the done thing round here?' she asked.

'Nooo,' he shook his head, 'you had to step out together for ages, endure endless teas on Sunday afternoons with aunts, uncles and all the cousins who got to run the rule over you to see if you were the right sort. She just appeared from nowhere, like she'd fallen from the skies, my nan used to say.'

'They didn't take to her then.'

'Maybe not but I reckon they'd have given her a chance.' He took another sip of his beer. 'She married my dad, got pregnant with my sister pretty much straight away and I arrived a couple of years later.'

'They must have been happy to begin with.'

He shrugged, 'Dunno,' and he said it like it was of no consequence.

'Did she leave a note?'

'Not really. She just wrote two words on a bit of paper and left it on the kitchen table for Dad to read.'

'Two words?'

'"I'm sorry".'

'And you never saw her again?'

He shook his head.

'Oh that's terrible, how old were you when she left?'

'Four.'

'Oh my God,' and he was struck by the look of genuine distress on her face.

'Hey, there's no need to cry about it, woman, it was nearly twenty-five years ago,' and she realised that the thought of the little boy he once was, being abandoned by his mother, had actually made her eyes water. She coughed and wiped them quickly.

'You must have been devastated,' she said.

'I'm sure I was very upset at the time but clearly I was better off without her.'

'What makes you say that?'

'Well, what kind of woman walks out on two kids aged six and four? The kind you don't need around when you're growing up, I'd say.' Tom shrugged. 'My sister and nan looked after me. My dad brought home the money. We did all right.'

'She must have been beside herself to leave you like that. I bet she thought about you all the time after she left.'

'How do you know what she was thinking?' he snapped, 'If she'd thought about us at any point she could have come back and seen us but she never bloody did.'

'No, you're right,' she said quickly, 'I didn't know her,

I'm sorry,' and she wanted to change the subject but couldn't think of anything to say.

Helen left shortly afterwards and Tom drank his pint then trudged wearily across the village. He was in a sour mood; annoyed at Helen, annoyed at himself for being annoyed at Helen and all over a woman he could only dimly remember. He didn't notice the car which sped past him as he walked.

When he reached the top of the hill, he realised two men were standing by the side of the road. One of them was leaning against a black Ford Sierra, the other standing on the path, blocking his way. As he drew nearer he was able to make them out more clearly. The one on the path straightened when he spotted Tom. It was clear they had been waiting for him. Tom had seen these men before and they didn't look happy.

Skelton held up his warrant card.

'Can I help you, officers?'

'Get in,' O'Brien told him, motioning towards the car that Skelton was leaning on.

'I don't think so.'

'Get in,' echoed Skelton, 'or we'll make it formal.'

'You're going to arrest me?' chided Tom, 'for walking down the street?'

O'Brien shrugged, 'Drunk and disorderly,'

'Get away. I've had three pints.'

'Attempting to drive a motor vehicle while under the influence of alcohol,' Skelton offered instead.

'Can you see a car?' Tom protested.

'Or how about we just skip straight to "assaulting a

police officer"? Would you prefer that?' asked Skelton. 'But mind you don't bump your head while you're climbing into the car.'

'Jesus, are you two for real?'

'Look, just get in and save us all a lot of bother, will you. We only want a word.' Skelton was in a bad mood, made worse by the fiver he'd been forced to hand over when they'd witnessed Helen leave the pub on her own.

'She looks pretty un-knobbed to me,' O'Brien had told him with a grin, then he'd held out a hand for his money.

Tom reluctantly walked towards the car and DC Skelton held open the rear passenger door. As Tom climbed in, he asked, 'Where are we going?'

The only answer he received was their presence as they joined him in the car. They didn't begin their questions until they had left the village. Tom began to feel uneasy. There were no houses here, just farmer's fields and he belatedly realised nobody had seen him climb into their car.

'What's this about?' asked Tom, trying not to sound concerned but once again his question was met with silence. Skelton increased speed and the car shot down the B road then abruptly took a sharp left turn linking it to another side road. Why weren't they using the main road that would bring them to the neighbouring town and police station? Instead, they were driving down a rural rat-run known only by the locals. The trees on the side of the road began to thicken and there were no lights overhead. The next time the car took a turning, the road became so small it didn't even have cat's eyes and there was only enough room for their car. Skelton was driving far too fast for oncoming traffic. Anything coming at them round the next bend would be forced off the road or it would hit them head on.

'Where are you taking me?' asked Tom.

'Shut up,' O'Brien told him.

There were more bends in the road until they finally reached a long open stretch of high ground with a flat section of land that was shielded by bushes. Skelton jerked the car to one side then slammed on the brakes. Tom was thrown sideways. He was about to protest when he realised that both police officers had turned and were now staring back at him from their front seats, looking as if they meant business, so he said nothing.

'Five miles,' said Skelton and though he was looking at Tom it seemed the comment was aimed at his detective sergeant.

'That ought to be enough,' confirmed O'Brien and Tom started to get a sick feeling in his stomach.

'What's this about?' he asked again, then he glanced around him to confirm his suspicion that they were in a completely isolated spot. A pregnant moon shone down on them and there was a light from the window of a distant farmhouse but that was the only sign of life.

'Your source,' answered Skelton.

Tom waited for further information and when none came he parroted back, 'My source?'

DS O'Brien nodded. 'The one who told you about Professor Burstow.'

'What do you mean?'

'That story didn't come from the man at the *Mirror*. We spoke to him and he denied it. He was even a bit pissed off he hadn't written it himself. We checked out the other journalists too. You are the only one who could have sold that story,' O'Brien told him, 'and the information must have come from a police officer.'

'You'd be surprised,' Tom tried to deflect them but he could see they weren't buying an alternative theory.

'Tell us who told you about the professor and you'll stay in our good books,' O'Brien told him.

'Yeah, right, I can see I'm in your good books. That's why you've driven me out into the middle of nowhere to scare me.'

'Frightened, are you?' asked Skelton. 'We haven't even started yet.'

Tom could tell that whatever rule book these detectives had been issued with, it had long since been discarded in favour of a results-are-all-that-matters approach. Had they been watching too much TV or were there always a significant minority like them in any police force, who just assumed rules were for other people? Right now Tom didn't care and he was certain of one thing. Whatever they did to him, he wasn't going to give them Ian Bradshaw's name.

'What are you going to do?' he asked them defiantly, 'beat me up? Plant some drugs on me? I'm not some striking miner or bolshie student with a placard. I'm a journalist working for the biggest newspaper in the country and I'll plaster you all over the front pages.'

'Hear that, Sarge?' Skelton smiled, 'I don't know about you, but I am quaking.'

'I told you we checked you out,' DS O'Brien said. 'You're not the only one with contacts. We know you are a probationer with a contract that hasn't got a prayer of being renewed. Is that why you sold your story to the *Mirror*? Don't suppose your current employers would be too chuffed to hear that.'

Tom's heart sank. He had been hoping he was dealing with two thick detectives who liked to throw their weight around but he'd underestimated these two.

'What story?' answered Tom. 'I sold nothing.'

'Your name wasn't on it but we know it was you,' O'Brien told him. 'The *Mirror* reporter up here is covering a court case. Every other journalist would want to give their own papers an exclusive. The only other possibility is that posh bird from the *Messenger*. She's bright enough to tap up one of our lot and fit enough to get him to spill but I can't see her risking her career this early and she hasn't got the contacts.'

'Which leaves you,' added Skelton. 'But you can't just go round paying police officers to leak information. We are looking for a missing girl here and you are harming our investigation.'

'I didn't pay anyone but I bet you've both taken back-handers from journalists before. Revealing that the police are being helped by a forensic psychologist is not going to prevent you from finding Michelle Summers or her killer. You have been using the media since this case began. We are your best chance of finding that young lass alive and you know it.'

'We've seen you drinking with Bradshaw,' Skelton said. 'You were with him tonight.'

'He's an old mate from school,' said Tom, 'and I barely exchanged three sentences with him tonight.' He was telling a version of the truth because it was easier to stick to if they kept on interrogating him. 'I don't have a source in Durham Constabulary but if I did, I wouldn't be naming him, particularly to bent coppers who threaten me.'

Skelton's face set into a snarl but O'Brien simply asked Tom, 'Is that your final word?'

'Yes,' he said it with more conviction than he was feeling.

'Get out of the car,' O'Brien ordered and when Tom didn't move, he repeated it slowly and more menacingly, 'Get . . . out . . . of . . . the car!'

Tom reluctantly complied. He opened the door and stepped out onto the grass verge by the side of the road, readying himself for the beating.

The two detectives got out of the car as well. Skelton put a firm grip on Tom's arm and pulled him out in front of it, leading him a few yards from the vehicle then spinning him round so he was facing the headlights, which had been set to full beam so that Tom was dazzled by them. Tom held a hand up to his eyes to block the light and Skelton retreated. Tom could just make out two shadowy figures either side of the car.

'Last chance,' DS O'Brien told him. 'Name your source and we forget all about this. Nobody gets to know that you told us; Scout's honour.'

'It's either that or you don't come back at all,' DC Skelton told him and there was something so chilling in those words that, for the first time, Tom started to feel that these two out-of-control police officers might actually be seriously thinking about killing him.

'Fuck off,' he managed weakly.

'Suit yourself,' Skelton told him and there was a change in the light as Skelton moved away from the car. Tom was completely dazzled by the headlamps and he braced himself for the first blow. When that did not immediately happen, Tom blinked at the car. He could no longer see either man. A moment later, he heard a door slam and then another. He listened as the car's engine started and got ready to run before they could mow him down then the headlights spun in an arc as the car reversed at speed. Tom watched dumbly as the car completed a perfect three-point-turn until it was facing back the way they had come. He watched in disbelief as the car abruptly drove away, leaving him standing there in the middle of nowhere.

'You are kidding me,' he said to himself and he finally realised the significance of Skelton's comment. 'Five miles,' he repeated idiotically.

Tom watched the rear lights of the car until it rounded a bend then disappeared. He waited to see if they were bluffing but soon realised they were not and he faced a very long walk back to Great Middleton.

Chapter Forty-Four

Day Seven

Tom stifled a yawn as Roddy scanned his notes for the relevant passage. Helen and Tom sat in silence, waiting for him. Helen felt sure Tom was avoiding her eye.

True to his word, Roddy had been ringing round and asking questions. He'd called them both that morning and arranged for them to drop by but now seemed to be having trouble locating the information he'd promised.

'Here we are,' he said finally, tapping his notes with a Biro, 'Jack Collier re-enlisted in his old outfit, the Durham Light Infantry, in 1937,' Roddy told them, 'they've a record of the date,' and he looked at them both significantly, 'about six months after Sean Donnellan disappeared.' Then he corrected himself, 'was killed I mean.'

'Why would he re-enlist if his brother was back with Mary,' asked Helen. 'From what Sam said, Jack's problems should have been solved?'

'Guilty conscience,' answered Tom, as if it was obvious, and his tone irked her.

'Who knows,' answered Roddy. 'Jack was part of the British Expeditionary Force that fought a rearguard action in Dunkirk in 1940. More than three hundred thousand soldiers were rescued from that beach. Jack Collier wasn't one of them.'

'To think he survived all that combat in World War One and came home for twenty years only to be killed in another bloody war,' observed Tom.

'His luck finally ran out,' agreed Roddy.

'So he didn't get away with it,' he said pointedly to Helen.

'And the younger brother; Stephen?' Helen asked, ignoring Tom.

'Dead too, I'm afraid.'

'I was hoping there was someone left alive who might know the truth about all this apart from old Mary Collier,' Tom said, 'because we won't get it from her.'

'We might,' protested Helen, 'if we can show her we know more than she thinks,' and she turned to Roddy. 'What happened to Stephen Collier?'

'Like Sam said, Stephen was institutionalised,' and he let the tip of the Biro float above his words until he found the necessary passage. 'In 1951 he was taken to Springton.' He put down his pen and looked at Helen. 'It wasn't far from here. When Stephen was taken there it was officially known as the mental asylum. I'm ashamed to say that when I was a kid we called it the loony bin. By the time it closed, about ten years ago now, it was a psychiatric hospital.' He smiled grimly. 'Progress of sorts, I suppose.'

'And Stephen died there?' Helen asked.

'I phoned someone who works at the council office in Durham where they keep all the old patient records,' said Roddy, 'nice lady, a bit of an amateur historian like myself, goes to the same meetings,' Tom resisted the temptation to drum his fingers on the table in impatience. He always wanted to edit Roddy's conversation to get him to come to the point. 'She called me back later,' continued Roddy, 'and said that Stephen was there right up until the end.'

'So who looked after him between Jack Collier re-enlisting and Stephen being carted off to Springton?' asked Tom. 'That's fourteen years. Did Henry take him in when he married Mary?'

'Must have done. He had nobody else.'

'What a sad way to end your life,' said Helen, 'in a place like that. What was actually wrong with him?'

Roddy shrugged. 'Back then they weren't too big on detail; nerves, probably.'

'Nerves?'

'It's a euphemism,' explained Tom, his tone impatient, 'a catch-all people used when they were trying to be delicate. They didn't like to talk about illness or disability when Stephen Collier was a lad.'

'Exactly, nerves was used to describe any one of a large number of ailments; from acute shell shock to hysteria, anxiety or postnatal depression,' explained Roddy, 'and a hundred other conditions that might fall under what we might now think of as a mental disorder. People didn't understand those things very well back then, so if somebody went off the rails they were pretty much considered barmy and put away. This was the dark ages. Between the wars they even locked up lasses for having sex before marriage.' His eyes gleamed mischievously. 'Imagine that now. There'd be no one left in the village.'

'There was a stigma attached to mental illness,' said Tom, 'the people affected were an embarrassment.'

'And they call it the good old days,' said Helen.

*

306

'I've got to go back to the office,' she told him when they left Roddy.

'Right,' he said, opening his car door.

'But I can meet again later if you like?'

'Sure.'

'What's the matter?'

'Nothing.'

'I thought only women were supposed to do that?' she frowned at him.

'Do what?'

'Pretend things were okay when they're not.'

'I don't get you.'

'I'm sorry if I upset you yesterday,' she said. 'You were right, I don't know a thing about your mother. I shouldn't have said anything.'

'Oh that,' and he shook his head as if he had already forgotten about it. 'It's nowt.'

'Then why wouldn't you look at me in there?' she asked. 'You were like a bear with a sore head every time I opened my mouth.'

'Oh come on,' he protested then he realised she had a point. 'Sorry,' he said. 'I didn't get much sleep last night,' the memory of the five-mile walk back to Great Middleton in the dark still rankled, 'and I'm under a lot of pressure right now.'

'All right,' she said, his apology calming her. 'Well, if you ever want to talk about it.'

'Why would I want to do that?' he was mock incredulous. 'I'm a Northern bloke, we don't talk about our problems, ever.'

'Sorry,' she said, 'must have slipped my mind.'

*

From his vantage point on the higher ground he could see right into the playground without even leaving his car but he wasn't interested in the horrible older kids, the ones who leaned against walls or play fought with each other on their way to smoke behind the rows of garages at the opposite end of the school. It was the young ones that interested him, only the girls; the little angels who still smiled sweetly and were without cynicism or manipulating ways, the ones who hadn't changed yet. He so badly wanted to save them.

His window was open and he could hear their laughter and squeals even from here. He looked down at the matchstick figures far below him with a sense of great sadness and he wanted to weep, for he knew two things. He would never be able to save them all and this couldn't go on much longer.

He'd almost been caught and the shock and sudden realisation of how close he had come to ruin had thrown him. He knew he could do one more, perhaps two or even three but eventually the net would tighten. Something would go wrong and he would be taken.

Perhaps he could just stop and then maybe then they would never find him. He could run away, go so far that nobody would ever imagine he could be the one they called The Reaper. It was an intoxicating thought. But no, who would do God's will then?

He knew what he had to do. St Augustine had told him, *'Pray as though everything depended on God. Work as though everything depended on you.'*

Helen spent the afternoon talking to a monosyllabic youngster who had just won a regional piano contest then went straight to an interview with the council's new Chief Executive for a profile piece in the *Messenger*'s so-called business pages. She arrived at the Greyhound that evening before Tom was down from his room. There was a rough-looking bunch standing at the bar and one of the men scowled at her. Frankie Turner must have belatedly realised Helen had conned him. Either Betty gave the game away the moment she left their house or he'd actually bought the local paper hoping to be in it and seen nothing there about hard-working families.

Helen quickly ordered a drink and sat down in a quiet corner. Tom didn't keep her waiting long but she could feel the atmosphere change slightly as he walked into the bar. There was a tangible sense that something had been brewing here. Some of the men had obviously been discussing them both.

Tom nodded at her and pointed to her drink. She shook her head, having barely started the one she'd ordered. When he ordered his own drink, Frankie Turner straightened and when he spoke, the words were loud enough for everyone in the room to hear.

'Your bird's over there.'

'Thanks,' replied Tom with a smile that said he wasn't taking the man seriously, 'but I've only got eyes for you, Frankie.'

Helen was immediately afraid he had gone too far. She wasn't surprised when Frankie didn't let it go. 'I'm surprised at you Colin, serving him.'

'How'd you mean like?' asked the landlord.

'Thought you said you were going to bar all of them journalists,' he said, while the landlord pulled Tom a pint, 'you said they were parasites, come to dance on a little girl's grave. That *is* what you said?' he reminded Colin.

'Aye, well, I wasn't meaning Tom,' the landlord replied, 'we've known him for years man.' Other drinkers were openly watching now.

'They're all the fucking same. He's not even with the local paper any more. I wouldn't use the one he works for to wipe my own arse.'

'You've started wiping your arse have you, Frankie?' asked Tom calmly. 'When was that then?'

There were one or two uncertain laughs from corners of the room but they stopped when they saw the look on Frankie's face. The big man took a step forwards. Tom picked up his pint and took another sip, a picture of steadied calm. Helen's heart was in her mouth, expecting him to be viciously assaulted at any moment.

'The *Messenger*'s a pile of shite,' Frankie told everyone in the bar, 'but it's nowhere near as bad as that lying Cockney rag he works for.'

'You didn't think the *Messenger* was shite when you won the leek show did you?' said Tom and Colin smiled knowingly. 'I've never seen anyone so chuffed to get his picture in the paper.'

'Fuck off, I never . . .' but Frankie Turner was already blushing at the memory.

'As soon as Johnny Patcham got his camera out, Frankie here was stood to attention next to a table piled high with his prizewinning leeks and onions. His shirt was so new it still had creases in the front and he'd even combed his hair, do you remember, Colin?'

'Aye, I do as a matter of fact,' the landlord smiled at the memory.

Frankie wasn't liking this one bit. There was a definite shifting of the balance of power; people were openly grinning at Tom's recollections. '"Make sure you get me onions in the picture, perhaps I could hold one of them up",' Tom mimicked.

'That's shite,' hissed Frankie.

'You remember Johnny Patcham, don't you, lads?' There was a murmur of agreement from the men. 'Five foot four in his stocking feet but he took one look at Frankie here and said, "Now listen here bonny lad I'm the photographer, not you, so we'll do it my way or not at all."' Tom pointed at the humiliated Frankie and said, 'And this dizzy twat just looked dumbstruck and said "Okay, mate."'

Frankie looked round to see everybody laughing at him, even his own mates; especially his own mates. The man seemed to shrink visibly in front of Helen, all the threat gone from him.

'Fuck off, the lot of you!' And he marched out of the pub to loud ironic cheers, leaving his half-drunk pint on the bar.

'You took a risk,' Helen told Tom when he sat down opposite her, 'not that you were even aware of it. You were as cool as a bloody cucumber.'

He regarded her oddly. 'No I wasn't,' he told her with a frown. 'I was bricking it. I thought Frankie was going to glass me. He's not a nice man, you know.'

'But you looked so calm.'

'Outwardly,' he told her simply, taking another big swig of his beer, 'inwardly, no,' and he grinned at her.

She opened her mouth to answer but any words she might have uttered were drowned out abruptly by an ear-splitting din from the opposite end of the bar. A man in his mid-thirties was clutching a microphone and staring determinedly at a screen mounted on a nearby wall as words began to scroll along it to the accompaniment of very loud music.

'Bloody karaoke,' shouted Tom, so she could just about hear him, 'it's everywhere these days. Whatever happened to coming to a pub for a quiet pint and a chat?' he added, sounding like an old man for a moment.

The singer was already destroying Neil Diamond's, 'Sweet Caroline' and as soon as *hands* started *touching hands*, Tom called to Helen, 'Come on!' and he rose from his seat, 'bring your drink!'

Chapter Forty-Five

They sat on the floor with their backs against the end of his bed. They'd been going over everything they'd learned about Sean Donnellan and his murder before moving to the disappearance of Michelle Summers and the previous victims of the Kiddy-Catcher.

'We're going round in circles,' Helen admitted eventually. 'There's nothing new, is there?' And when he didn't immediately reply, she asked, 'What is it?'

'I've been thinking about your theory on why the girls go with him.'

'Oh that,' she said, 'I could be very wide of the mark there.'

'And you might be bang on. It could be a woman who lures them to him – but I did have another thought.'

'I'm sure I'd prefer it, no matter what it is.'

'I got into a stranger's car recently,' he told her, 'but only because they flashed a badge at me. They were police, but what if they hadn't been?' And he turned to look at her. 'What if you were an eleven-year-old girl and a man with a fake ID told you he was a police officer and you had to get into his car?'

Helen looked at him intently, 'I'd get in,' she said finally.

Tom nodded, 'I think you would.'

Suddenly the volume of the music downstairs shot up. 'Bloody hell,' he said.

'Good luck getting to sleep with that racket.'

'I'll be all right if Colin doesn't have a lock-in.'

The unmistakable chorus of 'Delilah' could clearly be heard, even though it was muffled by the carpet and floorboards.

'I'd buy you another drink,' he told her, 'but someone's murdering Tom Jones down there.'

'I'm fine,' she said, 'I've got to drive back anyway and it's a school night, though I don't know how I'm able to look Malcolm in the eye now that I know about his little . . .'

'Side-line?' and he smiled. 'Don't worry about it. It'll all be forgotten in a day or so. No one takes Malcolm seriously.'

'I have to. It's all right for you.'

'Is it?'

'Yeah, I'm just starting out but you've already made it. You're in the big leagues.'

'Not quite.' Tom wasn't sure he wanted to be having this conversation because he found to his surprise that he actually cared what she thought of him.

Helen carried on as if she hadn't heard him, 'Whereas I've been doing this for five minutes and my name is already mud at the *Messenger*.'

'Only because you caught your editor up to no good.'

'It's not just that,' she admitted. 'Most of the time I don't feel like I know what I'm doing.'

'I used to feel exactly the same way,' he assured her, 'still do most of the time. Everybody does. They just act like they don't.'

'But you *do* know what you are doing,' she argued.

'Not always and only because I've been round the block a few times. I'm a bit older than you.'

'Only about five years older,' countered Helen, 'and that's not much. You're hardly the grizzled old veteran.'

'Reporter years are like dog years,' he assured her, 'five years in journalism is a lifetime. Look, don't worry about Malcolm. I reckon you're off to a flying start.'

'So you don't think I'm a soft, southern princess, living off my parents' money till I can slope off to get married and have babies.'

'No,' he told her emphatically.

'That's funny,' she replied, 'everybody else does.'

'No, they don't,' he informed her, 'they're just unsure of you, that's all.'

'Either way, it's not working out the way I expected.'

'It will,' he said, 'give it time. You're bloody good,' and then he added, 'and I ought to know.'

She smiled. 'Why, because you're bloody good too?'

'Exactly,' and he grinned at her.

'Then maybe, in five years' time, I'll be doing as well as you.' And he sighed and got quickly to his feet. 'What's the matter? What did I say?'

He was planning to lie to her but instead, for the second time since he'd arrived back in Great Middleton, Tom felt he could trust someone enough to reveal the truth. 'Things aren't going that well.'

'You're working for the biggest newspaper in the country.'

'No,' he told her, 'I'm *suspended* from the biggest newspaper in the country.'

'But I thought . . .'

'I'm not broadcasting the fact.' And she listened while he told her the whole sad story of Timothy Grady and the hookers, the barrister wife and her threats of litigation then about the Doc and what he was likely to do about it all.

When he'd finally finished Helen must have felt pressure to offer him a crumb of comfort. 'You're still young,' was all she could manage, 'you can bounce back.'

'I'm pushing thirty.'

'You're twenty-eight.'

'*That's* pushing thirty,' he informed her, 'anything north of twenty-five is pushing thirty.'

'What'll you do?'

'I haven't the faintest idea. This is all I've ever wanted to do. I mean I knew it wouldn't be easy and I know that editors sometimes lie or do stuff that's morally dodgy, I'm not naïve, Helen, but I believe that newspapers are a good thing, on the whole. I really do. Without them, rich and powerful people would do whatever they wanted, completely unchecked by a government that doesn't give a damn. We expose those people, hold them up for censure. Look at Grady. There have been rumours about that bloke for years. He's one of those people that everybody knows is bent but no one can quite prove it. There are business men, celebrities, football managers and politicians like that who all have the whiff of corruption about them. If we didn't keep at them until we've uncovered something dirty then they'd just continue to ignore the rules and trample on everybody.'

'You're still an angry young man then?' she said but not without kindness.

'If you lose the anger, what have you got left? You end up like Malcolm.'

She got to her feet then and regarded him carefully. 'What?' he asked.

'He's not fine with it,' she said suddenly, 'the journalism.' She looked tense. 'My boyfriend Peter, I mean,' she shrugged, 'since we are sharing.'

'Why not?' he asked her. 'What's wrong with being a reporter?'

'It's not the actual job. It's me being away and the possibility I might never get back, if I get opportunities elsewhere, if I choose to take them,' she added as if that might still be open to doubt. 'I think he worries about that. I reckon he'd be fine if I was working for his local paper.'

'Right,' he said, 'long-distance relationships can be tricky.'

'Don't say it like that.'

'Like what?'

'Like we're doomed or something.'

'I didn't,' he protested.

'He isn't horrible to me or anything, he's lovely most of the time. It's just . . .'

'Just what?'

'I sometimes think he wants me to get this out of my system then come home.'

'Oh,' he said.

'What does "oh" mean?' she asked suspiciously.

'It just means "oh",' he said, 'I didn't dare say anything really controversial like "long-distance relationships can be tricky".'

'Sorry,' she said, 'I didn't mean to be . . . I'm just a bit . . . it's difficult sometimes . . . I get so . . .' and she let out a noise that was an exasperated groan.

'I understand,' Tom told her.

'You do?'

'Yeah?' he assured her, 'I'm not fluent in *woman* but I speak just enough of it to get by.'

'Cheeky sod.'

'You're not the first to say that,' he admitted cheerfully, 'come on, I'll walk you to your car.'

'It's all right, you know,' she said, as they left the Greyhound together, 'I'll be fine.'

'It's late,' he reminded her, 'and there are some unpleasant people in this village.'

The high street in front of the Greyhound was a double yellow zone, so Helen had been forced to park a couple of streets away. When they reached her car she said, 'Thanks and I promise I won't tell anyone what we talked about,'

'You sure?' he smiled. 'It would get you back in Malcolm's good books. He'd love it.'

'I think I can resist the temptation,' she assured him, 'and don't give up. I know it's really tough right now, but it's often when life is at its lowest ebb that things suddenly start to take a turn for the better.'

'Thanks,' he said and she kissed him on the cheek, lingering there for just a second. Tom put his arm out and placed his hand on her waist. She glanced down but didn't move from him and when her head came back up again he leaned in and kissed her.

Helen did not push him away or fight him off, she allowed the kiss to happen, even returned his kiss, but suddenly it was as if a spell had been broken. Helen broke free from him and took a step back. 'What are you doing?' There was hurt and confusion on her face and he was shocked by it.

'I thought that . . .' but he already knew no words could dig him out of this one.

'I have a boyfriend!' she insisted, as if they had not just been talking about the idiot. 'I thought you . . .' And she shook her head angrily as if to clear it. 'Unbelievable . . . just unbelievable.'

Helen climbed into her car, slammed the door and drove off.

'Oh shit,' he said as he watched her go, knowing that he had just ruined everything but still clinging to the not-entirely-certain notion that she had kissed him back. He was sure she had kissed him back.

As he ambled back to the Greyhound, he caught himself absentmindedly putting a hand up to his lips. 'Idiot,' he cursed himself for that and the kiss that preceded it.

The wind was up, bending the branches of the trees at the edge of the common and rustling the leaves noisily, so he didn't hear the footsteps until the man was almost upon him. Tom managed a half turn but wasn't quick enough. The blow to the back of the head was delivered with such force it sent him sprawling forwards. He barely had time to put his hands out in front of him before crashing onto the concrete. Tom's palms took some of the force of his landing and he fell sideways on impact, with a searing pain in his head and a sick feeling in his stomach. Before he could pick himself up a boot went into his side, knocking the wind from him, leaving him sprawled helplessly on the pavement.

'Fucking bastard!' shouted Frankie Turner and there was another furious kick from the man he had humiliated. As the pain moved from his stomach to his ribs with the new impact, Tom was dimly aware that Frankie must have waited outside in the cold all this time, hoping he would leave the pub, which told him everything he needed to know about the man's fury.

'Don't you ever . . . take the piss out of me,' Frankie hissed, kicking Tom every few words, 'else I'll kill you . . . got that!'

For Tom, the fight had been over before it had even begun. This was not about having the will or the courage to fight back, he couldn't even get up. All he could do was use his arms to try to defend himself against the kicks while Frankie railed at him.

Then Frankie landed a kick right on the end of Tom's chin and the blow almost knocked him unconscious, ending his ability to even put his hands up. Frankie wasn't finished. 'You're leaving tomorrow. If you don't, you'll get more of this,' then he stamped hard on Tom's hand.

Frankie spat on the floor inches from Tom's head and walked away muttering to himself, 'Fucking mess with me, you little prick.'

It was minutes before Tom felt able to roll onto his

front then gingerly press down onto the concrete path with his undamaged hand, so he could push against it and attempt to haul himself to his feet. Everything hurt; his head, ribs, stomach, both legs and arms and especially his hand. There was sheer hatred in Frankie's blows and the man's retribution had been thorough.

Chapter Forty-Six

Day Eight

Tom woke in his room at the Greyhound the next morning. As he opened his eyes the memory of the one-sided fight with Frankie immediately came back to him, along with the pain, and he groaned. Every bit of him ached. The next thing he recalled was Frankie's threat: leave town or face another beating. As if he didn't have enough problems already. What was it Helen had said to him just before it, about life often getting better when you were at your lowest ebb? Surely his ebb couldn't get any lower than this.

He thought of Helen then and their aborted kiss. What had he been thinking? He'd probably blown it with her too. Was there no end to his troubles? He climbed out of bed, gingerly surveyed the vivid bruises on his torso in the mirror then turned on the television to catch the news. With typical bad luck, the first voice he heard was Timothy Grady's.

'I met with the Prime Minister this morning to tender my resignation from the cabinet,' he told a reporter standing outside the Palace of Westminster. 'I did this to prevent any distraction to the business of government. The Prime Minister reluctantly accepted my resignation but agreed with me that, until this matter has been satisfactorily resolved, I will be unable to devote myself fully to my ministerial position. The Prime Minister has made it clear that I continue to enjoy his full confidence and he has not ruled out an immediate return to government. That is all.' And Grady walked briskly away from the camera, ignoring the questions that followed him.

Tom grabbed the mobile phone and jabbed at the buttons. It rang first time for once.

'Hello,' Terry sounded preoccupied.

'It's Tom, I've just seen that Tory wanker on the TV.'

'Just a minute,' and there was silence for a moment while Terry presumably turned away from his colleagues, 'everyone has been watching it here too,'

'So he's gone from a position of "I will never resign" to one of "I am quitting to clear my name"; bloody marvellous!'

'Not for us it isn't.'

'Doesn't it show that nothing he says can be trusted?'

'Well no, he didn't want to go. He's been forced out by the PM.'

'Obviously,' said Tom, 'we've made him an embarrassment to his own government.'

'And that's exactly why it's so serious, Tom.' Terry sounded agitated. 'Don't you get it? If he wins his case against us, they'll say we ruined a previously unblemished political career and he will take us to the cleaners. This is a guy who could have been Prime Minister before we stuck our size nines into him. How do you put a price on that?'

'I don't believe this. The man sleeps with hookers then pulls up his trousers and goes off to make speeches about family values. Nobody has been more vocal about the harm single mums are doing to society.'

'With the possible exception of us,' Terry reminded him.

Tom ignored this, his anger at Grady rising, 'have we forgotten what makes it a story? Nobody cares if Joe Bloggs shags a prostitute but this is a government minister who's been telling us how we should be living our lives, the fucking hypocrite.'

'No one has forgotten that, Tom. We're just worried that's all, you know, about our futures, if the newspaper goes bust or most of us are sacked, trivial things like that. Can't you for once put yourself in our shoes? If he wins, everybody is fucked.'

'Well he won't win. A jury will see right through him.' Tom was expecting further argument from Terry but strangely there was silence on the end of the line. Tom started to wonder if he had lost the connection. 'Hello?' he prompted.

'We can't run that risk,' Terry's voice was calmer now and that was more chilling somehow.

'What do you mean by that?' there was another long pause, 'what do you mean by that, Terry?'

Terry sighed, 'the Doc is going to settle.'

'He's actually going to pay the man? You are not serious?'

'A sizeable damages pay-out, a very large retraction and an apology in a prominent position, maybe even the front page then perhaps all of this will go away,'

Tom couldn't believe what he was hearing. 'This can't be happening.'

'All we have is some photographs that show Grady

emerging from an apartment block on the same evening as a prostitute. That's not much. MPs stay overnight when they are working late.'

'He's MP for Kensington for God's sake. He's got a townhouse there.'

'But his main home is out in the country, he has an apartment and he stays in hotels as well.'

'The apartment isn't any closer to the House of Commons than his town house,' protested Tom. 'He uses it for his shags.'

'It doesn't matter as long as he has friends to corroborate it if he says he has meetings. His lawyers are claiming he's been canvassing support for his re-election campaign.'

'That's bollocks. Grady has one of the biggest majorities in the House of Commons. He doesn't canvas, he doesn't have to. He's MP for one of the richest parts of London. His constituents practically goosestep their way to the polling stations.'

'Yeah, yeah and they'd vote for Stalin if he wore a red rosette up your way too,' said Terry wearily.

'What about the girls? We have three of them willing to stand up in court and testify he paid them to have sex.'

'No Tom, no, we don't have three *girls* who are willing to testify. We have three *prostitutes* who are willing to testify, against one highly respectable pillar of society. The first thing any decent barrister will ask these girls, who are prepared to have sex with strangers for cash is, "Were you paid by the paper for your story?", which of course they were. That barrister will then speculate that they, their bodies and their words are all easily bought. The jury might just conclude that these immoral people are likely to say anything in return for payment. By that point they will be adding another nought to the damages.'

Despite his mounting frustration and anger, Tom could see that everything Terry had said was true. He just didn't want to believe it. 'Are you sure the Doc's going to settle?'

'It's the only option that's being discussed but no offer has been made yet and we don't even know if Grady will accept it. He might still want his day in court.'

'And if the Doc does settle,' asked Tom, 'where does that leave me?'

Again, there was a sizeable pause before Terry said, 'That's pretty hypothetical at this point,' and Tom didn't need to read too far between the lines to know he was fucked.

Chapter Forty-Seven

They boil the kettle a lot in a home that's had a tragedy. It was what you did when your world was turned upside down by unexpected death or horrific injury or, in this case, the sudden disappearance of your daughter with the odds against her safe return worse than one in a million. You put the kettle on, made everyone a cup of tea, then you put the kettle on again. Tom had learned you should never offer to help, never try to take the job of making the drinks away from the person who has offered to make them. They were the ones in agony, trying to work out why everything they had ever planned or dreamed of for years had suddenly come to an abrupt and shocking end. Filling the kettle, boiling the water, popping tea bags in the cups and carrying the drinks in on a tray with a sugar bowl and a spoon was the one thing they could manage to accomplish between the bouts of weeping, cursing of fate and railing at their god. It made them feel useful again, for about two minutes.

Tom was standing alone in Michelle Summers' bedroom while her mum made the tea. He knew coming down here to see Fiona like this was clutching at straws but maybe he'd discover something from this visit and, if it proved to be a dead end, then it was likely to be one of very many before someone finally blew this investigation wide open.

Tom was meant to be meeting Helen at Mary Collier's

house that afternoon but he seriously doubted whether she would show up. While he waited for Fiona to return, Tom looked around the missing girl's room but didn't touch anything. The place already looked like a shrine to a dead girl. His eyes took in the posters, the cheap ornaments she was probably a little too old for now: a snow globe, an old music box with a ballerina on it. The room spoke of the kind of hard-up childhood he recognised. It wasn't poverty exactly: there'd be food on the plate and they could probably afford to heat the place but there wasn't much left once the bills were paid. The things Michelle owned probably came from market stalls and the bargain bins from cheap store sales. Tom knew this because he'd experienced something very similar.

'I didn't know if you took sugar.' Fiona handed him a mug of very milky tea. 'Forgot to ask,' she added, in a tone that indicated she was forgetting a lot at the moment. Tom had never met Fiona before but she looked so worn out, he'd have been willing to bet she'd aged a decade in the past few days.

'It's fine as it is, thank you,' he said, taking a sip.

Fiona looked at him now as if he had suddenly come into sharp focus and he wondered if she was on strong anti-depressants. 'What was it you wanted again?' She seemed to be zoning in and out and, if she'd noticed his bruises at all, obviously didn't see them as worthy of comment. Instead, she'd meekly let him in as soon as he told her he was a journalist.

'I was wondering if you had a more recent photograph of Michelle,' he said. 'The one the police are using looks a bit out-of-date. A newer picture could help to find her.'

'We stopped buying the school photos,' she admitted, 'they're always so expensive. I don't know if I've got anything recent,' and her lip quivered as the realisation hit her. She had no up-to-date photographs of her daughter and might never get the chance to put that right.

'Can I have a look at these?' asked Tom, indicating a row of four cheap photo albums that took up half a shelf on a rickety wooden bookcase.

Fiona nodded her assent. 'They're just daft pictures of her and her mates,' she said.

Tom picked up the nearest album and leafed through it. It was a house party. The birthday girl looked about fifteen and so did the other kids who were smiling out from the first four pictures Michelle had taken, which had been carefully pressed onto the page then sealed in place behind a clear, plastic cover. The girls had made an effort to dress up but they were still learning how to look the part. Make-up was either non-existent or there was way too much of it. The boys mugged for the camera or wrestled each other in front of it. There were excited smiles and laughter but at their age the lads and lasses looked like two alien species that treated each other warily and had no idea how to communicate with one another. Tom turned over a page and then another until finally he recognised her.

Michelle Summers was standing next to a friend, grinning at the camera. Her stance and smile were still a little awkward but this was a very different Michelle to the girl in the picture that had graced the pages of every newspaper in the country. Made up like this, with her hair carefully styled, she looked closer to a woman than a girl. She had folded her arms across her breasts self-consciously for the photograph, as if she wasn't yet confident about the way her body looked. Michelle Summers was still a child but she didn't look a bit like the other victims of the Kiddy-Catcher.

'Could I take this?' asked Tom, 'I've got a contact at the *Daily Mirror*. They'll print it for you.'

'If you think it will help,' she said.

He didn't know if it would but he peeled back the protective film and put the photo in his pocket anyway.

They went down the stairs together and talked some more about Michelle but he knew what he was hearing was a distraught mother's edited version of a young girl's life: the cheeky grin, mischievous sense of humour, loving nature and occasional memory from a childhood holiday long ago but it didn't tell him anything that might reveal the reason why she'd run away from home or been murdered by someone. Michelle and Denny 'got on,' her mother said. Michelle's boyfriend was 'all right, I s'pose but she hadn't been seeing him that long.'

They talked for five minutes or more before the subject turned to school, which Michelle didn't like, 'but then they don't, do they, kids, I mean? Can't wait to be out of there, I was the same when I was her age,' so Tom asked her about the junior school, to fill gaps in the conversation while he finished his tea.

Fiona seemed to bristle at the memory. 'Michelle didn't like him at all. Had it in for her, he did.'

'Who?'

'Nelson, the headmaster. He was a bully. I went down there once.'

'What happened?'

'He hit her,' said Fiona.

'Nelson hit Michelle?' Tom had been brought up in an era when teachers routinely hit pupils with slippers, blackboard dusters and even hard-backed books but Michelle was a child of the late eighties and that sort of behaviour was supposed to be over by then.

Fiona nodded, 'slapped her right across the face he did. I can't even remember why but it was something-or-nothing. I went right down there to have it out with him. I threatened to report him and he couldn't say sorry quick enough; said he'd been provoked but admitted he shouldn't have done it and apologised.' She seemed to feel the matter had been resolved to her satisfaction.

Tom knew Nelson well enough and this behaviour was uncharacteristic, which meant Michelle had somehow managed to push her headmaster until he had done something that could have cost him his career.

Fiona took the empty mug from Tom and disappeared into the kitchen with it. It was while she was gone that he noticed the piece of lined notepaper on the dining table close by. It had been folded in two but he could still make out the word that was written on the front of the note in pen, *Fiona.*

The sound of clinking cups and a tap being turned on came from the kitchen.

Tom took a step towards the table, glanced back at the door and when no one stepped through it, lifted the note up with a finger so he could read the words that had been hastily scribbled on the other side, *I am so, so sorry but I can't stay here no more. Please forgive me. D.*

Tom remembered the stepfather he had seen in the press conference footage. He heard a footstep on linoleum then and immediately took his finger from the note, which closed obediently, then he took a step away from it and smiled as Fiona re-entered the room. 'If there's anything else I can do . . .' he offered.

She walked him to the front door and he asked, in what he hoped was a casual tone, 'Is Michelle's stepdad working today?'

She nodded but it was too quick and emphatic, as if she wanted to believe the lie too.

Unable to get a signal between Fiona's house and the Greyhound, Tom fed coins into the public phone at the pub then waited for Bradshaw to answer before identifying himself.

'I said I owed you one.'

'You do,' the detective agreed.

'You might want to check out the stepdad,' said Tom. 'I think he's moved out.'

'Moved out? Why would he . . . how do you know that?'

Tom recounted his visit to Michelle's home before adding, 'You didn't hear this from me.'

Bradshaw snorted, 'I'm in enough bother. I won't be mentioning your name.' But his tone softened slightly: 'Thanks. We'll check it out.'

'Any word on Sean Donnellan?'

'They're still looking,' said Bradshaw.

At least they are looking, thought Tom.

*

He swept past Vincent's desk on his way to the smoking room. His fellow detective did not look good today. Don't go sick on me now, you bugger, he thought to himself, I'm going to need you. Bradshaw knew this was his chance.

DI Peacock was having a cigarette with Skelton and O'Brien when Bradshaw walked into the smoking room, a recent innovation that had caused extreme annoyance amongst the twenty-a-day mob, who loudly proclaimed that smokers were being victimised, due to some entirely unproven theory on passive smoking. The air in the tiny room was permanently stale and rank with smoke.

'What is it?' asked Peacock irritably.

'Sorry to interrupt. I've got some information on the Michelle Summers case and I wanted to pass it to you straight away.'

'Let's hear it then.'

'Michelle's stepdad might have moved out.'

'Moved out?' answered his DI in disbelief. 'Did you know about this?' he looked at Skelton and O'Brien accusingly.

Skelton shook his head and O'Brien asked, 'What makes you think that?'

Bradshaw knew he was out on a limb now. 'I got a call from a neighbour. He wouldn't give his name but he knew me from my door-to-door. He reckons he saw a note Denny left on Fiona's table.'

'What kind of note?'

'An apology; saying he couldn't stay and he was . . .'

'What?' interrupted his DI. 'He was what?'

'Asking for forgiveness.'

'Bloody hell,' said Skelton, 'you sure about this, Sherlock? You haven't just imagined it, have you?'

Bradshaw ignored him but Peacock didn't. 'Shut up Skelton.'

'Let me track him down,' Bradshaw urged his DI.

Peacock turned back to Bradshaw and eyed him carefully. 'Reckon you could look into this without messing it up?'

Bradshaw nodded. 'Just give me the chance.'

'Do it then,' ordered Peacock.

'Should we go and see Michelle's mother again?' asked Skelton when Bradshaw had gone.

Peacock shook his head. 'She's not all there,' and he took a long reflective drag on his cigarette. 'Sherlock's out to prove himself, so let's see what he comes up with. If he can find out why Denny's been feeling guilty, I reckon we're halfway there.'

Vincent Addison was staring off into space when Bradshaw walked up to his desk and spread his palms on it, leaning in close. 'Remember all that bollocks I told you about us being a team and me needing your help when you were ready?' he demanded.

'Er, yes.'

'Well, we *are* a team and I do need your help but it cannot wait until you're ready,' he told his startled colleague, 'so grab your coat, 'cos we've got a job to do.'

Chapter Forty-Eight

He didn't expect her to show but he should have known better. Ever the professional, Helen Norton drove into Mary Collier's street at the allotted time and stopped in front of his car. Tom had parked some yards from Mary's house. If there was going to be a row he didn't want the old lady to witness it.

They both got out of their cars at the same time and he waited for Helen to say something about the kiss. He was expecting some form of telling-off but instead she said, 'What happened to you?'

He had forgotten about his bruises. 'Oh,' he said, 'I told you there were some unpleasant people in this village. Frankie Turner is one of them.'

'He did that?' she said and he was relieved to see she was still concerned. 'Have you reported it to the police?'

Tom shook his head. 'No point, Frankie will have half a dozen people lined up to say they were with him when it happened. The police won't be interested,' he was dismissive, 'and I'll live.'

Relieved she had shown up at all and not even commented on their kiss, he took her silence as his cue and said, 'Shall we see if she's in?'

Helen nodded and they started to walk up the street together.

This time Mary Collier was at home but their latest

attempt to see the old woman was thwarted by the arrival a moment later of a be-suited, middle-aged man who looked like an insurance salesman. While they were still some way from the old vicarage, the man emerged from a maroon Rover that had pulled up right by Mary's house. He knocked on the front door before being admitted by Mary's housekeeper.

'Bollocks,' muttered Tom.

'Should we wait?' Helen asked him.

'I have a feeling he's going to be a while,' Tom said. 'Fancy a walk?' She wondered if he meant the pub but instead they set off over the hill together.

'Where are we going?' she asked but he didn't answer. Helen didn't push the matter. She was just glad they were still capable of working together and relieved he had not commented on the night before, even to apologise, which would have been excruciating. When she had driven away, she'd been angry with Tom but even angrier with herself. He had kissed her, which was very wrong, but she had kissed him back, which was even worse for she was the one with the boyfriend. The guilt at this betrayal of Peter had been eating away at her ever since. It would surely have confirmed his worst suspicions about her and Helen's first instinct had been to phone him and tell him what had happened, for she had never kept secrets from him before. Something had stopped her from doing this though, an instinct that it would be too much for him perhaps and that Peter's pride would force him to end their relationship there and then. She felt almost as guilty keeping it from him as she did about the kiss. Now she walked silently next to the man who had caused the problem between her and her boyfriend, but all she experienced was relief that he felt no need to refer to it. It seemed they were both happy to forget the foolish events of the night before – or at least pretend they never happened.

For once, the weather was mild. The rain had stopped and there'd been enough time for the ground to dry. When they reached the bottom he steered her away from the main road to an unmarked track alongside farm land. There was a stile here and a sign denoting a public footpath. 'No Name Lane,' he told her, 'it leads down to the river. I thought you might like to see the spot where Sean Donnellan drew his landscapes.'

'Why is it called No Name Lane?'

'Because it doesn't have a name.'

'But everybody calls it No Name Lane?' she said.

'Yeah.'

'So it does have a name.'

'I suppose,' he said, as if it didn't really matter.

They rounded a bend and the river came into view, its level swelled by the recent rains till it threatened to burst its banks, the water flowing at an alarming rate. 'Funny to think this place hasn't changed one iota since Mary Collier walked here as a young girl.' Tom looked exasperated then. 'It's driving me crazy,' he admitted, 'we are so close to the truth but I wonder if we will ever really know what happened that night because everyone who could have told us is dead. My money is still on the soldier but a knife in the back doesn't sound like Jack Collier's way of doing things to me.'

'Does it sound like Henry Collier's way of doing things?' Helen asked disbelievingly, 'or even Stephen's?'

'A mentally disturbed man who lurks in the shadows, peeping on half-dressed girls, has violent episodes and blackouts and can remember nothing about them afterwards?' he asked. 'So what does that make him I wonder; a homicidal maniac or a simple-minded soul who doesn't understand that his actions are inappropriate? It's anyone's guess.'

'It doesn't sound like any of them, does it?' he admitted, 'but one of them must have done it – or all three. Who else could it have been?'

'Mary Collier,' she observed, 'according to Betty Turner. *It was you,* remember?'

'But did she mean it literally?' asked Tom, 'or was she saying it was Mary's fault, indirectly? I don't think Betty Turner knows the truth any more than we do but I'm sure the Colliers were responsible for Sean's death somehow.'

'Like you said, they're all dead. So we'll never know now, will we?'

'No,' he admitted, 'probably not.'

They had reached the famous part of the river, where the rains caused it to swell at its widest, deepest point and the water swept past them at great speed, as if in a rush to get where it was going.

'Beautiful, isn't it?' he said, as they watched the swell.

'And scary,' said Helen.

It had been a relatively easy matter to locate Denny that morning, for his movements tallied exactly with the itinerary he had submitted in advance to Durham Constabulary in case they needed to track him down if they got news of Michelle's whereabouts. The hard part was staying interested and alert as he covered mile after mile of motorway while they followed him at a discreet distance. Vincent and Bradshaw tailed him all the way down to Cannock in the West Midlands, where he unloaded a consignment of canned goods, then followed him back up the A1 again.

'Just what exactly are you hoping to find?' asked Vincent, not for the first time.

'I told you,' Bradshaw reminded him, 'I don't know. Something, anything, because this guy is not right. I am telling you, Vincent, that man is hiding something. I just know it.'

When his colleague failed to respond enthusiastically, he added, 'And I intend to find out what it is.'

They walked for nearly an hour along the river bank and talked about Mary Collier and Sean Donnellan. Then, when there was nothing new left to say on the matter, they transferred their attention to Michelle Summers' disappearance but were soon going over old ground here too.

It was Helen who changed the subject. 'Do you still have family up here?'

'Only my sister,' he said, 'she's married, lives in Newcastle, got two lovely little girls.'

'You're an uncle?'

'You sound surprised. I'll go and see them when this is all over. Everyone else is gone; Nan, Dad.'

'Do you miss your dad?'

'We never really got on. We used to argue all the time,'

'What about?'

'Everything – but the miner's strike really drove a wedge between us.'

'Didn't you agree with it?'

'It wasn't that. I just thought it was unwinnable and badly handled. He didn't see it that way or at least didn't want to.'

They arrived hopefully back at Mary Collier's home but the maroon-coloured Rover was still parked outside.

'Well, she won't go far,' he said. 'Let's get a bite to eat at the Greyhound.'

'Is that wise?'

'Fuck Frankie Turner,' he told her, 'if he walks in I'll belt him with a pool cue,' and she was left to wonder whether he was joking or not.

'What is he playing at?' asked Vincent as he watched the seven and a half tonne truck, 'he's been here over an hour and hasn't even left his cab.'

'Maybe he's been kipping in it?' suggested Bradshaw.

Denny's lorry was parked in the corner of the large, rough patch of muddy, pockmarked land that served as a car park. The truck stop was a few miles south of Wetherby. They had tucked their unmarked car in behind a large lorry with German plates, leaving just enough room to watch Denny's cab and the front door of the café but Michelle's stepdad didn't go into the greasy spoon. He didn't do anything at all, in fact.

'Join the police, they said. Crack some heads and nick some villains,' said Vincent, then sighed, 'and now look at me.'

'I don't recall anyone saying that,' Bradshaw corrected him.

'You know what I mean,' Vincent complained, 'what a

wasted day. I'll be getting piles from sitting here in the cold.'

'Stop moaning.'

Just then the door of the truck stop opened and a young girl emerged, dressed in a white shirt and black skirt, partly covered by a baggy anorak.

'Just a waitress,' Vincent said, for she could not have been anything else out here. When she started to cross the car park, however, Denny's cab door finally opened and they watched him climb down.

The young girl started walking more quickly then. While the watching detectives were trying to work out what was going on, Denny opened his arms wide and she marched straight into his embrace. He clasped his arms tightly round her for a moment then they broke off, but only so they could begin kissing passionately.

'Bloody hell, how old is she?' asked Bradshaw in disbelief.

'Sixteen,' replied Vincent, 'seventeen at a push.'

'The dirty bastard,' observed the detective constable.

Chapter Forty-Nine

A familiar car pulled up alongside Tom as he was leaving the pub.

'Get in,' ordered O'Brien.

'Again?' said Tom, 'get a life, will you.'

'What's going on?' asked Helen.

O'Brien ignored her. 'Our DCI would like a word,' he told Tom.

'So get in before we drag you in,' added Skelton.

Helen looked alarmed at that but Tom said, 'It's okay,' and Skelton held open the rear door for him. 'If I'm found hanged in my cell later, it was these two,' he told Helen then he winked at her and she was left standing there as they drove away.

At least this time they kept to the main roads and Tom was soon back in the town again. Skelton steered his Sierra into the car park of the cop shop, as the police station was known locally. Tom held his tongue as Skelton and O'Brien escorted him to DCI Kane's office but when he saw the senior officer sitting calmly behind his desk, he could no longer contain his anger.

'What's this about? Am I under arrest? On what charge?'

'Calm down,' Kane told him, 'you're obviously not under arrest. I'd like a word, that's all.'

'Really, well I like to have a choice about who I speak to. I prefer not to be lifted off the street by your goon squad and dragged here. So the answer is no, whatever you want. Now, are you going to take me home, do I have to order a cab, or are these two going to beat me up in a quiet cell somewhere first?'

'Relax, we didn't drag you here,' and then he noticed the sheepish looks on the faces of his two detectives. 'Bloody hell,' he told them in exasperation. 'I said to ask him nicely.'

'Sorry, Guv,' answered Skelton.

DCI Kane eyed Tom closely for a moment until the younger man cottoned on. 'Don't worry,' he said, 'the bruises were there already.'

'I never doubted it,' said Kane but he turned to his men then, 'be good lads and bugger off while I speak to this young man,' and they trudged out of his office. 'I'm sorry,' he told Tom, 'those two can be intimidating even when they're not trying to be but they are basically good coppers.'

'We'll have to agree to disagree on that,' replied Tom. 'I think they're a disgrace.'

'It's not their fault they've been keeping such bad company for the past twenty years. It tends to come with the turf.'

'Don't you think the lines get a little blurred after a while?' asked Tom, 'that the guys tasked with catching the villains can become almost as bad as the men they are after?'

'No I don't,' answered the detective chief inspector, 'that's a naïve view and you wouldn't share it if you'd done the job as long as they have. There's a very big difference between them and the villains they lock up. They might ruffle a few feathers along the way but they are on the right side of the law, believe me, which is more than can be said for some of your mob.'

'Yeah, there's bad journalists out there right enough, I'll admit that, but every one of them has two or three coppers on his payroll feeding him stories for beer money,' said Tom. 'Now, what exactly did you want to see me about?'

Kane regarded Tom for a long while, as if he was deciding whether to continue. 'I wanted to speak to you because I hear you are a good journalist, one of the better ones, and you're discreet.'

'Flattery will get you everywhere . . . just not with me. What do you want?'

'I have a story for you . . .'

'Oh here we go . . .'

'I don't want paying for it. It's not like that.'

'Go on, then.'

'This story . . . it's a big one, it'll do you some good and it's bound to leak sooner or later anyway. I reckon the public have a right to know about it and they can't hear it from me,' he shrugged, 'so they may as well hear it from you; if you are interested of course?'

Tom forced himself to calm down. He told himself the one thing he couldn't afford to do right now was pass up a good story. 'I could be,' he admitted.

'There's just one thing.'

'What?'

'This conversation,' Kane looked him right in the eye, 'it never happened.'

'Obviously.'

'I mean it.'

'So do I,' Tom said, 'a good journalist never gives up his source. Just ask your two goons out there if you don't believe me.'

'I did,' said the DCI, 'which is why you're here.'

'Out with it then.'

Kane leaned back in his desk chair and folded his arms. 'Well sit down and I'll tell you.'

Tom took the seat opposite Kane and let the police officer begin. 'You're familiar with Professor Burstow and his role in the Kiddy-Catcher case.'

'Of course,' said Tom but he still wasn't going to admit to writing the article that had made it public knowledge.

'His input has been to narrow down our investigation. It is his psychological profile that has enabled us to sift the many hundreds of leads received by Durham Constabulary. The detectives on this case have all basically been working for him, in a manner of speaking. If he tells us a lead is worth following then we follow it, if he says it's a dead end then we put it to one side, because he represents the new way of doing things, he is the future.' Kane said that last bit drily.

'I get the picture.'

'And it's not as if he isn't credible,' continued the DCI, 'I mean, he's got all those letters after his name and that glowing report from the FBI after all of the work he's done for them.'

'Where are you going with this?'

'But what if I was to tell you that Professor Burstow isn't who he claims to be?'

345

'How do you mean?' asked Tom. 'Are you saying some of his CV doesn't stand up to scrutiny?'

'Perhaps I'm saying that none of it does,' Kane admitted.

'Bloody hell,' Tom thought for a second, 'if you're telling me that the hunt for a multiple child killer has been going down blind alleys because the man who has been directing the investigation is a fraud then I would say that's a very big story indeed.'

'I thought as much,' admitted Kane with classic understatement.

'How the hell?'

'He's never worked with the FBI,' said Kane, 'nor helped a police force anywhere on any of their cases, least of all a murder enquiry. He's not a professor or even a doctor, his qualifications are fake. The man is a fantasist.'

'Jesus Christ!'

'It seems we were so desperate that the man who did the hiring didn't bother to conduct any background checks on Burstow. Instead he read all the testimonials on their headed notepaper, helpfully provided by the FBI and others, and took them on face value.'

'Oh my God.'

'All of this only came to light because an American tourist read a newspaper report in London on the Michelle Summers' case. The story contained a reference to a professor Burstow being heavily involved in solving a previous case in the U. S. Trouble was, this man was an FBI agent who worked that case and knew Burstow had nothing to do with it. Being a civic-minded soul, he called

346

to let us know. One of our detectives contacted the FBI in Langley and, lo and behold, they had no record of a Professor Burstow involved in that case or any other. It took us about an hour and a half to pick apart every other claim on his CV then we asked the good professor to come into the station and help us with our enquiries. Only this time he was on the wrong side of an interview table. He's down in the cells right now in fact.'

Tom could scarcely believe what he was hearing. 'Why did he think he could get away with it?'

Kane shrugged, 'because he's barking,' he said simply, 'I don't mean he's rolling-round-in-his-own-shit-frothing-at-the-mouth crazy, but he's clearly wired very differently from other people.'

'Has he admitted it?'

'He's not admitted or denied it. He's just acting like it doesn't make any difference. He knows who the killer is and he's going to help us find him, if only we'd listen. Big of him, isn't it?'

'Does anybody else know about this?'

'If you mean other journalists, then no.'

'Who does know about it?'

'Half-a-dozen senior police officers and a couple of panic-stricken politicians, including our esteemed local MP.'

'Wait a minute,' said Tom, 'they are not trying to put a lid on this?'

'What do you think?'

'But how can they?'

'Oh I don't know, get the charges dropped or perhaps have chummy down there sectioned under the mental health act; hope nobody notices.'

'And you don't want that to happen?' Tom narrowed his eyes, 'even though this could be very damaging to the force? Now why is that?'

'There'll be a shit storm,' Kane admitted, 'for a while, but I think there are more important concerns here, don't you? That man has endangered the lives of every young girl in this county by jeopardising a police investigation into a serial killer. I reckon it's time we blew the whistle, got it all out in the open. The public have a right to know.'

'Very noble,' and Tom regarded the Detective Chief Inspector with interest.

'What?'

'Professor Burstow was Trelawe's man wasn't he?'

'I believe Trelawe brought him in, so, yes, he was Trelawe's man, as you put it.'

'And what will happen to him?'

'I'm afraid Detective Superintendent Trelawe has been suspended, pending the outcome of an enquiry.'

Tom finally understood. 'So your boss could be for the chop and you don't want this hushed up while charges are dropped, madmen placed quietly in asylums and Detective Superintendents exonerated? That's how your lot normally operate, isn't it? But you want to see Trelawe hung out to dry.'

'Why would I want to see a fellow officer come to harm?' asked DCI Kane in a deadpan voice.

'Maybe you don't care for him or he doesn't like you. It could be that simple but my best guess is you're next up,' Tom told him, 'who is overseeing the Michelle Summers' case now that Trelawe has been suspended?'

'I am liaising directly with the Assistant Commissioner,' admitted Kane, 'for now.'

'Really?' Tom shook his head in disbelief, 'I've got to hand it to you, Kane, even if I don't believe a word of that story about off-duty FBI agents on holiday in London. Do me a favour. You checked out Burstow. You did the leg work your boss couldn't be bothered with, all the way back to the FBI in Langley. You invented that tip-off to justify it when you went over your boss's head. You've thrown him to the lions.'

'You've never had any dealings with the detective superintendent. If you had, you wouldn't be so shocked. He's a very political animal,' Kane informed him, 'and so, it turns out, am I.'

'You shafted him before he shafted you, that it?'

'Partly,' admitted Kane, 'but my main concern is his judgement, or lack of it. A police officer of his rank should have some don't you think, and that man is an empty uniform.'

'And when I write up this story, he'll be finished,' said Tom.

Kane shrugged. 'What do you care?'

Tom felt weary all of a sudden. 'I don't, not really.'

'Right,' DCI Kane's face hardened, 'so do you want this story or not?'

Chapter Fifty

This time Tom only gave Alex Docherty half an hour before calling Terry for a second time.

'Did you give the Doc my message?'

'Er . . . yeah, I did,'

'And what did he say?'

'Not much,' admitted the sub-editor.

'Well what, exactly?'

'You know the Doc.'

'What did he say, Terry?'

Terry sighed, '"*Tell him to go fuck himself.*"'

'Great,' answered Tom, 'that's just great.'

Tom hung up and dialled Paul Hill at the *Mirror*, then he called Helen.

As Tom made for the old vicarage, he walked past the pensioners' bungalows and the vacant lot which used to house the old brewery. It was amazing to think a village this size once had its own site for brewing beer but that was long ago and the building had lain empty for years before finally being torn down. The site had been grassed over and trees planted, some tall and mature but the ones nearer the road were more recent additions; little more than saplings, tied to thick wooden supports to keep them aloft while they bent and twisted in the wind.

Tom was in a more buoyant mood following his conversation with Paul Hill. With another story sold, he felt as if he was managing to build up a war chest, which might help sustain him when the time came for his inevitable dismissal from the paper. At least he could keep the wolf from the door while he worked out what to do next with his life.

He rounded the corner, his mind preoccupied with Mary Collier, which was why he didn't notice Frankie Turner coming towards him from the other end of the street until it was too late. The older man spotted Tom though and immediately broke into a run. 'Oh shit,' mumbled Tom as he belatedly recognised the snarling face powering towards him, 'not now.' Caught unawares, Tom had a split second to make a decision.

'Come here!' shouted Frankie and Tom made up his mind then. He turned on his heel and fled. 'Stay there, you bastard!' roared Frankie.

Tom disappeared back round the corner and Frankie Turner shot after him, determined to catch up with him, not quite believing that Tom had the sheer bloody nerve to stay in the village when he had been warned away. Frankie's anger lent him speed, 'Come here, you!' He was determined to catch Tom and give him another beating. Frankie went barrelling round the bend, praying he'd made up enough ground and hoping to see Tom just ahead of him.

But Tom was a great deal closer than Frankie was expecting. He was waiting just round the corner for his attacker to catch up with him. Before Frankie could do anything, Tom twisted his body and brought something crashing towards him. Frankie managed to put his arms up to parry the blow but Tom adjusted his stance and brought the wooden strut he'd pulled from one of the saplings down low so it missed Frankie's hands and face, instead landing a sickening blow to his torso.

Frankie groaned and gasped at the same time and went down hard, clutching his stomach. That blow would have been enough to end the fight on its own, because Frankie wasn't going to be getting up in a hurry, but Tom wasn't finished yet. He dropped the wooden strut and instead lashed out with a boot that caught Frankie full in the face, sending him hurtling backwards. Frankie groaned as he rolled along the ground. 'Did you think I was running away from you, Frankie? No chance! I've been waiting for this, you bastard!' The next kick went in hard on Frankie's knee and he cried out in pain. 'Did you reckon I was going to stand in the street and trade punches with you? No way. You like to fight dirty, well, that's fine by me.' The next kick was aimed at the face and Frankie tried to shield it with his hands but Tom anticipated that and redirected his kick so it connected with Frankie's ribs. He groaned again and tried to crawl away but Tom saw his opportunity and the end of his shoe went in hard between the other man's legs. Frankie let out a strangled, coughing choke and rolled over, clutching his balls.

'Not done yet,' Tom assured him, his fury increasing as he recalled the cowardly attack he had endured at Frankie's hands.

'No,' pleaded Frankie, 'stop,' he gasped.

'Fuck you,' Tom told him and the next kick went into Frankie's shin, causing another cry of intense pain as he rolled on the ground. Weeks of anger and frustration seemed to roar out of Tom then and Frankie Turner took the brunt of it all; his betrayal by the Doc, fury at Timothy Grady, anger at the two rogue detectives who'd left him stranded five miles away and, of course, there was Helen and her idiot boyfriend.

As Frankie took another blow from Tom's boot, he pleaded, 'Enough.'

'No,' Tom assured him, 'you don't get to decide when you've had enough,' and he knelt down next to the man, drew back his arm and punched him hard in the mouth, 'I get to decide!' another punch in the face then another, this time opening up a big cut above Frankie's eye. 'I get to decide!' he gripped the other man's shirt with one hand and it ripped as his other fist slammed into Frankie's face once more. Tom drew back his arm to administer one final punch.

'Tom!' screamed Helen and he looked up to see her standing there. He hadn't even heard her car draw up at the side of the road and now she was out of it and screaming at him, 'Stop! For God's sake, stop! You'll bloody kill him!'

Tom did stop then. He looked at Helen's wild eyes then glanced down at the man he had been pummelling. Frankie Turner was conscious, just, but his head was lolling and he was making an unnatural gurgling noise caused by the blood in his nose and mouth. His face was battered and bloody and there was no way he was going to be able to stand unaided.

Tom took a step away from Frankie and viewed his handiwork while Helen moved closer. 'Fuck him.'

'You can't just leave him in the street like this,' she told him, 'he needs help!'

'If you care about him that much, you help him!' he snapped and before she could reply he turned his back on her and was gone.

By the time Helen caught up with him again Tom was already sitting in the corner of the Lion, clutching a half-drunk pint but still flushed from the exertion of fighting Frankie Turner. Helen was breathless from the effort of catching up with him, which she did just as soon as she'd confirmed that Frankie Turner wasn't in a critical condition. He'd merely snarled at her and staggered to his feet, swearing and brushing her away before limping from the scene. She was stunned that he could walk at all after such a savage beating and she watched him until he disappeared round a bend, convinced he was likely to collapse at any minute.

'You'll be lucky if he doesn't press charges!' her voice was loud enough to attract the attention of the men in the bar, all of whom had been sensible enough not to ask Tom how he had bloodied his hands.

'Press charges?' sneered Tom. 'Frankie Turner? That's the last thing he'll do. He knows the police would shake me by the hand for giving that arsehole a beating.' Helen saw that the skin on his knuckles was broken and bloody. 'He came after me. It was a fight and he bloody lost. I gave him more chance than he gave me the other night and he'd have done worse if I hadn't got the drop on him.' He could tell she was unconvinced, 'I don't want to talk about it, Helen,' he told her firmly, 'I don't want to talk about anything.'

'Well that's going to be difficult, since we are supposed to be working together. Sulking isn't going to help.'

'I am not sulking.'

And she gave him a look that said *you clearly are* then reminded him, 'We were supposed to be seeing Mary Collier.'

'Just give me a minute, will you, for Christ's sake,' and when she said nothing. 'Can I not have just one minute to myself without you standing there, looking at me like that!' He drained the beer from his glass.

'Like what?'

'Like I've crawled out from under a rock. Can we not have a one-minute holiday from that?' He was scowling at her now and she was stunned by the ferocious look on his face.

'You can have as many minutes as you like,' Helen told him quietly and she walked away from him then, leaving Tom staring into the bottom of his glass.

Chapter Fifty-One

Mary Collier was alone that afternoon but she did not invite Helen in. 'What is it this time, Miss Norton?'

Helen was still angry after her argument with Tom and in no mood for chit-chat. 'We've been to see Sam Armstrong,' she informed Mary, 'he told us all about you and Sean Donnellan.' There was a look of resignation on the old lady's face then as she opened the door wider to admit her.

This time Mary poured two glasses of sherry and passed one to Helen, who took it from the old lady's trembling hand and sat down opposite her.

'Where's Tom,' asked Mary, 'you two had a tiff?' She looked Helen directly in the eye. 'You are sleeping with him, I assume?' she asked, catching Helen completely off guard. Mary smiled but there was no warmth behind the smile. 'I could tell he's interested you,' she explained. 'It's perfectly all right,' she added, 'it's the duty of every generation to shock the one that came before it? Though you'd have to do something pretty racy to shock the generation after mine.'

Helen surprised herself with her choice of words: 'Who I'm sleeping with is none of your business.'

'Quite,' agreed Mary, 'though you seem to think the whole world might be interested in who I may have been sleeping with.'

'Yes,' answered Helen, 'that's because your boyfriend was murdered.'

Mary let out something between a gasp and a startled laugh then she regained her composure. 'My boyfriend? He *was* a boy, a man actually, twenty-two years old when he came here, so young but seemed so worldly and sophisticated somehow and of course you want to know all about us, like we're public property all of a sudden.'

'I just want to know what happened to him, that's all.'

'Why?' Mary asked sharply. 'So it will make your name, set you on your way to a glamorous career as a journalist? Is that it?'

'Maybe,' conceded Helen, 'that's what we do. We find out what happened and we write about it and yes, if I can write a good piece about this then it might not do me any harm, but there's more to it than that.'

'How so?'

Helen could feel her anger rising at this old woman who seemed to care more for her reputation than the truth, 'a young man came to this village one day and never left. Something bad happened here and he was killed because of it and his body buried in a marshy field, with no headstone, no funeral and no mourners. He probably had a mother, a father, sisters, brothers, friends who cared for him. They never saw Sean again and if any of them are still alive I think they deserve to know what happened to him. I think this secret has been haunting you for years and you need to tell us the truth.'

'What makes you so sure about that?'

Helen opened her mouth to say something, but was interrupted.

'Because you're dying,' the male voice came from the doorway behind her and she spun round.

'The door was unlocked,' Tom explained, 'so I let myself in.' The look in his face told Helen he'd had enough of the usual niceties too. Tom looked grimly determined. 'I was going to call but I heard voices and, yes, I've been listening at the doorway. You can ask me to leave if you like.'

'Why shouldn't I?' Mary challenged him.

'Because Helen's right, you want to tell us what happened,' he sat down opposite her. 'My Nan had rheumatoid arthritis for years and she never had a tenth of the doctor's appointments or hospital visits you get through. I thought it was some fancy private health care scheme at first but then you had the visit from Graham Heath yesterday,' his tone was hard, unbending. 'I'm assuming our local solicitor was updating your will?'

Mary turned to Helen, 'Oh, he's good,' she said as if she was particularly impressed by a young protégé, 'he's very good. What a sharp one, he's so sharp he'll cut himself one day, he will. I'd keep this one if I were you, young Helen. You two could go far together.'

'So it's true?' asked Helen, 'you are ill?'

'Small cell lung cancer,' said Mary, 'sounds almost harmless, doesn't it? But those small cells are killing me. It's inoperable, at my age at least,' and she shook her head dismissively. 'Everybody smoked in my day. We didn't know any better and by the time we did it was too late,' she said the last part as if she really didn't care one way or the other.

'I'm sorry,' said Helen.

'Don't be,' she replied firmly, leaving them to draw their own conclusions about her desire to continue living, 'so, what's Sam Armstrong got to say about me?' she asked, drawing the subject to a close.

Mary didn't bother to deny any of it this time. Instead she listened without offering any response until they were done. Tom and Helen recounted everything they had learned from the farmer, expecting her to pick Sam Armstrong's account of her young life apart when they were through but instead she just said, 'The devil finds work for idle hands, as my father was fond of saying.

'He wanted me to be a lady and ladies didn't work. He wanted me to marry, keep house and stay out of trouble but it left me with too much free time. Teaching came later, during the war, when the men went off to fight.'

'What did you do all day?' asked Helen.

'Helped Mrs Harris, baked, read my books,' she said listlessly, 'and I used to go for a long walk every day on my own – a woman could back then and she'd be safe. My walks often took me down No Name Lane. Sean Donnellan was always by the river. I would stop and talk to him, little by little I got to know him and I realised I had been hasty in my judgement.'

'How so?'

'He was kind and considerate, he cared about my opinion on things, which was rare for a man in those days, still is, and he knew so much. Sean had read so many books, he had travelled, he knew writers, poets, artists and he had such big plans for his future. We became close. It was a gradual thing that happened slowly, over a whole summer.'

'What about Betty? They were courting weren't they?'

'Hardly,' she said dismissively. 'Sean stepped out with Betty for a while but it was never . . .' her voice trailed away then she said, 'men were expected to sow their wild oats before they settled down. Girls like Betty were foolish enough to let them. Sean never made her a promise of anything.'

'At least that's what he told you,' said Tom but she ignored this. Helen was trying to understand a society that expected men to sow wild oats while condemning the girls that granted them the opportunity.

'Sean wasn't courting anyone when it started and nor was I,' Mary insisted primly, 'I broke it off with Henry when I realised I had feelings for Sean.'

'How did Henry take it?' asked Tom, knowing the answer already.

'Badly.'

'Sam Armstrong said he pinned all his future hopes on you and when you broke up with him, he pretty much lost his mind.'

'He kept saying he had done it all for me,' she assented, 'made himself into something so he could be with me, pleaded with me to give him another chance but I just couldn't,' she said, then added, 'not then.'

'Most teenage romances end dramatically,' said Helen, 'but this was different wasn't it?'

'Yes,' Mary admitted.

'What happened?' asked Tom.

'Nothing for a while,' she told him, 'I stopped seeing Henry, much to my father's disapproval, and started to walk out with Sean.'

'Did your father know?' asked Helen.

Mary shook her head. 'He would never have allowed it,' her eyes widened, 'the vicar's daughter and the Irish Catholic boy? But it's impossible to keep a secret for long in a village.'

'There was gossip?' Helen asked.

'Someone saw us out walking together by the river and that was that; the fire was lit and Betty poured on the coals. She made sure everyone in the village knew I ended things with Henry so I could steal her man. Soon Mrs Harris heard about it and then of course my father.'

'What did he do?'

'He told me never to see Sean again.'

'But you saw him anyway?' said Helen.

'I was a wilful girl,' she explained, 'and he could hardly keep me locked up.'

'You were in love with Sean?' Helen prompted her.

'Yes.'

'And he was in love with you?' asked Tom.

'So I thought.'

'You don't sound sure,' he said.

'I wasn't,' and she looked down at her shoes as she spoke, 'for such a long time I wasn't.'

'Until they found his body in Great Middleton,' said Tom.

'Yes,' she admitted, looking up at him as if he had finally worked it all out, 'I thought he had left me, all those years ago and gone off to America without me.'

'Why did you deny it, Mary?' he asked her. 'If you loved this man, if he meant that much to you, then why not admit it when we asked you?'

'Because I was ashamed!' she told him, 'I married Henry and spent years living with that shame, hoping everyone would eventually forget about it or find something else to talk about behind my back.'

'Did Sean ask you to leave with him?' said Helen.

'He told me there was nothing for either of us here and I believed him. He said it was the only way we could be together. He asked me to leave in the night when everyone was asleep. We knew if we walked across the fields we could reach town by the morning and catch the first bus to Newcastle then take a train to Liverpool and a boat to America. He had just enough money to get us there but no more.'

'Is that why you stole the money from your father?'

'What?' her voice sounded distant.

'The sovereigns,' prompted Helen, 'we know about the gold sovereigns that were stolen from the vicarage in 1936. It was in the newspaper.'

'Oh,' she said, 'yes, of course, but I didn't take them.'

'Did Sean ask you to?'

'Yes,' she admitted and the admission cost her.

'You told him about them?'

'It just came up. We talked for hours about many things. One day I told him my father didn't trust banks and he asked me what he did trust. It sounds foolish to think about it now but we were talking about America and money. I was frightened we'd starve. What if no one wanted his drawings? What if he couldn't find work of any kind? We'd be in the gutter. Sean asked me if I could get money from my father.'

'When he said *get*, did he mean steal?' Tom asked.

'Well he wasn't going to give us any, was he?' she answered caustically. 'Sean said it would be like getting a portion of my inheritance early. He said I'd be disinherited for running away with him anyway so I should just take some.'

'But you didn't take the sovereigns?' asked Helen.

'How could I steal from my own father?'

'So Sean took them anyway,' Tom offered by way of explanation, 'he took the money because he knew where to find it.'

'That's what everyone thought,' she admitted, 'it's what I thought.'

Tom contemplated this for a moment. 'Where were you supposed to meet Sean?' he asked Mary, 'on the night you were going to leave with him.'

'At the end of No Name Lane,' she answered.

Tom looked at Helen. 'The lane runs right through the farms and carries on for miles, halfway to town.' Then he turned back to the old lady. 'What happened, Mary?'

'You want me to tell you what happened to Sean?' she asked. 'Well I can't.'

'Can't or won't?' asked Helen. 'Who are you protecting?'

'Or did you do it yourself?' Tom said. 'That's the first thing the police will ask.'

Mary shook her head as if Tom was a very dim pupil indeed. 'Do you actually believe I could have killed the man I loved, for any reason. Do you really think so little of me?'

'You wouldn't be the first.'

'Well, I didn't,' she assured them, 'though I don't suppose you'll take my word for it.'

'That depends,' answered Helen. 'Somebody killed him.'

'And if you tell us who it was, maybe we'll believe it wasn't you,' added Tom. 'Was it Henry,' he asked, 'or was it Jack Collier? We know all about him.' When she did not reply, he continued, 'Perhaps Stephen killed him, or your father?' he was offering up names so she could rebuff the more outlandish choices and at least narrow it down.

'I don't know,' she said. 'Don't you think I want to know the truth myself? Do you imagine I have thought of anything else since they found Sean's body in that field?'

'Then tell us what you do know,' urged Tom, 'give us the scraps Mary and let us piece them together, we're the only chance you've got of ever learning the truth.' When she didn't contradict him, he said, 'what happened?'

'It was such a long time ago and . . .' She waved a hand airily.

'I think you remember everything,' Helen told her firmly and when Mary looked affronted, Tom spoke to her.

'Try,' he urged, 'please.'

'I was going to leave with him,' she explained.

'So what happened, Mary? Why didn't you?'

Chapter Fifty-Two

1936

'Do you no longer knock?' asked Mary sharply.

'I'm glad I didn't if this is what I find,' replied Mrs Harris. She had entered Mary's bedroom to discover her packing a suitcase.

'It doesn't concern you,' Mary told her, 'you are not my mother.'

'Maybe but it would concern your father if he were here.'

'He's not here. He's staying with the Dean and it wouldn't matter if he was.'

'He'd forbid it.'

'Yes,' agreed Mary, 'and I'd still go.'

Mrs Harris seemed to lose all the fight in her then. 'Please Mary, I'm begging you not to leave with this man. He's not the right kind for you.'

'Why? Because he's not an Englishman, because he hasn't had my education, because he doesn't want to be a school teacher?'

'Because he'll tire of you!' she shouted at the young girl but then her shoulders slumped and she continued in a pleading voice, 'then where will you be? In ruination, that's where.'

'He won't tire of me.'

'He tired of Betty quick enough.'

'And what man wouldn't?'

'Is that any way to speak of your friend? You might be many things Mary, but you were never cruel. We didn't raise you that way. It's only since you've taken up with him. And what will happen to Henry? You'll be the ruin of him too. You've already broken him.'

'I can't help that!' protested Mary. 'Must I marry a man I don't love to spare him a broken heart? You stand there and say I'm cruel but I have no worse an opinion of you or Betty than you have of me. I know what they are saying about me in the village and I won't stay here. I won't!'

'So your mind is made up?' she asked. 'Are you leaving now?'

'Not now.'

'When then?'

Mary sighed, 'Soon. Go to bed. When you wake in the morning, I'll be gone.'

'Don't do this,' urged Mrs Harris, 'he'll trample on your heart. I know he will.'

'How?' asked Mary, 'how do you know it? Because someone broke yours long ago and you've not had a proper life since? Are you jealous because I have a chance of happiness and you never did?'

'Yes, a man broke my heart long ago. He tired of me quick enough and went the way of the drink instead, like so many others, and yes, Sean Donnellan reminds me of him but that's not the only reason. You've got stars in your eyes right now Mary and you can't see because of them. Don't throw your life away. Don't turn your back on your family because of this man you hardly know.'

'I do know him,' Mary wailed, 'and he's a good man. He makes me happy. He *will* make me happy. Now leave me alone!'

'I will, if that's what you want. I can see there is no reasoning with you and I'm sorry you think I've not had a good life but I have, living here with you and your father and that's why I don't want you to ruin everything for him. But if you're determined, there's nothing I can do to prevent it. I won't lock you in here but I will pray for you Mary. I will pray for you.'

Mary rounded on her then in fury. 'You'll pray for me! How dare you offer me your prayers like I'm some fallen woman!' Mrs Harris flinched at the ferocity of her words. 'Do you think I don't know about you? Do you really imagine I still believe you skulk round the house at night because you can't sleep. I know you're warming my father's bed and that's why he lets you stay but he won't marry you, will he? He's happy enough to lay down with you but he doesn't think you're good enough to be a vicar's wife, does he? Look to your own sins and save your prayers for each other. You're both hypocrites and he's the worst kind!'

Mrs Harris backed away from Mary's words, flinching at them as if they were blows. Mary pursued her until she was outside the room then she closed the door in the housekeeper's face, turned and flung herself on the bed, grabbed a pillow and brought it to her face to stifle the sound of her sobbing.

Moments later she heard a door slam but she did not go after Mrs Harris. Instead she lay for a while, revisiting the words they had spoken to one another in their anger and realised there was no going back for her now.

Mary got up and dabbed at her eyes with a handkerchief then forced herself to concentrate on the task in hand. The argument with Mrs Harris had delayed her and she was not even half packed. She would be late if she did not attend to the task,

Half an hour later, Mary had packed then re-packed a single suitcase, for that was all her lover would permit her to bring. When she was finally happy with the contents she wrapped a shawl around her shoulders, picked up her suitcase then slipped quietly out the back door of the vicarage to join Sean, experiencing a strange combination of fear and exhilaration at the thought of their new life together, far away from this one.

She followed the empty, dimly lit road till it took her up the hill, past the church then down the other side. There were no street lamps here. Mary stumbled in the dark and almost fell but as she straightened she found herself at the entrance to No Name Lane. Her eyes had become accustomed to the gloom by now and there was just enough moon that night to light her way. Mary had walked the lane so many times she knew every curve of it, even in darkness. The only sound was the river as it hurried along beside her with a great rushing that drowned out animal noises and the wind as it rustled the trees.

It took Mary a few minutes to reach the meeting spot they had agreed upon: a gnarled old tree that hung over the river as if stooping to take a drink from it. She rounded the bend fully expecting to see Sean standing there, for she knew she must be a few minutes late and assumed he would be early so he could wait for her. Mary squinted into the gloom but there was no one there and she immediately felt a surge of panic. She told herself not to be so foolish. She had been late herself and Sean must have been delayed too. He would be there presently, for had he not sworn to her that he would come? The thought comforted her as she waited by the tree.

Mary told herself not to worry. Sean was a man after all and the very best of them were never that reliable. He had been delayed leaving his lodgings, waiting for his landlady to fall asleep, and had encountered someone on the way and even now was hiding behind a hedge until they passed or instead he was making some excuse to them for his nocturnal wanderings. She didn't yet dare entertain the notion that he might not come. She had to believe he would, for the alternative was too dreadful to contemplate. There was no way Mary could return to the vicarage, not after the way she had spoken to Mrs Harris. She had said things that could never be unsaid and made it clear that Mary considered the older woman a fool. She had declared Sean her saviour. Mary forced herself to banish uncertainty and reject the humiliation she would experience if Sean had somehow changed his mind. It would be too much to bear if he was as feckless as Mrs Harris judged him to be.

No, there was no way he would let her down like that. Mary knew Sean too well and he wasn't the kind of man to lack the passion to see something through. They were leaving tonight and nothing would stop them. She told herself this when a quarter of an hour had passed, then again after half an hour and there was still no sign of

Sean. He had a reason, she assured herself, he would still come.

Then it began to rain and Mary was forced to endure it, for there was little shelter from the old, gnarled tree. It rained hard and before long her shawl became drenched. The night turned cold too and she hugged herself for warmth. Where was he? She had begun to feel exposed out here and was eager to get going before they lost half the night but where was her Sean?

After an hour, Mary was forced to admit that he was not going to come. Yet still she stayed; fear of the humiliation that awaited her back home kept her rooted to the spot by the tree. The rain continued intermittently through the night and several times she was soaked anew, shivering uncontrollably.

Only when she was drenched to the skin, bone cold and the sky had finally begun to lighten was Mary forced to give in to the inevitable. She picked up her suitcase in a freezing hand and trudged slowly home before early risers witnessed her folly.

She had hoped to at least slip in the back door unnoticed but Mrs Harris was up already and waiting in the kitchen. She looked as if she had not even been to bed. The older woman's face cracked in something like relief at the sight of Mary standing there, dripping water onto the floor.

'You came back Mary.' It was not said unkindly. 'You didn't go with him,' and Mrs Harris rose to meet her.

'He didn't come,' she answered flatly. 'Sean didn't come, so now you can tell me there's never been a more foolish girl.'

'Oh Mary, never mind about all that. You're soaked to the skin. You'll catch your death if we don't get you out of those wet clothes. Come here,' and she part-embraced and part-steered her towards the fire, removing her sopping shawl. 'I'll get dry things and some towels,' she told the frozen girl and she picked up Mary's suitcase and took it out of the kitchen, as if she was removing evidence from the scene of a crime.

Mrs Harris brought Mary a clean dress and helped her change into it. Neither woman spoke for a long time, as the housekeeper dutifully dabbed at her soaking hair with a fresh towel until eventually it was fit for brushing. Mary stared off into space while Mrs Harris took the silver brush and very slowly began to run it through Mary's long, damp hair. After a time she started to hum an old tune, which Mary only faintly recognised. As she sent the brush through Mary's hair, the humming took on the quality of a comforting lullaby that might have been sung to soothe a child.

When Mrs Harris finished brushing her hair they both turned at the same time and abruptly realised Mary's father was standing in the doorway, staring uncomprehendingly at them both. Neither of them had heard the Reverend Riley return. Mrs Harris got quickly to her feet and started an excitable explanation. 'My, you're back so soon,' she announced with a mock cheerfulness, 'we never expected you. Mary's been out already, in the pouring rain, silly thing, I made her change her clothes and dry her hair . . .' but she stopped as soon as she realised Reverend Riley was not listening to a word she said. He looked as if there was something he was unable to understand but instinct told Mrs Harris that the something had nothing to do with her or even Mary's dishevelled state. Her eyes went to the little wooden box he was holding loosely in his hand. It was empty.

'I'm ruined,' he said.

Chapter Fifty-Three

When Mary had concluded her story nobody spoke for a while. Helen realised for the first time that this poor woman had spent her whole life feeling like a bride that's been jilted at the altar. She tried to imagine what it must have been like to arrive at that spot on No Name Lane with hope in your heart then see it gradually eaten away, as you waited for a man who never came, not knowing that he was most likely dead already and buried just a few hundred yards from that same spot.

'There's only one question left to ask you, Mary,' and when she did not understand, Tom asked, 'Did you tell anybody else you were leaving?'

'No,' she replied.

'What about Sean? Would he have told someone?' Tom pressed,

She shook her head, 'Sean never trusted anyone from the village,' she said, 'with good reason.'

'So you only told Mrs Harris?'

'Yes,' answered Mary quietly, as if only now appreciating the gravity of that decision.

'Then she betrayed you,' he told her. 'Think about it. You never saw Sean again, so he must have been killed that night, you just didn't realise it at the time.'

'I think you're right,' she admitted.

'Who would she have told?'

'Who do you think?' answered Mary.

'Not your father, if he was away at the Dean's,' he said. 'I'm assuming she went straight to Henry or Jack Collier, perhaps both of them.'

'It couldn't have been anyone else,' she admitted, 'and I thought she forgave me when I returned. I remember thanking God for her kindness to me and to think she went to her grave years later still pretending to be my friend.'

'But how could they have known where you were meeting Sean and when? Did you tell Mrs Harris that?' asked Helen.

'No,' she said simply.

'She didn't need to,' explained Tom. 'All they had to do was wait for Sean to leave his lodgings and follow him. If you were meeting him in No Name Lane it would have been easy to confront him there or before he reached it.'

'I was a few minutes late,' she said in a dead voice, 'only a few,' and they realised she was wondering if those few minutes might have cost Sean his life and changed her future forever.

'A man like Jack Collier could have easily followed Sean and warned him off,' he said. 'If Sean stood up to him there'd have been a fight. If it got out of hand, maybe Jack used the knife to finish it. He'd killed men before in the war.'

'Perhaps,' answered Mary but Tom noticed the closer they were getting to the truth, the more weary Mary looked.

It was Helen who was brave enough to ask Mary the question, 'Could Henry have killed Sean?'

To Helen's surprise the old woman said, 'I don't know. I honestly don't. It's the question I have been asking myself since they found Sean.'

'He wasn't a fighter,' Tom reminded them. 'Maybe this was the only way to stop Sean from taking you away from him.'

'A knife in the back,' Helen observed, almost to herself.

'And you honestly don't know?' asked Tom, more in desperation than anything.

'How could I?' she asked him, 'I went to meet Sean. He never came. I waited for hours, long after I knew he wasn't coming, because I was too ashamed to go home.'

'But eventually you had to. And that's when you realised the gold sovereigns were gone,' said Helen.

'Yes,' Mary replied, 'all of them. As soon as Father walked into the house, he knew someone had been in his office and taken them.'

'And he blamed Sean?'

'Everybody did,' she confirmed. 'I couldn't explain why I was sitting there, dripping wet and Mrs Harris urged me to tell the truth, because she assumed Sean had duped me and, by then, so did I. I had to tell my father what happened.'

'That must have been awful for you,' said Helen.

'It was,' the old lady said quickly, as if she had no desire to relive the moment, even now. 'The police were called. They were sure they'd catch up with Sean eventually but they never did. He used to talk about America so everybody assumed he'd gone there with Father's money. He was never seen again. No one realised he was already dead.'

'No one except the person who put the knife in him,' said Tom. 'I don't see how Sean could have stolen the sovereigns while you were in the house. Whoever killed him must have done it afterwards while you were waiting for Sean and Mrs Harris was asleep. They wanted to make it look as if Sean had run off with the money. That part was genius,' he observed and Helen shot him a look to remind him they were dealing with an old woman's feelings, 'who was it, Mary? You said you'd only told Henry about the sovereigns.'

She nodded. 'And he in turn could have told his brother.'

'I think we now know most of what happened,' said Helen, 'but we have to accept we may never know who actually killed Sean.'

'But it seems certain it was Jack or Henry,' Tom said, 'either alone or working together. Jack was certainly capable of following Sean and overpowering him. He could have broken into your home in the night while you were waiting for Sean and stolen those sovereigns.'

'He did not have to break in,' Mary told him, 'we never locked our doors. I know it's hard to imagine now. All he had to do was prise open the drawer and take the box.'

'How did Henry act towards you afterwards, at first I mean?' asked Helen.

'He was . . .' and she searched for the right words, '. . . kind,' she settled on, '. . . and understanding. He knew that half the village regarded me as a slut and the other half a fool but he didn't care about that. He still wanted to take me on.'

'I'll bet he did,' said Tom, 'so you married him.'

'A few months later,' she confirmed, 'we had a quiet wedding.'

Tom got to his feet then and walked over to the bay window. Helen watched him as he gazed down onto Cappers Field.

'Did Jack attend the wedding?' he asked.

'No,' she said, 'he re-enlisted in the army a week before.'

'Leaving you with Stephen to look after?'

'Yes,' she said defiantly, 'which we did for many years.'

'Until you had him locked away in a mental home.' offered Tom.

'That wasn't our suggestion,' she told him.

'But you didn't fight it.'

'The man was peering through people's windows. He didn't understand what he was doing half the time. He used to frighten me.' Then her tone became defiant. 'We looked after him in our home for nearly fifteen years. You have no idea what that was like. Afterwards, I didn't want anything to do with him.'

Without turning back to them, Tom abruptly changed the subject. 'Did Henry own a lock knife, Mary?'

The old lady frowned but Helen couldn't tell if she was trying to remember or busy composing a lie.

'He did, yes,' she admitted finally, 'for fishing and other outdoor pursuits.'

Tom was still looking out of the window. 'They found one in Sean's back.'

Again there was silence while Mary thought. 'I remember . . .' she began but faltered and Tom turned to her then.

'What do you remember?'

'The knife,' she said, as if suddenly recalling something important, 'Jack took it off him.'

'What?' asked Helen, as this seemed far too convenient.

'Jack Collier stopped me in the street and told me I was to blame for driving his brother to despair. He said he had to take the knife from him in case he did anything stupid, told me Henry was stabbing it into a work bench over and over again for no purpose at all, so he took it off him.'

'Did you believe him?' asked Helen.

'Why would I not believe him?' and her face turned sour then, 'I believed most of what I was told in those days, more fool me.'

Helen and Tom exchanged a look. They were done here.

Before they left, Tom said, 'We brought something for you,' and this was the cue for Helen to reach into her bag and take out a large, rolled sheet of sturdy paper. 'Roddy Moncur thought you might like this.'

Mary unfurled it and was shocked to find herself looking down on Sean Donnellan's drawing of her younger self. 'Oh my,' she said and one of her hands went instinctively to her face.

'Roddy said it was a good likeness,' Tom told her.

They trudged back to Helen's car. It was still parked a few yards from the scene of Frankie Turner's vicious beating at Tom's hands and he half expected to see the man still lying there.

'I think we've got all we are ever going to get,' Tom reluctantly admitted.

'But is it enough for a story? I don't think Malcolm will think so. He'll be too worried to print any of it.'

'You could try,' he said half-heartedly, before reminding her, 'you can't libel the dead,' but then he thought for a moment. 'No, you're right, Malcolm won't want the *Messenger* to run a story implicating a former headmaster and his Dunkirk, war-hero brother in a murder when there's absolutely no proof. All we have is guesswork, based on the testimony of Betty, Sam and Mary, none of whom actually witnessed Sean's murder. Malcolm will say the man could have been stabbed by anyone and it might not even be Sean.' He sounded discouraged, 'Can't say I blame him really.'

'What?' she was surprised, 'You've changed your tune.'

'Malcolm hasn't written a controversial word in his entire career and he's been editor at that place for years. Look at me, I stuck my head above the parapet once and I'm finished already.'

'Don't think like that,' she urged him, 'you're ten times better than anybody at the *Messenger*. Please don't give up. Things could improve.'

'The last time you told me that I got my head kicked in,' and she gave him a helpless look. 'All right, admittedly it's not entirely doom and gloom at the moment. I did get a story this morning,' and he told her all about his meeting with DI Kane.

'You see,' she said, 'that's great,' before adding quickly, 'I mean, from a news point of view. It obviously doesn't help poor Michelle Summers or anyone else the Kiddy-Catcher has targeted.'

'Yeah,' he said, 'we should talk some more about that.'

'I can't now,' she said quickly, 'I've got to go.'

'Tomorrow, then?'

'Don't think I can tomorrow.'

'Why, what's the big story?'

She grimaced, 'the W. I. baking contest. I'm supposed to spend the whole morning in the village hall looking at cakes and scones then interviewing the winners. They even asked me to be a judge but I told them I needed to stay neutral if I am going to report objectively on it,' she added dryly.

'At least it'll fill your district page,' he said. 'I should come too. My Nan used to bake a mean vanilla sponge and I know my way around a maid of honour.'

'I bet you do.'

It was late and DI Peacock was just about to call it a night and get off home to his wife when Bradshaw and Vincent sauntered in with their news.

'So you were right,' he told Bradshaw, 'Denny did have a secret. He's knocking off a teenage waitress.'

'We followed them,' said Bradshaw, 'she's got a ground-floor flat. My guess is Denny is helping her with the rent.'

'It looks like he's moved in with her,' added Vincent.

'We went back and had a discreet word with the café owner too,' Bradshaw told Peacock, 'Denny's been using the place for a while. She's over-age, but not by much. The owner didn't know if she was seeing him or not but he didn't look like he gave a shit one way or the other.'

'Did you tell his missus?' asked Peacock in a tone that did little to indicate his feelings on the wisdom of that.

'We thought we should,' said Bradshaw, 'if she was protecting him or refused to think badly of him, this might be just what was needed to get her thinking more clearly about him and Michelle.'

'How'd she take it?'

Vincent shrugged, 'not well but . . .'

'She didn't say much,' admitted Bradshaw, 'just slumped there on her sofa and got a bit teary. Maybe she already suspected something or it just wasn't that important any more, with her daughter still missing.'

'She didn't give us anything we don't already have,' admitted Vincent.

'He's a bit of a one isn't he, this Denny?' asked Peacock, as if he was talking to himself, 'trouble is I don't know what this really tells us other than the fact that he likes teenage muff,' he added, 'and he's already getting some of that. Right now we can prove that Denny is an old perv but not that he killed his stepdaughter.'

'What more do we need?' asked Vincent but he said it quietly, as if to himself.

'We need a body,' Peacock told him.

Chapter Fifty-Four

Day Nine

Tom slept late that morning. There didn't seem to be any point in getting up early. He'd reached a dead end in the Sean Donnellan case, was reduced to peddling stories to a rival newspaper, was about to get his arse sued off by a member of the cabinet and then there was Helen.

The old familiar feelings of hurt and rejection swept over him now. This was exactly why he had always been so careful not to get seriously involved with anybody. Tom knew you could never fully trust or rely on anyone else in this world. He had learned that lesson from a very young age. Basically you were on your own and the sooner you accepted that the better but there had been something about Helen Norton that had made him forget all of his usual rules and he had stupidly let his guard down. Now he felt like an idiot and he was determined to take his mind off Helen and the way she had calmly driven off after their time with Mary Collier.

Something came back to him then: Fiona Summers' words about Nelson, the headmaster at Great Middleton School, 'slapped her right across the face he did. I can't even remember why but it was something-or-nothing'. This had jarred with him at the time, the notion of the in-control headmaster being pushed beyond his limit by the little girl and, even though the incident had been some time ago, in Tom's eyes it still merited an explanation.

Tom reasoned he was more likely to gain an audience with the oh-so-busy headmaster once the school day was over. He knew that Nelson liked to stay behind for a couple of hours after the children had gone. On arrival, Tom told the school secretary it was about a story that would be in tomorrow's paper but he was deliberately vague about this. It would do no harm to put the shits up the headmaster, as it was likely to be the only way he would be permitted to see the man at short notice.

Tom wanted to know why Nelson would slap a girl like Michelle Summers. What was it about her in particular that made the head lose control? Nelson's explanation might be a trivial one and was likely to have no bearing on the girl's disappearance years later but the incident had been nagging at Tom and he kept coming back to it. He knew it was liable to be a waste of time but there was no harm in rattling the headmaster's cage to see what would come of it.

The school reception was a sizeable open space with skylights and magnolia walls but no furniture. Tom occupied himself by taking in the gallery of photographs while he waited for the school secretary to return. It must have been a relatively recent addition, for he had never seen these pictures before. Generations of children were featured here in rows of framed group portraits. The headmaster must have reasoned the one thing the new school lacked was a sense of history, so he'd decided to import one, by fishing out these old pictures from the previous school building. The collection started at one end, with a handful of black-and-white images. Tom recognised Henry Collier in one of those earlier photographs, which, judging by the clothes he was wearing, dated from the early sixties. He had a serious but not unkind face and the children seemed relaxed in his presence, the boys in shorts and the girls in dresses, their hair tied in bows, an image of a more innocent, unknowing era. The one thing he did not look like was a murderer.

Tom worked his way along the wall, glancing at each photograph in turn, as the pictures slowly became more modern, the short trousers replaced by long ones, the black-and-white photographs by colour pictures as he finally reached the seventies, the decade that taste forgot. The male teachers had beards and long hair that covered their ears. They wore brown jackets in tweed or corduroy, while the women were decked out in shapeless dresses with coloured hoops or spots in green, brown and purple, or they wore pleated A-line skirts and white blouses with ruffled collars and beige jumpers. The kids wore chunky, hand-knitted sweaters with clumsy patterns, bright T shirts or coloured check shirts and there was a lot of gingham and even tartan, as if the brightly coloured clothes could make up for the drab days of power cuts and the three-day-week.

Tom wondered what these kids were all doing now and who they had grown up to be. Then he found what he was really looking for. It was an old, colour photograph, slightly faded from being in direct sunlight for a long time, but the figures in it were still recognisable. It was a group shot, around twenty years old, featuring two rows of children and a woman stood to one side of them. Mary Collier was dressed primly in a woollen dress, her hair tied back and pinned with a precision bordering on military. She could have been in one of those old war films that showed women in blue uniforms, moving toy planes around to chart the progress of the Battle of Britain. Mary Collier would have been ideal casting as a harsh, middle-aged NCO, disciplining the young WAAFs for lateness or wearing too much make-up on duty.

His eye left Mary and settled on the rows of children in her charge. They must have been aged about seven or eight.

'Are you in that one?' He had been so absorbed by the photograph that he hadn't heard the receptionist return.

He pointed at a short, worried-looking kid at the end of the front row. 'That's me.'

'Oh bless,' she said it kindly, 'you look like you've got the troubles of the world on you there,' and she was right, he did.

'He'll be finished in a few minutes,' she told him, 'would you like a coffee while you're waiting.'

'No thanks.'

'Then I'll leave you with your memories.'

When she was gone, Tom continued to gaze at the photograph, trying to remember how it felt to be that age. He looked so serious. Of course this could have been an illusion. Perhaps the shutter clicked at the wrong moment and he had been smiling and happy a second earlier but he doubted that. Tom knew it would be years before he could shrug off abandonment by his mother as something of no real consequence. He wondered what thoughts were going through that troubled little mind of his.

As he progressed along the line of photos, the pictures became brighter. This was the modern age of the new school and the images hadn't yet succumbed to the debilitating effect of the light. One photograph in particular caught Tom's eye and he stopped and stared at it.

At first he couldn't quite take in its significance, his interest was more instinctive than anything else, but he began to gaze closely at the faces of the little boys and girls and the teacher who was standing there with them until everything gradually came into view. A thought dropped into Tom's head and exploded there like a bomb. The sudden shock was a physical sensation that he felt in his blood and all over his skin, which prickled at the realisation.

Moments later the headmaster finally emerged. Mr Nelson pushed open the swing doors hard so he could make his point. He was far too busy to waste any more of his precious time with journalists but as he came through the door and out into reception he stopped in his tracks and looked disbelievingly around the room, because there was nobody there. Tom had gone.

Tom rang the doorbell and waited until he heard footsteps coming down the stairs, then the door finally opened.

'There's something I want to ask you,' he told Andrew Foster from his doorstep. 'It's important.'

Chapter Fifty-Five

'Really?' his friend seemed perplexed by his directness. 'Everything all right, is it?' and he made a show of looking beyond Tom to see if something was going on outside that he didn't know about. Did the teacher seem nervous? 'Okay, mate. Come in then.'

Tom followed Andrew into his front room, which was exactly as he remembered it from the night they had been drinking together, minus the vodka bottle but with the addition of sunlight through the windows.

'Ask away.'

'It's about Michelle Summers,' he said, 'the missing girl.'

'Right.'

'That night when we first met in the Lion, you said you didn't know her.'

There was a fraction of a second's hesitation. 'I don't.'

'You said you'd never known her, that she was before your time.'

'Yeah,' answered the teacher, 'that's right.'

'But that's *not* right is it, because you do know her, or at least you did.'

'I don't follow you, mate.'

'You taught her, for a whole year. In 1988, the first year you were at the school in fact, she was in your class.'

Andrew was trying to force a bemused look onto his face but it wasn't working. The only genuine emotion that

Tom could see written there was fear. 'I've seen the class photo on the school wall. It might be five years old but there's no mistaking her.'

'It can't have been her, mate. One ten-year-old girl looks very like another, that's all. You've seen another girl and thought it was Michelle what's-her-name.'

'Her name is Summers; Michelle Summers.'

'Yeah, right.'

'Say it then.'

'What?'

'Say her name.'

'Why?'

'Because I want you to,' insisted Tom, 'say her name.'

'Michelle Summers,' Andrew gave Tom a look like he was humouring a drunk, 'happy now?'

'No. Christ, man, she's standing next to you at the end of the row in the picture. It's her. There she is in your first school photo as a teacher, part of your first form class, which had to be a big deal for you, and she's standing next to you. Yet you told me you never even knew her.'

'Hang on,' Andrew held up a hand in an 'I can explain' sort of way.

'No, you hang on. I want to know why you said you never knew her.'

'Tom, relax will you. You've got the wrong girl, I'm telling you.

'No, I haven't. I know I have the right girl because I checked. That's what journalists do, we check things, and I checked this. I've just been to see Michelle's mother and I asked her. You definitely taught her.'

'Okay, okay, I'll take your word for it. So it was Michelle

and I'm sorry for being such a forgetful tosser but I don't get that attached to the kids, mate. It's just a job,' and he shrugged in an exaggerated manner, 'I didn't realise she'd been in my class. It was five years ago and I forgot about it, all right?'

'No, not all right. I don't believe you, Andrew, and do you know why?'

'What the hell is this, Tom?'

'Do you know why?' Tom shouted it at him.

'No, I don't. And I want to know just what this is actually, Tom. I want you to tell me.'

'Because when I went round to see Michelle's mother, do you know what she told me about you? Do you?'

'How could I?' Andrew Foster looked very rattled now. 'Only good things.'

'Right, well then,' he seemed relieved.

'Lots and lots of good things and all because Michelle thought you were the best thing since sliced bread. Apparently you were all she talked about for a while there. It was Mr Foster this and Mr Foster that.'

'Well, that's okay isn't it?'

'According to her mam, Michelle had a bit of a school-girl crush on you but she didn't mind because you helped her daughter with her reading and handwriting, which was always so untidy before Mr Foster got involved, giving her extra help, a bit of one-to-one tuition. Fiona even made a point of thanking you at the parents' night.'

'That's not my fault,' he swallowed as if his mouth was suddenly dry, 'if she had a bit of a crush. It can happen to any teacher; male or female.'

'Yes and it's not as if you were likely to reciprocate were you, not at her age? You're not a paedo, after all.'

'Of course not! How could you even say something like that? She was only ten.'

'Yeah, only ten back then,' said Tom quietly, 'but she was fifteen when she disappeared.'

There was a long pause. The silence stretched out in front of them. Each waited for the other to speak. More than once Andrew opened his mouth to say something but no words came out. Eventually he settled on, 'I don't know what it is you think . . .' then he shook his head as if he felt his friend had gone crazy.

'It's very simple. I think you are hiding something, Andrew. I was pretty sure of it when I came round here. I'm certain now.'

'What do you mean?'

'You're scared. In fact you're shitting it, which makes me wonder what you've done. You've lied about a missing girl. She thought you were the doggy's little bollocks but you denied knowing her . . . and now she has disappeared,' and he reached into his jacket pocket and took out the mobile phone. 'So if you won't tell me, it'll have to be the police.'

'Oh come on, don't be stupid.'

Andrew's house was on high ground so Tom managed to get a signal and he started to dial.

'Don't call the bloody police, mate,' Tom finished dialling the number and they listened as the faint sound of a ringtone began. 'What are you going to say? They won't take you seriously!'

Tom knew he was right. All he had was a hunch that his friend had something to hide but there was not a shred of real evidence that Andrew had anything to answer for, except a poor memory. Tom was bluffing him. And it looked as if Andrew was going to call that bluff. The phone rang out for what seemed like an age. He had dialled the direct line for the station that he knew by heart and they were taking a bloody long time to answer it but that was just as well, because Tom had no idea what he was going to say when they did. Tom and Andrew watched each other as the phone continued to ring and ring.

'This is just . . .' and Andrew shook his head again, '. . . madness.'

Finally the ring tone stopped and a voice said 'Police?'

'Hello,' said Tom and all he could think to add to this was, 'Sorry, wrong number' but before he could say it, Andrew took a step forward and spoke.

'Wait, I'll explain,' he urged Tom, 'I'll explain it all. Please.'

Tom hung up without another word. 'What have you done, Andrew?'

Chapter Fifty-Six

'Just give me a moment, wait there,' Andrew Foster was an agitated man, 'there's something I have to show you. It will put your mind at rest, I promise. Just wait there.' He was waving his arms in an effort to reassure Tom and keep him from moving then he disappeared and could be heard running up the stairs.

Tom was left on his own to attempt to put his thoughts in some sort of logical order. This was crazy, Andrew Foster wasn't a murderer, surely; the man he had grown to know over pints in the Greyhound and the Lion couldn't be a killer, could he? But what else could explain his bizarre behaviour? He had reacted like a man whose life depended on quickly coming up with answers he didn't possess and he had been desperate to prevent Tom from talking to the police.

And now he had disappeared upstairs. To do what? Escape from a first-floor window or to get something? Tom looked at the living-room walls with their bayonets and the weapons suddenly took on a more sinister appearance. Tom had Andrew pegged as an immature loner with a liking for boys' toys but what if he was a crazy man who'd become a teacher so he could get at little girls? Could Andrew be the Kiddy-Catcher and if he was, would he let Tom Carney back out into the world so he could tell everybody about it? What if he had used one of those bayonets on Michelle? What if he owned a gun? Christ, if Andrew was mad enough to try and shoot Tom to keep him quiet, would it be any consolation that the teacher would be arrested as soon as the shots were heard? Not if he lay bleeding to death on the living room carpet it wouldn't.

It was too late to do anything about that now. He could hear Andrew's footsteps on the stairs. The teacher was coming back down. Tom told himself that his new friend was unlikely to try and kill him in his own front room in broad daylight but, up until a few minutes ago, he would not have suspected the man of murdering a schoolgirl. Tom tensed in readiness so he could rush Andrew and disarm him if he had a weapon, but he didn't fancy his chances.

The living-room door swung open and Tom's gaze immediately went to Andrew's hands, which were empty. Any gratitude Tom may have felt for that small mercy was instantly forgotten when his gaze travelled upwards and he took in the scene in front of him. Tom's mouth fell open in astonishment and he felt his skin tingle. 'You have got to be kidding me?'

'No, Tom,' admitted Andrew, 'we are not kidding you.'

But Tom Carney ignored the words of his friend. He was too busy gazing at the figure standing behind the school teacher. She was a slight young girl with dark hair, a faint trace of lipstick on her mouth and a silver chain around her neck with a St Christopher medallion attached to it. Michelle Summers wasn't dead or buried in a ditch, miles from Great Middleton. She wasn't Girl-Number-Five, the latest victim of the Kiddy-Catcher, and she wasn't a teenage runaway, sleeping rough in London or Manchester and getting mixed up in drugs or prostitution.

Michelle Summers was very much alive.

She looked well, with no signs of ill treatment, and she was standing in Andrew Foster's living room, less than a mile from her mother's house.

'Jesus Christ,' said Tom, 'she's alive.'

The teacher nodded, 'and completely unharmed,' Andrew assured him with a benign look on his face, as if that would make it all okay somehow.

'Oh my God,' Tom was struggling to find the words, beyond a succession of callings to the Almighty, 'what have you done, Andrew?' he asked again.

Then Andrew did a strange thing. He turned back to the girl he had been holding captive in his home, while the police frantically searched for her all over the country, and said, 'Tell him, darling. I think it should come from you.'

Tom was struggling to process the information he was receiving now. Did her abductor just call Michelle Summers, darling? What kind of brainwashing was this?

'It's very simple,' the girl told Tom with a steely confidence that belied her years. 'We knew this day would come sooner or later. We want you to listen to us, to hear us out, before you call the police, I mean. We'd like to explain everything, so everybody knows and understands why we did it,' and if all of this wasn't astonishing enough, the young girl then did something that sent Tom's world rotating on its axis. She reached out an arm to one side and the schoolteacher took her hand in his, then they held on to each other like the star-crossed lovers they were convinced they'd become.

'We are going to tell you everything, Tom,' said Andrew calmly. 'We want you to hear our story.'

'He loves me,' said the girl with conviction, 'and I love him too.'

Chapter Fifty-Seven

Tom took some persuading. His first reaction was to reach for his phone again and call the police. 'Please don't do that!' begged the girl. 'Not yet. Everybody has to know the truth first. Otherwise there's no hope for us, ever! Don't you understand?' she seemed frantic now.

'No hope for you? Are you crazy?' Tom asked Michelle. 'Don't you know what's been going on while you've been hiding in here? A nationwide man hunt! Every police officer in the country has been looking for you. Have you any idea how much of their time and manpower you've wasted or the hurt you've caused?' He then looked into the calm face of his friend. 'Oh I just remembered, you don't read the papers or watch the news,' he told him, 'but you must have bloody known!'

'Yes Tom, we did know,' Andrew continued to talk to him as if he was an entirely reasonable man who was trying to calm somebody down, 'and that certainly wasn't our intention. Things just spiralled out of control – but I know you will understand when you hear what we have to say.'

'Understand?' then he remembered something. 'Was she here when I came back for that drink? Was Michelle hiding upstairs while we were downing your bloody vodka? She must have been!' He was furious then.

'Just give us a few more minutes, please, then you can call anyone you like.' Tom hesitated. 'Please,' Andrew said again. 'It's a good story and that's what you wanted, wasn't it? A really good story.'

Tom shook his head, 'I must be crazy.'

'Thank you,' said the girl, beaming at him, as if her problems were solved instead of just beginning.

'You won't regret it,' Andrew told him.

'I already am.'

Ian Bradshaw sat at his desk at HQ thinking about his partner, if that was the right word to describe his unofficial pairing with Vincent Addison, and the fake professor, both of whom had let him down badly. He was praying that Burstow's intense questioning would not reveal the private conversation the mad fantasist had enjoyed with DC Bradshaw in the pub, for no good could ever come of that. If Bradshaw was annoyed at himself and more than a little embarrassed at having been taken in by the fake professor, he was hardly alone, however. The entire Durham force had been listening to the lunatic's theories for weeks and it was all the fault of one man. Detective Superintendent Trelawe had told them Burstow was an expert, so why would they ever have cause to doubt him? Still, it galled Bradshaw that he had ever taken the trouble to listen to the man's bullshit, assuming it to be science and not fantasy.

Then there was Vincent. Like Bradshaw, he had been discouraged by the realisation that although they'd rumbled Denny as a pervert, with a liking for girls who were borderline legal, they were unable as yet to pin the disappearance of his young stepdaughter on the man.

When they'd been out on the road tailing Denny,

Vincent had seemed livelier and more positive than usual. Bradshaw reasoned his partner secretly enjoyed doing a bit of real police work for a change, even if he was unlikely to admit it. DI Peacock's grim assessment of the lack of evidence connecting Denny to Michelle's disappearance seemed to dent his partner's morale, however. Sure enough, when Bradshaw enquired after his whereabouts the next morning he was told by Peacock that Vincent had gone sick with depression, the DI adding the word 'again' to his sentence, before concluding, 'He's about as much use as a toffee kettle and just as reliable.'

Bradshaw was gutted. He had spent the rest of the morning on the admin that plagued every modern detective: statements, filing, endless form filling, the stuff they never showed you on TV. Now he was eager to get going once more. He had an idea that this might be a good time to revisit Michelle's mother. If he could have another word with her in the cold light of day, once she'd had a few hours to allow Denny's betrayal to sink in, she might prove more open; freed from a conflicting loyalty, Fiona might remember something significant. It was certainly worth a try but he would have liked Vincent to be in the room with him. One of them would make the tea and provide sympathy; the other could derail Fiona with a few harsh questions about the appropriateness of Denny's relationship with Michelle. Good cop, bad cop this time. He wanted to get back out there with Vincent and show everybody just what they were capable of when they put their minds to it but it seemed his new partner just didn't have the stamina to see things through to the end, so Bradshaw was on his own again.

*

They sat together on Andrew's couch; the schoolteacher and his underage lover, still holding hands. Tom sat in the chair opposite them. He placed his tape recorder on the arm of the chair and turned it on then took out his pen, placing the pad on his knee.

'I'm listening,' he told them. 'You've got five minutes, no more. I'm going to burn in hell for giving your mother five more minutes of anguish, so this better be one amazing explanation. We'll start with you, Andrew. Just what in God's name did you think you were doing, bringing her here?'

'I didn't do it deliberately, Tom, you have to understand that. It all began because I bumped into Michelle again, purely by chance.'

'At the bus stop?' asked Tom, as it was the last known sighting of the missing girl, and she nodded.

'It was pouring down that night,' added Andrew, 'I was walking back from the pub when I saw her standing there. She looked wet through and so cold. I didn't know who it was at first but then I realised it was Michelle. I'd taught her years ago, like you said. She was just a little girl back then of course but now here she was again, all grown up.'

'Not quite,' Tom reminded him but Andrew ignored this.

'We talked for a moment but she was shivering and I offered to drive her home. I'd only had two or three and you can never rely on that last bus.'

'Go on,' he urged his former friend, needing to hear something, anything that might justify the decision to hide a girl from her family for so long.

'I agreed to go with him,' Michelle explained, 'he was just being kind.'

'Was he?'

'When we got to my house she was still dripping wet so I said she could come in and dry her hair. Her shoes were soaking too.'

'They weren't the best pair for weather like that,' the girl admitted with a sheepish grin and Tom stared at her as if she was mad.

'Anyway,' was Andrew hesitating now, as if his well-rehearsed justification was about to sound distinctly weak when told to an outsider? 'I gave her a towel, made her a hot drink and we started to talk. She told me there was no hurry to get home; her mother would be asleep, her stepfather out in the lorry, so there was no rush.'

'We just talked and talked,' the girl explained, 'well, mostly, I talked and he listened. I think he was the first person to listen to me in years.' And they smiled at the shared memory, grinning like simpletons. It was if they were a proper couple at a dinner party, telling everyone the story of how they first met.

'What was inappropriate about it?' asked Andrew innocently. 'We didn't *do* anything, just talked.'

'Aside from the fact that she is fifteen years old and you are a teacher?' Tom shook his head. 'Why didn't you just take her home?'

'The more we talked, the more I learned what a special and delightful young girl Michelle had become and how unhappy she was at home.'

'That's no reason to keep her here.'

'I didn't keep her,' answered Andrew, 'she stayed of her own free will.'

'Why?' asked Tom incredulously.

'Well . . . and this where things got a bit complicated, it

became late and I said I'd make us another drink before driving her home. At this stage we thought she could just slip in through the front door and nobody would notice. Her mother's practically an alcoholic, doesn't care about her at all in fact but that's by-the-by. Even if she did wake up, Michelle could just say she was out walking or called in at a friend's, so nobody would get into trouble.'

'*Nobody* meaning *you*, you mean.'

'I went back into the kitchen and put the kettle on again but by the time I came out with the hot chocolate, Michelle had fallen asleep on my couch.'

'And you didn't think to wake her up?'

'I was going too,' he admitted, 'but she looked so sweet and pretty and peaceful lying there that I just thought it would be a shame to.'

'So what *did* you do?'

'I covered her with a blanket. Then I sat down in the chair you're sitting in and figured she'd probably wake up eventually and I'd drive her home but she didn't wake up and I fell asleep too. I didn't open my eyes until six in the morning and by then it would have been too late to drive her back home without a lot of very difficult questions.'

'But I don't understand. If you'd done nothing? I mean, what you did do was bloody stupid and you would have been in trouble but if you hadn't touched her . . . wouldn't it have been better to just bring her home? The grief you've caused?' Tom asked, confused.

'But I didn't want to go home,' Michelle answered, 'I begged him to let me stay.'

'And by that stage, well, I didn't know what else to do, so I let her.'

'You mean you went off to school as if nothing had happened?'

'What choice did I have?'

'What choice did you have? A bunch of them! You could have chosen to end the misery of a family who thought their little girl had been murdered by a serial killer. Are you both completely out of your minds? You must be!'

'By then I think we both knew something special had happened between us, something permanent,' Andrew told him with the wide-eyed zeal of a religious convert. Tom opened his mouth to speak but couldn't find the words. How could he reason with somebody this deluded? 'Every night we said we would give ourselves up in the morning but we just couldn't bring ourselves to do it. We knew it would end eventually and we would need someone to tell our story,' he continued. 'Then I met you in the pub and I just knew you'd be the right person to do it. I nearly brought Michelle down that night you came for a drink but we wanted to be together a bit longer. I've never felt so alive,' Andrew assured him, 'but you must understand that I didn't touch her. I didn't view her like that.'

'You didn't touch her?' Tom repeated.

'No,' Andrew assured him, as if he was determined to be portrayed as a man of honour, 'sex wasn't important to either of us,' then he cleared his throat, 'at first.'

'At first?'

'That didn't happen till later,' he said.

And before Tom could respond to that, Michelle interrupted, 'And when it did happen, I instigated it. It was my decision.'

Tom stopped writing. He put down his pen and pad

and stared at them both, 'Oh well,' he told them scath-ingly, 'that's all right then!' He shook his head. 'Teachers can't just have relationships with schoolgirls!'

'Why not? We're not the first and we certainly won't be the last. Is it better for her if she goes with some spotty sixteen-year-old who has no idea how to treat her? I love Michelle and she loves me. Please be happy for us. I thought you might understand this.'

'Understand it? Me? Are you completely barking? You're banging on about love and things being perman-ent? Can't you see it, Andrew? You're going to jail! They are going to throw the bloody book at you!'

'I don't think it'll come to that,' answered the teacher, 'but even if it did, that's a risk I'm prepared to take, for Michelle,' he squeezed his lover's hand and she smiled at him reassuringly, 'and no matter how long it takes, she will wait for me.'

'You idiot,' Tom told him, 'you still don't get it, do you. Your whole life is fucked, Andrew, you're going to prison and when you get out you won't be able to get a job, you'll lose your house, everything and there is no chance they are going to allow you to contact her. None! Can't you see that? If there is one thing I am certain about, it's this: when I make this phone call you will never see Michelle again, ever. That much is bloody guaranteed!' and he picked up the mobile phone and began to dial.

For the first time Andrew looked rattled, as if the thought of being denied access to his one true love had never crossed his mind. 'Well,' he said uncertainly, his voice cracking a little when confronted with Tom's certainty, 'we'll see, won't we?'

Chapter Fifty-Eight

Bradshaw was still annoyed at Vincent, who was physically no sicker than he was. The man was suffering from an attack of laziness or an onset of the blues but, if it really was depression that had caused Vincent Addison's current absence, then he would get no sympathy from his younger colleague. If Bradshaw had to carry on and muddle through whenever the black dog of his own depression was biting down hard, then why shouldn't Vincent? His absence was all the more frustrating because of its timing. Vincent had gone home to his bed just when they had begun to make some serious progress. What chance did they have of ever being taken seriously, if his partner abandoned a case at such a critical point because he wasn't feeling up to it?

Well, Bradshaw wasn't going to allow that to happen. He'd dug out Vincent's address and he was going round there to talk him back onto the Michelle Summers' case. Bradshaw was on his feet, a second from leaving HQ, when his phone suddenly rang. He almost didn't pick it up at first then he cursed and answered.

'Bradshaw,' he said.

'Ian, it's me, Tom Carney.'

'And I was having such a good day,' said the detective. 'What do you want?'

There was a slight delay on the line while Tom Carney

seemed to be trying to find the right words, then he said, 'I have found Michelle Summers.'

'What?' Was this some kind of sick joke?

'I have found . . .'

'I heard what you said,' interrupted Bradshaw, 'but what do you mean? How could you have . . . Are you saying, you've found her body?'

'No,' said Tom, 'she is alive and . . .' Could he use the word 'well'? He decided on 'unharmed'. She's been staying with a teacher in Great Middleton. His name is Andrew Foster.'

'Jesus.'

Tom Carney gave Ian Bradshaw the address then and sealed the teacher's fate.

'She's in Great Middleton?' asked Bradshaw and Tom was glad he wasn't the only one questioning his own sanity.

'You can come and get her,' said the reporter quietly and he hung up.

For a second Ian Bradshaw stood holding onto the phone as he struggled to digest the significance of this while everybody else in the room carried on working, oblivious to the news he had just been given. Bradshaw had become convinced Denny was responsible for Michelle Summers' disappearance, refusing to believe any other theory, but now he'd been told she was alive and well and hiding in the village whose front doors had become so familiar to him lately. He glanced towards Peacock's office and realised the DI wasn't there, then he looked around the room at the detectives manning their desks, calmly taking calls and making notes. He asked them all, 'Where's DI Peacock?' When nobody answered him Bradshaw called louder, 'Where's the boss?' but all he got in return was an uninterested 'Dunno,' from his nearest workmate.

Bradshaw surveyed his uncomprehending colleagues and felt a rising anger at their lack of urgency. 'Where's Peacock?' he shouted at the top of his voice and everybody froze. They all stared back at him like he was mad but at least he had their full attention now. 'Where's the boss?' he shouted once more.

'I think he's in the smoking room with the DCI,' answered Marie Ryan, one of Durham Constabulary's few female detectives. 'What's up?'

'Go and get him,' Bradshaw demanded as he pulled on his jacket, 'get them both and get them now! Michelle Summers has been found!' He thrust the address he had scribbled on the paper towards her, then raced from the room with every eye upon him.

When Tom Carney phoned Michelle's mother to break the news, he did it quickly. 'I have found Michelle and she is alive,' he said, in case she assumed the worst.

'Oh my God, oh my God!' Fiona was hyperventilating on the end of the phone. 'Oh God, I don't believe it, oh God.' Then finally, when the news had sunk in, she asked, 'Where is she?'

'In the village.'

'In the village?' She wasn't expecting that; she was clearly assuming London or at least Birmingham but not *in the village*. 'Where in the village?'

Tom told her, then he hung up and made one last call.

*

Afterwards, Ian Bradshaw would be unable to remember anything about the journey to Great Middleton that day but he took every twist and turn at speed, shouting, 'Come on, come on,' at any driver who moved too slowly in front of him.

Eventually, he reached Great Middleton and chose the first turning that would take him up the hill, almost losing the back end of his car in the process. At the top, he took a sharp right which brought him into the street Tom Carney had mentioned then he sped along it, scanning door numbers till he reached the right one. He slammed on his brakes, abandoning his car in the middle of the road, not even bothering to close the door as he alighted.

Only then did it cross Bradshaw's mind that if Tom Carney was somehow wrong, deluded or just winding him up, he would be in the kind of trouble it would be impossible to come back from. Surely Michelle Summers could not have been staying at this quiet, little house nestled in a row of similarly innocuous properties, right in the heart of her village, without anyone knowing about it? It didn't seem possible.

Bradshaw was about to bang on the door when it opened. Tom Carney was standing there. The journalist did not say a word to the detective. He simply held open the door to admit him, then stepped aside.

Bradshaw walked straight into Andrew Foster's living room and there in front of him was a miracle. Tom Carney had not been deluded, nor was he winding Bradshaw up. Seated on a sofa was a young girl. Though he had never met her, Bradshaw instantly recognised Michelle Summers from her description and photograph. Even if she was a little more grown-up than the image the police had been using, this was clearly the same child. It was almost too much to take in at first. Against all the odds of probability, Michelle Summers was alive and seemingly unharmed.

The young girl was sitting next to a man in his twenties who Bradshaw had to assume must be the teacher Tom had mentioned. They both had anxious looks on their faces and if the sight of them sitting together was not shocking enough, Bradshaw suddenly realised they were holding hands.

'Michelle?' asked Bradshaw in disbelief, and when the girl slowly nodded, he demanded of them both, 'What the bloody hell has been going on here?'

Andrew Foster opened his mouth to answer on their behalf but his words were drowned out by the sound of police sirens.

Helen was the first reporter on the scene, if you didn't include Tom Carney. She heard the sirens of multiple police cars and instantly abandoned her post at the W. I. event because that kind of din could only mean something major had happened or was just about to.

As she left the village hall, Helen looked towards the sound just as it dimmed. Ahead of her was a small village green in front of a steep hill, with two public foot-paths snaking up it, one on either side. They rose until they combined at the top as they reached a road and a row of small houses set back from it on the high ground. Three police cars were parked carelessly outside an insignificant-looking house with whitewashed walls. They blocked the road, their lights blinking pointlessly, the officers having seemingly abandoned their vehicles to attend to something urgent inside the house.

As Helen climbed the hill three more police cars suddenly sped into the village with lights flashing and sirens blaring. As she reached the top of the footpath they screeched to a halt in front of her. A half-dozen uniformed officers and several plain-clothes detectives spilled from them, then darted into the house.

It was a scene of exhilarating chaos and Bradshaw found himself numbly taking charge, buoyed by the knowledge that, whatever had been going on here, it did not constitute murder and for once, there would be some good news to report to a salivating media. The uniformed officers who arrived shortly after Bradshaw happily obeyed his instructions to keep the public back from the house and take Andrew Foster in for questioning. Michelle would be leaving for the station too for her own safety and to ensure a proper explanation for her disappearance was secured.

Aware that their noisy arrival would soon ensure a crowd of onlookers, Bradshaw said, 'Get them out of here quick.' Then he glanced at Tom. 'And you're coming too,' he ordered.

Helen waited outside, watching the comings and goings at the house from the top of the footpath at the other side of the road. Neighbours were beginning to emerge and other onlookers began to congregate, drawn to the scene by the police sirens. Two uniformed policemen pushed and waved them back to create some space. They did not have to wait long to witness the cause of all the excitement. First, a man that she had seen talking to Tom in the pub came out through the front door, manhandled by two burly policemen who did not look happy. His arms were pulled back behind him and his head pushed down but he managed to raise it and, for a second, his gaze caught Helen's and he looked right back at her, his face a picture of resignation. They bundled him into the back seat of a police car and Helen watched them speed away.

Next, Tom emerged from the house with the detective she had seen in the Red Lion. What was going on and what was his role in all of this? Had he discovered the teacher was up to no good or merely received his confession like some parish priest? Before she could consider this latest complication further, something else happened, something that put a seal on the whole day.

Another person came out of the house then, accompanied by the police. Helen knew her in an instant, for her face had been on TV and in every newspaper. It was Michelle Summers; a young girl thought taken, a lost innocent, presumed dead. And here she was. This was the end result none of them could have hoped for.

It was too much for Helen to take on board at once and it was clear that the small band of onlookers felt the same way. Aside from a few gasps and one or two cries of 'Michelle' and 'it's her', nobody did anything. They simply stood and stared at the girl as if she was an apparition.

Just when she was wondering if Tom had somehow

solved the mystery of her disappearance and rescued the girl, another familiar figure arrived. Michelle was halfway up the front garden path when her mother suddenly appeared, red-faced and breathless, for she had been forced to run halfway across the village to the school-teacher's house. Fiona saw her daughter and let out a loud cry of, 'Meee-shell!' then she ran forward to embrace her, almost knocking her off her feet in the process. The police stood back and let her do it and Bradshaw did not inter-vene. It would have been a brave or foolish man who would have tried to come between a mother and her daughter at the moment. Instead they stood back and watched, looking on as Fiona Summers clasped her daughter to her so tightly it looked like she might break the girl in two. Her mother was sobbing and reciting the same words over and over again like a mantra, 'Oh my God, Shell . . . oh my God, Shell . . . are you all right? . . . oh my God, Shell . . . what did he do to you? . . . did he hurt you? . . . did he touch you? . . . the bastard!'

Helen couldn't make out all the words of Michelle's reply but she did hear, 'It wasn't like that, Mam . . .' before Michelle Summers' voice dropped to a level where noth-ing more was audible. Helen watched as her mother released her and Michelle presumably began an explan-ation for her presence in the village. Helen could see the young girl's face and it looked as if Michelle was trying to calm her mother, while explaining something to her that was actually very simple and that all was really quite well with the world

When Fiona Summers answered her daughter, Helen heard everything.

'What?' the single, startled word encapsulated her mother's shock. Fiona Summers was staring at her daughter through disbelieving eyes, her face still streaked with tears.

The girl continued her explanation at a level only her mother could make out. And, just when the surrounding group of officers had begun to relax and enjoy the reunion between the relieved mother and the naïve girl wrongfully imprisoned by the older man, a strange thing happened. The mother took a step forwards and hit her.

Fiona Summers struck her daughter hard, right across the face.

It wasn't a small slap. This was a full-on, wide-arm blow that made onlookers wince and instantly turned Michelle Summers' cheek bright red. 'How could you do that!' hollered Fiona and she aimed another slap which, fortunately for her daughter, missed its target as she tottered backwards, merely catching the ducking girl a glancing blow on the top of her head. This was the signal for the shocked police officers to belatedly intervene, wading in between them to drag Michelle's mother away from the young girl, though she was still flailing her arms. 'How could you do it?' she screamed once more as she was dragged backwards up the garden path. 'He's left me!' she hollered, 'he's fucking left me! Because of you! All because of you! Are you happy now? Are you?!'

Michelle Summers' face bore the lurid welt from the first blow and she was already catching up with her mum in the waterworks department; her mouth was clamped shut and her bottom lip began to quiver. Then the tears came and she started to sob uncontrollably. Suddenly she looked exactly what she was: a small, frightened child snapped back into the real world, being led away by the police.

Helen watched Michelle climb into one car with a police-woman, while two male police officers led her mother to a different one. 'You've got her back,' Bradshaw reminded Fiona. 'At least you've got her back,' and he opened the door for the weeping woman.

Chapter Fifty-Nine

When the cars started to pull away, Helen walked over to Tom.

'Did that just happen?' she asked dumbly.

'Michelle and the teacher?' he asked. 'Yes. Think they're Romeo and sodding Juliet.'

'Oh dear God,' she said, 'all this time and everyone thought she was dead. Are they crazy?'

'I think they are,' he agreed, 'or at least deluded.' Then Tom shook his head as if he couldn't believe their idiocy. 'And he is going to burn for this.'

They watched as, one by one, the remaining police cars made careful U-turns in the road, all except the last.

'I have to go too,' he told her. 'They want my statement.'

'How did you know?' she asked him.

'It was just something he said, about not knowing Michelle,' Tom explained, 'but I found out he taught her.'

'Is that all?'

'Yeah.'

'Bloody hell.'

A tape recorder whirred in the background and DC Ian Bradshaw listened intently while Tom Carney told his version of the events of that day and, as he did so, the room began to fill up around him; first DI Peacock, then Skelton and O'Brien and finally DCI Kane.

When his statement was complete, the tape recorder was turned off and Kane spoke.

'If we hadn't heard it from them and you,' Bradshaw told him, 'I doubt we would ever have believed it. Does that teacher not have any idea of the grief he has caused everybody?'

'No, I don't think he does,' confirmed Tom, 'though I suspect he is about to find out.'

'Oh yes,' said Kane, 'he will be left under no illusions as to the severity of his situation.'

'Can we do him for kidnap?' asked Skelton.

'Not when she went voluntarily,' Bradshaw told him, 'and she did go voluntarily, right?'

'So she says,' said Tom.

It was the DI's turn now. 'But we have got statutory rape of a minor, wasting police time, obstructing justice and that's just off the top of my head. I'm sure I can think of a few more,' said Peacock.

'No need,' said Kane. 'Cleverer men than us are currently formulating charges that will guarantee that bastard jail time. The ACC won't be happy till he gets ten years.'

'That won't happen,' muttered O'Brien.

'No but he'll definitely see prison,' Kane assured his DS. 'He embarrassed several police forces, caused us all untold grief and damaged a few important careers along the way, so an example will be made, of that you can be certain.'

'And he ran off with an underaged girl,' Tom reminded him.

'The least of his crimes,' said DI Peacock and there were a few wry chuckles at that one.

When the formalities were over, Kane said, 'you can get off now if you want. One of our lads will run you back.'

But Tom didn't move. 'There's still a man out there,' he said significantly, 'killing little girls.'

'What's your point?' asked Bradshaw.

'Helen Norton and I have been talking about the Kiddy-Catcher and we think we might know how he's doing it, how he is getting them to come with him,' Tom told him. 'We have a couple of ideas in fact, but you're probably not going to like either of them.'

'Go on.'

First Tom explained Helen's theory, causing murmurs all around the room. That told Tom they were taking the female accomplice idea seriously but were all really hoping it wasn't true.

'Okay,' said Kane, 'that we can look at.' And he turned to Peacock. 'Start with any known offender with a partner who could be an accomplice. Most sex offenders are so pathetic they couldn't possibly get a girlfriend but there are some who could persuade lasses to help them. Let's track them down and see where they were on the nights our girls disappeared.' He turned back to Tom. 'What's your second theory?'

'I think he might be impersonating a police officer,'

'What?'

Tom shrugged, 'I've accepted lifts from strangers lately, but only because they showed me a warrant card. That made me feel safe somehow,' and he gave O'Brien and

Skelton a wry look. 'How else does he get the girls to climb into his car?'

'All of us have been wondering about that,' said Kane and he turned to the other officers. 'Has anyone been pulled up for impersonating a police officer? Not just recently, check the records, go back a few years then have a word with them all. Do they have alibis for the nights when the girls disappeared? Look out for fake IDs and warrant cards. Spread the word but do it quietly and discreetly. I don't want anyone from the press picking up on this and running with it or nobody will trust us again, and that includes you,' he jabbed a finger at Tom.

Tom nodded. 'Don't panic. I'm not about to create a news story out of nothing more than my own half-baked theory.'

'Really, I thought that's what you guys always did,' Kane told him with a half-smile. 'We'll look into it and thanks for rumbling the teacher. You did a good job.'

When Tom was finally finished with the police he was driven back to Great Middleton. This time he went straight to the Greyhound. After the excitement of the day's events he knew he was beginning to crash. He'd eaten nothing for hours so he ordered crisps with a pint of IPA and took them to a table. He sat there numbly, trying to put some level of sanity into the events of the past few days.

The place was quiet and Colin was going round the room, collecting glasses.

'Now Tom,' he said, 'have you heard about that bloody Tory?'

'Which one?'

'That Grady fellah you wrote about.'

'Oh, him,' answered Tom without enthusiasm, 'what's he done now.'

'It's been all over the news. I thought you were supposed to be the journalist.'

'Yeah, well, I've been a bit busy today.'

'Where've you been like?'

'Andrew's house,' he replied mechanically, not wanting to go into it all just then.

'Oh right,' said Colin. 'Expect he'll be in later,' he added absentmindedly.

'Doubt it,' said Tom and he took a long, deep drink.

'Looks like you needed that,' said Colin

'I did,' agreed Tom then he remembered what Colin had said. 'So the right honourable Timothy Grady. What's he been up to then?'

'So you really haven't heard what's happened?'

'I said, didn't I?' snapped Tom.

'Right,' Colin nodded, 'well I'm about to make your day then.'

'Why?'

'He's been arrested.'

'Arrested?'

'Aye.'

Tom regarded the landlord doubtfully. Colin was a good man but not the world's most reliable narrator and he really didn't want to get his hopes up, only to have them dashed later when he discovered Colin had been wildly misinformed.

'Are you sure we are talking about the same guy?'

'Yeah,'

'Timothy Grady?'

The landlord nodded.

'The former government minister; the man trying to sue me and my newspaper?'

Colin nodded again.

'Has been arrested?' Tom didn't understand how he could have been.

'That's what they're saying, like.'

'Arrested for what?'

Colin did make his day then. 'Kerb crawling.'

Chapter Sixty

Colin turned on the TV in the bar and they waited for the early-evening news. There was no doubting the lead story. Former Defence Secretary Timothy Grady had been arrested by police in the early hours of that morning, on a side street close to King's Cross station, in a notorious red light district. The story hadn't leaked till mid-morning but it had quickly gained legs and now everyone was running with it.

The TV report wasn't holding back, which meant Grady had to have been caught bang-to-rights. There was even a mention of a second person arrested at the same time in connection with the incident; a seventeen-year-old girl who, for legal reasons regarding her age, could not be named.

There was footage of a very rattled-looking Grady leaving Paddington Green police station that afternoon with photographers all around him.

'What was he thinking?' asked Colin. 'I mean, how daft can you be?'

'He wasn't thinking,' explained Tom. 'Men like that think laws don't apply to them.'

'But he could have gone to a hotel. Why drive down to King's Cross and pick up a teenage hooker?'

'Because of the risk,' said Tom, who immediately understood. 'Cheating on your missus and putting two fingers up to the Prime Minister, while shagging escort girls in discreet hotel rooms isn't exciting enough for men like Timothy Grady. No, he needs a hurried blowjob in his car down a side street filled with used condoms and syringes. The excitement of getting caught is probably the only way he can get off.'

'Well he was caught all right, stupid bastard.'

'Yes he was,' smiled Tom, 'and you know what that means?'

'What?' asked the landlord.

'I am back.'

Tom phoned the office of Alex 'the Doc' Docherty and Jennifer answered. He asked to speak to the Doc and, for once, was put straight through, which didn't entirely surprise him.

'Tom!' exclaimed Docherty cheerfully. 'What a bloody result! Eh? My giddy aunt! Who could have predicted that?' The Doc could not have been in a better mood. 'The man's about to destroy us all then he ruins everything because he can't keep it in his trousers for another few weeks. I don't know what this country's coming to, I really don't,' he said gleefully.

'I always said he was dodgy.'

'You did, son, and so did I. But that's not what counts, remember?'

'It's proving it that counts, right?'

'You're learning,' the Doc told him, 'which is one of the reasons why I am delighted to welcome you back. Thanks to our contacts, I've already got the inside story.

Grady was caught by two police officers with a seventeen-year-old prozzy. He had his flies undone and she had his cock out,' the Doc laughed. 'Even he couldn't talk his way out of that one. I hope he enjoyed it, because this is likely to be the most expensive hand job in human history.'

'It couldn't happen to a nicer guy,'

'The claim for libel has already been dropped, leaving Grady with a colossal legal bill, a furious missus and a very disgruntled Prime Minister, who's getting it in the neck for publicly backing the man. The police are going to charge him with perverting the course of justice and the Crown Prosecution Service are looking into some serious, long-standing fraud allegations against him and his bitch of a missus, now that all of their powerful friends are running for cover. Grady has managed to lose his marriage, his career and a large chunk of his personal fortune in a single day. That's some achievement.'

'Single mums all over the country will be dancing in the aisles at Asda,' said Tom. 'So, am I off the hook?'

'You? Of course! It's over, my son. In fact I want you back down here ASAP. I'm going to do a big follow-up piece on exactly how our crack investigative team brought down the sleazy government minister with his hypocritical family values.'

'There is still the small matter of my contract?'

'Consider it renewed. There, I said it. Now, how's that for a weight off your shoulders? Feel better? I only wish I could have told you sooner, Tom, but you know what it's been like here. Where are you anyway?'

'I'm still in the north east. I've been following up the disappearance of Michelle Summers.'

'The Kiddy-Catcher case?'

'Yes, well, no. That's what everyone thought but it turned out she wasn't Girl Number Five after all. She'd just run off with her old school teacher.'

'No?'

'Yep,' and Tom explained it all to the Doc.

'That's amazing! What a bloody story. I hope Jake's all over it.'

Tom knew The Paper's Northern correspondent was not all over it. 'Want to hear something that's even more amazing?'

'What?'

'I found out about it before the police and got their side of the story,' Tom informed the editor, 'the girl and the teacher.'

'You're kidding me?'

'Nope and I'm the only one who's got it. They arrested the teacher afterwards. They'll be questioning him for the next couple of days while they piece it all together but they haven't formulated the charges yet, so this could all be published in tomorrow's paper without prejudicing a court case. "Our story", by the teacher and the teenage runaway who hid while her mother thought she'd been murdered.'

'Oh my God! I don't believe it, son. That's incredible. You are one in a million! Get yourself down here pronto, next train, you hear, no, forget that. I'll arrange for a car to pick you up. We'll get you to Newcastle airport and fly you down. Write your notes up on the plane and Jennifer can type them up for you when you get here.'

'You think it's a good story then?'

'A good story? This is bloody dynamite!'

'So it's worth a few bob?'

There was a silence on the line for a moment. 'Oh, I get it. It's like that is it? Listen son, I know you're a bit narked at me right now but . . . I'll see if I can't bump your salary up when you get back here,' Tom stayed silent, 'and we'll get you two or three grand extra in readies as well. You know, a nice brown envelope to welcome you back. How does that sound?'

'Two or three grand for this story? You know the other red tops would all pay ten times that and don't try and tell me you haven't got the authority to match them, because I know you have.'

'Match them? Are you kidding me? You work for me, son or have you forgotten that, so don't come over all lippy just 'cos you fell on a story while you were on gardening leave, 'cos it won't wash.'

Tom stayed silent again until the Doc calmed down. 'Okay, he added finally, 'I'll up your pay by ten grand a year and I'll slip you ten grand in readies from the kiss-and-tell fund.' Tom could tell the Doc was excited, champing at the bit for this story. The doc chuckled, 'We won't tell the tax man if you don't. How does that sound?'

'Not good enough, I'm afraid, Doc.'

'What?'

'I think I'll be taking my story elsewhere, if it's all the same to you. *The Mirror* has already offered me forty grand.'

'Elsewhere? Have you gone stark raving bonkers? You work for me, you ungrateful little shit, which means that everything you write belongs to me! It's called intellectual property and we'll bloody sue you if you try to give it to anybody else. Now get your arse back down here! You can kiss that ten grand goodbye for starters, which will teach you never to piss me off again! Have you finally got it, you stupid bastard?'

'I have, Doc,' answered Tom. 'I fully understand about the intellectual property argument. I got it in one, in fact. There's just one little problem.'

'What's that?' snarled the doc.

'My contract with you expired two days ago,' Tom said and there was another lengthy silence on the line while Tom allowed the Doc to digest that piece of information, 'which means I'm officially freelance, so I can sell my stories to anyone I want and right now I want to sell this one to the *Daily Mirror*. I believe you once sacked their current editor? They're actually gonna pay me extra because they know how pissed off it'll make you to see my story plastered all over his front page. Enjoy reading that over your cornflakes.'

The Doc went mad then. Tom had never heard anybody lose it to quite such a degree. Nobody had, in fact. The entire newsroom stopped what it was doing and collectively turned to listen as Alex 'The Doc' Docherty unleashed an absolutely unparalleled deluge of four-letter filth down the phone at Tom Carney. The tirade went on for a good two minutes.

Tom listened calmly until the Doc was finally spent. When the editor had at last run out of breath and invective Tom could finally get a word in edgeways. 'You finished, Doc? Calmed down have you? Good,' said Tom. 'Now do me a favour and go fuck yourself.'

Tom had the last word, but only because he managed to hang up before another foul-mouthed blast began.

Tom Carney became a legend in the newsroom that day, chiefly for being the cause of the Doc's most violent meltdown, even though he didn't get to hear the culmination of it. As soon as the Doc realised he had been entirely shafted by his former junior reporter and that Tom was no longer on the line, Alex Docherty ripped his phone out of the wall by its socket and hurled it as far away from him as possible.

Jennifer was still sitting outside the great man's office, trying to make herself look very small indeed until her boss's fury finally died down. She had seen the Doc lose it before, but never quite like this. Even she jumped at the almighty crash as the Doc's phone came flying through his office window, shattering it in the process, showering glass all over the carpet and her desk while her boss let out a cry like a wounded bull, which had everybody wondering how they could vacate the building discreetly. Jennifer went and hid in the ladies.

Tom dialled Paul Hill at the *Mirror*. 'You can have everything,' Tom told him. 'I've enough on the teacher and his runaway pupil for a front-page splash and a double-page spread inside.'

'Nice one,' said Hill, 'our editor is well happy with you right now.'

'Thought he might be and I've got another story he's

going to like. My inside angle on the Timothy Grady take-down. How we got the story, how we trapped the Lion and I've a nice angle on how he used British libel laws to stifle freedom of speech. As a bonus, I'll even add a few hundred words on why Britain's biggest-selling newspaper bowed to pressure from his lawyers and threw me to the wolves.'

'Ooh,' said the voice on the end of the line, 'I like that last bit.'

'I thought you might,' said Tom. 'There's just one small thing.'

'Name it,' said Hill.

'I want to write the headline.'

The next morning Tom rose early and drove to the Rose-wood café. On the way there he bought the newspapers and placed them on the table so he could read them while he ate his breakfast. Tom ordered a fry-up with coffee then turned his attention to that day's front pages, all of which were running with follow-up stories on the wreckage of Timothy Grady's career and marriage. The front page of the *Mirror* was particularly striking, with a banner headline promising the inside story of a Romeo teacher and his gymslip runaway pupil, while underneath there was a lead story about the Defence Secretary that this time proudly carried Tom's by-line. This was followed by a detailed analysis of Timothy Grady's career implosion, including his wife's conniving, malevolent influence and the strong whiff of corruption that surrounded them both.

The headline read: 'The Lion, The Bitch and The Fraud Probe'.

Chapter Sixty-One

Day Twelve

Three Days Later

'What on earth do you think you're doing?' he asked the girl and she visibly jumped. 'Don't you know there's a killer out there? Don't your parents read the newspapers?'

The girl was frightened to death of him, he could see that. She had already started edging forwards out of the bus shelter in case she had to run for it or shout for help. Instead of answering him, her eyes were darting around looking for someone to help her in case he was a crazy man.

'It's all right, love,' he told her wearily and he reached into his inside jacket pocket, brought out the warrant card and showed it to her. 'I'm a copper.' Then he said, 'It's okay, you are not in any trouble. What's your name, eh?' and he smiled at her in what he hoped was a reassuring manner.

'Kimberley Russell.'

'And how old are you?'

'Eleven,' she looked a bit older but it was so hard to tell these days.

'Well, Kimberley, you shouldn't be out this late, not on a school night, not on any night at the moment. Should you?'

'No, Sir,' she automatically afforded him the courtesy she was used to giving her school teachers, 'I had Guides.'

'Girl Guides?'

She nodded.

'That explains it,' he put on his most kindly face. 'Used to be in the Boy Scouts myself. Be prepared eh?' And she smiled nervously at that.

'Live near here, do you?'

'Church Street.'

'Climb in the back and I'll drive you home. Save your parents worrying about you.'

She hesitated then. He could tell it was against her better instincts. She was wavering, they always did for a moment, and a little flash of panic ran through him. He was about to start the car and drive off before she could clock the registration then he composed himself and went for the tactic that always worked; the voice of authority, for she was used to obeying her elders and betters. 'Don't mess about, Kimberley,' he barked, 'get in the car,' and he frowned at her like the important man he was. 'I haven't got all night.' She hesitated for just a moment longer then relented, eager to avoid his disapproval. She walked to the door behind him. He heard it open and the swish of her skirt as she slid onto the seat behind him then the soft click as she closed the door.

'I don't think you shut it properly, Kimberley,' he told her, his heart pounding like it was about to burst, 'try it again, love.'

Silence. Should he not have used the word love? Could she actually hear the nervousness in his voice? Was she going to make a break for it? He heard the door swing open once more and for a moment he was convinced she was going to run off, then it slammed back hard and she gasped a little, as if she had put all of her strength into it.

'There's a good girl,' he told her.

He had another look round to make sure no one had seen her get in. Not a soul nearby. He put the car into gear and moved away. He knew a quiet spot nearby where he could quickly drag her from the back seat and throw her into the boot then he could take his time, transporting her to the place he had chosen: the old quarry. No one would be able to see or hear her there.

Soon he would save another one.

Suffer the little children to come unto me.

Three days after Tom's front-page story, Helen finally gave up waiting for him to call her and walked into the Greyhound.

'He's gone back to London, pet,' Colin told her from the other side of the bar.

'Is he coming back?' she asked, ignoring the scrutiny of the Greyhound's curious regulars.

'Don't know,' he said, 'but he took all of his stuff with him. He said something about a job down there,' and he must have seen the disappointment in her face because he added, 'I expect he'll let you know.'

'Thanks,' Helen said, feeling a lot less sure about that than he seemed to be.

'I'll tell you what this is, shall I?' offered DC Trevor Wilson, as he scrunched up the packet of chips and threw the empty newspaper and its greasy wrapper out of the car window into the nearest bush.

'If you like,' answered Bradshaw, knowing that he would anyway, whatever his reply.

'A waste of my time,' and he exhaled loudly, 'and yours,' he added, almost as an afterthought.

'Not a lot of choice in the matter though, is there?' Bradshaw told his new partner. Vincent Addison was still on the sick so the two DCs had been on nights together for three consecutive days now, flagging down passing motorists at random to see if they knew anything about the disappearance of the missing girls. There had been a justification of sorts from their DI but they both knew it was little more than a box-ticking exercise, so that DCI Kane could say he'd come up with some new tactics to apprehend the Kiddy-Catcher, now that he was officially in charge. Detective Superintendent Trelawe was gone and he wasn't coming back. The shit had really hit the fan following that newspaper piece on the fake professor and now everyone reckoned Trelawe was for the guillotine.

The Michelle Summers case had been solved and public interest in the body-in-the-field had begun to wane, so DI Peacock had taken Wilson and Bradshaw off the dead-wood squad and reassigned them, along with some of the less indispensable members of the larger squad. Six detectives were now working in pairs on roads connecting key spots in the Kiddy-Catcher investigation, backed up by uniformed officers who patrolled these 'arteries' as the routes were known in the incident room.

The two men were on the Durham Road, a few miles outside Great Middleton, and so far, in three nights, they had pulled over eighty-six motorists. Aside from a few drivers that were over the limit and a couple of common-or-garden perverts who had no good explanation for why they were out after dark, all they had uncovered of a criminal nature was one man with a boot full of lead he had just swiped from a church roof.

Now they sat in Bradshaw's car with two uniformed officers backing them up in a marked police car, waiting for their next flag-down.

'How many we got so far then?'

Bradshaw checked his records, 'Eighteen tonight,' just as a car's headlights came into view at the opposite end of the long straight road they were blocking.

'Your turn,' said Wilson smugly because the rain was lashing down now.

'Bloody hell,' moaned Bradshaw but he climbed from the car anyway.

Bradshaw watched as the car's headlights came into view. It was moving pretty briskly so he bent low enough to speak to the officers in the squad car, who turned on the flashing lights. PC Harrison got out of the driver's side. The advancing motorist saw the lights and began to slow before he reached the cones and the warning sign with 'Police – Stop' written on it. Another sign with an arrow guided him to the side of the road where Bradshaw was waiting to begin the usual round of questions. Harrison stood nearby, holding a torch.

The car was a boxy old Volvo, about as boring as you could get. When Bradshaw approached it, the driver's side window wound down with a squeak then an arm came out. The hand attached to it was clutching a warrant card. Normally Bradshaw would have relaxed at that point but he had been in the room when they first discussed the possibility that the Kiddy-Catcher could be impersonating a police officer, so he had to be sure. He bent to look into the car and a familiar face blinked back at him.

'Bloody hell, Vincent,' smiled Bradshaw, 'what you doing out here? You come to take over? We could do with a break.'

'Sorry, mate,' came the soft reply, 'still on the sick, just out for a drive. I find it helps when I'm feeling bad.'

'At this hour?' asked Bradshaw and he immediately regretted it. He knew that, like himself, Vincent had his problems and probably dealt with them in much the same way as he did. In Bradshaw's case, his demons sometimes left him with little or no energy to do anything but there were other occasions when he would suddenly feel a manic vitality that could only be calmed by a blaze of activity, when a week's chores could be completed in an evening. That mania sometimes culminated in a long, fast drive down empty motorways or silent country roads in the middle of the night. Maybe Vincent needed similar therapy. 'Sorry for flagging you down. We've been pulling over everyone; Chief's orders.'

'No problem.'

But Bradshaw didn't wave Vincent through because he knew he was just about the only one in CID who bothered to speak to him these days and he felt guilty for judging him so harshly when he first went on the sick.

'Dreadful bloody night eh? I'd be tucked up at home with some hot chocolate if I were you, or maybe something stronger.'

'Insomnia,' said Vincent, 'I get it terrible. I've tried sleeping on the couch, watching TV, reading books. Only thing that works sometimes is if I go for a drive, until I start to feel tired.'

'I get that sometimes,' said Bradshaw. 'I wake up at four in the morning and can't get back to sleep, my mind's racing so much, know what I mean?'

'Yeah.'

The windscreen wipers on Vincent's car were still going full pelt and one of them stuck on something but kept going. It made a squeaking sound that was jarring and both men were momentarily distracted. Each time they swept back and forth the rubber from the nearest wiper caught on some invisible obstacle and shuddered then squealed in protest before continuing its task. 'Kill that for a sec, will you,' winced Bradshaw, 'it's like nails scraping a blackboard.'

Vincent complied with the request, killing the windscreen wipers but not the engine. The squealing ceased and now the only sound was raindrops hitting the car and the low murmur of its engine. Then Bradshaw heard a door open and he turned to see Trevor Wilson leaving the car, which surprised him because Wilson had been moaning incessantly about the rain. His colleague marched towards the bushes, presumably to empty his bladder.

Bradshaw was about to share a joke with Vincent about what a nightmare Wilson was to work with but he was distracted again, this time by a noise.

'What was that?'

'What?' asked Vincent.

'That sound?'

'I didn't hear anything.'

'Shhh!' hissed Bradshaw and he strained to hear it.

There was silence, apart from the staccato pat-pat of dozens of rain drops on the roof and bonnet.

'What are we listening for?' asked Vincent.

Bradshaw held up a hand to silence him and they both froze for a moment while Bradshaw listened. Then it happened.

A thump.

The hollow sound of something hitting metal.

'That,' said Bradshaw, but he was still unsure of the source.

'What?' asked Vincent stupidly, but he must have heard it, thought Bradshaw.

'That,' said Bradshaw when the thumping happened again, twice more.

'Oh,' replied Vincent, 'that,' but he offered no further explanation.

'Is that coming from . . .' this time the thump was louder and there were three beats, not one.

Bradshaw turned towards the noise and tried to comprehend its source. The sound came again: thump-thump-thump.

'Have you got something in your boot, Vince?' Bradshaw looked at his colleague again. 'Have you got a dog in there or . . . something?' And Bradshaw realised how absurd that notion was.

'No,' answered Vince but that was all he said.

Thump-thump-thump.

Bradshaw couldn't think of a good reason for the sounds emanating from Vincent's vehicle and his colleague didn't seem to be about to offer one. Vincent wasn't looking at Bradshaw any more. Instead he was staring straight ahead, both hands gripping the steering wheel. At that moment the words of his DCI came back to Bradshaw: 'Look out for fake IDs and warrant cards.'

Bradshaw stared at the blank expression on Vincent's face, heard the thump-thump-thump one last time and said quietly, 'Could you get out of the car please, Vincent?'

Vincent didn't move.

'I'd like you to get out of the car and open the boot for me, Vincent,' Bradshaw said, still clinging to the hope that this was just some strange misunderstanding that could all be resolved if only Vincent would cooperate and open the boot of his car.

But Vincent didn't get out of the car. Instead, in a fluid and determined movement he reached sideways and thumped the door lock down

'Vincent!' called Bradshaw and he leaned through the open window to try and grab at the keys and wrench them from the ignition but before he could accomplish that, the car shot forward, straight through the sign and cones. Bradshaw was knocked to the wet ground but, as Vincent sped away, he shouted at the uniformed officer. 'Get in!' yelled Bradshaw, 'start the car!'

Bradshaw was back in his own car before Harrison reached his. A quick glance at Trevor Wilson revealed his colleague way back by the bushes with his back turned to them, calmly doing up his fly, completely unaware of what was going on. Bradshaw couldn't wait, so he sped off without him.

Behind Bradshaw, the uniformed boys attempted a swift three-point turn. They slammed their car into reverse but when they hit the ground behind them it was slick with mud and the rear wheel slid backwards. Harrison had to slam on the brakes to prevent the car from falling into a ditch. As he tried to get the car back on the road, the wheels span. He tried twice more without success until PC Lumley jumped from the car and gave it a shove while he drove it out. Lumley jumped back in the car, while Wilson looked on. 'What the hell's this?' he asked but he did not try to join them and, seconds later, he watched as the rear of their vehicle disappeared from view as it shot down the road.

Chapter Sixty-Two

Bradshaw called in his status and location then took a deep breath and explained who he was following to a disbelieving control.

'Suspect is one of ours,' he called, 'Repeat – one of ours. Failure to stop at a road block. Suspect is DC Vincent Addison.'

'What did you just say?' a disembodied voice crackled back at him.

'Repeat, suspect is Vincent Addison, DC Vincent Addison.'

'What?' it was said in disbelief.

'You fucking heard me!' said Bradshaw as he nearly lost it on a bend. 'Oh, screw this,' and he dropped the radio, so he could grip the steering wheel with both hands. Control would just have to sort out back-up.

Bradshaw had never driven a car at this speed before and real roads were nothing like the skid pans and race tracks on training days. This was unblinking, white-knuckle, pedal-to-the-metal driving just to keep Vincent within sight, who was propelling his boxy, old car as if he didn't care whether he made it out of the next tight bend or not.

There was no time to wonder what the hell had got into Vincent Addison. All Bradshaw knew was that there was someone in the boot of that car. Vincent made a sharp

437

right turn then and the back end of Bradshaw's car slid alarmingly as he followed. He wrestled the steering wheel, narrowly avoiding crashing into a stone wall as Vincent continued to push his car around every bend, while Bradshaw said a silent prayer of thanks that there was no one else coming the other way on this narrow road in the middle of the night.

For five long and terrifying minutes, Bradshaw followed Vincent along tight roads and through blind bends, his own car clipping the edge of tracks that were little more than country lanes and skidding as he forced it to follow the suicidal speeds Vincent dictated. Bradshaw watched Vincent power his car towards a T junction up ahead and could only gaze helplessly as he showed no sign of stopping. Instead his colleague propelled his vehicle straight across the road and smashed through a wooden fence, obliterating it on impact and sending huge splinters showering down behind him. He heard the sound of Vincent's engine alter as he changed gear and sped across a grassy farmer's field.

Bradshaw had no choice but to go straight across the road without stopping and through what remained of the gate, skidding as soon as his tyres touched the mud and careering sideways until he at last got the car under control. Then he took off after Vincent, who had a head start of a hundred yards or so.

Moonlight glinted off the water ahead and Bradshaw realised where Vincent was heading. He was driving straight for the dark, freezing waters of the river.

'Jesus,' said Bradshaw as he watched Vincent's car build speed, as the man he was pursuing turned his vehicle until it was facing the fast-flowing water, swelled by the recent rains. Bradshaw watched helplessly as the car shot across the grass, dipped as it hit the low ground by the river's edge, was catapulted upwards by the river bank then seemed to take flight as it flew over the open water, until gravity intervened and sent it nose-diving straight into the icy river.

Bradshaw's car reached the river bank just as Vincent's ploughed into the water, sending frothing waves out in front of it. Without thinking, Bradshaw was out of the car and running towards the water. He could see the dim figure of Vincent in the moonlight and he watched helplessly as the driver's window came down. At first he thought Vincent was trying to escape but the big man made no attempt to leave the vehicle as the car started to tip forwards. Bradshaw realised Vincent had opened his window to hasten the car's descent into the river.

Bradshaw shook off his jacket, pulled off his shoes and ran towards the water. It had been a long while since he had won a swimming gala but he could still remember how to dive and he threw himself forwards, landing in the freezing water with a heart-stopping impact that was like a million needles piercing his skin and left him gasping in shock as he came back to the surface. He thrashed towards the sinking car just as the water was about to reach the open window. Its front end was virtually nose-down now and he knew he only had seconds left.

Bradshaw reached the car just as it went vertical, which meant the back end was pointing upwards and he couldn't even reach the boot from his position in the water. He cursed in frustration but the car soon moved again, as the water finally reached the open window and began to rush inside. Immediately the car dropped several feet as the weight of the incoming water dragged it downwards and Bradshaw was at last able to reach the boot. He pressed the catch hard but it refused to budge and he realised it was locked. There was no way he could hope to open the boot without a key, even if he was on dry land with plenty of time, but he only had a second or two left before the car filled with water and sank. There was nothing he could do.

He could hear whoever was imprisoned in that boot thrashing around and it was breaking his heart. Bradshaw had never felt more helpless. The water reached a critical mass inside the car then and it was suddenly and abruptly dragged forwards and down. He was forced to let go as it was pulled completely beneath the water.

Bradshaw could hear a siren in the background as the uniformed police finally caught up with him and he made a decision. He was not going to give up.

Bradshaw dived beneath the dark water and powered after the sinking car, locating its back end by touch and immediately pulling on it to propel him down its driver's side. He couldn't see anything at all in the inky water but he felt the rear window and he pushed himself downwards until his left hand touched the frame of the open driver's window. His free hand went through the window and his arm brushed against something that moved. It was Vincent, but he ignored the man and groped blindly inside the car until his hand hit the steering wheel. He knew he was close now so he wrapped his hand round it and groped for the keys with his other hand. He snatched at them once, twice and finally a third time and they came out of the ignition.

Bradshaw was about to kick against the side of the car to break free from it when a strong grip fastened on his arm and the two men struggled but Vincent was absurdly strong and Bradshaw couldn't break free. Vincent was determined to take Bradshaw with him. They were both going to drown down here.

Suddenly there was a jolt as the car finally touched bottom and the impact of the river bank was enough to throw both men off balance. Bradshaw seized his chance and used his left hand to power a fist through the water, which impacted on the side of Vincent's head. The blow was powerful enough to make the man loosen his grip slightly and Bradshaw kicked against the side of the car and broke free.

He knew he had very little time left but Bradshaw managed to pull himself to the rear of the car, which was stable now on the bottom of the river. Frantically he felt for the boot mechanism while rubbing his other hand against the keys he was holding. He couldn't see them but he could tell there were two; one fat bulbous key with a plastic surround that he had ripped from the ignition; the second a tiny metal key that, please God, had to be for the boot. Groping blindly he managed to bring one hand to the other and trace a finger on the boot release until he found the tiny indent he was aiming for. Keeping his finger on it he brought the key towards it and stabbed it into the lock. The first time it grazed against metal but did not go in, the second time the metal parted for him and the key slid inside. Bradshaw turned it and the lock popped open but instead of a spring release like a jack in the box there was a frantic tug of war between the air bubble in the boot and the weight of the water outside pressing it down. Bradshaw heaved and the boot began to prise open. He wedged a shoulder under it and groped inside the boot until his hand felt something; a coat? He tugged with all of his might and a small, limp body was pulled free.

Bradshaw dragged the body out of the sunken car and pulled it to him. He reached with his foot until he found the metal bumper of the car and pressed hard against it, using it for leverage. Bradshaw and the girl were catapulted to the surface, leaving Vincent behind to drown alone in his car.

As soon as he broke the surface of the river, Bradshaw took in a huge lungful of air, then he looked into the pale, unconscious face of the girl in his arms and hoped he was not too late. Bradshaw could see Harrison on the river bank and he rolled onto his back, kicking while he clutched the lifeless girl to him. Their progress was slow because Bradshaw was forced to fight the current of the fast-flowing river.

Bradshaw was exhausted and the freezing water was sapping what was left of his energy. As he drew closer to the river bank he managed to push the limp body of the girl towards it with one last burst of strength. Harrison stretched out a hand but he wasn't close enough. Brad-shaw tried to shout something at him but all that came out was a gurgle and he swallowed river water, which made him gasp and choke. He kicked to try and get nearer to the policeman, who stretched out as far as he could. With one last huge heave Bradshaw pushed the little girl towards his colleague who stretched further still and grabbed at the collar of her coat. Bradshaw let go and he could hear the strain in the officer's voice as he pulled the sodden child towards him, the wet clothes doubling her weight. Then he fell backwards and watched as the girl was hoisted clear of the water.

Bradshaw had nothing left inside him then. All his strength had been used to get the girl out of the car and push her towards the river bank. It felt as if his body was closing down. No way was he going to make it to the bank himself but something deep inside him didn't care any more. The girl was out of the river. He'd achieved that much at least and he prayed she was still alive so this wasn't a wasted death. He let his hand trail away from the bank and the water swept him further from rescue. He got a last glimpse of Harrison putting the girl on the river bank, then turning back towards Bradshaw with a shout of alarm as he realised he was too late. Bradshaw knew that he was finished. Then he was swept away.

Bradshaw's face went under the water before he had the chance to take a big enough breath to sustain him. The water was so cold he knew he wouldn't be able to survive more than a couple of minutes more at this temperature, even if he didn't drown. The river buffeted him and he sank further before bobbing back upwards again, his senses bombarded with the noise of the fast-running river and dark images of the underwater world he would soon be consigned to.

He had messed up again, it seemed, but maybe this time it didn't matter quite so much. Bradshaw let his body go limp and waited for death.

There was another rush of water then and a sharp pain in Bradshaw's side as he smashed into an object or more likely it crashed into him and, before he could work out what it was, he was being dragged along by something. In his panic and heightened senses he had the impossible idea that some underwater predator was trying to take him and he thrashed his arms wildly.

The response he received was a hard bang on the head that knocked all resistance out of him and then he realised he was moving again. His face was out of the water and he gasped for sweet air, then turned his head. A strong arm was around him and he was being propelled slowly back towards the river bank. It took him a moment to realise it could only have been the second police officer, Lumley, who had run down the river bank then jumped in to save him. He must have landed virtually on top of Bradshaw just as he was about to drown, which explained the crashing feeling and sharp pain in his side. The thump to his head was standard practice for lifesavers, who prevent people from drowning both themselves and their rescuers with their panicked thrashing by giving them a hefty blow to temporarily disable them. Once Bradshaw's fevered brain had worked that out he went limp again and lay there, completely exhausted, as his rescuer got them both back to the river bank.

Chapter Sixty-Three

Day Thirteen

They'd insisted he stay in the hospital, at least for a night, while they treated him for exposure. He promised to comply but only if they told him about the girl.

'She's alive,' the nurse looked at him with something that resembled pride. He wasn't used to that. 'She's poorly but she'll live, thanks to you. I imagine her parents will want to thank you themselves but we'll keep them away for now so you can get some rest.'

She made as if to leave.

'Nurse,' he called and she turned back to him, 'what's her name?' For some reason that seemed incredibly important to him all of a sudden.

She smiled again, this time kindly. 'Kimberley Russell.'

'Kimberley Russell,' he said it aloud to himself to help him remember. Little Kimberley, he thought then he closed his eyes and slept for nine hours.

Bradshaw woke feeling ravenous but there was no one around so he decided to get out of bed. He had no idea what time it was and his watch and wet clothes had been taken from him but it was light outside. He was in his own room even though he didn't have private health care, so there was no one to ask. He padded barefoot down the corridor, feeling groggy, as if he had slept for days, and he decided to look for the canteen, though he had no money. Maybe he could somehow run up a tab for food, he reasoned.

He walked down two long corridors before he came upon an open door that led to a lounge where recuperating patients could watch TV. It was empty but the news was on with the sound turned right down and he saw a picture of a girl who looked vaguely familiar. Was this the little girl he had rescued? It certainly looked like her. They cut back to a newsreader in the studio then and he would have liked to have listened but he couldn't see a remote control anywhere so he just stood in the doorway, watching. Then his picture appeared.

It was an old photo, taken when he had joined the force and he looked ridiculously young, like a matinee idol from the fifties. Bradshaw watched the rest of the report, which included a film clip of the fast-moving river taken that morning and a short, silent interview with DCI Kane, who looked very serious, as well he might, considering it was one of his own officers who had taken the girl. Bradshaw doubted he would ever be able to come to terms with the fact that his partner turned out to be a madman.

The final piece was another interview but this one shocked him rigid. What the hell was Alan Carter doing in the studio and what was he saying? Bradshaw cursed the lack of volume as he watched the lips move on the expressionless face of his wheelchair-bound former colleague and could only guess what Carter might be telling the world about him.

*

Ian Bradshaw was discharged that afternoon. He was surprised to find that a WPC had been entrusted with the keys to his flat and had gone round there to find him some fresh clothes, which she then personally brought to his bedside. His first thought was what a kind, caring and pretty girl she was; his second that it was a bloody awful shame he hadn't known she was going to go round there in advance, because the place looked like a pig-sty. He was willing to bet she thought he was a right saddo, now that she'd seen the way he'd been living, but she seemed both warm and genuine in her congratulations.

'You were incredibly brave,' she assured him. 'I wouldn't have jumped into that water.'

Bradshaw certainly didn't see himself as a hero just because he jumped into the river and got the girl out. What else could he have done? Watch her drown?

'The DCI wants you to go in once you're feeling well enough,' she said.

He was about to question her about Vincent and how everyone in CID was taking it but what she said next stopped him from thinking about anything else.

'Oh and Alan Carter's wife has been on the blower,' the WPC told him. 'He wants you to visit him.'

'Thanks for popping round, mate.'

'No problem, I came as soon as I could.' Bradshaw wasn't kidding about that. He'd come straight from the hospital.

'No, I mean it,' Carter assured him, 'I appreciate it, I really do.' And he smiled. 'Were your ears burning this morning? I was on the news talking about you. They wanted to speak to one of your friends to find out what you were like but none of your serving colleagues were allowed to talk to journalists, for some reason.' Bradshaw knew the reason. He'd heard news reports on his car radio and no one had yet admitted that Vincent Addison was the man in the car or that it was a police officer who was responsible for the girl being in the water in the first place. 'Anyway, someone suggested me, so they wheeled me into the studio, quite literally,' and he grinned at that. 'Don't worry, I didn't say anything bad about you. Bloody well done as well.' He regarded his former colleague carefully but Bradshaw didn't know what to say, so instead Carter changed the subject. 'I know why you stopped coming, by the way.'

'You do?'

'Carol told me. She told you it wasn't doing me any good but she was wrong,' he waved a hand dismissively, 'I mean, it's not her fault or anything but she was mistaken. Your visits were a good thing, I looked forward to them,' and he smiled again. It was only a half-smile but Bradshaw had not seen smiles on Carter's lips since he had fallen twenty-five feet through the plate-glass skylight of that factory and landed on a hard wooden work bench. 'I know it didn't look like it and I'm sorry for being such a grumpy bastard but,' and he half-smiled again, 'in my defence, I have had a bit on my plate,' and he tapped the side of his wheelchair.

Bradshaw didn't know what to say.

Carter interjected for him, 'This is the bit when you're supposed to say, "No problem mate, I fully understand."'

'Oh, God, yeah, I was thinking it, I just didn't say it out loud, sorry, mate.'

'I'm taking the piss out of you, man. We used to do that quite a lot as I recall. Have you forgotten?'

And Carter was right, they did; spending all those hours driving round together, ripping it out of each other, but it seemed a very long time ago somehow. 'Yeah,' he said. The lack of banter from his fellow officers was one of the things Bradshaw missed most about being persona non grata these days. Back in the day, there had been a lot of near-the-knuckle humour to get them through the stressful days and many of those had ended with long sessions down the pub. Carter was particularly keen on those booze-ups and more than once Bradshaw had to ensure he got a cab home to Carol before his legs gave way or he fell asleep in a corner of the pub.

'Well, I don't blame you. I haven't been a barrel of laughs to be around these past months. I admit that. I've been an awful dad, a shit husband and a crap mate, no, Ian, I have, hear me out. I just wanted to say thanks for all the times you came. None of those other twats from the station bothered to come a second time. I haven't seen any of them in a year. You're the only one.'

'Well, I felt . . .'

'Obliged?'

'No,' and Carter raised his eyebrows in a questioning gesture, 'well maybe a little, no that's not it, not obliged, no, more . . .'

'Responsible?'

'Yes,' and a funny thing happened to Ian Bradshaw

449

then. He started to feel tears in his eyes and he knew he wouldn't be able to stop them, so he didn't try.

Carter carried on talking, as if the sight of a grown man crying in front of him was entirely normal. 'I've been thinking about that too. I've been thinking about it a lot. I've wanted to blame everybody for what's happened to me: the little cunt who broke into that factory and went through the skylight with me but walked away with a few broken bones. I've blamed the force for putting me in that position. I tried to blame God but I don't think he was listening and then there was you. There, I'll admit it. I've even tried to blame you.'

'I know,' Bradshaw was crying openly now, weeping like he hadn't done since he was a small child, 'it was my fault. You told me we shouldn't go up on the roof, you said it wasn't worth the bother, we were right near the end of the shift, you said to just leave the call for someone else, the uniforms, but I wouldn't listen. If I'd listened to you . . . if we'd done what you said . . .'

'I never would have gone through that bloody skylight?' 'Yes.'

'Maybe,' Carter admitted, 'and that's why I blamed you at first, along with that robbing little bastard whose fall I cushioned, but you didn't push me through that skylight, Ian, and I didn't have to try and grab him when he made a break for it. I did it without thinking, it was instinct and if I could go back in time and replay it I would have let him dash past me and get away,' he said, 'or maybe I'd just trip the little idiot up and he'd go through the skylight on his own this time.' He smiled again. 'Yeah, that's what I'd do.'

Bradshaw didn't know how to respond so Carter continued.

'I want to tell you something, Ian, and I want to do it now because I think you need to hear it from me, then I don't ever want to talk about it again, you hear?'

'Yeah.' Bradshaw was bracing himself.

'You're not to blame for what happened to me. You were there with me when things went pear-shaped and I am fucked for life as a result of it. You could have done things differently but then so could I. I hate myself for trying to tackle that bloke on the roof. If you think I have blamed you for being paralysed then you have no idea how many times I've blamed myself. But, when it comes down to it, it was an accident. I fell. End of story. What I am trying to say, Ian, is it wasn't your fault. The fact that I am in this chair is not your fault.'

Ian Bradshaw let the words wash over him before taking a number of deep breaths. Only then could he summon the strength to say 'Thank you,' before he broke down and cried like a baby right there in the room.

At that exact moment, Carol walked in with a tray of hot drinks. She stopped suddenly, took in the sight of their good friend Ian Bradshaw weeping uncontrollably in front of her husband, who perversely looked more calm and serene than he had done for months, and she froze. Bradshaw hadn't heard her, his back was still to her and his head was down, face in his hands, a wretched, pent-up, strangled, sobbing sound coming from his mouth. She looked to her husband for guidance and he quickly shook his head. Carol silently retreated from the room.

Chapter Sixty-Four

Day Fourteen

'Where the bloody hell have you been?' demanded Helen. She'd been walking past the Greyhound and glanced through the window. She was stunned to see Tom sitting there.

'You sound like my Nan,' he made a point of looking at his watch, 'is it past my bedtime or something?'

One or two heads turned at the bar, regulars who were amused to see Tom finally getting it in the neck from this fiery young woman who'd been looking for him for days.

'Why didn't you call me?'

'I had to send the mobile back,' he said, as if there weren't any other phones in the world that he could have used.

'You've been gone for days.'

'Yeah,' he admitted, 'and it looks like I missed all the fun.' And when she stared blankly back at him he explained, 'They caught him; the Kiddy-Catcher.'

'Yes,' she said, calmer now, 'they did.'

She joined him at the table and her voice was lower now, causing the boys at the bar to lose interest in them. 'Where've you been?'

'London,' he explained, 'sniffing out a couple of jobs.'

'Anything good?'

'Maybe; the *Mirror* like me but I'm not sure if I want to be tied to a tabloid contract again.' And he told her about his phone conversation with the Doc.

'Blimey, I saw your name on the *Mirror*'s front page,' she said. 'At least they ran something on Michelle Summers and the school teacher.'

'Did Malcolm spike your story?'

'No but he edited it . . . with a chainsaw,' she admitted, 'we were left with *Missing Girl Found Safe in Village* but precious little else.'

'What did you expect?'

'I don't know,' she admitted, 'something . . . anything . . . more than that. You were right about him and the *Messenger*. As soon as I can I'm going to leave and work for a proper newspaper.'

'Good for you,' he said.

'You said there were a couple of jobs?'

'There's another one working for a new magazine. It's a completely new concept. They're calling it a lads' mag and aiming it at young males; lots of photographs of girls in bikinis and interviews with minor celebrities. I'll be doing the interviewing, not the photographing of girls in bikinis.'

'Are you going to take it?'

'I think so. The money's pretty good, so why not?'

'But I thought you were a proper journalist,' she said.

'I am,' he protested, 'I was . . . it's just too bloody hard sometimes. The last few weeks have worn me out. This would be easy money and my articles won't get spiked or changed beyond recognition.'

'Good luck with it then,' she said, 'no, I mean it,' before adding sullenly, 'I thought you'd gone already.'

'Wouldn't you have preferred that?'

'Don't be stupid.'

He watched her for a moment. She seemed unhappy and on edge. Like him, Helen had been scarred by their recent experiences. Without giving it any thought he suddenly blurted, 'You could come with me?'

'What?'

'Come to London,' he urged her, 'you'd get something down there easily.'

'I can't just drop everything, leave everyone and come to London with you.'

'Why not?'

'Because I have a life. I have a job and a family and . . .'

'A boyfriend?'

'Yes, a boyfriend.'

'And you love him?'

'That's none of your business.'

'I think it is my business, under the circumstances.'

'You can think what you like.'

'And you can do what you like. It's allowed. People go off and do things they want to do. They don't have to stay where they are if they are unhappy.'

'People don't just abandon other people like that.'

'Yeah they do,' he said drily, 'believe me.'

'And I can't believe you are seriously suggesting it, after what you went through,'

'I was four, he's twenty-four. He'll get over it!'

'Do you realise how cold you sound when you talk like that?'

'And do you realise how wrong it is to stay with some-one if you are not happy with him? It's unfair on him and it's not fair on you.'

'Who says I'm not happy with him?' Tom let out a snort of derision and she rounded on him then, 'You don't know everything about me!' Helen stormed out of the Greyhound, causing every head at the bar to turn in her direction.

When he left Alan Carter's home, Ian Bradshaw felt com-pletely drained. All he really wanted to do was go home. Reluctantly he drove to the cop shop and went straight to Kane's office.

'We could do with a bit of good news at the moment,' the DCI told him, once he had established that Bradshaw was basically okay, 'what with Vincent Addison about to give every police officer in the country a bad name, so you're going to be made a DS,' Kane told him, 'acting, to start with, obviously.'

Bradshaw wasn't expecting that. He had half-expected a telling off when Kane called him in, for breaking some ill-defined, unwritten police rule about health and safety when he took off after Vincent then dived into that river.

'The chief constable wants his picture in the paper with you,' Kane added wryly, 'so you are going to get a com-mendation too. He reckons we could use a few heroes right now and I can't argue with that.'

Bradshaw said nothing. It felt as if Kane was discussing somebody else, not him.

'Anyway, you did well out there,' and when Bradshaw still did not respond, he added, 'well done.'

'Thank you, Sir,' he managed.

'I'd say this is your chance, wouldn't you?'

'Sir?'

'To put things behind you and turn your career around,'

'Yes, Sir.'

'So don't fuck it up,' Kane told him, 'there's a good lad.'

'No, Sir.'

'Anyway,' and he regarded Bradshaw thoughtfully, as if he couldn't quite believe that he was indeed the officer about to be honoured and promoted, 'that'll be all for now.'

This time Tom had to run to catch up with her and their argument continued all the way down the hill, until they reached Roddy Moncur's house. It was just beginning to get particularly heated when Roddy, showing a level of poor timing and insensitivity that even Tom would not have given him credit for, opened his kitchen window and leaned out to call to them.

'Oi!' he shouted, 'I've been looking for you two! Where've you been?'

'Don't you bloody start!' Tom shouted back at him and Roddy belatedly realised that he and Helen were both red-faced and looked furious with one another.

'Oh,' he said, 'well, maybe this won't interest you then but I thought it was important.'

'What is?' demanded Helen, 'for God's sake can't you just explain yourself for once, man!'

Roddy seemed taken aback at being shouted at by Helen, but he recovered sufficiently to say, 'I dropped a bit of a bollock.'

*

Roddy looked agitated when he opened his front door to them.

'I saw her, you see,' he began to explain, 'at a meeting,' and they followed him into his kitchen.

'Who?' asked Helen, not bothering to hide her exasperation.

'Wendy, my contact who works at the council records office, the one who told me all about Stephen Collier.'

'Right,' she said.

Roddy hesitated before continuing. 'And it turns out I made a mistake. A pretty big one, actually.'

'Go on,' Tom urged.

'I asked her if there was anybody still alive who might remember Stephen, someone who might be willing to talk to you, so you could learn a little more about him and what happened.' Roddy seemed embarrassed at the recollection.

'And what did she say?'

'She said, "Why don't you just speak to Stephen?"'

It took a moment for Tom to take this in. 'Talk to Stephen? You mean he's alive?'

'Apparently so.'

'But you said he was dead.'

'That was the mistake,' he admitted, 'when I spoke to her on the phone, I thought that's what she was telling me. She said "Stephen was housed at Springton right up until the very end," so I took that to mean he was there until he died.'

'Right,' Tom was trying to keep the excitement from his voice.

'But she meant the end of *Springton*, when it was closed

in 1980. When Springton was shut down, Stephen was transferred.'

'Transferred?' said Tom, 'Transferred where?'

'Milton Mews.'

'Where's that?'

'Newcastle. It's a residential care home for the elderly, which houses low-risk mental patients.'

Tom blinked at Roddy, 'So you're telling me the one person left alive who might be able to fill in the gaps of the Sean Donnellan murder is living in a care home a few miles from here?'

'Yes,' replied Roddy, 'that's exactly what I'm saying.'

Chapter Sixty-Five

Tom was striding towards the car, Helen struggling to keep up with him.

'Do we even know if he's compos mentis?' she asked.

'No.' He was almost at the car. Helen had never seen him move with such purpose.

'He could be completely senile,' she reminded him.

'Yep.'

'Or just not all there to begin with,' she said, breathlessly.

'True.'

'He might not know anything about what happened that night,' she concluded.

Tom climbed into his car and started the engine, just as the passenger door opened and Helen climbed inside. Tom turned to look at her. 'You're coming then?'

'Too bloody right I'm coming.'

They thought they would need a cover story so they worked one out on the way there: they were cousins from a branch of Stephen's family and had only just discovered they had a relative in the care home. Luckily they were met a by a young, trusting employee who let them into Milton Mews as soon as they announced they were there to see Stephen Collier.

'He's in the lounge,' the young girl told them as she led

the way along a corridor carpeted in threadbare Axminster. 'I've never known him have a visitor before. I didn't know he had any family left,' she told them and Helen just smiled back at her disarmingly but made no comment. They walked silently along three narrow corridors until the girl said, 'Here he is.'

They entered the room and Tom silently prayed they would find somebody capable of engaging with them. Half a dozen old ladies were seated here, dozing or reading newspapers half-heartedly. They followed the girl up to an old man who was sitting on his own. He was staring through a large window that overlooked rose bushes and a freshly mown lawn, 'Stephen, you've got visitors,' she said to him, but he didn't react.

Stephen Collier was a small man dressed in ancient carpet slippers, baggy grey trousers and a cardigan that must have been hurriedly done up by a carer that morning because the buttons were askew. His skin was grey from years without enough sunlight and he had liver spots on a face that was lined but bony, giving Helen the impression that he did not eat enough. The young girl persisted. 'There's someone here,' she told him, 'family to see you!' she called as if he was deaf. She placed her hand gently onto Stephen's arm to gain his full attention, 'That's nice isn't it?'

Stephen Collier turned his uncomprehending face very slowly towards them and Tom expected him to ask who the hell they were but he seemed calm enough. The carer concentrated her efforts on levering him out of his chair. 'Let's get you into your room, shall we, where it's nice and private.'

It took a long time for Stephen to shuffle along the corridor in his slippers and they were both filled with nervous excitement. They knew that at any moment someone in authority could come along and demand to know who they were before kicking them out, ending their last opportunity to get to the truth. Finally they reached a sparsely furnished ground-floor room and the carer sat Stephen in a shabby armchair. There was one other chair by the door but Helen perched on the end of Stephen's bed so she could face him and Tom stayed on his feet.

'Would you like a cup of tea?' offered the girl, then she turned back to Stephen. 'I'm sure I can sort one out for you and your visitors,' she told the silent old man.

'We're fine, really,' Tom told her.

'Okeydokey, I'll leave you to it then.'

Tom waited until the girl was halfway down the corridor before he spoke. Stephen was staring through his bedroom window, as if they weren't really there.

'Hello, Stephen. This is Helen and I'm Tom.'

There was no response from the old man and Tom began to fear that years in an institution had robbed him of all of his remaining faculties. 'We came to visit you today because we would like to ask you a few questions.' The old man continued to stare blankly ahead of him. 'Would that be all right?' and when there was still no reply, Helen added, 'It won't take long.' She gave him a big, beaming smile. 'Wouldn't want you to miss your dinner, would we?'

Tom watched Stephen Collier. There was the merest flicker from the old man at the sound of the pretty girl's voice then he turned his head slightly towards Helen, took in her presence at the foot of his bed but said nothing.

'Can you hear me okay, Stephen?' asked Tom. 'Do you understand why we are here? We just want to ask you a few questions.'

Helen opened her mouth to add something but Tom gestured to her and she stopped. Tom felt that if they both carried on talking at the old man he would never take the trouble to reply. Eventually the silence stretched out so far in front of them it became clear Stephen was not going to say anything. Tom sighed, 'I think we could be wasting our . . .'

Before he could complete the sentence, Stephen Collier finally spoke but his voice was a low whisper and neither of them made out the words. 'What did you say?' Helen prompted him and Stephen started to cough. Once more Tom found he was holding his breath, hardly daring to breathe. He wanted so badly to get through to this old man.

'I'm not daft,' said Stephen suddenly and once again Helen and Tom exchanged glances. 'I can hear you.'

Tom nodded at her, prompting Helen to address him.

'Nobody thinks you are daft, Stephen.'

'They do,' his voice was a rasp but they could clearly make out the words now. 'They all do in here.'

'Well, we don't,' answered Helen, 'you're clearly not daft.'

'No,' he continued. 'I can't do adds and takeaways, that's all,' and he tilted his head so he could look at Helen directly, 'and if I try to count to a hundred I get confused and have to stop,' he told her earnestly, 'but that doesn't make me daft.'

'Of course it doesn't,' she assured him.

Tom noticed the way the old man suddenly seemed to lock on to Helen. He was looking at her smiling face as if she'd been sent from heaven to greet him.

'Helen here will be asking the questions today,' Tom said, hoping she would understand.

Stephen frowned then. 'Who are you?'

Tom cut in before Helen could answer: 'We're the people who are asking the questions, Stephen. That's all right, isn't it?'

'Questions?' he asked suspiciously, 'what about?'

'Something that happened a very long time ago,' Helen explained. 'We want to ask you what you remember about a night many years ago when you were a young man.' Did Stephen look a little nervous then?

'What night?'

Helen glanced at Tom but he just jerked his head in a gesture that meant 'Go on.' She was nervous herself now, fearful of messing things up if she upset the old man.

'We need to hear what happened that night, Stephen,' she forced her voice to sound calm, 'when the Irishman had an argument with your brothers, Jack and Henry. You remember, don't you?' No reply from Stephen. 'Sean Donnellan quarrelled with your brother in No Name Lane, perhaps both of them, because he was going to run off with young Mary, Henry's fiancé.'

The old man lowered his head, his face a picture of confusion, or was it fear. 'You don't have to worry about any of it. We just want to clear it all up, that's all,' said Tom.

Nobody will get into trouble,' added Helen, 'it was all such a very long time ago and everybody is gone now, so there can't be any harm in telling us the truth, can there?'

'I don't want to talk about that,' said the old man firmly.

'Please, Stephen,' Helen urged him, 'we know almost all of it anyway. You wouldn't know about it, living all the way out here, but they found Sean Donnellan,' Stephen Collier seemed to flinch slightly then, 'his body I mean. We know there was a big quarrel about Mary. Henry was very upset and Jack wanted to help him by making the Irish man go away. We understand all that.' No response from Stephen. 'We also know there was a fight and, during that fight, Sean got stabbed with Henry's knife.' She watched Stephen closely for signs of recognition but his face betrayed nothing. 'All we need to know is how it happened, that's all,' and Helen waited for an answer. When none was forthcoming, she asked, 'Was it Jack,' to no response. 'Was it Henry?' Again, no reply.

Then Tom interrupted, 'Or was it you, Stephen?' And the old man took his gaze from Helen and turned it on Tom. 'Is that why you won't tell us?' Tom noticed that Stephen was wringing his hands now, becoming agitated as the questioning continued. 'Of course, it could have been an accident,' offered Tom, 'maybe nobody meant to stab Sean but somebody slipped during the fight. Perhaps he fell on the knife or he was pushed against someone who was holding it. It would explain why you had to bury the body. You were probably worried nobody would believe you. Is that what happened? You can tell us. It's okay.'

'I can't remember,' said Stephen, finally.

'You can't remember?' repeated Tom. 'Now that I don't believe, Stephen. I've forgotten a lot of things in my time but I know I'd never forget the day I saw a knife go into the back of someone. That kind of thing stays with you.'

'Please tell us, Stephen,' urged Helen. 'If it was Jack or Henry, then what harm could come of it? They are both gone now. We just want to hear the truth.'

'No,' he told her firmly, shaking his head, 'mustn't tell!'

'And if it was you,' she offered, 'then it must have been an accident. Everybody would understand.' Silence from Stephen. 'And if it wasn't an accident? If you killed Sean because he was in a fight with your brother and he was hurting Jack, well, people would understand that too. I know they would.' Then she tried a new approach. 'It must be terrible, living with a secret like that, all of these years.'

'It is,' he told her quickly, as if he couldn't help himself.

'There you go then,' Helen smiled at him once more and he gazed back at her. 'You'll feel so much better when you tell us. I promise.'

Stephen Collier opened his mouth to say something. Helen and Tom waited to learn the truth. 'No,' and he shook his head violently, 'you can't make me.'

Helen pleaded, 'Please, Stephen,' but he remained unmoved.

'It's no use, Helen,' Tom told her, 'we'd better just go. We'll never get the truth like this,' and he took a step towards the door. Confused, Helen stayed where she was then Tom said, 'It's quite clear to me now. I am sure I know what happened. Stephen here killed Sean. It's obvious.'

'No,' protested the old man and he turned to face Tom.

'He stabbed him with that knife, murdered the poor man in cold blood,' continued Tom, 'that's why he won't tell us the truth.'

'I didn't,' Stephen shook his head again, the gesture making him appear childlike, 'I never.'

'It doesn't matter,' Tom told him, 'you won't tell us what happened, so we'll just have to tell the authorities you won't cooperate with us and you know what that means.'

'What?' asked the confused old man.

'Well they are not going to want you here now, are they?' Tom told him firmly. 'They can't leave a murderer in an old folk's home.' He shook his head, 'No, they are going to want you out of here straight away.'

'No,' Stephen looked terrified, 'they can't.'

'Tom,' cautioned Helen.

'They can and they will,' Tom took a step towards the man and went down low so he could speak more softly. 'They'll kick you out on the streets if you don't tell us what happened that night.'

'Tom!' called Helen but he wasn't listening to her, just staring at the terrified old man.

'You've been in trouble with the police before, haven't you?' Tom told him. 'You'd better tell me now, before it's too late.'

Stephen Collier looked as if he might be about to crack when the young carer walked suddenly back into the room. She had obviously heard a little of what Tom had said from the corridor. 'I want you to leave,' she told him.

'No,' replied Tom firmly and the girl looked stunned by his defiance.

'You have to leave,' she told them both, 'you're not family. He hasn't got any family. They just told me. I never would have . . .'

'We'll go in a minute.' Tom turned to her. 'Stephen has something very important he wants to tell us first, don't you, Stephen?'

'You have to leave now,' she snapped, 'or I'm calling the police.'

'Do what you want but I'm not leaving,' he told her, 'not until I've heard what he has to say.'

'Right,' huffed the girl and she left the room and marched down the corridor.

Tom turned back to the old man. 'Last chance, Stephen. You heard her, she's calling the police.' The old man looked like he was about to drop dead from the shock of that. 'They'll take you away if you don't tell the truth, so tell me now, quickly, before they get here.'

'Jack never meant it to happen,' Stephen blurted suddenly.

'Go on,' urged Tom.

'He took the knife off Henry, in case he did something daft with it. It was in his pocket but when he went to see the Irish he still had it on him.'

'Tell us what happened, Stephen.' Helen and Tom could hear animated voices at the end of the corridor now.

Stephen managed to confirm what they already knew or had guessed: that Mrs Harris had come to their house and warned them Mary was going to leave with Sean Donnellan,

'Jack went down there to have it out with the Irish. He

told Henry and me to stay at home but after a while Henry went after him.'

'What did you do, Stephen? Come on?' The voices were getting louder.

'I went after him too,' confirmed Stephen. 'We followed Jack and we hid and watched him. We saw the Irish coming out of the house and Jack followed. We followed Jack but we stayed back a way, because we knew he'd go mad if he saw us. The Irish went down No Name Lane and Jack went after him. When we got there the two of them were already fighting. They'd taken their coats off and they were punching and kicking and braying each other. It was awful.'

'Was Sean winning?' asked Tom, assuming it would not have been so awful for Stephen if Jack had been in control of the fight.

'Only 'cos he was a dirty fighter,' protested Stephen, looking hurt by the accusation, 'or Jack would have had him. He can fight anybody,' he told Tom proudly, holding up a fist, as if his older brother was still alive and not dead for more than half a century, 'but the Irish fights dirty, butting and gouging, and he was telling Jack that he was going to kill him if he tried to stop him.'

Helen could hear the voices drawing nearer now, animated conversation between women who sounded as if they were in positions of authority. Tom closed the door then he kicked the other armchair until it slid towards it and blocked it, the back wedged under the door handle so it couldn't be turned from the outside.

'Who stabbed Sean, Stephen? Was it Jack, Henry, or you?'

Stephen was shaking his head, tears streaming down his lined face now. 'Our Jack was on the floor and the Irish was kicking him in the head,' explained Stephen. 'I didn't think he was going to stop.'

'So you picked up Jack's coat to get at the knife?' Tom prompted him.

'No.'

At that moment the handle of the door turned slightly but wedged against the chair. Someone tried to push it open and Helen watched as it rattled a little but the weight of the chair held it firm.

'Open this door!' a woman shouted.

'Who did it, Stephen? Was it you?'

'The police have been called,' the same woman shouted through to them and another shrill voice added, 'They're on their way, they're coming!'

'You heard her!' called Tom and he pointed to the door. 'The police are coming for you, so you'd better tell us now or we won't be able to help you. Who did it, Stephen?' Tom demanded and he put both hands on the old man's shoulders and shouted, 'Who?'

Stephen Collier gasped and sobbed then it was like a dam had burst and a great torrent of words followed. 'He thought Irish was going to kill Jack. I didn't even see him get the knife. I didn't even see him pick up the coat. One minute the Irish was standing there over our Jack, about to kick him again. Next thing he's opened his mouth like he's going to say something and all this blood came out. I didn't understand. I didn't know what had happened. Then he just dropped. He fell to his knees like he was praying in church and when he fell I saw him.'

'Who did you see?' urged Helen.

Stephen's face took on a look of wonder, as if he was seeing the whole thing again in his mind's eye but for the first time, like he'd blotted out the entire memory so that it was just as shocking to him this time around.

'Henry,' he said. He was standing behind the Irish. The Irish man fell forwards and the knife was sticking out of his back.'

Helen heard the sound of a police siren.

'Henry killed him?' asked Tom and the old man dipped his head and nodded sadly. Helen and Tom looked at one another. They had finally discovered the truth.

'What did Jack do?' Tom asked.

'He went mad,' said Stephen, 'he took one look at what Henry had done and he hit him. He kept saying, "What have you done? What have you done," and "all for a stupid little girl." It took him ages to calm down.'

The police siren was getting louder and louder. The women from the home had stopped pushing at the door.

'But he did calm down,' Tom prompted him, 'and he got rid of the body.'

'We all did. Jack made me and Henry carry the Irish into the marshland, because the reeds were high and no one could see us, while he ran back home to hide Sean's bag and fetch the shovel. Then he dug a hole in a dry spot on Cappers Field, dropped Irish in it and covered him over.'

'Why didn't he get rid of the knife?'

'It was still stuck in him,' explained Stephen, 'we left it in him to stop blood going on the grass when we carried him but we forgot about it when we stuck him in the hole.

When Henry remembered, Jack said it's too late now but it doesn't matter. Nobody is ever going to go digging here. He told Henry to buy a new knife and say he'd lost it.'

The siren was close by and its volume wasn't changing. Helen realised the police car was in the car park.

'And the money?' Tom asked. 'Who took the money from the vicarage?'

'Jack did. We watched in case anyone came.'

'He stole the money so you could blame it on Sean Donnellan?'

'He said it was the only way to make Mary believe Sean had left without her. He was right. It's what everybody believed.'

'What happened to the money?'

'Jack threw it at Henry.'

'Jack didn't want it?' asked Tom.

'No,' the old man said, 'Jack didn't want any of it.'

Helen started as loud banging came from the door, 'Police! Open up! Open this door now!'

Tom stood straight then went towards the chair and dragged it away from the door, opening it. Two huge, uniformed police officers were standing there. 'I'm sorry, officer, there seems to have been a bit of a misunderstanding . . .' said Tom, hoping to defuse their anger.

At the sight of the police officers, Stephen screamed then went into a wild panic. 'Don't take me away!' wailed the old man, 'Please! Don't take me away!'

'Jesus Christ,' said one of the officers, 'what have you done to the poor bastard?'

Chapter Sixty-Six

They spent more than four hours in the cells before they were released. 'We're not charging you with anything,' the desk sergeant looked at Tom like he was the worst kind of parasite, 'but if it was down to me, I'd have thrown away the key.'

'Good job it's not down to you then, eh?'

'Scaring a helpless old man like that, you're bloody vermin,' and he raised his voice as Tom went through the front door of the station, 'and if you didn't have friends in high places, you'd still be in here!'

'Friends in high places?' asked Helen as they walked to the car.

'I used my phone call to get through to Ian Bradshaw,' explained Tom, 'asked him if he couldn't get someone to have a word with his Geordie counterparts, see if he could clear this mess up.'

'And he did?'

'Seemingly.'

'And it *was* a mess,' she told him, 'I've never even been arrested before, much less spent time in a cell.'

'Worth it though,' he said, 'to finally get to the truth.'

'I don't know,' she replied, 'was it?'

''Course it was,' he assured her. 'You're out now, aren't you?'

'I meant Stephen.'

'Oh, him.'

'Yes him; you scared an old man witless,' and when he said nothing, she added, 'you don't seem to care.'

'I didn't scare an old man witless,' Tom explained, 'I interrogated someone who got away with murder years ago, or at least helped his brother to get away with it. All his life, Stephen escaped punishment for what he and his brothers did, never having to account for any of it. None of them did. Henry Collier should have gone to the gallows for that. Instead he got on with his life as if nothing happened.'

'You can't know that.'

'He killed his rival then married the girl,' said Tom, 'got the wife he wanted, carried on teaching, even became headmaster and all the while Sean Donnellan's body was rotting in that field on the edge of the village. Christ, Helen, does none of that make you the least bit angry?'

'Yes it does. I already told you it did but his simple-minded brother wasn't to blame.'

'He helped to bury the poor bastard, didn't he? Then he kept quiet about it all these years.'

'What choice did he have? He was living with his brothers. He was entirely dependent on Henry,' then she added, 'until they carted him off to an institution.'

'It was too late to dob his brother in it by then and nobody would have believed him.' Tom sighed. 'The other brothers are almost as guilty as Henry. Even at today's rates they'd all be doing serious jail time. You know they would. Instead they got away scot-free.'

'I suppose.'

'You know I'm right, Helen,' he told her firmly, 'deep

473

down you know I did the right thing. If I hadn't scared that old man we'd still be charging round trying to discover the truth.'

'Maybe,' she conceded, 'but I can't help liking you a little less because of it.'

'Ha,' he snorted, 'and that makes a difference to us exactly how?'

'How long are you going to keep on hating me?'

'I don't hate you,' he replied, 'the exact opposite in fact.'

'Just get in the car,' she told him.

They drove in silence all the way back to Great Middleton. They both knew where they were going without mentioning it. Tom parked outside the old vicarage. Helen rang the bell and when Mary answered she said, 'Can we come in?'

The sound of Stephen Collier's voice filled the room, followed by Tom's. *'He said it was the only way to make Mary believe Sean had left without her. He was right. It's what everybody believed.'*

'What happened to the money?'

'Jack threw it at Henry.'

'Jack didn't keep it?' asked Tom.

'No,' the old man said, 'Jack didn't want any of it.'

Tom reached for the tape player and turned it off before the sound of banging and the shouted commands of the police officer. The old woman regarded it silently. Even though it had been in Tom's jacket pocket, every muffled word was still discernible.

'Are you all right?' asked Helen.

Mary took a moment to answer and when she finally did she said, 'Lord no,' then added, 'how could I be?'

474

'Would you like a glass of water?' asked Helen and Mary nodded weakly. Helen walked into the kitchen, filled a glass and returned, handing it to Mary. Tom watched as she gulped the water then Helen took the glass from her shaking hand.

'Did you know?' asked Tom simply.

Mary shook her head, 'No, not all of it but . . .'

'You had your suspicions?'

'Not at first,' and she started to cry then. 'For a long time I thought I'd been love's biggest fool. Imagine the guilt I have borne all these years. I spent most of my life imagining that the man I loved had conned me, stolen my father's life savings then abandoned me. Now I finally know the truth and still the guilt won't leave me.'

'I don't understand,' said Helen, 'why would you feel guilty now?'

'A man was killed because of me, a good man committed murder because of me.'

'Was he a good man?' asked Tom but she didn't answer.

'I was a disappointment to my husband,' Mary said, 'I've known that for a long time. He wanted me too much, you see. No one could possibly live up to that. I know I couldn't. I knew it on our wedding day when I walked up the aisle and he beamed at me like he couldn't quite believe I was entirely real. In the end I was a disappointment to him and to my father.' She dabbed at her eyes with a handkerchief, 'Father never really looked at me again,' she said as if this was entirely to be expected, 'and I never saw him smile. Not once.'

'There was only one man I didn't disappoint and for fifty years I thought he never really wanted me. Can you imagine how that made me feel? Do you understand why I was so pathetically grateful when Henry forgave me, how astonished I was when he offered to take me back, to act like nothing had happened, even though I wasn't pure? I thought what a good, noble, honourable man he is to take care of me like this. And he was of course, in many ways; just not then, not that time.

'I think that was why he worked so hard with those children. To make amends. He knew he'd done a terrible thing and could never tell anybody about it, even me – especially me – and he knew I wasn't worth it in the end. I couldn't even give him children and he'd have loved to have been a father. He must have realised he should have let me leave with Sean and found someone else. I think the guilt and the shame knocked years off his life.'

'When did you first suspect?' asked Tom and Mary looked as if she was about to deny suspecting anything but either she was too tired or she knew he would have seen through that.

'I have something to show you but you'll have to be patient,' she said. 'I'll need your help to climb the stairs.'

Tom held out a hand and she planted her cold, tiny hand in his. Her skin was paler than parchment paper and he could see the blue veins that ran beneath.

Together they shuffled out of the living room to the stairs. Helen followed their tortuously slow progression and they eventually reached the landing where she unlocked the room and they went inside. Mary opened the drawer then she took out the leather-bound journal and an old mahogany box.

'My husband died quite suddenly and I mourned him,'

she announced, 'he was only fifty-five and never had the time to get his affairs in order. It took me nearly a year to sort everything out; his personal things, papers, everything. Then one night, more than twenty years ago now, I went up into the loft. I wanted to see what junk he had stored there. I found this.'

She handed Tom the wooden box and he opened it. Helen and Tom stared at its contents: four gold coins.

'The sovereigns,' said Helen.

'Some of them,' said Mary, 'not all. After my father died we bought this house. Henry said we could manage, even on a school teacher's salary, and I accepted that. Back then, women didn't question their husbands where money was concerned; housekeeping perhaps, but not on the big things. Love, honour and obey, that was the vow. I should imagine that in some warped way, by buying this house for us, my husband felt he was keeping the money in the family. He never spent any of it on anything else, as far as I am aware.'

Tom closed the box and placed it back on the dresser.

'Henry took them,' she said simply. 'It was him, whether Jack broke into that drawer or not. Henry stole the sovereigns from my father. Not because he was greedy or needed them. He took them so everybody would blame Sean. I didn't want to believe it when I found them. I kept thinking of ways that he could have come by them innocently but he wasn't there to ask and . . .' she sighed to show that she had never been able to find a rational explanation for their presence in her attic, '. . . then I simply tried not to think about it because the alternatives were too awful.'

'That Sean was dead and your husband responsible?' he asked her.

'I didn't make that link, honestly I didn't, even then. Instead I wondered if my father had somehow left some coins in the attic and forgotten about them but he hoarded his money like a miser. Then I wondered if he had perhaps given Henry some money without me knowing about it or perhaps not all of the coins had been stolen and these were left behind. On darker days I wondered if Henry had stolen all of the money himself but blamed it on Sean's disappearance. I never once thought that he could have killed Sean,' she told them, 'but then I wasn't in the least surprised when they found his body. Devastated yes, but not surprised.'

'That's because you knew all along,' he said and she looked shocked.

'But I just told you . . .'

'Deep down, I mean. You couldn't bring yourself to entertain the one possibility that turned out to be true but when Sean's body was found it all fell into place.'

She nodded slowly. 'I think I always knew that Sean hadn't just left me and when they found him in that field I suppose I felt vindicated in a way. Isn't that awful? If I really loved Sean I should surely have preferred him to have run off with Father's money for a new life in America.'

'So Henry Collier was a thief and a murderer and he left your father penniless.'

'He could hardly have given the money back to my father,' said Mary, 'those sovereigns were an alibi, weren't they? They explained Sean's sudden disappearance in a way that everyone accepted. Sean was the thief, he'd taken the sovereigns and run away. If people couldn't find him, it was because he didn't want to be found. Nobody realised that he never left the village.'

'I spent my whole married life thinking I was the wicked one; that Henry rescued me from myself. It took me thirty years to realise my husband might be a thief and a liar and another twenty to discover he was a murderer, though I couldn't be sure of that until you finally told me.'

'I'm sorry,' he said.

'Well, you shouldn't be. I should know the truth after all these years. I didn't go out for days when I found what was left of those coins. I just stayed in the house and cried and cried.' She must have seen her reflection in the dressing-room mirror then, 'They used to say I was a beauty, years ago.'

'You *were* a beauty,' said Tom, 'we've seen the drawings, remember?'

'But I'd have been better off plain. Don't you think I'd have been happier? I do. Looks aren't a blessing, they're a curse, if they make a man steal for you, fight for you, do anything to keep you, even kill another man.'

She handed him the leather-bound book then.

'My journal. I used to keep one, back when I was a silly young girl. This volume goes right up to the time when I agreed to marry Henry. It's all in there. The whole story; everything that happened and how I felt about it at the time. I've kept it all these years. It's yours to do with as you please.'

Tom took the slim volume from her hand then opened it. The ink on the yellowing pages had faded over the years but it was still faintly legible. Tom recalled the portrait of the young girl who had written them all those years ago. As he turned the pages of Mary's journal and her story unfolded he noticed how her words became more unruly, spilling onto the pages, like frightened people stumbling from a burning building. He could see the haste here and the distress. This wasn't a story, it was a scream.

'I do have one condition,' Mary said, snapping him out of his thoughts.

'What's that?'

'You wait till I'm in my grave.'

'Before I write the story, you mean?' he looked decidedly uncomfortable about that.

'I have months. Three they think, six if I'm lucky, but no more than that.'

'But you don't want to be lucky, do you?' Helen said.

'My life is already over,' she explained. 'It ended on a filthy night more than fifty years ago. God has been punishing me every day since and I am more tired now than I ever imagined it was possible to be.'

'You still believe in God?' asked Helen.

'Oh, I know there is a God and I know he is waiting but what more could he do to me? I spent my life with the man who murdered my Sean.' She shook her head, as if trying to compose herself. 'And children . . . we never had children . . . couldn't have them . . . my fault, apparently. That's why I know there is a God. He was punishing me for what I did. He chose to deny me children but kept me wedded to that man.'

'But you didn't do anything,' protested Helen.

'I betrayed Henry, I planned to run away with Sean, so Henry killed him. It was my fault, all of it.'

'No!' Helen shook her head. 'You didn't force Henry to do what he did.'

'Please tell me you don't think you're going to hell,' Tom said.

'Hell? Do you know what hell is?' she asked. 'Hell is knowing your entire life has been a waste, founded on a lie. That's hell, Tom.'

Chapter Sixty-Seven

Tom needed a drink. He had just spoken with an old lady whose life had been ruined before she'd reached the age of nineteen, a woman who had spent the past fifty-seven years torturing herself every day because she thought God had chosen to personally punish her for her sins. So Tom definitely needed a drink. But when they came out of Mary Collier's house they found Detective Constable Bradshaw waiting for them. He was leaning against his car and seemed calm enough. 'You owe me,' he told Tom matter-of-factly. 'My colleagues at Northumbria police think I've been hanging out with the wrong sort.'

'What are you doing here?' asked Tom.

'You weren't hard to find,' said Bradshaw. 'You've just caused a ruck at an old folk's home housing Mary Collier's brother-in-law. I figured you had a reason and this would be your next port of call. So spill,' he demanded.

Tom figured they really did owe Bradshaw and there was little point in trying to hold out on him, so Helen, Tom and the detective walked together and the two reporters took it in turns to fill in the gaps of Sean Donnellan's story. They were halfway across the village by the time they had finished.

'Bloody hell,' said Bradshaw, as he sat down heavily on a bench by the common, 'so the future headmaster of the village school murdered his love rival?'

'Yes,' said Tom, as they joined him on the bench, 'fifty-seven years ago. It took that long for the truth to come out.'

'I've only just received confirmation that Sean Donnellan disappeared back then and was never seen by his family again. It looks like we can finally wrap this all up and put a pretty bow on it.'

'You seem pretty relaxed about it,' said Tom.

Bradshaw shrugged. 'Well, let's see,' he ruminated, 'one of our own men, a guy I have been working with personally, turned out to be a multiple child killer and he killed himself in front of me. Compared to that, this is a walk in the park.' And he let that sink in before adding, 'And who are we going to arrest? The murderer is dead, so is his elder brother and Stephen, from what you tell me, isn't fit to stand trial.'

'No,' admitted Tom reluctantly, 'he probably isn't.'

'Case closed then,' Bradshaw said and when Tom failed to contradict him he added, 'So, what does the future hold for you now? You off back to London?'

'He's been offered a job on a lads' mag,' Helen said before Tom could answer.

'A job on a what?' asked Bradshaw.

'It's a new magazine for men,' Tom said. 'They want me to interview a bunch of celebrities, actresses, models, singers, easy work.'

'I guess it would be for most people,' said Bradshaw. 'How do you mean?'

'Won't you get a bit bored? I mean you've got a skill, anyone can see that. You're more like a copper than a reporter.'

'I'll take that as a compliment,' said Tom guardedly, 'but only because it's coming from you.'

'Be a shame to waste it though.'

'I haven't said I'll take the job,' said Tom, deliberately not looking at Helen. 'I might not. Maybe I'll stay up here for a while. Do a bit of freelance.'

'The North East is a big place and if you had a bit of inside knowledge,' Bradshaw was regarding Tom intently, 'then who knows what you might turn up?'

'What are you saying?'

'Cards on the table, eh?' Bradshaw looked tired then. 'We are about to take a pounding from all sides. One of our own men turned out to be the one we were looking for all that time and we had no bloody idea. The press will say there's no trust left between us and the people we police any more. They will try to paint a picture of an incompetent force that couldn't spot a certified nutter when he was sitting in their own canteen.'

'Well,' answered Tom, 'it's true, isn't it?'

'I thought you might have been a bit more understanding,' Bradshaw told him, 'since you've been drinking with a paedophile.'

'Fair point,' conceded Tom, 'so you're saying guys like that just can't be spotted.'

'I don't quite know what I'm saying, except that there are still good people in this force and their morale is on the floor right now because one lone crazy man completely lost touch with reality. Maybe you could write something to that effect.'

'How do you mean?'

'Vincent Addison was completely unhinged but he

appeared quite normal to his colleagues, well, reasonably so.'

'That's just your opinion. What would I base it on?'

The detective constable reached into his pocket and pulled out an envelope. 'DCI Kane wanted you to take a look at this.'

'So Kane sent you,' accused Tom.

'Nobody sent me. I came to talk to you about the Sean Donnellan case,' and when Tom gave him a disbelieving look he held up his hands. 'All right, Kane gave me the letter and asked me to show it to you when I saw you next. He knows we . . .' and Bradshaw seemed to be searching for the correct phrase, 'cooperated,' he explained. 'We found this at his home. He didn't even hide it, just left it on a table for us in case anything happened to him.'

'What is it?'

'An explanation,' and Bradshaw took the letter from the envelope and handed it to Tom, 'of sorts.'

Tom took it gingerly, 'but this is evidence isn't it? I'm not supposed to see this,'

'The man's dead. There won't be a trial. Just say it's from a police source and leave it at that,' he instructed Tom. 'Kane's already cleared it,' he added, 'at the highest level.' Bradshaw avoided letting Tom know of his resentment at the way DCI Kane managed to get a leak to a journalist officially sanctioned, when his own unofficial leaks to Tom Carney had come so close to costing him everything.

'You mean your top bosses know you are showing this to a journalist?'

'They are not stupid people. The alternatives don't play well for anyone.'

485

Tom opened the letter and was immediately struck by the erratic handwriting, which seemed to have been put down on the paper at speed and with some force.

He showed it to Helen and they read the letter together silently.

Vincent Addison's words were a rambling, paranoid, delusional attack, on society in general and women in particular, whom he appeared to blame for all the troubles of the world. The letter was an unstructured diatribe, which quoted bible verse as a justification for his murders. Most strikingly, he seemed convinced that he wasn't actually harming any of his victims, he felt sure he was saving them in fact.

'*I am not killing little girls,*' his spidery scrawl concluded at the foot of the page, '*I am making angels. Suffer the little children to come unto me.*'

When Tom had finished the letter, Bradshaw said, 'Now you can see what we were up against.'

Tom was still contemplating the motives of a man who had murdered four terrified, little girls for nothing, so they could be transformed into angels. 'He was a madman,' he said. 'All of this suffering because of a twisted belief in God.'

'Much of the evil in the world is committed in the name of religion,' the detective reminded him, 'always has been, always will be.'

'I'll write a piece,' Tom told him.

'And your angle?'

'That nobody could have spotted this delusional madness festering inside any man.'

Bradshaw thanked him. 'I guess I'll be seeing you around then,' he told Tom before he left.

When he was gone, neither Helen nor Tom felt like talking for a while. Instead they sat on the bench watching as pedestrians and passing cars went by. Helen marvelled at the way the village just seemed to carry on. She knew it was ridiculous but somehow she wanted it to stop and collectively acknowledge the seismic events it had just witnessed. Instead the scene looked as calm and peaceful as ever.

She couldn't have known it but, next to her, Tom was thinking too. He was struggling to find the right words. Tom knew Helen would soon announce that she had to be going and that, once the spell of working on this murder together had been broken, once the unreal bubble they had been encased in for days had burst, they might not have a cause to ever see each other again. Right now, for reasons he didn't want to think too closely about, Tom was desperate to avoid that happening. He needed to explain to her that she was wrong to stick with this boyfriend who would never appreciate her or her career. He wanted to say that though he had no idea what his future would bring, he wanted her to be some part of it.

He also knew Helen well enough to realise that if he said any of this right now, she would panic. He'd be left feeling like an idiot while she swiftly disappeared from his life forever.

'What?' she asked him suddenly.

'Nothing,' he said, 'I didn't say anything.'

'But what are you thinking?' she prompted and she

seemed a little nervous then, as if she was concerned at what he might say next.

'I'm thinking,' he began, 'that after the day we just had, I could really use a drink,' then he looked at her hopefully. 'Can I buy you one?'

'No,' she told him firmly, 'you can't,' and before he could protest she climbed to her feet. Just when he thought she was going to leave him sitting there on that bench all on his own, she stretched out a hand to him and said, 'I'm buying you one. Come on.'

Acknowledgements

I would like to say a huge thank you to everyone at Penguin Random House for their faith in this book. In particular I owe a massive debt to my editor, Emad Akhtar, for believing in *No Name Lane* and working tirelessly with me to improve it. It has been a pleasure grafting with him and we didn't come to blows once.

I am lucky enough to be represented by the best literary agent in the UK, Phil Patterson at Marjacq. I would like to thank 'Agent Phil' for all of his help, good judgement and friendship over the years and for always believing in me. I would also like to thank Luke Speed at Marjacq for his hard work on film and TV options and Sandra Sawicka for her dedicated handling of foreign rights.

No Name Lane wouldn't have been a Howard Linskey book without the fine judgement and attention to detail of Keshini Naidoo. Thanks for helping me get to the end, Keshini.

A special thanks to Ion Mills and everyone at No Exit Press for giving me a big break and exhibiting grace and class at every turn along the way. My thanks also to Peter Hammans and all at Droemer Knaur in Germany.

The very fine actor of both stage and screen, Dave Nellist, also deserves my gratitude and respect for bringing my work to life in the audio books.

I would like to thank the following for their help, kind words and faith, all of which sustained me during the years when a more sensible person would have given up entirely: Adam Pope, Andy Davis, Nikki Selden, Gareth Chennells, Andrew Local, Stuart Britton, David Shapiro, Peter Day, Tony Frobisher and Eva Dolan.

My lovely wife Alison has put up with my writing for years now, along with all the ups and downs that go with it and she never stopped believing I would make it into print. I couldn't have completed this book without her unflagging support, for which I thank her wholeheartedly.

Finally, I must thank my wonderful daughter Erin, who makes me smile every day and turns my world into a much better place. Thanks for your love and very kind heart Erin. Your dad couldn't have done this without you.